SOLDIERS!

A Chronicle from the 31st century

Part One

John Dalmas

Sky Warrior Book Publishing, LLC.

Published by Sky Warrior Book Publishing, LLC.
PO Box 99
Clinton, MT 59825
www.skywarriorbooks.com

Editor: David Lee Summers.
Cover art: William R. Warren Jr.
Publisher: M. H. Bonham.
Cover Layout: Mitchell Davidson Bentley
Printed in the United States of America
    0   9 8 7 6 5 4 3 2 1

Dedication

*This novel is dedicated to gamers, who
in the story universe, kept military science alive
and viable through nine centuries of blessed peace,
till their talents became needed and their foresight validated.
And in our world to my good friends: Sgt. Phil Yarborough,
Cory Rueb, the late Rod Martin, and the late Bill Cooper.*

*And finally
to the memory of the most distinguished warrior
I have personally known, Captain William C. Ashby,
187th Airborne Regimental Combat Team,
Korean War, 1950–1953*

Introduction to SOLDIERS!
the Story Behind the Story

SOLDIERS (at that time without the exclamation point) was published as a mass market paperback by Baen Books in May 2001. Jim Baen liked it well enough to make it a list leader for the month, with an expensive brushed metal cover illo. The sell-through of copies shipped was 79.2%, which was and is outstanding.

It had its season in the sun. Now it's out of print, the rights have reverted to me, and I'm releasing it as an e-book. Aiming it at new readers, including readers who don't often read science fiction. There may be, though, readers who read it before and would like to revisit it. They are more than welcome.

Of all my novels, SOLDIERS! is my favorite. I say this with some trepidation, but it's true. SOLDIERS! *is* my favorite, and the people dwelling within it are among my favorite fictional (creations? personalities? souls?): Jael, Esau, Qonits (the Wyzhñyñy scholar), Sergeant Arjan Hawkins Singh, Charley Gordon, Admiral Soong, Ophelia…. (From where did they come? How did I know them?)

Some gamers complained, even bitterly, at the book's dedication to gamers, **because it is not well suited to gaming.** They took me by surprise. It wasn't written to be adapted for gaming. Rather, among other things, *it is an appreciation* of the potential role of gamers in keeping military science alive through a long time of peace, despite social/cultural disapproval.

Several reviewers commented on its human aspects —

"One develops a real affection for many of the characters…" James K. Burk

"Dalmas focuses not on the experiences of an individual soldier or the whys and wherefores of strategy and tactics, but on the social pressures and changes that war causes." Carrie Barrera

"Slam-bang action…with a heart and a soul." William C. Dietz

"Too many military SF novels ignore the essential unevenness and tragedy of war. John Dalmas knows better. His *Soldiers* have both courage and heart." David Brin

SOLDIERS! is rooted in a supposition—that over time, humankind will evolve mentally, emotionally, and culturally. And explores what we might be like in 900 years, with a future history that includes "the Troubles" (pretty much the entire 22nd century)—94 harrowing years of terrorism and low-grade warfare tailored to avoid large scale disasters—including generations of martial law. I've actually assumed we're on our way to being more civilized, sane and just, an evolution driven by history, and by *memes* (the term *truisms* fits here) rather than *genes.*

Further, in my story universe, humanity has become driven less by a compulsion for novelty or self-aggrandizement than for humanity, ethics, tolerance, and environment. But we remain notably flawed, troubled, and sometimes self-righteous—for starters.

Meanwhile, the Troubles has made all things "military" anathema, and political and religious zealotry are looked at as almost obscene. For a time there were "return to the past" movements, in the form of ethnic and religious agrarian communities on Earth. But at about the same time, a hyperspace drive was developed that enabled deep-space exploration. More and more habitable worlds were discovered, and colonization inevitably followed, a sort of cultural safety valve helping us through early racial adulthood. Tentatively at first, then more confidently, this grew into "the Dispersion" of the 23rd and 24th centuries—mainly of groups avid for a self-sufficient world of their own, where they could live the way their version of God, or of good sense, would most approve.

And zeal satisfied tends to be zeal deflated. Depressurized.

Even with the more fervent dissident groups gone to the stars, Terra still has prejudices, differences of opinion, disputes, but they've become less angry, more civil. While on the colony worlds?—a sect with a planet of its own is less subject to wounds and abrasion; it experiences far fewer insults and resentments, and its assumptions are subject not to suppression but to testing.

In a word, humankind has become *peaceful!*

Meanwhile, space exploration has failed to turn up compelling evidence of non-human spacefarers. And as centuries pass, it seems more and more that we may actually prove to be the only high-tech life form in our galaxy. Thus while alien boogymen still lurk in the depths of human imagination, they lack substance, and there seems little point in maintaining a military that might conceivably turn and bite us.

That is the state of human affairs when our story begins— *with another space-faring life form showing up in the fringe of human expansion.* A life form with genocide fixedly in mind— and an armada of 16 thousand ships! And suddenly a military seems urgently important and effectively absent.

So: Come with me, and we'll visit a space ship very far away.

Chapter One
The Wyzhñyñy

Grand Admiral Quanshûk shu-Gorlak waited. "Thirty-nine," the ship counted. "Thirty-eight, thirty-seven..." *After eleven years in hyperspace,* Quanshûk asked himself, *how can these final seconds seem so long?* Eleven years of wondering what he'd find. Probably, hopefully, nothing basically unfamiliar.

Most of his people had spent the entire eleven years in a sleep so profound that aging was suspended; even he'd spent alternate months in a stasis chamber. Eleven years of hyperspace, mostly between spiral arms. On the screen's display of the F-space potentiality, there'd been whole months without the matric distortion of a single star. Only today had they seen two on a watch, both clearly unsuitable. And now a third. Judging by its mass not a promising third, but it was time to emerge, examine the starscape.

"...twenty-four, twenty-three, twenty-two..."

He glanced around at the bridge watch, all of them tense. Not so much as an ear flicked. But Quanshûk was not deceived. Those long brain cases harbored thoughts. Anticipation. Apprehension.

"...thirteen, twelve, eleven, ten..."

The word "ten" focused him. His eyes gripped the matric distortion caused by the massive stellar object, with a lesser distortion showing "nearby." Unexpectedly he too was gripped by apprehension. Intense apprehension. His bowel wanted to void right there on the bridge.

"...five, four, three, two, one..."

Stars exploded onto the screen, glorious, a panoply of brilliant points almost stunning in their collective beauty. For a moment Quanshûk's emotions soared, then responsibility took command. Responsibility for 26 million people. What would they find in this distant place, or what would find them? Every earlier swarm, over the centuries, had expanded the empire's existing boundaries into space already probed by scouts. But this—was territory totally unknown.

The brightest star was brilliant blazing red, the primary of this system. Ten degrees to its left was the next brightest, a planet orbiting it.

Reaching, Quanshûk pressed a key, and on the screen, reality was replaced with a system mechanics simulation, and a data menu. Already navcomp was identifying and computing provisional orbits for the system's planets, along with their masses, spectra, solar constants... Perhaps one of them would prove habitable despite the red giant primary.

Shipsmind would inform him promptly of any technically produced electronics.

◇

The living gas bag was both ancient and young, had identity without a label, and thought without words. For its kind, language had long since become not only needless, but pointless. It floated in the uppermost atmosphere of a Jovian giant, enjoying the radiation—the sunshine—on its huge balloon-like body. Meanwhile it composed/produced what, for lack of a more suitable concept, might be termed music. An activity carried out jointly with its play companion, fifteen degrees of arc—10,000 miles—distant on the same latitude.

A sudden awareness interrupted their activity—interrupted the activities of all the gas bags around the planet. Something else sentient—some sapient presence—had manifested within their perception. An armada was not part of their experience, but the concept intuited within the group mind, and expanded to comprehend the beings operating the ships.

Together, the thousands of great globules contemplated this new phenomenon, among other things perceiving its reason for coming there, its purpose and intentions.

They made a decision.

◇

What happened next intensified the newcomers' earlier apprehension. For brief minutes they'd been in a planetary system which their navcomp made perfect sense of. A locatable system in real space, F-space. Even now, shipsmind could tell

Quanshûk where that system was, relative to their home sector. Even though thousands of parsecs from it—11.26 hyperspace *years,* rounding off.

Then for a moment the navcomp had blacked out so to speak, as the Wyzhñyñy had. Both had completely lost orientation— and Quanshûk's armada was suddenly at a different location. A location without any recognizable reference point.

The ship insisted that the change had occurred in zero elapsed time, and that they had not left F-space. They'd simply— translocated. Instantaneously. Meanwhile Quanshûk and most of the bridge watch stood frozen, transfixed. Only one had lost consciousness, and toppled to the deck.

For a full half minute—a half minute with millions of star reads and trillions of computations—the navcomp labored to determine their new location. Without success. What it was able to do was begin creating a new star chart, centered on current ship position. Which was effectively stationary, relative to galactic coordinates. Clearly they were not in the outermost fringe of a spiral arm, as they had been moments earlier. They were well within whatever galaxy this was.

Acknowledging that was the first step in recovery. Quanshûk's muscles twitched. Tremors flowed across his hide. His hair bristled from nape to withers to tail. Bypassing the ship's captain, who still stood cataleptic, Quanshûk called the flagship's medical center and ordered the fallen crewman tended to. Then he ordered the ship to generate hyperspace and proceed to the vicinity of the nearest promising star.

To give that order had taken a major effort of will, but he was grand admiral, with all the responsibilities thereof. He tried not to wonder what might happen next, or what it might mean to this migration, this out-swarming he led.

Chapter Two
Pirate Base

The planet had no official name; its system hadn't yet been visited by a Survey ship. Unofficially it was called "Tagus"— short for Tagus Cove—by the only humans who knew it existed. Actually, the small part of the planet they were interested in didn't look at all like the historical Tagus Cove, which lay on the west shore of Terra's Isla Isabela, in the Galapagos Archipelago. But both were, or had been, pirate hangouts.

Also like the Terran Tagus Cove, this deep-space location was equatorial and volcanic, though the vulcanism had long been dormant. But the base itself was twelve miles from the planetary ocean, and had no shortage of drinking water. Instead of scrub, it bore magnificent rainforest, with towering trees, lush green foliage, and colorful darting birds—red, yellow, blue— even more vivid than the flowers.

And numerous technological improvements: a system of tunnels and chambers cut deep behind the craggy wall of a basaltic plateau. These tunnels accessed, among other things, comfortable dormitories and mess halls for raiders, and both family-style and bachelor lodgings for base keepers. Caverns sheltered and concealed the fighting craft and "bag ships," whose long absences provided the reason and wherewithal for the base. Entrances were inconspicuous, opening into a narrow gorge eroded into one flank of the plateau. The excavation rubble was visible from overhead, of course, but resembled natural rockfall.

Everything at the base was designed to elude detection from both space and atmospheric reconnaissance. Even the geogravitic power converter, that provided the base's energy, was too deep to be detected. As was the emergence wave detector. Hyperspace emergence waves pass through rock as freely as neutrinos.

Not everything could be concealed, of course, but what couldn't was designed to mislead. The electronics scanners had been installed in the roofs of what looked like a fishing resort, on the coast twenty miles from base. There, except for the scanners, everything was exposed: lush lawns and gardens, tennis courts, comfortable cottages and cabañas, dining hall, large pool, boat houses... There were almost always off-duty base personnel and crewmen there, who came on AG scooters to enjoy their free time.

An innocent vacation spot with little to hide, a secluded, low-gravity stop for the space-touring wealthy. Though it was a long way to go for a vacation.

All in all, Tagus seemed a harmless place, without so much as a pod beacon in the system's fringe.

◇

Henry Morgan was Tagus's founder and (often *in absentia*) ruler. He'd borrowed his name from a 17th century Welsh buccaneer, and it was the only name he admitted to. Like the original, this latter-day Henry Morgan was Welsh, born in Swansea, but he'd grown up in the North American city of Omaha. Remarkably, his birth name was Edward Teach, a name he shared with an 18th century pirate, but the earlier Teach was more barbaric than his namesake cared for. In fact, this latter-day Morgan and his personnel were generally civilized, even amiable, with a leaning toward nonconformity and adventure. Morgan thought of his crew and himself as gentlemen adventurers—daring, risk-taking, colorful. An attitude shared vicariously by many "good Commonwealth citizens." On Terra, from time to time, pirate dramas were popular, in the form of books, videos, and cinemas.

Henry Morgan was eating lunch in his living quarters when his yeoman knocked, audibly agitated. "Commodore!" he said, "come quick!"

Morgan stopped his fork in mid-course. "What stung your ass, Jerzy?" he called back.

"Sir, it's emergence waves, sir! All over hell, sir!"

Frowning, Morgan lay down his fork, with its morsel of sea turtle fried in nut oil, got to his feet and left, hurrying down the corridor. In his forties and moderately overweight, he still moved well. The wall screen in his office showed a three-dimensional coordinate model of the local solar system and environs. And thousands of hyperspace emergence loci! A footer said 16,297.

Sixteen thousand space craft! And Jerzy's "all over hell" summarized the situation nicely: the loci formed a diffuse lenticular swarm in the Tagus System's farside fringe. Some were out—hell!—close to 5 billion miles, according to the grid. Others were less than 2 billion. Allowing for distance, the size of each locus indicated the mass of the emergent ship, and virtually all were far larger than anything his two small squadrons of corsairs had. Larger than anything the Commonwealth admiralty had, excepting a handful of prototypes.

For just a moment Morgan stared, then sat down on his command seat and pecked at his key pad. An overlay, a chart, popped onto the screen, its numbers telling him more than he cared to know. Centuries of galactic radio monitoring had turned up nothing remotely convincing—threatening or otherwise—in the way of alien radio traffic. But in his youth, Morgan had read disreputable novels in which the Commonwealth was invaded by aliens. So the concept of alien invasion was familiar to him, and it seemed the only possible explanation of what he was looking at. Sixteen thousand alien ships! While the Commonwealth had half a dozen squadrons—frigates and (mostly) corvettes—for piracy suppression. That was the sum of its space defenses.

Sixteen thousand! And unless their hyperspace navigation was incredibly poor, they'd come a *very* long way; otherwise they wouldn't be so dispersed. After—what? Years? After years in hyperspace, it seemed likely they'd explore a bit before moving on. Look over the neighborhood, establish references.

Morgan frowned. "It's going to take them weeks to re-form formations," he said thoughtfully. "Days even to form up an assault group, if they're interested." He turned grinning to his yeoman. "Tell me, Jerzy, if you were me, what would you do about this?"

The young man blinked. "Why sir," he said, "I'd order all hands to prepare for evacuation. In case the intruders move insystem."

Morgan laughed. "Sounds like a winner. Let's do it."

◇

Preparing ships would take a day or so. The on-world squadron parked in the hangar caverns had recently returned from a long sweep. The loot was still being transferred to the bag ships, and Morgan was short on AG cargo handlers. And till now there'd been no hurry.

The only data he had on intruder ship positions was when the instantaneous hyperspace emergence waves were received. The emergence loci were an unchanging record of something that had already happened. They told him nothing of subsequent ship movements. Equally important, Morgan was unfamiliar with either the intruder's intentions or procedures, and his working assumptions were incorrect. Nor, of course, could his sensors see into warpspace, to detect ship movements there.

◇

He left his office and strode back to his apartment. He was someone who didn't hesitate when something was necessary, however unpleasant, and he was about to throw away a secure base he'd developed over a dozen years. Entering his younger brother's room, he stepped into a fragrance much like Terran night jasmine. An orderly on an AG scooter had collected them from the forest roof; she collected some fragrant species or other every morning. It was more than a duty. It was an expression of fondness for Robert Teach. Robert was a pudgy, disarmingly sunny man, a thirty-one-year-old child liked by everyone. Beginning with his older brother, who'd rescued him after their mother suicided.

Just now, Robert was sitting at his computer terminal, playing with the ephemeris for Epsilon Indi. He could compute in his head—if compute was the word—the moment-to-moment positions of the planets of every inhabited system in the Commonwealth, for any moment you'd care to give him. What he could not do was read, above the primary level, or write at all beyond a carefully lettered "signature." He even had trouble buttoning his shirt. Med-tech Connie Phamonyong did that for him. Robert didn't like Press Close or pullovers. He liked buttons. They were nicer.

"Hi, Robert," Morgan greeted. Robert didn't reply. The words hadn't registered; he was utterly engrossed. Connie came out of the kitchenette and gave her commodore a hug and kiss. A fond, familiar kiss. They'd been together for fifteen years.

Morgan nodded toward Robert. "I need his help," he told her. "I need to contact the prime minister and the admiralty."

Her eyes widened, but she asked no question, simply nodded. Turning, she spoke to Robert, the words a command hypnotically programed years earlier. He didn't hesitate, didn't even blink, simply turned his chair, got up, stepped to a nearby couch (it once had graced a yacht owner's saloon) and lay down. Connie pulled the computer chair over to it and sat, then looked questioningly at Morgan.

"Just the two for now," he said, "the P.M. and the admiralty."

She turned to Robert, and spoke with a calm she did not feel, a standard prolog to whatever the message would be. Then she looked again at Morgan, and briefly they waited.

◇

On Terra, in the palace penthouse at Kunming, a young man not basically unlike Robert Teach sat at a keyboard, playing a flowing improvisation based on a Chopin nocturne. Abruptly he stopped, and turned to his attendant. "It is something for Mr. Peixoto," he said. Then getting to his feet, he stepped to a nearby lounge and lay down. The attendant clicked a switch on his belt and sat down beside the young savant.

At the same moment, half a mile away, a tiny aging woman at a computer screen broke off her inspection of commercial freight schedules at the Kinshasa terminal; she could have recited it verbatim, it and numerous others. Turning, she spoke to her attendant, not a frequent event. When a communication triggered a trance, her speech was quite clear, not at all like her usual lisping voice that resembled a three-year-old's. Her attendant helped her to her couch; the old woman couldn't walk unassisted. She'd never been able to.

◇

When the two communicators on Terra had responded, Robert Teach spoke again. "They are ready," he said. Then his elder brother began to dictate, identifying himself by both his legal name and pseudonym, Robert passing them on precisely, mentally. Instantaneously. Without a qualm, Morgan gave his galactic coordinates, then described what his emergence wave detector had shown. Those same emergence waves had reached Terra at the same instant, of course, but at that distance—hundreds of parsecs—they'd been far too slight to register.

◇

It would be an historic event: the first planetary capture by the Seventh Wyzhñyñy Swarm. The flagship's bridge was bright with officers of the exalted genders, their fur blue, except for the ridge of cardinal that began at the withers, and in the master gender culminated in a cranial crest. Amongst the reddish-brown of the crew and subordinate officers, they were vividly dominant.

Their flagship was equipped with the best sensory system the empire could provide. Within minutes, the grand admiral knew the location and approximate orbits of all the system's planets, and their first-order environmental parameters—mass, solar constant, magnetic field, surface temperature, approximate atmospheric composition... Also the presence of technical electronics—that had been recorded almost at once—and the curious absence of any apparent pod beacon.

With those data established, Grand Admiral Quanshûk shu-Gorlak had ordered the fleet of one pre-selected tribe—transports, cargo ships, armed escorts...to head in-system. While inbound, all colonists were to be revived; all but the matrons were soldiers. The bombardment ships and ground-assault craft would emerge from warpspace close to the inhabited planet, move in, and wipe out all military installations and population concentrations. That accomplished, ground forces would seek and destroy all remaining native sophonts. With mop-up underway, they would commence base construction.

Nothing was said about prisoners. The only prisoners the Wyzhñyñy ever took were for interrogation, and only as ordered by their high command. Without such an order, all alien sophonts would be killed. Of course.

◇

The tribal fleet, or most of it, emerged from warpspace and approached quickly in gravdrive. Its scouts quickly found the sole source of technical electronics—the "resort." Eight miles out, Support Force Commander Kraloqt stood on the bridge of his flagship, frowning. Was this all? The place didn't appear dangerous. He ordered a single pulse fired, adequate to obliterate the central building, hopefully drawing fire from any defense forces.

It did the first but not the second.

Perhaps the defenders were in subsurface installations. Kraloqt ordered a spray burst, each pulse more powerful than the single first shot. The resort site exploded, lofting a large cloud of smoke and dust, leaving a twenty-acre crater field.

He then ordered in an elite infantry battalion, to scout the surrounding forest and flush out the enemy. The first assault lander had barely put down when a small spacecraft emerged unexpectedly at the surface, twenty miles east-northeast of the landing zone, accelerating outbound as strongly as its crew could tolerate. Another quickly followed, then a third, a fourth. By that time the first had generated warpspace on the run, and was essentially out of harm's way. The others followed suit.

Kraloqt's battlecomp had peripheral attention better than any living organism's; it was never distracted. In the same moment that its alarm system squalled, his flagship fired a series of pulses at the location from which the alien craft had appeared. Kraloqt ordered a bombardment ship into action.

To hunt fleeing craft in warpspace was impractical, and at any rate not Kraloqt's responsibility. His job was to destroy the planet's surface defenses and prepare it for occupation. He radioed a report to the Grand Admiral (it would take a dozen hours to reach him), then ordered another elite battalion to the site of the alien launch. In less than a minute, the battalion's armored assault landers were on their way, with gunships flying cover.

◇

When the resort's electronics reported bogies entering

F-space only 90,000 miles out, the surprised Morgan had ordered all base personnel to board their assigned ships for evacuation. They were to be fully secured for flight within ten minutes, and depart on his command. His own yacht would leave after the others were clear.

But again the invaders surprised him. While the transports and cargo ships entered F-space 90,000 miles out, the assault force had continued in warpspace, and emerged unexpectedly overhead at only 63,000 feet.

Despite his surprise, the intruders' haste grabbed Morgan's curiosity, which at times could be stronger than his good judgement. Thus, though Connie and Robert were still in his apartment, he was reluctant to leave his office. The intruders might try to communicate via computer. It seemed probable.

Before the ten minutes were up, communication with the resort was cut off. Two minutes later the shock wave of its destruction hit the subterranean pirate base, and Morgan's hopes crashed and burned. He knew at once there'd be no negotiation, or even an ultimatum, just destruction. A touch on his keypad showed he still had communication within the base. Biting the words out, he called Flight Control. "Drago, it's time to vamos. Are all ships secured and ready?"

"All but yours, boss."

"Leave without me. Now! No delay! I'll follow when I can. Till then, you're in charge."

"You're the boss, boss." Drago paused. Morgan could hear him talking laconically to someone else—Hideo Pienaar, Morgan's own first officer, who would serve as launch control till Morgan boarded the *Delight* with Robert and Connie.

Then Drago was speaking through the base communication system. "Emergency evacuation! Emergency evacuation! Standard rendezvous! Standard rendezvous! All cradles except the commodore's yacht cradle will power up to launch. NOW!" There was a brief lapse, then Pienaar was speaking. "Launch One!" Pause. "Launch Two!" Pause. "Launch Three." Pause. "Launch Four."

Morgan felt the rock shudder much more severely than

before, a series of heavy shock pulses hammering the plateau top directly overhead, and the upper face of the gorge. He hadn't imagined such a quick response. His hands clenched the arms of his chair. Objects fell from shelves. A vase waltzed briefly and toppled, spilling flowers and water across the surface of his desk, wetting his lap. He swore. Jabbing a key on his pad, he called, "Damage report!"

"Boss, this is Hideo. Ships one through four got out. Then we took multiple hits, and a lot of rock came down. Both ports are blocked by rockfall. Doesn't seem to be any interior damage though."

Thank God for any favors, Morgan thought. "How long will it take to clear the ports?"

"An hour at least. Likely four or five. We need to get the dozer running."

"Okay, do it."

It was as if the invader had been listening. There was another, longer series of shocks, and Morgan's line with damage control cut off. Along with any prospect of getting the ports cleared at all, he told himself.

Opening a desk drawer, he took out a remote control and shoved it into a pocket. He had no doubt intruder scouts would be along soon, checking the target area. *We'll really be in the soup then,* he told himself, *unless the ports are so thoroughly blocked, the bastards don't notice them. We'll likely have their version of marines in the tunnels with us.* Or worse, some explosive aerosol that would blow the base all to hell from the inside out.

Defense was out of the question. Moving more quickly than he had for years, Morgan headed for his apartment, to find Connie standing round-eyed with worry, Robert beside her. Pointing at Morgan, Robert laughed. "You wet your pants!"

Morgan looked down where the water from the vase had spilled on him. "Well I'll be darned," he said. "Look at that." Then he stepped to the phone and keyed base security. That line was working. The speaker was on, and Connie and Robert listened.

"Prieto," a voice answered.

"Have we got visitors yet, Léon?"

"They just landed. They will be knocking at our door in a few minutes. Our monitor eyes are all inop, but I have men peeking over the rubble blocking the work port." Prieto laughed. "Maglie says they are the centaurs from hell. Then he said no, they are centaurs from the Jurassic." Léon paused, then continued: "I think they will blast their way in."

"Look, Léon," Morgan said, "if you think it's best, surrender to them. I'm giving you full authority. Meanwhile I need to get Robert out of their reach. One way or another."

"Got it, boss."

Morgan switched off. "Robert, Connie, let's go." They followed without questions. Nearby was a dead-end corridor. As they approached it, he took the remote from his pocket, and aiming it at what appeared to be solid rock, he touched the switch. Groaning, the rock slid aside about five feet, a steel panel with rock slab veneer. He gestured Connie and Robert through the gap ahead of him. "Hurry!" he said, and even Robert hurried. Then he pointed the remote again, and the gap closed.

The tunnel on the other side was narrow, crudely finished, and unlit. It smelled moist and fusty, as if not serviced by the base's ventilation system. Morgan pressed a second switch, and the remote became a flashlight. Turning, he directed the beam down the tunnel. Blackness swallowed it a hundred feet ahead.

"Morgan," Robert said, "I'm scared." His voice was a little boy's now, despite its tenor pitch.

"It's okay to be scared, but you'll be all right. I'm your brother; I take care of you." Gently he rumpled Robert's close-cut hair. "We're going to a *secret* place. The bad guys don't know about it. No one does except us three."

Then he led off along the tunnel.

<>

It went farther than Connie had expected. Half a mile at least, she decided, and except for the first hundred yards or so, it climbed. Not steeply, but enough that Robert got a bit querulous. "You'll make it, brother," Morgan told him. "You're doing great. Our father used to climb mountains, and we inherited his legs, you and I."

"Really? What mountains?"

"He used to climb Mount Snowden every chance he had. When I was little, back in Wales. A couple of times he even went to Scotland to climb; he climbed Ben Nevis there, and Ben Macdhui. Once, after we moved to Nebraska, he took mother and me to Colorado, where there were even bigger mountains. He climbed one of them, too. I wanted to go with him, but I was too..."

A faint tremor shivered the rock beneath their feet, interrupting Morgan's recitation. He didn't get back to it, simply walked faster.

Connie's knowledge of Terran geography pretty much ended with what was taught in middle school, and in high school in connection with history. It didn't go much beyond the more important places and historical events. Her mind couldn't create an image of Wales on the map, but she was pretty sure it was part of Great Britain. Scotland she could image. On the map it looked like the profile of a dowager, with a feathered hat from some far-back time—the 20th or 21st century. Before "the Troubles." As for Colorado—she'd heard of it. It was in North America.

She wondered if Henry was telling Robert the truth. She'd never known him to kid his brother, but over the years she'd learned he could lie when it suited him.

After what might have been twenty minutes, the flashlight picked up a steel door ahead, with what looked like a wheel on it. Like much else in the base, it was from a waylaid ship—the security vault door of a luxury cruise ship. It wasn't locked; Henry simply spun the wheel and pulled, then ushered them in and closed it after them.

He didn't take time to show them around. Leaving them in the dark, he disappeared through another door. Half a minute later she could hear humming. From wherever the machinery resided that provided the utilities—a small geogravitic power converter, water pump, sump pump, air circulation... Lights turned on. Seconds later she heard water running.

After Henry returned, the rock shuddered again, this time more strongly than in the tunnel, though nothing like they'd felt in the apartment. He went back into the machinery room, and while he was gone, the shudder repeated strongly enough to worry her.

◇

They made love that night for the first time in a week. Afterward, over brandy—short drinks; they needed to be frugal with it—Henry told her more about what had happened. Including the tremor in the tunnel, and those they'd felt since then. The first, he believed, was the intruders blasting their way into the base. The second was the use of concussion to kill everyone inside. "And the third—" He exhaled gustily through pursed lips. "If the alien charges didn't collapse the base, I wouldn't want them to find this place. And years ago I had charges set to bring down the corridor leading here."

He reached, and patted her hand. "There's a way out though, and enough food to keep the three of us for a couple of years if need be. Meanwhile I'll be doing things, finding things out, and you and Robert can help me communicate what I learn to Terra." *Though what it might be,* he told himself, *or what good it might do them, God only knows. Sixteen thousand, for godssake!*

Chapter Three
Chang Lung-Chi and Foster Peixoto

President Chang Lung-Chi's chauffeur had let him off 300 yards from the palace. Three hundred esthetic yards, pregnant with history. A long, initially turbulent history. After the Troubles, the Commonwealth of Worlds had undertaken to recognize and honor its diverse roots. And for Chang, walking through Peace Garden was to celebrate those roots. He strode briskly between vivid red and white flowerbeds, past the tall, crystalline Fountain of the Heroes, then across Unity Square, to mount the broad, low marble stairs of the Palace of Worlds. There he entered through the Portal of Admiral Gavril Apraxin.

The president was a man of less than ordinary height; without exception his bodyguards were taller. They didn't march; didn't even keep to any particular configuration. They could almost have been walking together by chance. And if you watched them, not knowing who they were, it would be Chang Lung-Chi your eyes would follow. His somewhat portly sixty-year-old form was straight-backed, and he had presence.

The vast lobby was busy, though the senate and assembly would not be called to order for two more hours. Staff members bustled on errands. Bureaucrats and members of parliament sauntered in conversation. Families and other early sightseers circulated, examining displays and memorials, or gazing at the shafts of colored light from reflectors overhead.

Security was inconspicuous but excellent. Concealed surveillance cameras recorded everything. They were not sapient, of course, but they were programmed to notice—and correlate—face and form, bearing and demeanor, clues subtle as well as overt. And to inform as appropriate.

The president passed the broad corridor that led to both senate and assembly, proceeding instead to a secure express tube to the next-to-top floor, where his offices and apartment were. When he stepped out into the eighty-sixth-floor's east elevator bay, the prime minister was waiting for him; the surveillance system had more than just security functions.

"Mr. President!" the prime minister said. "Something has come up which urgently requires our joint attention."

Chang Lung-Chi raised his eyebrows. "Well then," he said, without asking what. It seemed to him he could guess.

Foster Peixoto had already turned, starting down the corridor to his own wing, which was larger than the president's. It was not a matter of rank or prestige. The prime minister was head of government, which in the Commonwealth meant its director of planning and operations. He required a larger staff. The president was head of state: its spokesman, setter of directions and goals, co-setter of policies and priorities.

Physically they were not at all alike. Peixoto had lived the first fourteen years of his life on Luna. Not surprisingly he was nearly seven feet tall, though weighing less than the president. And their differences went beyond body type, yet they'd been friends at first meeting, and close friends almost as quickly. They even complemented one another. Peixoto was an analytical thinker who dealt well with details. The president was intuitive. His mind cut quickly to the core of a problem.

Peixoto's office was spare, and strictly utilitarian. The few art pieces had been supplied by the General Services Administration. Folding his long body onto his desk chair, he rested his hand by his key pad. The president, a frequent visitor, seated himself.

"The alien armada has attacked another world," Peixoto said. "This time the Gem of the Prophet. My communicator learned of it only minutes ago. You'd already left the airport, so I decided to wait." He tapped a short sequence of keys. A picture lit a wall screen, of a youth, a savant lying in trance. President Chang knew the young man, whose talents went far beyond his musical virtuosity. He lay in a penthouse apartment overhead, but his words originated on a world so distant, its sun was not nearly visible to the naked eye.

The savant spoke in Terran, in the first person. After identifying the system, he began the message. "Two hours ago," he said, "bombardment craft, parked out of sight overhead, began to destroy our towns. They ignored our attempts to communicate. Now not a town remains standing. After you forwarded the report of Morgan the pirate, this unit was ordered to the Mountain of the Poet, where the invaders have not yet found us."

So, Peixoto thought, *the aliens, the intrusion, are real. This leaves no doubt.*

The words continued. "They have landed ground forces at numerous locations. Video signals show their soldiers as having six limbs, and like the mythical centaur, they walk on four of them. The other two, the arms, are on an upright torso that rises from the withers. The head looks reptilian, despite fur and external ears, and the tail is like that of an ass. They wear no clothing, only harness to which their gear is attached. They run briskly, and even ignoring the upright torso, their body appears larger than the largest dog.

"They attack fiercely, and have rejected, or failed to understand, offers of surrender. They simply kill, the unarmed as well as the armed."

There was a long pause. "They have detected us. Our..." Briefly the savant shifted on the couch, then lay quiet. His attendant moved into camera view. "Ramesh has lost contact," he said. "We will continue to record further communication, if there is any."

Peixoto touched a key and the screen went blank. Chang's head had bowed as they'd listened. Now it raised. "Faith has gotten itself tangled in the thorn hedge again," he said. The Faith Party was small but sometimes pivotal. When the report from Tagus had been released, Faith had been vocally upset with it. Their pacifism had been threatened, and they'd denied vehemently that there was such an armada. It was impossible, a pirate ruse.

They'd have a hard time calling this report a pirate ruse. And Faith depended on the perception that their positions and statements came to them from the deity. "Faith will lose more than face," Chang went on. "To the 800 million Muslims on Terra, traditional and reformed, the Gem of the Prophet has been the crown jewel of their colonies. Now Salam will disassociate itself from Faith." His gaze sought Peixoto's. "This will help you get a war powers act through."

Peixoto nodded absently; a thought had taken his attention. "We must somehow establish communication with these... centaurs. Negotiate with them."

The comment took the president by surprise. "Of course," he said. "But meanwhile we'll promote a war powers proposal to parliament. Rearming will require immense focus, unswerving determination—and discipline." Chang paused, peering carefully at his friend. "Do you actually suppose these creatures might negotiate?"

Peixoto shook his head reluctantly. "I hope, but I do not expect. We must try."

The president nodded. "I agree, my friend, we must try." He frowned, then gestured at the wall screen. "Call up a space chart. Centered on the azimuth of Gem."

Peixoto's forehead furrowed, and he tapped keys. A three-dimensional star chart appeared on the screen, with a thin green line that extended from Terra through the Gem of the Prophet. "Now show me where Tagus is," the president said.

Peixoto's lips framed a silent "oh" of realization, and he tapped keys again. The primary of the Tagus system showed a pulsing red. It was not far off the azimuth that ran through Gem.

"Now show the Gem-Tagus bearing, enlarged."

Peixoto's fingers busied. The image jumped, showing a line from Tagus to Gem. Several labeled systems lay near it; one had a colony. A touch of the arrow gave its name: The Star of Hibernia.

"Does our embassy there have a communicator office?"

All colonial embassies were authorized one, but there were more embassies than suitable savants. Once more Peixoto's fingers tapped, and names appeared. "Yes," he said.

"Contact them, right now. We must know."

"Of course, Mr. President." Peixoto phoned his communicator's apartment, and gave quick instructions. Then they waited. It took a few minutes; Ramesh had gone to the roof garden with his attendant, to enjoy the flowers. It was something he did daily at about this time. Like most idiot savants, he was happier, and healthier, when his work day was organized around things pleasant and predictable. Meanwhile the prime minister and the president waited without a word, Peixoto wondering how he and his staff had managed to overlook the Star of Hibernia. Finally Ramesh was back on his couch. Peixoto told the attendant what he wanted, and the attendant instructed the savant.

Chang was not surprised when the embassy on Star did not respond. "Burhan, is there any possibility that their communicator is engaged in something that prevents his answering?"

"None that I'm aware of, Your Excellency," the attendant said. "There should be at least an autonomic response, even if asleep, or deeply engaged in something."

"Ask Ramesh if he gets any sense of how things are on Star."

Burhan passed the question to his ward while the two executives watched the screen. The tranced savant did not reply.

"As you see," the attendant said, "he says nothing. But I can sense his distress. Something bad has happened there."

Peixoto nodded. "Thank you, Burhan. And if it seems appropriate to you, thank Ramesh for me. For myself and the president."

The slender, youthful-looking attendant nodded soberly. "I will forward your excellencies' appreciation to Ramesh."

Peixoto broke the connection. *"I can sense his distress,"* Burhan had said. It could well be true, but it was a frail basis for decisions. He looked at Chang Lung-Chi, who looked back grimly.

"How," Chang asked, "could the intruder armada—the *invader* armada—have arrived at Star without our being notified of their emergence?"

"I can think of a possibility. It is the beginning of the rainy season at New Kerry. The whole planet celebrates, drinking intoxicants, squirting water on people... Perhaps no one was tending the detector at the time... Or the invader may never have emerged there. Their savant may simply be ill."

Chang's only comment was his wry expression. "Call a cabinet meeting," he said, "for 1000 hours if possible, with Shin and Kulikov sitting in. Invite Thorkelsdóttir to sit in for Faith. By Faith standards she's a pragmatist; she will actually listen to what others say." *Against a set of 20th century preconceptions!* "We face the biggest threat in the history of the human species.

"We need a plan on how to contact the invaders, and a strategy for negotiation. Establish a peace committee; Thorkelsdóttir can be vice chair. Then keep it focused on specifics: how to contact the alien, how to communicate with them. How to begin learning their psychology. How! How! How! We must focus!"

As Chang spoke, the enormity of the task struck Peixoto.

"There will be a language problem," Chang went on. "And the invaders will travel in hyperspace. Probably in an invasion corridor centered on the Tagus-Gem axis. We'll have to predict where they'll emerge, and decide on how to intercept them."

The prime minister nodded, but his heart was a stone in his chest. The prospect of negotiation seemed zero.

"Meanwhile I'll meet with Diderot and Gordeenko. We need to plan the evacuation of colonists in and near that corridor." The president paused. "Sixteen thousand ships! Phew!" The number itself was overwhelming. "You realize what this means," he said.

Peixoto had no idea what Chang referred to, and waited for him to answer his own question.

"We may face a folk migration instead of simply a war."

Peixoto gnawed a lip; he could see the logic. "If that's true," he said, "the situation is less severe than it might be. Every transport means one fewer warship."

"Ah, but my friend, a folk migration suggests they do not have the option of returning home, wherever that may be. And they are a different life form than we are. They may all be warriors. Born warriors. Then every transport is a troopship!"

Again the president paused, then the flow of words resumed, more measured now. "We must see to the requisition and conversion of all available shipping, to evacuate colonies. And expand our war and shipbuilding industries as rapidly as possible. Recruit and train armies! Build hundreds on hundreds of warships, and train crews for them! It will require complete and rapid mobilization of human and industrial resources—the biggest challenge in human history!"

The prime minister almost stared, attention fixed less on the enormity of the task than by the president's sudden energy. "With a population that hasn't fought for centuries," Peixoto pointed out. "Many with the conviction that to fight is immoral. That in the long run, the results of surrender are best. But seemingly this is an enemy that does not accept surrender."

Chang seemed not to hear. His mind was busy. "Evacuees will be our best source of recruits. Their lives will already have been disrupted." His focus returned to his prime minister. "We must approach negotiation as if there were no chance at all of winning a war, and we must prepare for war as if there were no chance of successful negotiation. In the meantime, victories in battle may give us leverage."

Chang Lung-Chi rubbed his hands.

Good God, the prime minister thought, *he is savoring the challenge!*

<>

Peixoto watched the president leave, then breathed a deep sigh. *We have no actual defense forces at all, beyond a few squadrons to suppress pirates. Contingency plans and industrial mobilization plans—yes. A small cadre of warfolk, yes, some active, some retired, but none with combat experience. Trained on sophisticated electronic war games. Limited experience with prototype weapons and virtuality trainers. But armed forces? A war industry?*

We'll have to start with recruitment and industrial mobilization. He realized he didn't know enough to evaluate either the problems or the prospects realistically. *Kulikov and Shin will know as much about that as anyone,* he thought, and reaching, keyed his phone.

Chapter Four
Chief Scholar

Quanshûk shu-Gorlak touched keys on his[1] command panel, then spoke into his communicator. "Chief Scholar, please report to my quarters at once."

"As you command, Admiral."

Quanshûk turned and crossed the bridge, his dull claws inaudible on the acoustical surface. He was aware that his executive officer, Rear Admiral Tualurog, was folowing him with his eyes. *I have been brooding,* Quanshûk realized, *and now I will discuss my thoughts with Qontis instead of with him.* On a flagship, a certain tension was natural between the XO, who was operations officer, and the chief scholar, who was not military. It would rarely cause serious difficulty—the separation of functions was hard-wired—but it could distract the XO. *I will,* Quanshûk decided, *set his mind at ease later. Somewhere other than on the bridge.*

When the grand admiral arrived at his suite, he found Qonits zu-Kitku already waiting in the corridor. Quanshûk placed a palm on the security plate, then pushed the stateroom door open, and gestured. Both stepped inside, the door closing behind them. The admiral poured nuts into two bowls, handing one of them to Qonits with a brief, casual gesture of blessing. Then he lowered his hindquarters onto a cushion, much as a dog might sit.

Qonits followed his example, then ate several nuts. "How can I serve you, my lord?" he asked.

"I need your ears and your responses." Quanshûk paused, gathering his thoughts. "I have been analyzing our experience in this new region. It has troubling aspects."

"Ah."

"The three worlds we have taken were all occupied by the same species. And their ships generated strange-space, which almost certainly means they have hyperdrive.[2] Is that not so?"

"It is hard to imagine otherwise, your lordship, considering that the ships were small for faring deep space in warpdrive."

"Yet the sapient populations of all three worlds were very small. One was no more than an outpost. Correct?"

"Unarguably."

"Therefore they could not have been self-sustaining. They must have been part of an empire."

Qonits bobbed his torso from the waist, a formal Wyzhñyñy nod. "True."

"And clearly they were only recently colonized, so this is an expanding empire. But even so, within a month or two— three at most—we will reach their core worlds. And with their technological level, they will no doubt defend themselves vigorously."

Qonits shrugged with his hands. "One would think so."

"Ours is the greatest swarm ever assembled, and far the most powerful. So we will continue in the traditional manner, neither hastening nor dawdling. Thrust into the heart of this empire like a great spear, pausing to put a tribe or tribes on every suitable world along the way. That should force their warfleet to come to us, away from the advantages of established defenses.

"And if they will not be drawn, we will continue. Eventually they must fight, and we will crush them. After that, the remainder of their worlds can be occupied without concern."

Qonits bowed deeply. "Your lordship," he said quietly, "you did not call me here to lecture me on the obvious."

"True. But it was necessary to set the table." Quanshûk's thick lids lowered to half-mast, a Wyzhñyñy frown. "But there are peculiarities in this situation, are there not? Why have these aliens not provided their outposts with meaningful defenses? War ships parked outside the radiation belts. Things to bleed us."

His fly-whisk tail waving slowly, Qonits considered the statement. "Who knows how these aliens think," he replied, "or what they value and do not value. Perhaps, my lord, they are sufficiently powerful, sufficiently dominant in this sector, that they did not foresee an invasion."

Quanchûk filed the reply and continued. "The rulers will

soon know of our arrival, if they do not already. Ships escaped worlds one and three, and presumably world two as well. After a day or so, they would have emerged into F-space to launch message pods, warning their nearer colonies, the nearer core worlds, and their crown world." Absently Quanshûk nibbled nuts. "But..." His gaze intensified. "Does it not seem that on the worlds we captured, their ships escaped with remarkable alacrity? As if they already knew of us, and were prepared?"

"They could have acted on the basis of our hyperspace emergence waves, which surely they found alarming."

Quanshûk licked air in apprehension; a gesture that might have embarrassed him with someone other than Qonits. "There should have been *some* defenses. Unless their rulers are indifferent to their outpost worlds."

"They may simply keep the core worlds strong and the outer weak, to ensure obedience. Depending on coercion instead of loyalty, in which case it must be a young empire. As dispersion grows, coercion becomes self defeating." Qonits paused. "Or this life form may be so remote, it doesn't recognize the danger."

Quanshûk considered the reply. "I must have information," he decided. "What are they like? How large is their empire? Their fleet? At the next world we capture, we will take prisoners. You will learn to question them and understand their answers. Shipsmind can develop a translation program. The Second and Fourth Swarms did it."

Again Qonits nodded. "True," he said. "But such a program requires much linguistic data, along with time and caution. Prisoners may lie. As for capturing them..." He paused, not liking to point out the obvious. "Enemy wounded are potentially dangerous. It is natural to kill them."

Quanshûk flicked a hand as if at a fly. "The physical presence of a commander enhances compliance. I will go insystem with the assault force, to demonstrate the seriousness of my order; they will feel constrained to abide by it."

Qonits' next bow expressed deference, but when he raised his torso, he did not avert his eyes. "You will be risking your life, Lord Admiral, and you would not easily be replaced. You were anointed by the emperor."

Quanshûk answered mildly. "We have yet to encounter meaningful resistance," he pointed out. "And if I deem the situation dangerous, I will stay away."

Qonits placed his palms together in a formal nod. Clearly the admiral would not be dissuaded. And the nature, extent and intensity of the system's technical electronics output would suggest the likely level of danger. "Of course, lord admiral. And if we gain no more than some insights into their psychology, they may well prove useful."

"Thank you, chief scholar." Quanshûk stepped to his small bar. "Will you drink with me before you leave?"

◇

After Qonits had left, Quanshûk poured another drink. He felt much better than he had. But even so, the situation had peculiarities.

◇

The chief scholar settled himself at his terminal and turned his attention to the multi-faceted entity known as shipsmind. "Librarian," he ordered. And a moment later, "Give me all you have on the interrogation of alien captives." It wouldn't be much, and who knew if any of it would be pertinent here. But it was a place to start. He watched the annotated source list form on the screen. *We might learn a great deal,* he told himself, *or we might harvest confusion and lies. But it will be interesting. I can monitor their brainwaves, their electrical fields...* He began to like the idea of prisoners.

◇

Footnotes:

[1] English doesn't provide pronouns to deal with the varied Wyzhnyny genders. For simplicity, the masculine—he, him, his—will be used to cover them all.

[2] Strange-space is a collective term for two different phenomena—warpspace and hyperspace. Warpdrive utilizes warpspace, and hyperdrive utilizes hyperspace. The strange-space generator can generate both.

The Terran term "warpdrive" grew out of a 20th-century theory that 4-dimensional space could be warped, permitting faster-than-light travel. Though the concept would prove unproductive, the term was familiarized by space fiction. Later, by extension, the first drive to actually bypass the speed of light was dubbed "warpdrive," though it has nothing to do with warping 4-dimensional space.

Chapter Five
Eric Padilla

When the Wyzhñyñy arrived at distant Tagus, few people on Terra had heard of Doctor Eric Padilla, humanity's pioneer in cyborg engineering. There weren't many experts. A one-handed man could count them on his fingers. But the technology had survived in old training cubes, and tangentially in the fields of neurosurgery and pseudo-organic engineering. In fact, given a two-week training intensive, numerous neurosurgeons and roboticists, working together, could function as cyborg engineers.

Unfortunately there were no such training intensives. Cyborg engineering had been proscribed by law, and abandoned by universities, and by science in general. Such thorough abandonment would have been impossible before the Troubles, but the drive to innovate, to search deeply and build daringly, had faded during that period. The Troubles: nearly a century of martial law, chaos, terrorism, and intermittent, cautiously tailored warfare. A period during which distrust of government, of corporate greed, of innovation and activism had all intensified. The result had been a combination of technological and business conservatism, and social liberalism. Over subsequent centuries these persisted, though somewhat changed in their expression.

There had also been growth toward a spirituality relatively free of boundaries and mostly of creeds. A growth abetted by the emigration of many unhappy sectarians to the stars. In the new spiritualism, the main approach to dogma lay in pacifism and human rights doctrines. And even these were mostly not zealous. Zeal was suspect. The urge to combative idealism had become much less common. It had served its purpose. The public cynicism it helped sire had largely dissolved political, racial, and ethnic chauvinism in the Sol system, leaving occasional dull scums of prejudice. And scattered, hard and bitter nodes of hatred, like social gallstones, to dissolve gradually, one by one, without surgery.

In the process, the cynicism too had faded.

Meanwhile, pacifism and the long peace had minimized and marginalized the military. Even military fiction had become socially disrespectable: a ghetto genre with a low profile. The child Eric Padilla had grown up in Denver, in the Colorado Prefecture. He'd been part of that ghetto. By age ten, his favorite reading had been regimental histories, novels set in historical wars, and especially yarns in which aliens invaded the human worlds. He rented them from private libraries, or bought them on the ether, or borrowed them from friends, hiding them in his pocket reader.

His mother would have been prostrated, had she known. But she didn't snoop his activities; unconsciously she feared what she might find. His father knew, and had reluctantly supported young Eric's habit. While trying to keep his wife from learning of it, and hoping his son would outgrow it.

Which in a sense Eric did. At age thirteen he announced to his parents an interest in neurosurgery. At the same time his grades surged from decent to excellent, allowing his selection into prep school, which was quite demanding. Three years later he qualified for university, and begged his parents to send him. University educations were expensive, but with loans and a scholarship, they'd managed.

They hadn't known his motive. His reading had stimulated the belief that aliens would in fact invade Terra someday. To his young mind it seemed inevitable; occasionally he even dreamt of it. And from this and playing war games, he'd developed a powerful interest in the concept of the military cyborg.

In fact, he intended to build one! In an era of peace and technological stagnation, he was a century and a half ahead of his time.

When he left for university, he knew that to be a neurosurgeon, one must first be an M.D. But he hadn't realized how little latitude his scholarship left for courses outside premedicine. Over three years he managed to schedule only two courses in pseudo-organic engineering—courses focused on industrial applications and information technology. And having no interest in an actual medical career, he found himself impatient, and in danger of losing his scholarship.

All of that was to change. At a war-game "convention," in an old warehouse in Cheyenne, he met an officer from the small, low-profile Bureau of Commonwealth Defense. Colonel Roger Kaytennae sometimes visited such conventions, where he might quietly talk an especially promising youth into a military career.

Kaytennae had himself grown up in North America, in the Arizona Prefecture. Eventually to become director of the Defense Bureau's War Games Section, where the army prepared in virtual reality for what they believed was inevitable alien contact, quite possibly hostile. Impressed by young Padilla's intelligence, vision and dedication, Kaytennae hired him as a civilian intern, where he could observe his talent, adaptability, and judgement. Within a few weeks the colonel had decided, and contrived a scholarship for his young fellow-American, dipping into the Bureau's discretionary funds.

He then enrolled Eric in Kunming University. There, with Kaytennae's participation, a professor of neurological physiology, and another in pseudo-organics, tailored a curriculum for the young man. This put him close to his military sponsor, and far from his parents, who were relieved if uneasy about their son's education being financed by the government.

His scholastic performance proved exemplary, and the colonel was soon satisfied that the young man's potential was as good as he'd hoped. Kaytennae then approached a wealthy manufacturer he'd cultivated, and got him to finance several scholarships. From the ranks of games enthusiasts, he'd already recruited several youths to fill those scholarships. Because Eric Padilla would need skilled collaborators and assistants.

At age thirty-seven, Doctor Eric Padilla personally and successfully removed the living central nervous system—the CNS—of one Carlos O'Brien. O'Brien was a thirty-year-old ex-construction worker who'd lost both arms and his eyesight in an explosion. Removed and transferred his CNS live, into a bioelectronic interface unit (BEIU, or "bottle") where it underwent hormonal detraumatization. Then he successfully installed the "activated" bottle into a newly designed prototype infantry combat servo. When fitted with the activated bottle, the servo provided a ruggedly formidable, prototype fighting machine.

This epochal operation was carried out with great care for secrecy. For the human rights movement had gone full circle, and begun to eat its own tail: to protect human rights, it undertook to deny them.

Normally Padilla was calm, unflappable, but he found the operation nerve-wracking. Not because of any possible leak and criminal prosecution; he gave that scenario almost no attention. But because neither he nor anyone else had ever performed such an operation on a live human being, and no one knew with certainty what the result would be. Of necessity, the servo's inputs to the overall sensorium were extremely complex, and though analogous, were quite unlike any a human CNS had experienced before. And especially troublesome, the procedure was not reversible. The human core of the cyborg could not be put back in its original body.

To function effectively for an extended period, the CNS requires an integrated set of inputs from its new body. Inputs producing a broad spectrum of information and responses that include, among other things, esthetics, orientation, discomfort, even a modified sense of pain. In fact, pretty much the same spectrum provided by human bodies. Padilla and his collaborators had spent a great deal of time and care in designing, testing, and fine-tuning the servo's quasi-organic nervous system, along with the manifold neural connections of the bioelectronic interface.

But the tests had used devices, not the human brain. There was no way Padilla could know, really know, how Carlos O'Brien would find life as a cyborg.

◇

That had been 157 years before the capture of Tagus Cove. Carlos O'Brien had wakened to life as a cyborg and found it mainly interesting, not traumatic. Certainly it was far better than his brief experience without arms or vision. Also it gave him a job—helping test the prototype. And the series of prototypes that followed, for if O'Brien could never wear a human body again, the bottle that held his CNS could be removed and installed in other servos. The more sensitive procedure had been installing the CNS into the bioelectronic interface unit—the BEIU, the bottle—attaching pseudo-organic neuro-connectors to biological nerves.

Then someone blew the whistle. The Respect Movement was outraged, and bottling was made illegal. And of course, careers were ruined, among them Eric Padilla's.

◇

Eventually the Wyzhñyñy arrived in the fringe of Commonwealth space, Henry Morgan's savanted message reached Kunming, and the news galvanized the Commonwealth. (Changing it forever, though just then no one gave "forever" much attention.) At that time, five manned servos existed, all secret. Five actual manned servos, but many virtual, generated in the computers that drove the Commonwealth military's virtual reality trainers.

Five manned servos, none of them military. That would quickly change. The Office of Industrial Mobilization would see to it.

Chapter Six
Maritimus

David MacDonald sat at the sundeck table, wearing shorts and Sunsafe, and reading a task report from *Submersible 4.* From their office, his wife's voice interrupted, loud and agitated. "David!"

Afterward it seemed to him he should have known, given the reports from Morgan the Pirate and Gem of the Prophet. But his immediate thought was that she'd cut herself, badly. In an instant he was on his feet and through the door. "What is it?"

"It's happened." Her agitation was gone now, leaving anger and chagrin. She pointed at the wall screen. "The hyperspace emergence detector just kicked in. There are 16,212 blips on the screen."

He turned and stared. A vast display of icons—mostly of large ships—was spread across a perspective representation of the Maritimus System.[1] A footer gave the number. Briefly he stared. "Good God," he muttered, then shook his head. "At least we're prepared for them." Most personnel, and all children but one, had been evacuated to Terra. Those who'd stayed had a very simple plan: if invaders arrive, get the hell out of F-space.

He turned to his wife. Yukiko Alegría Gavaldon—all five feet three inches and 115 muscular pounds of her—stood with hands on hips, face grim. They had eight years of work and dreams invested in Maritimus. His fingers tapped instructions on a key pad, and a klaxon began to blare over the master comm system, both on Home Base and at work locations—a sound that could waken the dead. He gave it ten seconds before switching it off and speaking into the microphone: "All personnel, this is Mac. All personnel, this is Mac. This is *not* a drill; repeat, *not* a drill. We've got 16,000 bogies in the fringe. That's 16,000 bogies. Carry out Plan 1-A promptly. Carry out Plan 1-A promptly." He gave them another five-second shot of the klaxon, then repeated his announcement, followed by a roll call.

The fourteen humans who'd remained on Maritimus had

told themselves the invaders might miss the system. But they'd retained the hyperspace vessel *Cousteau,* moving it to a cave that opened onto the sea, forty-one miles up the coast from Home Base. They'd also restricted their studies to a travel radius of two hours from Cave Bay, and kept their radios on at all times. Thus almost everyone responded as he read off their names. The two who didn't were accounted for. There were no questions.

His last order was to Dennis Bertrand: to message Terra of the invaders' arrival. The project's communication savant and her attendant lived aboard the *Cousteau.*

With roll call completed, Yukiko went to the spacious bedroom she shared with her husband. They kept partly packed bags in the closet; filling them would take only a few minutes. David stepped back onto the sundeck to grab his reader from the table, then went to help her.

First they finished packing. Then, while he carried their bags to the scooter shelter and stowed them, Yukiko ran a computer check on the status of the computer-destruct systems at the various locations. The Emergency War Directorate on Terra didn't want the invaders laying hands on a Commonwealth data base. Not that it was likely, if the invader's penchant for indiscriminate destruction was as bad as reported. The checkout was a stepwise procedure, requiring that she confirm each step. She considered the human confirmation needless, but did it as prescribed.

When she'd finished, David rechecked all manned locations. Everyone was to meet at Cave Base, aboard the *Cousteau.* The Talacogons had already left North Bay, and the Mellstads had left Cleaver Station. Ngozi and Hogan were about to leave Atoll Station. At Home Base, Marcel Kwong was loading his scooter just two hundred yards up the inlet from the MacDonalds. His wife Jeanne had just arrived in a jet boat, from an aborted run to service plankton traps. They'd leave within ten minutes.

With that information in hand, David activated the remote timer program for the destruction of all but the base at Cave Bay. If they lucked out and the invaders bypassed them, he could cancel it. *Fat chance,* he told himself. Aloud he said, "That is the hardest thing I've ever had to do."

Yukiko nodded. "Let's hope they leave without moving insystem. Given the descriptions from Gem, they're not remotely an aquatic life form. And if it's living space they're looking for, they won't find much here."

An exercise in false hope, she chided herself. Without a fly-by, the intruders wouldn't know that Maritimus was an ocean world without a single real continent. And if they came close enough for a fly-by... Even parked a few billion miles out, they'd have picked up the base's electronics signature as soon as they emerged from hyperspace. They'd know there was technology here. And judging from Tagus and Gem, they'd come in with death and destruction on their minds.

"I'm going down and let the dolphs know," she said. "We can't leave without telling them."

"Go ahead," David answered, then turned and left the room. The house was cantilevered over the inlet, some fifty feet above the Tufftile dock where *Submersible 1* lay secured. The rear of the house, however, opened on the cliff top, where a three-walled shelter of deep-jade Tuffglass housed their travel scooter. He took their bags to it in two trips, loading them in the already half-filled luggage compartment.

On the first luggage trip, he saw the Kwongs' scooter start off across the inlet. Now everyone except himself and Yukiko were at or on their way to Cave Bay. After the second load, he returned to the deck and looked down through a Tuffglass panel at *Submersible 1*. Its hatch was open: Yukiko was still talking to the dolphs via the speaker. While waiting, he found himself fidgeting, and wondered why. It would take hours for invader ships to arrive by warpdrive. Finally Yukiko emerged, shut the hatch behind her, and started for the stairs. David went back to the scooter and activated the AG.

Two minutes later, she came out carrying a padded beverage basket. "Brandy," she said, holding it up. "In case we have something to celebrate, or for night caps if we don't." She put it in the luggage carrier, then climbed into the cab. Their weight, when they sat down, activated the restraint fields in their seats.

David's fingers tapped a brief instruction, then at his practiced touch on the joy stick, the scooter rose slightly, moving out of the shelter.

When they were clear, he accelerated, the scooter curving smoothly out over the inlet. Yukiko looked down past her feet at dark water. *So much to learn here,* she told herself, *and so much potential.* She wondered if they'd ever come back. It seemed to her she should have been incarnated a dolphin. Maybe next life.

So far they'd found no evidence that Maritimus had any sapient native life form: terrestrial, aquatic, or avian. But they'd released thirty dolphins to assist in a survey of native marine life, and Yukiko was—or had been—in charge. Now she felt as if she were running out on them. But the dolphs were smart and resourceful, and they knew the situation.

The scooter had crossed the inlet, and they were low over Dolerite Point, when Yukiko became aware of the cold. She frowned. "David..." she began.

"I feel it," he answered, and tapped brief instructions to the scooter, his eyes on the resulting heads-up display. "It's the AG cooling system," he said. It was almost the only thing that went wrong with scooters.

"Can we make it to Cave Bay?"

"We'd better." He veered the scooter out over the ocean's edge. If the drive shut down, they wouldn't be able to stay aloft for long; they'd coast down on whatever azimuth they'd been flying, modified by the wind. With considerable momentum and no control at all. And if they were over the rugged coast when they hit, they'd likely be killed.

Yukiko switched her microphone on. "This is Yukiko," she said. "Dennis, we're on our way, but we're having AG trouble. We're on our way, but having AG trouble. Do you read me? Over."

Dennis Bertrand was their licensed hyperspace navigator, stationed at Cave Bay. His wife, Ju-Li, was the attendant of the project's savant, who was also her baby sister. "This is Bertrand," he said. "I read you, Yukiko, loud and clear. Marcel is about a dozen miles south of here. I'll have him turn back and follow you in, just in case. Over."

"Thank you, Dennis. Yukiko out."

David set a course that would keep them near the shore without taking them over land till they crossed Cedar Point. After Cedar Point they'd have a straight shot over water to the *Cousteau* in its cave. *If we get that far,* he thought. The cab was getting *really* chilly.

He'd barely thought it before the drive choked, nearly died, cutting back in just long enough that he initiated a turn shoreward. Then it cut out entirely, leaving the turn incomplete. Bracing himself, David opened the door on his side. He wanted to keep it open just a little, like an off-center drag chute, to complete his shoreward turn by air resistance. Which was stronger than he'd anticipated. He hadn't tightened his restraint field, and the door jerked him half out of the scooter. For a moment his joints turned to water. His mind knew that the restraint field, even lax as he'd left it, would keep him from being pulled out, but his body didn't believe it. Then the handle ripped free of his clutch, and the door banged back against the scooter's side. But not before nudging the craft almost directly toward the rocky shore. Heart still hammering, he tightened his restraint field.

They were losing elevation more rapidly now. Marcel wouldn't get to them till well after they were in the drink, and with the decay of the scooter's residual AG, they wouldn't stay afloat long. Punching the fat mayday switch in front of him, David let anyone within range know they were about to crash. Some distance ahead, surf raised on a rocky shelf, to slam against massive basalt blocks fallen from the cliffs behind it. Ahead to their right, a low rocky islet stood just above the sea.

"Yukiko," David said, "open your door. And hang onto it as hard as you can!"

She realized what he had in mind, and didn't hesitate. She cracked the door, and instantly the air jerked it wide. Her seat restraint field held her securely if resiliently. The door jerked her shoulder muscles painfully before tearing from her grasp. Now they were headed almost toward the islet, though well short of it. "David," she said, "the seat cushions…"

She didn't finish; he already knew. Holding their breath, they stared at the onrushing water. David shut his eyes, felt the scooter hit, skip, hit again, skip again, and again, each skip shorter than the one before. One final time it struck, nosing into a swell, jarring hard, then stopped. Their restraint fields had eased the shock while pressing the breath out of them.

David's eyes had popped open, and he pushed his restraint release, then looked at Yukiko. She was already free of hers. Water was spilling in over their feet. A touch on the control panel slid the cab's tinted hood back. A swell lifted them. David rose from his seat, snatched up its cushion and thrust his arms into the straps. "Go!" he shouted, and jumped.

In the water, another swell raised them. Beside him and slightly ahead, the scooter lifted again, less buoyant now. His eyes found Yukiko perhaps fifteen feet away and slightly to his rear as the swell left them behind. When the next swell lifted them, they saw waves breaking on the point of the small islet, ahead and a little to their right. The scooter would be carried past it, toward the surf crashing on the rocks some three hundred yards ahead.

"Swim for the island!" he shouted. "Don't let yourself be carried past it." Then he began kicking his feet, swimming toward it himself. *Marcel will find us,* he thought. *And if he doesn't, the surf may be less dangerous when the tide recedes.* Not that the tides amounted to much.

◇

Marcel Kwong had received the mayday signal, but gotten only an azimuth, not a location. Not knowing of Yukiko's delay to message the dolphins, he assumed the two were somewhere north of Cedar Point. When he reached the point without spotting them, he turned back, flying higher to see more area.

After flying halfway back to where he'd received the mayday, Marcel consulted briefly again with Bertrand, then turned south once more, seriously anxious now. The sun was low, cut off by the cliffs now. This time he crossed Cedar Point instead of stopping. Seventeen miles from Home Base, his wife spotted the twisted, surf-battered scooter on the rocks, each successive breaker compounding the destruction. Angling lower, they approached it at an altitude of twenty feet. Not surprisingly its cab was empty, its hood torn half off. He made two sweeps above the shelf, watching for bodies, and found none. That didn't surprise them either. There'd be an undertow here, and a south-flowing current offshore.

He switched on his microphone. "Dennis," he called, "this is Marcel. Dennis, this is Marcel. We've found the wreckage of a scooter on the shelf rock nine miles south of Cedar Point. But no bodies or survivors. We need help in finding either bodies or survivors. Over."

"Marcel, this is Bertrand. Elisio and Nona just arrived from North Bay, and Ngozi is on her way from the atoll. How badly was the scooter damaged? Over."

"It was utterly demolished, and I can't picture a human surviving the breakers here. There's shelf rock and lots of boulders. Over."

"All right, follow the offshore current south. They could be riding it on their seat cushions, watching for a gap. My chart shows a good-sized stream coming down off the plateau about four miles south of the wreck. There'll be a break in the boulder line there, and the outflow current should make the surf less dangerous. Over."

"Got it. We'll follow the offshore current south. Marcel out." He angled southward at about fifty feet above the waves.

He glanced at the time display: 1714 base time. It seemed to him they needed to find David and Yukiko today. Tomorrow would be too late.

◇

Footnote:

[1] Normally, in the Commonwealth, when a system is settled, it is named for its first colonized planet. The exceptions are systems with well-known names of long standing.

Chapter Seven
Reconnaisance

For a pirate, Henry Morgan was amiable. Almost always.

Seven years before the Wyzhñyñy arrived, his Squadron One had captured the hyperspace yacht *Guinevere,* whose owner/master was identified in the yacht's records as Gomer Colwyn. Though Morgan at first didn't know that. Trapped in F-space and under the pirate's beamgun, Colwyn had asked for quarter, and Morgan, as always, granted the plea. In the case of merchantmen, his practice was to disarm the ship, then loot it before giving it back. But the *Guinevere* was well suited for use as a corsair. So when she hove to, Morgan decided to load her personnel and passengers aboard a lifeboat and send them off, then put a prize crew aboard the yacht to fly it to Tagus.

The yacht's master had other ideas. After accepting the pirate's clemency, Gomer Colwyn had drawn a blaster from inside his blouse. With shocking quickness and force, Morgan disarmed and disabled the man. Colwyn cursed him then— surely those were curses—in a language unfamiliar to the crew.

Morgan's face turned stony hard, and he replied in what sounded like the same language. Then he ordered all the captives manacled, and told Colwyn to flip a coin for each of the twenty others the *Guinevere* had carried. Heads they lived, tails they died. Either that or choose ten to live. Colwyn wilted—he couldn't do either—so Morgan decided for him. One by one, ten of the yacht's eleven male crew—stoic or struggling, pleading or praying or silent—were jettisoned out the trash lock. To float as corpsicles in the empty vastness between Not Worth Much and New Pecos. The yacht's second officer he spared.

Morgan's boarding party was stunned. A few were near mutiny.

The eight passengers remained. A broken Colwyn pleaded for their lives; one was his wife and another his daughter. After listening, Morgan had all eight loaded into the forty-foot lifeboat with the second officer, and let them go. When they were gone, he told Colwyn he'd had the lifeboat's strange-space generator disabled. It would take them decades to reach a habitable world. Except of course they couldn't; not alive. In a few months they'd run out of food.

At that, Colwyn went psychotic. Morgan had him strapped screaming into a workboat, personally disabled its drive, then set it adrift.

When it was gone, Morgan sagged. With the boarding party, he returned to his modest flagship, leaving only the six-man prize crew. Then he generated hyperspace, set course for Tagus, and retired to his suite.

What, if anything, he told Connie Phamonyong, none of his men knew. But after comparing notes, there was one thing they did know: their commodore had *not* had the lifeboat's strange-space generator disabled. Only the workboat had been sabotaged. The yacht-owner's family and guests, and the second officer, were safely on their way to whatever world they'd chosen. In that, Morgan had been merciful. Not that it made up for murdering eleven people, only one of whom had done anything to earn it.

<>

In his suite, Morgan told Connie nothing, simply opened a bottle of brandy, and drank from it. He *had* known Colwyn, but hadn't recognized him till Colwyn cursed him in Welsh. Then Morgan had identified himself. Morgan had been eleven the last time they'd seen each other, and Colwyn had been in his twenties—his father's first cousin, his own second cousin. Colwyn had always treated him badly, pouring sarcasm over him, sometimes slapping him around. Though never abusing him sexually. That right his father reserved for himself. As a young man, Morgan had suspected his father had sodomized Colwyn when *he* was a child, and that Colwyn took it out on him.

If he hadn't told Colwyn who he was, this wouldn't have happened. Not that he regretted deep-sixing him. What troubled him was having killed the ten crew members. Telling himself he'd been insane at the time hadn't helped.

◇

An hour later, Morgan had moved into a vacant crew cabin. When he finally emerged again, three days later, he smelled of brandy. But although he may have been drunk much of the time, he lacked severe tremor, and showed no sign of hallucinating. So, two days drunk and one getting well, the crew concluded.

Meanwhile, even those who'd been most disturbed by their captain's actions aboard the *Guinevere* had recovered from their shock. Largely because of their commodore's reaction to his own deeds. It was agreed he must have known the yacht's skipper earlier in life.

After emerging from his isolation, Morgan began showing up for meals, saying something now and then, and sweating regularly in the workout room. His second continued to run the ship. He also moved back in with Connie and Robert. Long before they reached Tagus, Henry Morgan seemed normal once more, and the crew was at ease with him again.

All of that, though, had been seven years earlier, and seldom did anyone, including Morgan, think of it anymore.

◇

The first night after the Wyzhñyñy arrived, Henry Morgan wakened from an ugly dream, its events remaining sharply in his mind. In the dream he'd been a little boy. His father had been flogging Morgan's mother with a large penis, like a horse's, while she'd cried bitterly. Then he'd turned to Morgan, raised the penis, and began to beat him too.

It was then Morgan had wakened, to find his face and pillow wet with tears. It had been a very long time since he'd revisited those days. The stories he told Robert were fictions. He wasn't entirely sure what Robert might have experienced or remembered. He himself had run away — escaped—at age fourteen.

Apparently he'd been crying aloud, or perhaps thrashing around, because Connie was awake, her eyes wide, and white by the nightlight. Without saying anything, he'd patted her shoulder reassuringly, then got up and went into the small kitchen, to drink himself into a stupor. Something he hadn't done since just after the *Guinivere.*

◇

When next he awoke, it was in bed. Obviously he'd gotten there himself; Connie was too small to have managed it. His stomach was queasy, and there was a hard, heavy pain behind his forehead. Groaning, he found the bottle lying unstoppered on its side. It still held a shot or so, trapped by the bottle's shoulder, and he swallowed what was left. Then he asked Connie to make coffee. While he waited, he marched in place, raising his knees high and swinging his arms. When the coffee was ready, he had bread and jam with it, then read to Robert from the savant's favorite storycube. Afterward he planned, as far as it made sense to. He would, he decided, remain holed up for four weeks. "The invaders will either leave or stay," he told Connie. "If they're going to leave, they should be gone by then. And if they stay, they'll have had time to decide there aren't any of us left."

Electric torch in one hand and a C-sized power slug in a pocket, he'd ventured up the tunnel and stairs that led to his bolt hole. He wasn't surprised that the first 200 yards were intact. It was the last dozen he'd worried about, where the protective rock overhead thinned as he approached the tunnel's opening. The part that worried him most was the steel door. It had been installed to slide open and shut, and the bombardment might have deformed the rock, holding the door immovable. He installed the power slug in the door mechanism, and holding his breath, pressed the switch.

The door slid back smoothly, and the weight of the world lifted from Morgan's shoulders. Beyond the door were three more yards of tunnel, cut to resemble a natural break in the rock. It opened inconspicuously near the bottom of a draw, 0.7 mile from the gorge the invaders had pounded so severely. Cautiously he crept far enough to peer out. The bombardment had reached here, too; the forest was a shambles of broken trees.

Silently, thoughtfully, he withdrew back down the tunnel, and closed the steel door behind him. It seemed to him things were better than he deserved.

◇

Henry Morgan tended to be a patient man, and he stuck to his decision to stay holed up for four weeks. Meanwhile he spent more time than usual with Robert, telling him stories that grew more outlandish with time, making the savant whoop with laughter. Some of them even made Connie laugh. She had a pleasant sense of humor, but wasn't much given to laughing out loud. They were remarkably happy for three people hiding in a tunnel thirty yards underground. Morgan wasn't sure if they were the happiest four weeks of his life, or whether he simply had more time to appreciate them. It occurred to him the two might go together.

He also inventoried their supplies. For some of them, the need had been foreseen. Others had been stashed "just in case." He worked up two ration schedules—one for twenty months and one for thirty—and a chart on which Connie could keep a record of use. It wasn't something he considered vital; if they were somehow rescued, it would likely be sooner than twenty months. And if they weren't, then sooner or later they'd have to surface anyway, and forage for their keep. So he'd chosen the twenty-month version; they could back off on it later if it seemed best.

There was also a box of aerial stereo-pairs he'd had taken of that entire end of the continent. From them, the base computer, now undoubtedly destroyed, had produced a set of large-scale topographic maps with forest shaded green. There was little which wasn't forest: the "resort," and an occasional marsh or rocky prominence. The photography and maps had seemed like a good idea at the time. Now he was truly glad to have them.

Meanwhile he undertook to overhaul his body, for he was overweight and out of shape. He began to eat less, while following a modest kung fu regimen. He'd learned it as a youth and small-time criminal, at Kip Poi's Hall in Vancouver. Not that he imagined kung fu would prove effective against invader soldiers, but it improved his endurance and flexibility. He also did strength exercises that some spacers used in relatively confined quarters. Emphasizing his legs, because when he resurfaced, they'd be his only means of travel.

◇

When finally he emerged beneath the sky, he carried a pack, binoculars, and a short-barreled blaster with a fully-charged power slug and spares. *Now,* he told himself, *we'll see how effective that exercising was.* He marked the tunnel opening with a sort of mini-cairn, thirty yards away in the bottom of the draw: a thirty-pound chunk of stone atop a larger. It was something a snooping invader was unlikely to recognize as meaningful. Then he re-shouldered his pack and headed on a compass course for the ex "resort."

For a hundred yards he picked his way through forest debris from the invader attack, the damage thinning as he went. Then he was out of it, in peaceful forest, where he settled for an easy pace and a short day. Exercising underground didn't prepare the feet for hiking in boots not well broken in, and blistered feet didn't fit his plans.

One of his maps showed a rocky knob less than three miles from the site of the old resort. On its top, the trees were sufficiently sparse and small that the computer had mapped it as bald. He climbed it late on the second day, and standing beneath a stubby, umbrella-like tree, trained his binoculars on the distant clearing where the resort had been.

A month earlier, he might not have seen the clearing from where he stood; certainly not much of it. It had been only twenty acres, and all but a very small part would have been screened by bordering forest. Now he guessed its area at perhaps a square mile. From its borders rose the haze of burnt-down fires, no doubt of woody debris from land clearing. Through the haze he made out buildings and activity. Tiny figures moved about on machinery and afoot, figures minute with distance, but clearly not human.

Morgan took a deep breath of relief. This part of the continent had always struck him as fertile enough, and the ancient volcanic surface was mostly not rugged. But the planet had what seemed to him more promising land for colonizing, much of it on other continents. He'd feared that when they'd destroyed what they could find of human settlement—this one tiny area—they might leave, and settle halfway across the planet. And that wouldn't have served his purpose.

His lightweight binoculars weren't powerful enough to show him much detail. As he watched what he could see, he plotted his next move. He would, he decided, approach the fringe of the opening that day, and lay up overnight. At dawn he'd move closer, and see what he could learn, then return to base and see if he could get inside through one of the hangar openings. Hopefully he could work his way to his yacht. There was something he very much wanted to get from it.

Chapter Eight
A Scarce Resource

The voice on the phone was the prime minister's. "Mr. President," it said, "I have granted Dr. Farrukhi an audience, and you may want to be present. It is about the savant situation of course."

"When?"

"At 11:30—in forty minutes. The hour will help him be brief. He called only moments ago." Peixoto chuckled. "He wanted to bring Ho and Sriharan. I told him to come by himself."

Chang glanced at the screen. On it was page 17 of a hypertext document on Masadan military training, and its applicability to the Commonwealth's new army. He was skeptical; the Masadan culture was far more homogeneous than the Terran. Unlike any other human world, Masada had maintained and cherished a tradition of compulsory military training. Through centuries without enemies. From a 30th century viewpoint, it was one of the more unlikely marvels of human social behavior.

"Eleven-thirty? I will be there," said the president, and disconnected. Unlike himself, the prime minister preferred electronic conferencing. "People need not leave their desks," he'd explained. "And we are more concise. There is less protocol and small-talk." Occasionally he asked someone to his office, especially if they were officed on the same wing and floor. But for those like Farrukhi, officed elsewhere, such requests were rare.

The president tapped an alarm instruction on his timer, giving himself thirty-five minutes, then returned his attention to the Masadan document, and continued reading as if he'd never been interrupted.

◇

He arrived on the dot, to find Farrukhi there ahead of him, not yet seated. The psychologist was a thin man with an apologetic expression, and a fringe of black hair framing an expanse of bald brown head. If allowed to, his blue jaw would grow far more hair than his cranium. In other company he would have seemed tall, but in the same room with Foster Peixoto...

Farrukhi worked in the Office of Technical Recruitment. The previous afternoon, he'd sent Peixoto a brief description of a problem. Without suggesting possible action; a lack the prime minister despised. But the description seemed to say it all: War House had issued a confidential document outlining the intended conduct of the war. A description that, if carried out, required more than twelve hundred savant communicators. However, Farrukhi pointed out, only 447 suitable savants were known to exist. Nearly three hundred of them were at Commonwealth embassies on colony worlds, their only effective means of communication with Kunming.

The prime minister waved his two guests to chairs. "So," he said to Farrukhi, "what do you suggest?"

The man squirmed. Literally. "I hesitated to enter this into the system, but there are many verified savants in institutions, in very delicate health. With critically defective hearts or immune systems, or with physiological processes that fluctuate beyond sustainable limits. Most die in childhood. If they could be transferred...their central nervous systems that is..." His dark face grew even darker with blood. "Transferred into mobile life support modules..."

Say it, man, Chang thought. *The word is "bottled!"* But the idea was excellent, a potential solution.

"Unfortunately..." Shrugging, Farrukhi spread his hands.

"I know," Peixoto finished. "Bottling is illegal. But with our new war powers, that will be changed by supper." *To be followed by outrage,* he added silently.

The psychologist nodded. "I am also aware of another at least potential source. Worldwide there are many...'defective' children not identified as savants. And most in fact are not, but surely some are. If we could screen them... But..."

"But unfortunately," Peixoto finished for him, "it will further outrage our watchdogs."

Again Farrukhi's head bobbed. "And equally important is the matter of finding suitable sensitives to serve as attendants, to manage their communication function."

"Surely there are more psychically sensitive persons than there are savants."

"I'm sure there are. But again, the problem is to identify them. Many will seem quite ordinary, and prefer to keep their sensitivity private."

The president spoke now. "How have they been identified in the past?"

"In the past, sensitives were hired who were already known to institutions researching the field."

"Ah!" said Chang, "but surely some of the anonymous sensitives associate with others. Identify such groups and their meeting places. Post notices on the Ether: 'good money and secure, satisfying jobs for qualified sensitives.' Make the wages suitably attractive; perhaps equivalent to a PS-12. Consult with the attendants of savants already in government service. Ask their advice."

Farrukhi's face brightened. He shifted to the edge of his seat, as if to dash out and get started.

"Doctor," the prime minister said, "the president and I thank you for your astute help. I want you to sketch out quickly—before you break for supper—a rough plan to carry all this out. Now, don't let me keep you from getting started."

Abdol Farrukhi's long legs raised him from his chair. "Thank you, Mr. Prime Minister," he said, then looked at Chang Lung-Chi. "Thank you, Mr. President."

When he had gone, Peixoto turned to Chang. "It distresses me," he said glumly, "to outrage the honest if mistaken scruples of so many people. It could lead to demonstrations."

Chang grunted; his own distress threshold was higher than the prime minister's. To him there were reasonable people, and there were problem people, the latter including the chronically indignant. "We do what we must," he said, "and when we've won the war, or lost it, any demonstrations will be forgotten."

"Nonetheless…" said his friend, and shrugged. "Why don't we have lunch together? On your balcony over the rotunda. We can talk about other things than problems."

The president agreed, and they did their best to talk about grandchildren, the food, and the weather. It wasn't much of a conversation, but they'd get plenty of practice before the war was over.

Chapter Nine
Drago Draveç

The flood of early human migration to outsystem worlds was almost entirely atavistic—agrarian, ethnic, sectarian, or some combination of them. By the 26th century, however, humankind in the Sol System had evolved enough, socially, politically and spiritually, that sectarianism had greatly shrunken. Ethnic and racial mixing was widespread and accepted, chauvinism had lost its edge, and tolerance had far outgrown intolerance. As a result, colonization almost stopped; only nine new projects left Terra in the 26th century.

It picked up strongly, though, in the 27th, with new projects directed largely at the Ultima Fornax Sector, to facilitate eventual intercolonial commerce—a factor ignored during the centuries when colonists sought isolation. Most of the new colonists wanted to expand financially, and felt inhibited by Terran legal and cultural restrictions, or by established competitors, or both. Or simply wanted to start over on a virgin planet, this time to "do it right." In any case they had the goal of creating interacting, high-tech societies, using Terran technology and experience. As a result, by the 29th century, interplanetary commerce had become significant in the remote Ultima Fornax Sector.

> *Syllabus of Human History*
> Collegiate Books,
> Lyon, France

Sky Harbor was the political and commercial capital of Hart's Desire, and Drago Draveç, Henry Morgan's surrogate, knew it well. And while he had nothing to fence this trip, Morgan had done business there with Harlan Cheregian for more than a decade. And Cheregian, who knew everything and everybody worth knowing on Hart's Desire, also had the ear of government there.

The monsoon had arrived, hot and humid, and Drago Draveç set the *Minerva* down at the port of Sky Harbor in an afternoon deluge. (The squadron's other three ships had put down at Nuevo Oaxaca, far from Harts' central government. Summers at Nuevo Oaxaca were relatively cool and dry, the entertainment district less restricted, and the port authority more flexible. And Harlan Cheregian had a branch office there.)

A cabby had seen the *Minerva* land, and moved hopefully to her pad. Draveç sprinted the few unprotected yards to it, jumped in and slammed the door behind him, somewhat less than soaked.

"Where to?" asked the cabby.

"The roof of the Cheregian Building."

They expecting you?"

"I wouldn't go if he wasn't."

He. The cabby nodded. The spacer was indifferently dressed, but he'd arrived in what appeared to be a very expensive yacht, and gave the impression of someone in charge. Cheregian probably did expect him. The cabby lifted his floater against the downpour, riding lights flashing a penetrating blue, then swung toward the commercial district, headed for the Cheregian Building. "You from offworld?"

"Yep."

"Did you hear about the alien invasion?"

"Yep."

The spacer's answers didn't inspire follow-ups. Minutes later the floater hovered inches above the Cheregian Building's passenger pad, as close to the canopy as the cabby could get it. A flunky in a suit waited with an umbrella. The cabby turned to Drago, expecting plastic, and wondering what sort of tipper the guy was. Instead of plastic, the spacer handed him a Commonwealth 50-credit note, and got out saying "keep the change." He'd hoped for more, but it wasn't too bad.

Drago had been to the Cheregian Building before, and remembered his umbrella-carrying guide, who asked his name but didn't request identification. They rode a drop tube down a single level to the seventh floor, then followed a clean-carpeted corridor to a suite. The suite and its furnishings were like the building, the corridor, the carpet—not imposing, but they indicated money and conservatism. A receptionist buzzed Cheregian and announced "Mr. Draveç." Drago did not doubt that Cheregian was watching on a screen.

The receptionist looked up at Drago's guide. "Take Mr. Draveç in," she said.

The first thing Cheregian said was, "I presume you know about the aliens." Everyone on Harts knew. The Gem of the Prophet had been captured, and apparently the Star of Hibernia. Darwin's World was also in the invasion corridor, not so far from Star. So the Commonwealth embassy there had evacuated to Hart's Desire, which seemed to be safely clear.

Drago nodded. "The aliens don't fool around. They started pounding Tagus the same day they arrived in the system."

"I suppose you have nothing to sell this time," Cheregian said.

"Right. What I'm looking for now is a favor."

Cheregian's rambunctious eyebrows rose. "I suppose you know that Commodore Morgan warned Kunming. A selfless act. What favor do you have in mind?"

Warned Kunming? This made things look more promising. "I want to use the Commonwealth embassy's savant, to propose something to Kunming. But if I simply knocked on their door, I'd probably end up in jail. So I hoped you'd refer me to them. Call me an ex-employee you haven't seen in years..."

"Hmm. And what is this proposal to Kunming?"

Draveç smiled wryly. "For three years I was a midshipman in the Space Academy. I want to scout the aliens. Sting them, see how they respond. Learn whether they have force shields, that sort of thing. Then duck into warpspace and let Kunming know by savant. Which means I'll need to take one with me."

"Aha. What do you suppose the odds are that the aliens will let you escape, after you've, ah, 'stung' them?'"

"I've got four ships. I'll stand off, send them in and watch, then generate warpspace and report to Kunming. I've talked it out with my captains, at rendezvous." Drago paused. "The aliens moved in and started blasting without any communication whatever. As if they preferred killing to negotiation. So our prospects of survival—mine, the Commonwealth's, the human species'!—look rotten. And this just might help."

Cheregian nodded, thinking *sixteen thousand ships.* "I'll see what I can do," he said, then tapped keys and spoke to his phone. He was put on hold, but only for half a minute. Meanwhile he keyed the call to his desk speaker, so Draveç could hear both sides of the exchange.

A woman's voice spoke. "This is Ambassador Khai. What can I do for you, Mr. Cheregian?"

"I have a gentleman in my office, a Mr. Drago Draveç. He was referred to me by a business associate who feels I might have more influence with you than he would. Mr. Draveç would like to propose something to you regarding the alien intruders. And he seems to me worth listening to. He's one of Commodore Morgan's associates."

"Indeed! Well." There was a moment's silence. "The alien intruders." Another silence. "I'll send a car for him. It should arrive at your roof in—ten minutes. Considering what Commodore Morgan has done for humanity, we owe him that."

With eyebrows raised questioningly, Cheregian turned again to Drago, who nodded. "He'll be waiting," Cheregian said, then disconnected.

<><>

Drago went to the embassy in the ambassador's chauffeured floater. She didn't ask many more questions than Harlan Cheregian had. She'd already alerted her savant's attendant. Now she talked her way to Admiralty Chief Fedor Tischendorf himself. With Tischendorf "on the line," she turned the session over to the pirate, prepared to assist if necessary.

Savant communicators duplicated not only the speakers'

words, but their voice, tone, and emphasis, as nearly as their vocal equipment allowed. Which was nearer than a listener might think possible, given the typical savant's mental and physical difficulties. To Drago it was almost like listening to the admiral himself, who took him seriously, and definitely seemed interested. Tischendorf—famous for his recall—remembered Drago from twenty years past. The pirate had been a promising midshipman, till he'd been expelled for repeated unacceptable behavior while on pass. The space academy was fairly lenient about minor misbehavior on pass, but Draveç's had outgrown minor. His loyalty and command potential had never been questioned. His problem had been impulsive mischief or violence, usually inspired or aggravated by alcohol.

The admiral and the pirate rather quickly agreed on what Drago could reasonably hope to learn about the aliens, and how to approach the mission. Then Tischendorf spoke with Ambassador Khai again. "Madam Ambassador, I'd appreciate it if you'd arrange the transfer of Ambassador Rees's savant to—um—Commodore Draveç. And the savant's attendant, of course. Can you do that?"

Rees, Drago realized, had to be the Commonwealth's evacuee ambassador to Darwin's World.

"I'll propose it to Ambassador Rees."

"Do you expect him to balk?"

"I don't expect him to, no. He doesn't need a savant; he no longer has an embassy. And he's been an agreeable guest."

"Good. Let me know when it's arranged. And Drago, keep me informed of your progress."

◇

Though she couldn't have said why, Ambassador Khai had felt a moment's misgiving when Tischendorf asked her to arrange the meeting with Rees. When she went to Rees's small embassy apartment and broached the matter, the man's face went—wooden was the best description. But he agreed to talk with Draveç.

Ten minutes later she brought Draveç to Rees's living room. "Mr. Ambassador," she said, "I'd like you to meet Commodore

Drago Draveç.   Commodore Draveç, this is Ambassador Llewellyn Gustavo Rees."

Now Rees's face was more stony than wooden. Drago realized something was seriously wrong, but extended his hand. "I'm pleased to meet you, Mr. Ambassador."

Rees's arms remained stiffly at his sides. "I had never," he said, "expected the pleasure of meeting one of Morgan's men under such—gratifying circumstances."

Drago frowned, his extended hand lowering. "It seems you don't like me," he said slowly. "Care to elaborate on that?"

"First let me say how pleased I am that your nest of hoodlums has been destroyed. And if you think I dislike you... I hate your master, Henry Morgan, with a passion you could never understand."

The pirate's gaze was mild, but it didn't soften Rees. "I got that," Drago said, hoping to get the meeting back on the subject. "And I suppose it's appropriate for you to hate him. And me. What do you think about the aliens?"

"I prefer them to you.   They perform their atrocities against foreign life forms. You perform yours against your own species."

Drago stood quietly, groping for a useful response, something that wouldn't torpedo his proposal. "Ah... Meanwhile the matter at hand is a reconnaissance of the alien armada. And I need your savant to make it work."

"You shall not have her, sir. First of all, you intend no reconnaissance. That is a cover, a sham. Your intention is to get hold of a savant for your own piratical purposes. And my savant is female—I'll wager you'd like that, wouldn't you?"

Drago's hands took them all by surprise. Quick as snakes they grabbed Llewellyn Rees by the shirt front and jerked him close, even as the seams split. The violence shattered the man, who began to babble. But to Drago the babbling made sense. "Do you remember the yacht *Guinevere,* Mister Pirate? Do you remember the officers and crew jettisoned out the trash lock? One of them was my younger brother! Murdered! Cold-bloodedly, without even being accused of anything! Our sister was Gomer Colwyn's niece, sent off in a lifeboat. It was she who told us what happened."

Rees was panting and trembling with repressed hysteria.

Drago stared and let him go. All he could say to the man was, "I'm sorry. I understand." To Ambassador Khai he said, "Let's go."

Two minutes later they were alone in her office. The emotional encounter had left her almost as shaken as Rees, but she'd remained oriented on Drago's mission. "You'll have your savant," she said. "I'll message Kunming, tell them I'm going to let you take Peng, and I'll take Lew's Lovisa to myself. I'm in charge here; I have the authority. And if they have misgivings, I'll refer them to Admiral Tischendorf."

She paused, looking at Drago, really seeing him for the first time. "Would you like a short drink before you return to your ship?"

"Yeah, I could stand a drink."

"I have several mild liquers..."

"Scotch and water if you have it."

She poured first for him, then for herself, and they sipped. "Lew really lost it this evening," she said.

"Ambassador Rees? Yes he did."

"You handled it effectively."

Drago shrugged. "It's a good thing he didn't see the *Minerva.* My ship. She's the old *Guinevere,* renamed for the Roman goddess of martial prowess."

"Really!" She paused. "What is there to Llewellyn's story?"

He told her. He hadn't actually been there; as Morgan's principal captain, he'd been off with the other squadron, and heard the story after returning to Tagus. From the man who'd brought the *Guinevere* in as a prize.

"Morgan got back a month later," he went on. "The Morgan I knew, had known for years, was easy to get along with. The boss, but even-tempered. I'd seen him annoyed, but that was unusual. And I hadn't been able to reconcile the man I knew with the story I'd heard. So one evening over cognac I asked him about it."

Drago paused, pulling threads, retrieving memories. "And he told me. Things he'd never told anyone, he said, not even Connie. His father had been an abuser. Abused him sexually and generally. And the owner-master of the *Guinevere*—the ultimate in coincidence—was a cousin named Colwyn, maybe ten years older than Morgan." Drago fished for a moment and came up with the first name. "Gomer Colwyn. Morgan's dad had abused him, too, and Colwyn took it out on Morgan. They hadn't seen one another since Morgan ran away from home, barely in his teens. Made a living as a petty criminal, and worked up from there.

"Anyway Morgan recognized Colwyn. Who tried to get the drop on him. The boss got the gun away from him, and things were said. In Welsh. Until Morgan totally lost control, and did what he did. Afterward, according to the crew, he locked himself in a cabin and stayed drunk for days."

Khai sighed gustily. "Gentle Buddha," she said, "the things people do to each other!" And wondered how Drago Draveç had wandered into piracy.

When they'd finished their drinks, her chauffeur took Drago back to the *Minerva.* She'd been tempted to invite him to spend the night. She was only forty-three, and her mirror told her she was still attractive. Drago Draveç was probably still short of forty, and the most vital man she'd seen since…ever, she decided. And she hadn't had a man in her bed since she'd left Terra. Her husband, the director of a major art museum, had refused to follow her off-world, and she'd never been seriously tempted to indulge herself in the opportunities on Harts.

It's best not to this time, either, she'd told herself. *It would complicate things.*

◇

She awoke to someone pounding on her bedroom door. A marine guard, a sergeant; she recognized the voice. "All right!" she called, "I'm awake! I'm awake!" Muttering, she swung her legs out of bed; dawnlight filtered through one-way windows. Slipping into her robe, she went to the door and opened it. "What is it?" she demanded.

"Ma'am, it's Ambassador Rees! He's been found bound and gagged in a closet, with a lump on his head! When he woke up, he made enough noise, thumping around, to wake up his orderly."

Her eyes widened, then narrowed. *Draveç. It had to be Draveç.*

"And ma'am, his savant is gone! And her attendant!"

Good grief! she thought, *and right under the noses of marine security.* The *Minerva* would be gone, too, from Sky Harbor and probably from F-space. The Ministry would cry bloody murder, and look for someone to blame. Her.

She looked at the situation. If War House backed her, it might not turn out too badly. In these times, War House would outweigh the Ministry. And Österdorf wasn't deputy minister for security anymore.

Security. She wondered if her marines had anything to do with this, then shook her head: surely not.

Chapter Ten
Esau Wesley

The trees were tall for a heavyworld. Mostly their branches were strongly upsweeping, but remained subordinate to the strong central trunk.

This was old forest, the ground marked by fallen, "mossy" trunks of an older generation gradually converting to soil. Scattered patches of green shoots broke the sodden layer of last year's fallen leaves. Here and there were clusters of delicate pink —the first spring flowers.

Esau Wesley was adding his own dynamic to the ever-fluctuating system. He swung his ax again, and a chip flew from the steelwood tree. Then "chop!" and "chop!", and another flew. He continued, working his way around the tree without pause, cutting an unbroken ring through the hard bark and outermost layer of wood. Only then did he pause, removing his sweat-stained, lightweight leather hat and wiping his forehead on a homespun sleeve. It was early spring, and cool, but he was sweating. Steelwood was exceptionally dense and hard, even for New Jerusalem, but it favored the most fertile sites. And Esau was ambitious, and a bear for work.

He was also tall—five feet eight inches in his bare feet—and on Terra would have weighed a lean 227 pounds stripped. On the scale at the flour mill, however, he registered 322 pounds; gravity on New Jerusalem was 1.42 Terran-normal.

The years too were long. Esau was fourteen and a half by the calendar of New Jerusalem. On Terra he'd have been reckoned nearly nineteen. His frame was broad, his bones thick and dense, his heavy muscles powerful. And he was agile. Wrestling was a popular youth activity, and he was exceptionally good at it.

Thirty generations after the colonization of New Jerusalem, bodies more or less like Esau's were the rule. Bodies created by ruthless selection and strong gravity. And by the vigorous lives to which the colonists had been committed, in accordance with what the founders considered the Will of God.

The people of New Jerusalem were aware of space flight, and that their long-ago ancestors had come from distant Terra, where people lived ungodly lives, in technological sloth, and fought wars—the greatest evil of all—killing each other in droves. That was pretty much all the Jerusalemites knew about their ancestral world, and even that was incorrect. The last war on Terra had been fought before their forefathers left it.

The Commonwealth maintained a small embassy on New Jerusalem, though beyond the upper hierarchy, almost no Jerusalemites knew or cared anything at all about what went on there. Which wasn't much. Through the church hierarchy, the embassy purchased certain local products. For silver and gold. The Jerries had no electronics, rejected paper money, and disapproved almost all proposed imports. All in all, the embassy had virtually no impact on the lives of New Jerusalem's citizens. Though it was about to. It had been put there mainly to confirm that New Jerusalem was part of the Commonwealth.

The Church of the Testaments taught its people to read scripture, write letters, and do basic cyphering. Nonbiblical history, even of their own world, was not taught, except as morality and precautionary tales. The only books were on paper—scripture, hymn books, prayer books, and Elder Hofer's *Commentaries on the Testaments.*

The Jerusalemites, of course, sinned like anyone else. They murdered, abused, lied, seduced, cuckolded, even occasionally blasphemed!—but rarely stole. Mostly, in fact, they were a law-abiding people who generally trusted the officials of their theocracy. Theirs was a peaceful, stagnant, patriarchal, and rather tolerant backwater. Occasionally someone went berserk—perhaps assaulted a family member or neighbor with ax or gun, or themselves with gun or rope. But there were no psychologists to point the finger at depression growing out of frustration. The preachers had their own explanation: the evildoer had been led astray by Satan. And whoever doubted, kept it to themselves.

The summer after his thirteenth birthday, by the New Jerusalem calendar, a youth took a farm. Unless, of course, he was in line to inherit one. With family help, he might buy one in his own neighborhood—complete with buildings and mortgage—if one was for sale. But more often he moved to the frontier, and claimed new, wild land at the edge of settlement. Land surveyed by the Church, which valued orderly ways. There, with the help of neighbors, he built a log house, a log barn, and sheds, and began life as an adult. He might bring a wife from his old community, or marry into the new, and over the years they'd produce a brood of their own, to repeat the cycle.

His first winter on his homestead, he'd hire himself out to an established neighbor, clearing land. And on his own holding, clear a garden patch, and "deaden" timber. The ax-girdled trees died a year later, and their roots and stumps didn't sprout. No one on New Jerusalem could explain why, physiologically, or felt any need to; it was simply a fact of life. Afterward, "grass" grew beneath the dead trees, providing pasture for livestock and attracting wild herbivores—wild meat. Certain food plants could even be grown in the much reduced shade. And by the time the deadened trees had been felled, cut up, dragged and burned, the roots were much decayed. The settler then had a field, hard won but ready to plow.

Thus the typical Jerusalemites were strong, tough, self-reliant. And subject to the authority of their physical environment and the hierarchy, both of which they accepted matter-of-factly. They were a matter-of-fact people.

Meanwhile they were unfamiliar with ethnic or religious diversity. Their immigrant ancestors had been fervent sectarians, "full of the spirit." On Terra, they'd been fearful and indignant toward a society abounding with subcultures, where political, social and religious varieties sometimes yammered, and occasionally squabbled. Despite which there was already widespread mixing, intermarrying, blending.

From the beginning, the goal of the founders had been emigration, and a life of their own. It had taken courage, dedication, zeal, and pretty much all their earthly wealth to organize and incorporate a colonization company, lease emigrant ships, meet the requirements for the Commonwealth's approval to launch, and leave behind almost everything familiar except each other. Many families were divided, and some, when it came down to it, backed out.

Of those who'd followed through, the most common trait had been zeal.

Those born to New Jerusalem were different from their migrant ancestors, though they didn't know it. They'd been inculcated from infancy with, and only with, the dogmas, values and customs of those ancestors. As modified by the early experiences of life in a heavyworld wilderness. A world where the severe difficulties of heavyworld pregnancy, and gravity-induced, early deterioration of joints and organs, culled the early generations ruthlessly, shortening lives, and helping menfolk value their wives and daughters.

Whatever religious zeal they felt was seldom fervent. Like Esau Wesley and his wife Jael, they took their religion for granted. Its strictures seldom seemed onerous to them, and most were reasonably content with their lives.

Lives to be lived doing worthwhile things deemed pleasing to the Lord, finding satisfactions in farming, and in their offspring and each other. Given the effects of gravity on human physiology and anatomy, the Church had recently condoned the use, after five births, of a contraceptive herb known as lamb bane. This after three generations of earnest but confidential consideration and discussion at the highest hierarchical level.

The founders would have been horrified. But even given the generations of culling by New Jerusalem's gravity, deaths in childbirth left too many husbands alone on the farm with a brood of children to care for. And available widows were far fewer than widowers.

◇

Esau Wesley rarely thought about such things. He was young, sure of himself, and found pleasure in work. After wiping sweat, he'd picked up his ax to assault another tree, when his hound Clancy began to bark. Esau knew from the tone that the dog sensed a human coming, not a predator. Someone the dog knew.

"Halloo!" the young man called, then "Clancy! Shut up!" From a little distance came an answering halloo. A minute later, a man on horseback rode into sight among the trees: Speaker Martin Crosby from Sycamore Run,[1] one of Jael's uncles.

"What brings you, speaker?" Esau asked. Crosby hadn't been there since the parish had raised Esau's house and barn the summer before, though he'd seen him at church often enough. The older man looked more serious than usual. Outside of church, he was inclined to joke and laugh a lot.

"Got news," he said. "Big news." From his face, it was bad.

"Such as?"

"Such as—a war."

"A war?" Esau was mystified rather than alarmed. War on New Jerusalem was impossible.

"Word just came from Terra."

"Terra? What's that got to do with us?"

The older farmer sighed gustily and shook his head. "Elder Fletcher is sending word to all the people." He paused, as if what followed was so unreal, he lacked the words. "Satan is coming through the worlds, with his demons. They've got the body of a donkey, with a sort of man stuck on where the neck out to be, and a head like nothing you'd ever imagine."

"You sure someone hasn't been japing you, Brother Crosby?"

The man reached into a saddlebag, brought out a folder, and leaning down, handed Esau a piece of durable paper. A photocopy from the Commonwealth embassy, printed on both sides, with a picture. It had begun as a mental image, crossing the parsecs to Terra instantaneously, from a savant on a world called Maritimus. It was almost the last thing the water world's savant saw before blacking out, a strange phenomenon even for savants. From Terra the image had been forwarded to the embassy, and sketched by the savant there. Brother Crosby knew none of that, of course. It was enough that Elder Fletcher accepted it.

"Keep it," Crosby said. "I've got more than enough.

The demons know how to find people hiding, and got ways of killing them from the sky. That's what's said, anyway. There's 16,000 ships full of them, giant arks for flying between the stars. They've come to various worlds that's got folks living on them, worlds way far off, and killed everyone there, man, woman, and child. Butchered them, and wrecked everything."

Esau looked at the picture, then back at Crosby, still not convinced, but troubled. Brother Crosby took out another folder, this time with sheets of writing in quill pen and ink, copied at the embassy by some Terran artifice.

"This one's written by Elder Fletcher, in his own hand, telling us what we might do. Not have to, but might. When you go up for supper, read them with Jael. See what you think. I got a bunch more of these to take around."

The older man turned his horse then—what passed for a horse on New Jerusalem—and trotted off. Esau stood where he was, and read what Elder Fletcher had written. When he was done, he felt a deep misgiving. Without ringing another tree, Esau Wesley picked up his ax and started home. It seemed to him his whole world was about to come down around his ears.

◇

Footnote:

[1] On New Jerusalem, "sycamore" was not an imported species of the Terran genus Platanus, nor the Eurasian Acer pseudoplatanus, but a native tree with pale smooth bark.

Chapter Eleven
The Task

Joao Gordeenko was not at his best. As Deputy Czar of Resource Allocation, he'd worked till 0320 that morning, then slept on his office couch till 0730. Which had left time for only a hasty shower and shave, a cup of strong coffee, and to get dressed before receiving his first visitor. Breakfast would wait, probably till lunch.

The visitor, a new staff assistant, was very pretty, very bright, and very sure of herself. And well recommended. He hoped that Sarah Asayama would prove as able as her recommender claimed, but he was skeptical. She spoke well, but she'd never had anything approaching the responsibility of her new position. There was a lot of that in the burgeoning war bureaucracy. It was unavoidable. There were too few people with the knowledge and experience needed. Some would learn successfully on the job, coping, learning, innovating. Others would be replaced, sent elsewhere.

With Sarah Asayama's looks and personality, people tended to pull for her success, but as she talked, Gordeenko's misgivings grew like his workload. He wasn't surprised. This first assignment was in part a test of her readiness for it.

She sat six feet to his right, displaying her three-quarter profile as she spoke, while controlling the screen display with her pocket keypad. Under other circumstances he might have better appreciated her looks, but her words and the chart on his wall screen held his attention. "Unfortunately," she was saying, "the invaders' approach is taking them through a sector well populated with colonies, and on an approximate intersect with Terra."

Does she imagine I don't already know that? he wondered.

She switched charts. "Here is a list of the planets we need to evacuate, and their populations. The job will require a minimum of 2,900 ships, depending on the types selected." She turned, looking crisply professional. "I'm afraid it cuts rather heavily into the total."

Great Gautama! he thought. *An intelligence score of 123, and no concept whatever of the overall problem!*

Again she switched charts. "I've listed existing ships by types and classes, with their estimated capacity for stasis lockers. I realize this draft proposal requires review, and perhaps some modification, but given the colonial populations, we have little choice." Once more she turned to Gordeenko. "The less review time, the better. We need to refit the ships as quickly as possible, and get them underway."

Gordeenko nodded thoughtfully. It seemed to him he needed to make an impact on the young woman. *But be kind, Joao, be kind,* he reminded himself. "I agree," he told her. "The process must be expedited." He laid his hand on his desk keypad. "But first—First I need to clarify some things for you. I see now that you needed a much fuller briefing than you were given." His thick hairy fingers touched keys. The chart on the screen was displaced by another. "As you have implied, the number of merchant vessels in the Commonwealth is finite. As for warships—we have no fleet, as I'm sure you know. Only a limited array of prototypes. And of course a few score patrol ships, small, with utterly inadequate armament, designed only to discourage piracy. Just now, every shipyard in the Commonwealth has begun building *warships,* or is being overhauled in order to build *warships.*"

The young woman interrupted, honestly confused, her crispness gone. "But sir! I was talking about ships already built."

He raised a constraining hand. "I'll get to that, but first you must understand the problem. There are seventeen shipyards on Terra, eleven others scattered from Luna to Titan, and three each in the Epsilon Indi and Epsilon Eridani Systems. And that is all. In the entire Commonwealth! Not enough, Ms Asayama! Not nearly enough!" Now Gordeenko began to apply the heat. "We are beginning or planning the construction of more than *a hundred* other shipyards, of which fifty must be operating inside of six months! Can you conceive of what that means?

Everything must be done differently than ever before, if only because of the extreme shortage of shipwrights!"

"But sir…"

Gordeenko waved off her interjection. "And how will we provide the metals? Or transport the shipyard machinery?" His intensity caught and held her. "The demand on existing shipping will be extreme. Most of the new shipyards will be in space, in the belts of the various systems. And where will the workers live? In *ships,* Ms Asayama! Hastily converted dormitory *ships!* The same is true for the thousands on thousands of new asteroid miners and smelter workers who will provide the metals!"

Sarah Asayama looked ready to collapse. She'd known the Commonwealth was drastically unprepared for this war, but she'd never considered what dealing with it might involve. She'd given no attention to media discussions of such matters. On her brief internship her days had been long, spent on her own narrow duties. While away from the office, her attention had been on theater and young men. Thus Gordeenko's exposition had been overwhelming.

"That," he added quietly, "is a *very* brief summary. Very very brief. I'd assumed you'd ask questions, where you didn't know." It struck him then that she hadn't known she didn't know. "Like every other war activity," he went on, "we suffer a great lack of suitably prepared personnel. Thus we turn to persons like yourself: bright, energetic, patriotic…but with limited relevant experience, or none at all."

Reviewing the problems for her, he realized, had stirred his emotions—a mixture of repressed anxiety and dismay at the enormity of the task. Pausing, he inhaled deeply, and shifted gears. "We expect to evacuate not more than forty to fifty percent of the colonial populations in the invasion corridor. It may prove to be more, but we're starting with that estimate. Consider: most colonies grew from religious or ethnic groups or political dissidents who withdrew into space to live in their own narrow communities. And to a considerable degree, the original colonists have forwarded their beliefs through the generations. Thus we expect that many of their people will decide to stay at home. To take their chances where they are.

"Many colonies are so distant, the aliens will reach them before evacuation ships can. You've already allowed for that."

He exhaled heavily, and brushed back his thick pompadour. "Aim at fifteen hundred ships. Get with Al Vorselen, the director of transport; he knows what there are and where. Sort out the possibilities with him."

She stared. "But Mr. Gordeenko! We can't leave people out there! They'll be killed! We can't just abandon them!"

His gaze hardened, and his voice became crisp. "If you have a magic wand, Ms Asayama, I grant you all the ships you can conjure out of nothing. Or better yet, conjure the aliens back to wherever they came from. Meanwhile, tell Vorselen that you and he must give me your final figures no later than tomorrow."

"Tomorrow?" she squeaked.

"By 1600 hours. And the figures must be realistic. Then I can start requisition proceedings. They'll go swiftly; I have the necessary authority." He made a shooing motion. "Go now."

As she reached for the door, he stopped her with a closing statement, his voice low and confidential. "And Sarah, do not think of it as saving people. Because if the invader isn't stopped, we're all dead. The evacuees, you, me—all of us. Dead! So think of your ships as transports bringing military and labor recruits to Terra. But do NOT call them that, not to *anyone*. Not to your sister, your boyfriend—*anyone*. The evacuees are vital to us, my dear. Vital to the human species."

She paled and nodded, then hurried out. It seemed to Joao Gordeenko that she really did understand. She might work out after all; he'd know tomorrow before supper.

He hadn't mentioned the problems of training qualified workers, qualified ship's crews, qualified fighting men. He hadn't wanted to shock her into coma. Looking at his own chart, still on the wallscreen, Gordeenko felt overwhelm wash over him. Opening a desk drawer, he took out a small bottle of vodka flavored with *Vaccinium_myrtillus.* For just a moment he hesitated, then removed the cap, took a swig, and felt the heat spread through his belly. With sudden resolve he stepped to his small sink and poured the rest down the drain. The solution to overwhelm was not alcohol. It was more sleep, and working smart. Starting today he would quit at midnight. Or...better make that one o'clock, then sleep till 0700. And during the day take two twenty-minute naps. One at least.

He was fooling himself of course.

Chapter Twelve
Observations

On returning to his hidey-hole, Henry Morgan was welcomed tearfully by Connie Phamonyong. The tears took him by surprise. He'd recognized his scouting expedition was dangerous, but his imagination hadn't built on it. She'd managed not to infect Robert with her worries though; he greeted his older brother with casual cheer.

Almost the first thing Morgan did, with Connie and Robert, was message the prime minister and the defense office, newly named the Defense Ministry, or War House. Not that he had much to tell them, other than that the invaders had been clearing land. But he wanted them to know he was still alive, and intended further scouting.

This time he got more than brief acknowledgement; both the prime minister and War House thanked him for his efforts. They also told him about the Star of Hibernia and the Gem of the Prophet. But they didn't tell him about Drago Draveç reaching Hart's Desire; they'd wait till something had actually happened with that, besides a kidnapping.

Nor did they tell him to be careful. *Careful,* he thought wryly, *isn't what they need from me.*

The next morning he returned to the surface, this time headed for the gorge into which the hangar exits had opened. He set out with a blaster on his belt, and a lunch and heavy torch in his day pack. And a nervous stomach. Not because the invaders might have posted guards there; that seemed highly unlikely. His concern was that rockfall from the bombardment might keep him from getting inside.

Lack of rope was his first problem. Seen from the top, the gorge side appeared impossible to climb. Previously trees and shrubs had found rootholds on the precipitous slope, and where it had been bare, the rock had been solid. Now the trees and shrubs were mostly gone, and the surface rock extensively fractured. If he'd been an accomplished rock climber...but he wasn't.

He got around this literally, by hiking half a mile up the gorge, beyond the bombardment, picking his way down, then hiking back to a point from which he could size up the situation from the bottom. Hiking in the bottom wasn't easy, either. It held a lot more broken trees and rock than before. In places they'd impeded the streamflow, and he picked his way above the resulting pools.

A bloody mess, he told himself. *But war always is.* When he got there, the depth of destruction was worse than he'd foreseen. The gorge wall had been destroyed back nearly to the hangars themselves, and overlying rock had collapsed into the openings. The mass of rubble had one apparent opening, but from the bottom he couldn't tell if it went all the way through. *Hell,* he thought, *the hangar roofs might even have collapsed.*

The great pile of debris at the gorge bottom provided a start up; it required tricky scrambling, but not scaling. Above that it became more difficult. A couple of times it seemed to him he'd cliffed out, but each time he found handholds, a place to put a boot, and somewhere to go from there. After a bit, scratched and sweaty, he reached the opening, widened by invaders removing fallen rocks. The hangars had not collapsed.

"Centaurs?" Morgan muttered. Nothing horse-like had climbed this. *They must have used AG boats,* he thought, *or be more like goats than horses.*

Inside was dark, and musty with the smell of old death -- of bodies scavenged and desiccated—and dried animal excrement. But his torch beam found no carnivores. They'd been there, done what they did, and left. Bones and tattered cloth were abundant, and all the bones were human. And the spacecraft had open hatches; the people aboard them had come out to fight.

He went directly to his yacht, the *Delight.* She hadn't been destroyed, merely killed. The invaders had slapped magnetic "bombs" on the command panels of her bridge and engineering section, and fried her "brains." They'd also dug through all cabinets and lockers, but except for weapons, which were gone, they'd left the rest strewn around. Mostly they hadn't even taken the trouble to vandalize. Apparently if it didn't look dangerous, any damage was incidental.

He entered his suite with concern, saw the carrying case opened and empty on the deck, and felt sharp fear. Then his torch-beam found the telescope itself on the bed, where it had been tossed. He carried it out, set it up, and tried it. It was all right.

Now to find some cordage, he thought. Putting the scope back in its case, he left with it.

<><

He spent the next day with Connie and Robert. Then he left again, this time with eight days' rations in his pack, the scope in its case slung on one shoulder, and of course a blaster on his hip. The scope weighed far more than all the rest of it, and was awkward. He'd take a break every hour, he told himself.

He felt cheerful about the situation, and after leaving the zone of bombardment damage, made good progress. On the second afternoon he reached the prominence he'd climbed before, and started up the side away from the alien clearing. At the top, he selected the same scrubby tree he'd sheltered beneath before, and set up the scope in its shade. Here lay a certain risk. He'd brought his belt recorder, and both it and the scope were powered by power slugs. If the invaders were monitoring the electronic environment, they might just possibly detect them, though it seemed doubtful.

Setting the scope at 10X, he focused on the distant opening. It had rained, enough to soak out the fires and lay the dust. He began scanning, increasing and decreasing magnification as needed, pausing to describe anything that seemed worthwhile. His voice activated the recorder. Building construction continued. Here and there large machines—crawler tractors!—moved across the clearing, apparently cutting the coarse root network of the cleared forest. The activity left little question: the aliens planned to stay, and grow crops.

He focused on one who appeared to be a supervisor. It stood sideways to the telescope, watching builders at work, seeming to comment to a recorder of its own. The long head had upright ears, and overall it had reddish-brown fur. Prieto had said they looked like "centaurs from the Jurassic." *He should have said Miocene,* Morgan thought, *or whatever period it was when Terran mammals were trying out bizarre body forms.* He was pretty sure, though, that there'd been no six-limbed mammalian species in Terra's history.

It hadn't occurred to him to bring a vid. He didn't realize he could let Connie view the cube, and the prime minister's savant would see what she was seeing, via Robert.

So he described the alien in words, portraying the features of face and harness, the articulation of the limbs, and the four fingers and two thumbs on each hand. The feet were obscured by vegetation. From what he could see, the teeth were "cone-shaped and not particularly large," but the back teeth could be different.

Then the creature strolled to one of the buildings being assembled, and disappeared inside. Morgan shifted focus to another alien then, this one the color of wet sand. It stood on a gently sloping roof, using what appeared to be some sort of spotwelder. The feet had two splayed toes, suggesting a camel's but with heavy claws. Blunt claws, he thought, for traction instead of fighting.

He thought of measuring its height, but that required knowing its distance, and this was not the place to use his rangefinder. *Use your map, and estimate,* he decided. His computer made the worker's height twenty-eight inches at the withers. He couldn't get a figure for height to the top of the long skull; torso and neck were bent forward, eyes on its work.

"Not as big as I thought," he said, "and not horse-like at all." Again reducing magnification for scanning, he found a dozer piling sections of fallen trees. As Morgan watched, the operator began flailing its arms, and jumped from the driver's platform with the dozer still running. Its legs gave as it hit, but it was back on its feet in an instant, arms still flailing, hind feet kicking.

Morgan stared. The machine, he realized, had disturbed a nest of Tagus's version of hornets. The operator's dance became extreme, then it fell, limbs thrashing. Quickly Morgan increased magnification till he could glimpse the hornets, big as his thumb joint, strafing the invader until its limbs went slack, and its head flopped sideways on the ground.

"Jesus!" Morgan murmured. He'd been stung a few times himself—twice just the day before; presumably he'd gotten too near a nest. It hurt like hell when they hit, but it hadn't laid him low like that. Of course, from what he could see, the alien had gotten stung a lot more than twice. But still…

He cut magnification, and scanned for reactions by other workers who might have seen it happen. Two had left their machines, each holding what might have been a spray can, but instead of running to help their comrade, they watched from a distance. Moving nervously, apparently anxious, as if they wanted to move in, but were afraid. Morgan reported that, too.

◇

He continued scanning and recording for another half hour, feeling increasingly edgy. Abruptly then he made a decision, and after disassembling the scope, packed it in its padded case. Then he loaded his gear on his back and picked his way carefully down the knob. At the bottom he stashed scope and case beneath the trunk of a large fallen tree, and set out for home.

If I hike till deep dusk, and get an early start in the morning, I can get back to Robert and Connie by noon, he thought. *And debrief myself to the P.M. and the military.*

It seemed very important.

Chapter Thirteen
Language Lesson

David MacDonald heartily disliked the awkward commode they were expected to use. It was ill-suited for humans: a dry ceramic box perhaps sixteen inches high, and wide enough for two of the alien invaders to back up to at once. He sluiced it clean with the hose provided, then in lieu of paper, hosed his behind with a needle spray setting. He wondered how the aliens managed to hose their rears. Probably they didn't, he decided. Their arms were too short. And horses got by without it, and dogs.

Fortunately, alien hygiene arrangements included soft soap in bowls, and he made use of it now. He didn't particularly like making a spectacle of himself for the multi-lens monitor that left no part of their cell unobserved. When they'd wakened on the shuttle that had brought them to this—station? Ship?—they were naked. But of course their captors were naked too, except for equipment harness.

He looked at Yukiko, sitting crosslegged on the other side of the room on a sort of futon. Annika lay still and pale, her head cradled on his wife's lap. Yukiko stroked the girl's short, blond, cap-cut hair, crooning softly to her. That the savant had been captured told him that even with no exposed structures, the Cave Bay station had been discovered. Probably from its electronics signature. And the *Cousteau* had obviously not gotten offworld, because Annika would have been on it.

Ju-Li would have fought a squad of hyenas to protect her, so the others must be dead, he thought. Yukiko agreed. Probably Dennis had sent the others out hunting for them, when they all should have been headed outsystem in warpdrive.

David shook his head. He and Yukiko were together, and when they'd been put aboard the shuttle, Annika had been given into their care. If any of the others had been taken alive, it seemed to him they'd all be together. The only apparent alternative was for each human to be held in solitary, and obviously they weren't.

"How's she doing?" he asked.

"Fine," Yukiko answered. Her attention remained on Annika. "Just fine. Annika knows we're with her, taking care of her. Don't you darling?" she crooned, and continued to stroke. "She's just resting her eyes. She looked at me a minute ago."

David didn't take his wife's words at face value. She'd said what she had at least partly to sooth Annika, reassure her. It might take quite a bit of that before the child came out of whatever state she was in: a coma or stupor—whatever. The child. It occurred to him he didn't know how old Annika was. Eleven or twelve he guessed, but mentally equivalent to four or five. If "equivalent" meant anything in cases like this.

A sound caught David's attention, and he turned. The door was sliding open, and two aliens looked in from the corridor, sidearms in hand, long reptilian jaws closed. The eyes were squarely in front, presumably providing binocular vision.

The weapons, David guessed, were stunners of some sort. But not the variety familiar from crime dramas; he and Yukiko had been stunned while being picked up on the islet, and there'd been no hangover. "Look who's here," David said. "The hyena twins, Ugly and Uglier." His eyes were intent on their faces, which he could not read. But he got an impression of wariness, as unlikely as it seemed. The two walked through the door, then stepped aside. A third one, larger, walked in between them, seemingly unarmed. The first two were reddish brown. This one had vivid blue sides; the upright torso and head were teal blue. The face was marked with red, and the seemingly clipped crest was scarlet. To David's eyes the colors seemed natural. Its own eyes intent on David, the latecomer spoke, the words recognizable despite very approximate pronunciations. "How do you feel?" it said. The eff sound was approximate.

It's got no lips, David realized. The alien's eyes were on him, and for a moment David thought the creature wanted to know. But then it answered its own question. "I felt vetter".

Before he got it all out, the creature's gaze had moved to Yukiko. "How do you *suffose* I feel?" it said, then answered its own question. "Cratty." It looked from one human to the other, then made what might have been a smile, and touched its upright torso where its heart might might have been but almost certainly wasn't. "Qonits," it added. "Qonits!"

"Yukiko," Yukiko answered promptly, and touched her chest.

Ah-ha. It's begun, David thought. He remembered now: the first sentence had been what he'd asked Yukiko when she'd wakened— "how do you feel?" —and the follow-up had been her reply. "Cratty" was as close as their interrogator could come to "crappy." The aliens had been monitoring more than their movements. They'd recorded their words, run an audio-analysis, then this one had practiced the Terran phonemes, words, and sentences. They wanted to learn the language.

The chain of realizations had been more rapid than speech; the oceanographer didn't miss a beat. "David," he said, touching his thatched chest.

It was indeed the beginning. There was a wall table in the room, its height suitable for an alien to work at, but too low for a standing human; David and Yukiko would have to kneel. Qonits stepped to it and gestured. Gently Yukiko laid Annika's head down on the futon, and whispered to her. Then she and David joined the alien, who promptly walked the four fingers of one hand along the table's surface, and made a sound. Probably the word for walk, David decided. He repeated it back as best he could, and walked two of his own fingers on the table, human style. "Walk," he said.

The alien repeated the word he'd used, and both adult humans tried to duplicate it. The alien's eyes were unreadable. Again David's two human fingers walked along the table. "Walk!" he repeated, forcefully this time. "Walk! Walk!"

The alien tried it again, and David glowered deliberately, wondering what, if anything, the alien made of human facial expressions. Shaking his head, he galloped his fingers along the surface. "Run! Run! Run!" he barked.

The alien stared, appraisingly it seemed, then walked his fingers again. "Wahk," he said. "Wahk. Wahk."

David didn't let him get by with that. "Walk!" he snarled,

"not *wahk!*" You're not a duck, you're a goddamn…" He paused. "Hyena!"

◇

When Qonits left, some while later, he'd learned not only run and walk, but hungry, eat, drink, scratch (or itch?), wash, bathe, breathe, heart, urinate, and defecate. He could also count to ten. And considering the undoubted differences in his vocal apparatus, approximated the sounds rather well.

He'd also proven a quick study, which did not greatly cheer the oceanographer. David had no doubt the words were recorded in the ship's computer, but what it might make of them, he had no idea. *Not much,* he guessed. *Not yet.* It lacked the workhorse words: *is* and *are* and *were*; *you* and *me; but* and *and; here* and *there*… But it was a beginning. Meanwhile he'd established a kind of fragile dominance, though what good it might be, he had no idea.

Chapter Fourteen
Goosing the Tiger

Drago Draveç had learned something: that a near-suicide mission weeks away can be planned more or less matter-of-factly, but close at hand it was a meaner breed of cat. Not that *he* was thinking of backing out. But here he was, newly emerged in the far fringe of the Hibernia System—in its cometary cloud—with only two of his three other ships. Several minutes had passed with no sign of Indio Fuentes and the *Aztec,* and even after one minute, the odds of their showing had become microscopic.

That son of a bitch! he thought, but without heat. Fuentes, a skilled captain, had been with them eight hyperspace hours earlier, when they'd emerged to compute their approach shot. Now he wasn't.

So they'd do it without him. Drago realized how lucky he was that *Bachelor* and *Ludmilla* had hung tough. He was asking a hell of a lot.

Drago pulled his attention to his sensor reads. He was always better at disconnecting from his emotions than at dealing with them. From time to time they'd pop up later, unbidden and out of context. That was a major reason even he was sometimes surprised by his actions; even jerked by them.

He tended to cherish those unexplained surprises. He'd told himself more than once they kept life interesting. He'd even told his probation counselor that once, at the Academy. The guy's comeback had been "don't fall in love with your faults, Drago. It's like sleeping with rattlesnakes." But Drago hadn't taken the psych seriously. He felt confident in his intentions, and in his ability to make things turn out right.

The main thing that had gotten him in trouble over the years was liquor, and he'd become good at refusing drinks. He'd said more than once, "a couple of drinks and even I don't know what the hell I might do." He didn't allow booze aboard ship, except for his crew's rum ration—three ounces at supper, actually 50/50 rum and water. And he left even that alone. Didn't even keep a bottle in his room back at Tagus, though he'd sometimes share a drink with Lu, his base wife.

His sensors showed him the location of the alien's system defense force, in the planetary fringe roughly 90° from the primary, some 11 billion miles insystem. While close to the colony was a smaller force, probably a planetary guard flotilla. Unless they had more sensitive hyperspace emergence detectors than human technology had come up with, which seemed doubtful, there was a good chance they hadn't picked up the emergence of his own three small craft.

And his EM signature wouldn't arrive with them for seventeen hours, so he radioed his other two commanders.

"Fuentes isn't going to show," he said, "so we'll do it without him. Give me your location fixes on the system defense force."

They did. Both agreed with his.

"Okay. I'm going to let Kunming know we're here and set to go. Then, on my count, we'll move in, just as we planned. And good luck. A lot depends on us."

He counted, then jumped.

◇

If warpspace emergence produced waves, no human devices had ever detected them. But from this close, the three pirates' electromagnetic signatures reached the aliens in microseconds. They'd already be icons on the alien screens. That's why they'd jumped to emerge between the system defense force and the Star of Hibernia. Hopefully they'd be mistaken for small members of the alien's planetary guard.

Drago had no way of knowing how close to the system defense force he'd be on emergence—100 miles, 500, 1,000... It turned out to be 83. As planned, the pirate ships didn't pause to size things up. They could do that on the move. Nor did they break radio silence. Instead, as agreed earlier, the two subordinate pirate vessels began at once to move in grav drive toward the alien battle group, neither hurriedly nor hesitantly, as if this were routine. Drago followed more slowly, letting them open a larger gap. To sit motionless at a distance might bring questions he could neither answer nor read. Meanwhile *he* had the savant, and the responsibility to let War House know what he learned. Otherwise the mission would be wasted effort, and any lives lost, thrown away.

On emergence, the *Minerva's* sensors and her shipsmind had begun recording everything they could perceive about the enemy. Not everything a warship would perceive, but a lot. On his screen, the alien formation showed as an array of icons. He locked his sensors on one of the five largest, its mass not greatly less than a loaded ore carrier. Surely a battleship. He called for an actual image, and magnified it against a scaling grid. She was huge! By comparison, the pride of the Admiralty, the prototype cruiser *Yangtse,* was a dwarf. Of the alien's outriggers, the only one Drago could identify with confidence was the strange-space navigational sensor array. Others, less conspicuous, might or might not be communication equipment and targeting locks.

His own small, base-made torpedoes were designed mainly as threats, though they could easily disable or kill a merchantman.

So far his sensors had detected no changes in the alien radio traffic. To Drago even their code sounded somehow laconic. Hopefully this meant they'd accepted his three small craft as normal.

The pirates slowed their approach now, as if to join the battle group, intending to come alongside one or more of the large ships. Drago's fists and belly had clenched. "Not yet," he muttered, "not yet... NOW!"

It was as if the *Bachelor*'s master had heard him; less than a mile from the nearest cruiser, he released three torpedoes. A moment later there was a great flash, the explosion driving the cruiser sideways. Magnified on his bridge screen, Drago saw flame and debris vent from the breached hull. Even as he'd fired, the *Bachelor*'s skipper had activated his strange-space generator. A second later the pirate vessel winked into warpspace.

Drago emitted a single explosive "yeah!" Then his gaze fixed on the *Ludmilla,* intense again. She'd been trailing the *Bachelor* by about two miles. This was a delicate moment.

Kunming's most urgent question was whether the aliens had force shields. The *Ludmilla*'s skipper was to hold his fire until they'd had time to generate shields, if any. *Then* they'd surely generate them, if they had them.

Seconds passed—dragged—three, four, five... No shields. It seemed to Drago they'd had abundant time. Meanwhile the *Ludmilla* had slowed to avoid overrunning her target. "Not yet," he muttered. "Not yet. Not..." Then, faintly luminous in the blackness, shields began to form. "Now!" he shouted. At that instant the *Ludmilla* launched her salvo. Almost as quickly the battleship's war beam hit her, and seconds later the pirate's unarmored hull blew apart in a widening sphere of gassed metal and debris.

Time to leave! The *Minerva* had half closed the gap. As Drago activated the strange-space generator, her light hull resonated to an alien target lock. Had it been a torpedo lock, he'd have been in warpspace before the torpedoes reached him. As it was, a war beam began its non-explosive but sustained and intense energy transfer an instant before the *Minerva* left F-space.

An instant too short for human reaction, though the temperature increased. Then Drago stared at his screen. It showed not the indigo blue his shipsmind used to represent warpspace, but the restful yellow it showed for hyperspace.

"Gracious god," he breathed. He knew exactly what had happened. In the moment when warpspace was generating— in that small fraction of a second—the beam had corrupted his warpdrive, and he'd entered hyperspace instead.

His first officer too sat staring, then finally spoke. "Looks like we're screwed," he said softly.

"Screwed, rolled over, and screwed again," Drago answered, then paused. "Take the helm. I've got a report to make." Getting up, he started aft to the cabin shared by his savant and her attendant.

◇

It had been evening in Kunming when Drago Draveç notified War House of his emergence in the Hibernia System's cometary cloud. So instead of going to his apartment to sleep, Admiralty Chief Fedor Tischendorf had lain down on the couch in his office, just a few strides down the corridor from his savant's suite. When Drago's next savanted contact arrived, the admiral's night yeoman woke him. The admiral was off his couch instantly, wide awake and energized, and reached the savant's couch in under a minute, his shoes on but unsecured.

The savanted exchange was recorded and backed up on War House's AI. And on the admiral's powerful mind, where it instantly began to make connections, tying it into the extensive interconnected matrix that was his understanding of reality—his personal, internal version of the universe.

The session took nearly an hour, the information sometimes coming slowly: the size of the system defense force and the planetary guard flotilla; their distances from Star; descriptions of the enemy warships; the masses of the battleships and cruisers, their outrigs…and of course their shields, beam locks and radio frequencies. Important stuff.

Tischendorf imagined the pirate screening his cube— visuals and data—deciding what was meaningful and what wasn't. And when in doubt, telling it. Better the error of excess than to leave something out that might prove important. Invaluable.

The admiral wasn't surprised that one of the corsairs had funked out. He wouldn't have been shocked if none had carried it through.

The last thing Draveç mentioned was being scorched by a warbeam in the moment of escape.

"Did you take damage?"

"It knocked out my warpdrive and FSP dish. So I can't use the F-space potentiality to navigate, and I can't use dead reckoning like I could in warpspace. I'll pop into F-space from time to time though, if I can, and see if I can figure out where I am and what direction I've been going. Ever hear of anyone making it back like that?"

The admiral pursed his lips, then answered. "No, Drago, I haven't. But I'll put someone on it; see if we can come up with something useful for you. Maybe we can. We've been performing wonders on industrial mobilization. We've got the beginnings of a real fleet under construction, and your information will be extremely useful. All of it. We'd hoped the aliens hadn't developed shield technology—it would have given us an important advantage—but just knowing it will help us plan, and save lives and ships."

He paused. "And Drago, check in with us from time to time, just so I know you're alive. For what it's worth, I wish you well. If you make it back, and if you're interested…the fleet can always use more good officers."

◇

A very long way off, in another, very different universe, Drago Draveç grimaced at Tischendorf's words. If Henry Morgan was dead, and he just about had to be, then Drago owed loyalty to no one but his crew. They'd waited three long days at rendezvous, and Morgan hadn't shown. While *Minerva, Bachelor, Ludmilla* and *Aztec* had arrived within minutes of each other. Presumably Morgan was dead.

"I'll think about it, admiral," Drago said. "Meanwhile do me a favor: pass along my apologies to Ambassador Khai." Only now did he realize he didn't know her first name. "I expect I made a lot of trouble for her. And she's a quite a person, quite a lady. Maybe I should have let her handle things, but I didn't trust that bastard Rees. Basically he's psychotic."

◇

They wound up the session then. War House's master artificial intelligence had not only backed up the recording of the session in realtime, it had uploaded a copy to the prime minister. Meanwhile, for Tischendorf, it was less than two hours before time to get up, so he simply took off his shoes and lay down on his couch again.

Where he dreamed of drifting derelict in hyperspace.

Chapter Fifteen
Recruits

Bulk carriers were well suited for conversion to "snooze ships"—stasis ships—for evacuating colonies. They were extremely large, and their holds readily segmented by decks, dividing them into numerous levels.

In Esau Wesley's broad, low-ceilinged compartment, the aisles between the stasis lockers were packed with men; the sexes had been separated when they'd come aboard. Which left Esau uneasy, because he didn't know where his wife was. Women and men, they'd been told, needed to be put in separate holds for pre-stasis processing. "Processing," he discovered, meant getting ready for three and a half months of stasis; a kind of deep sleep, they'd been told. "Standard" months, whatever that meant. They'd also been told they wouldn't get any older in stasis. He'd wondered if that meant setting back their birthdays three months, but hadn't asked. The man who'd told them things had one answer for all questions: the single word "later."

They hadn't even been fed since the night before boarding the ship. By then they'd had to show their nakedness to what he supposed were physicians, who among other things had stuck them with needles, drawn blood, looked at their teeth, and shamelessly examined their private parts.

After that they'd been given a thin, soft, snug-fitting one-piece suit to wear "for while you're in stasis." There were no seams in them except in front, where they'd been open from throat to crotch. Like winter underwear but without buttons or a trapdoor. After they'd got into them, men had shown them how to fasten them by pressing. He hadn't known the whys for any of it. Then, at their command, he'd rolled up his homespuns, tied them with a tape they'd provided, and fastened his high-cut moccasins to the bundle with another tape. All the while wondering if he'd ever see his real clothes again; they were a lot better than what he'd been given.

When he wakened, the lid was open on his stasis locker,

and there was a faint smell in his nose, mildly sharp. He wasn't groggy, but he was briefly confused. Then he remembered. Meanwhile his bundle lay on his belly, moccasins included. At least the Terrans didn't seem to be thieves.

Then a whistle had blown, and a loud voice had bellowed instructions. Esau had climbed from his locker and changed into his own clothes, he and all the other men in his compartment. They filled the aisles. Nobody had said much, and most who spoke, spoke quietly. His stomach growled, and he felt strange.

The whistle shrilled again, cutting off the soft refugee murmur. Again the loud voice spoke, seeming to come from all around them. "ATTENTION ALL PASSENGERS! ATTENTION ALL PASSENGERS! YOU ARE ABOUT TO BE DISEMBARKED. YOU ARE ABOUT TO BE DISEMBARKED. STAY ALERT AND FOLLOW INSTRUCTIONS. STAY ALERT AND FOLLOW INSTRUCTIONS. WHEN ORDERED, FILE OUT IN AN ORDERLY MANNER. DO NOT PUSH. WE DO NOT WANT ANYONE CRUSHED, OR KNOCKED DOWN AND TRAMPLED. WHEN YOU GET OUTSIDE, LISTEN FOR YOUR NAME. WHEN YOU GET OUTSIDE, LISTEN FOR YOUR NAME."

Esau was pretty sure the voice wasn't human. They'd been warned that Terrans used machines to do all sorts of things for them; apparently that could include talking. As for "disembarked"—he supposed that meant getting off the ship. And they'd be calling off names! He'd listen for Jael's, and go to her regardless of anything. Anyone got in his way, too bad for them.

Meanwhile he waited. He didn't know whether three and a half months had passed, like they'd said, or three weeks, but he was pretty sure it was less than three years and more than three days. There was a vague sense of time having passed, and an even vaguer sense of having dreamt. But however long it had been, they seemed to have arrived, presumably on Terra.

Somewhere, someone must have given an order, because now the packed humanity in his aisle began to move. It was a main aisle, leading directly to an open door, toward which they moved slowly under the scowling gaze of a very tall man. He held what the refugees took to be a hand weapon of some sort. Esau's column flowed rather smoothly, out the door into a wide corridor. Like an aisle-wide subcurrent in a river of humanity, some of whose currents were female.

"You got a wife here somewhere?" asked a voice beside him. It belonged to another youth, a bit shorter but similarly built.

"I sure hope so. I did when I got on this thing."

"I wonder what it'll be like outside."

Esau had no reply for that. Just now his attention was on how he felt physically—light-footed, even light-headed. "Do you feel like I feel?" he asked.

"Might be. How's that?"

"Kind of strange. Light."

From behind them another voice spoke. "We all feel it. Things weigh less on Terra, including us. Back home I weighed 330 pounds. Here I weigh 230."

Esau looked back at the man, a man about his own age. And like himself, rather tall by the standards of New Jerusalem. But not as strong looking as most; he didn't have the look of a farmer. Also he wore eyeglasses. Esau decided he must be a speaker of the books. Or judging by his age, a student speaker.

"How could that be?" Esau asked. "We don't look any thinner than we used to." "Because the gravity is different here. A pound at home only weighs point-seven pounds here."

Esau wondered what a "point" had to do with it. And grabbity? "What's 'grabbity'?" he asked.

"Gravity," the fellow said soberly, "is what God created for things to weigh differently on different worlds."

Esau didn't ask anything more. He didn't think much of the answers he'd already gotten. Besides, they were spilling down a ramp now, into a cold drizzle. It had been early summer when they'd left home. Here it felt like fall. *Three months then,* he told himself, *or a little more. Seems like they told the truth about that.* Combined with not stealing his clothes, it made the Terrans out to be not so bad as he'd feared. Maybe they'd changed over the centuries.

He was glad he had his homespuns on again, and not the thin Terran clothes he'd slept in. Wool would keep off the drizzle better. At the foot of the ramp, tall men dressed like the armed guards in the corridor directed them into separate columns of twos. There was a certain amount of confusion, and the guards had to do some pulling and pushing. When one of them pulled on Esau, he didn't seem very strong, just tall. Esau told himself he could take the guy down and sit on him if need be. But it went all right, though one of the guards cursed way worse than Esau had ever heard in his life. The columns separated somewhat, eight or ten feet apart. Then someone up ahead shouted "halt" in another really loud voice, and after some jostling and piling up, the columns got themselves stopped.

Looking sideways down the gap between his column and the next, Esau saw a man talking into something he held one hand. The words came out loudly enough, it seemed to Esau he could have heard them a quarter-mile. The man said that when their name was called, they should go to a flag that someone up ahead was waving in the air. Then a bunch of names were called, some of men, some of women. After a bit they got to the *W*s—there was even a Wesley—but no Esau or Jael. Then the process started over again at a different flag.

Esau stood there in the rain through several rounds of that, while the drizzle started to soak through. The column had got a lot thinner before his name was called—his followed by Jael's—and he took off at a trot. Running was so easy, he began to believe in grabbity. Jael had already been somewhere up near the flag; now he could see her standing by it. She'd seen him, too, and was waving her arms overhead.

◇

Their group was led to a large sort of tent, the biggest he'd ever seen. Light passed through it, but he couldn't actually see through it. There they were given a kind of food—crunchy flatbread that tasted decent enough—and water to wash it down. Then they'd been lined up, each line leading to a different man at a different table. He and Jael stayed together now, determined not to be separated again, Esau first, Jael close behind. These lines also moved slowly; another kind of "processing," Esau decided. The people doing it to them wore clothes just alike, as far as he could tell: greenish-brown. When he reached the table for their line, the man sitting there had him say his name to a small box.

"Esau Wesley," Esau said, then gestured. "Hers is Jael Wesley."

The man ignored the last part. "Esau Wesley, you need to make a decision now, the one they told you about before you left New Jerusalem. There are two kinds of jobs available to you. You can either be a soldier, and protect humankind from the invaders, or you can be a laborer. The choice is yours. But I must tell you that if we get too few soldiers, the invaders will win, and kill us all."

Esau's jaw jutted. "I'll be a soldier if my wife can be. We've got to stay together."

"No problem," the corporal said. "Now I'm going to give you instructions. Answer when I tell you to. And speak clearly." He paused. "Do you, Esau Wesley, understand that you are volunteering to be in the Commonwealth Armed Forces? And that you will be subject to all military rules and regulations? Please answer now, yes or no."

Esau wasn't entirely sure what "military" meant, but "rules and regulations" was clear enough. "Yes," he said.

"Good. Congratulations, Recruit Esau Wesley." The corporal was supposed to shake Esau's hand then, but shaking the hand of one Jerrie had been more than enough. He simply pointed. "Get in line behind sign *C* over there. To get your physical exam and army clothes." He knew from an earlier shipment that some off-worlders didn't know the word *uniform*.

Esau frowned at him without moving. "I'll wait for her," he said, gesturing at Jael. "We'll go together."

The man's face and voice turned impatient. "Recruit Wesley, that is not possible. You'll be naked for your physical exam, so it's men with men and women with women. You can be together later. Now go get in line C."

Reluctantly Esau left. Then the corporal repeated the procedure with Jael.

◇

Jael felt mildly anxious that she couldn't spot her husband. Though not as anxious as she'd been aboard ship, and that had worked out all right. There were lines of one sort or another all over the huge tent, and she'd been directed to one consisting solely of women. Most, like herself, were young, and either single or childless, she supposed. It seemed unlikely that soldiers could take care of their children. Surely not in a war. Within thirty minutes, she'd been checked out by medics, inoculated, and issued a uniform. After changing clothes, she was directed to a mixed line. Esau wasn't there, either. *He's still waiting for his physical exam,* she told herself, but again anxiety gnawed her gut.

That line took her through the drizzle to a large nearby tent called a mustering shed, where she still couldn't see Esau. Here there were quite a few women, and most of the men appeared older. Her anxiety grew. Again names were called alphabetically, recruits gathering behind a man called ensign something. Something outlandish. When a company had received its complement of newly processed recruits, it left. Then a new ensign replaced the old, and the process repeated, starting with *A* again. When at last Jael's name was called, she fell in as instructed. And now she felt the beginning of panic, because Esau's name wasn't called. Hers followed Warner, and after it came Whitney, Wilcox, Williams and Yancy.

After the name Yancy, the ensign called, "All right, follow me!", and led off toward an exit, another man following to herd stragglers. Jael stepped out of line and ran to catch up with the ensign. "Sir," she said, "my husband isn't here!"

He glowered but did not slow. He was the tallest man she'd seen, even among the Terrans, a lantern-jawed giant. His skin was brown, his arms and hands long, and his eyes were hooded by thick slanting lids. "Soldier," he ordered, "get back in line. If you've got a problem, it can be handled at the waiting shed. We'll be there in a minute."

Not relieved, she fell in immediately behind him. In two minutes they arrived at another large tent, where a lot of people waited. The ensign told his charges to sit down on a block of empty benches he pointed to. They all did except Jael. She stood determinedly.

"All right, soldier, what's your complaint?"

Briefly she explained. Without answering her, he took a phone from his belt. "Provost Station, this is Ensign Adrup Gompo, 3rd Processing Company, at Station E. I have a recruit with a beef. This one needs an arbiter." He put the phone back on his belt and looked at Jael again. "Sit down, soldier. That's an order. Someone will come to take you to an arbiter. He'll fix what needs fixing."

She stood half numb. She'd only half understood what he'd said. A runner arrived, and led her to one end of the tent, to a room walled by plastic curtains hung on wires. Inside sat a burly, middle-aged man. A placard on his desk read Sgt. Major Nguva. His skin was almost black, his short salt and pepper hair formed tiny tight curls, and he wore a plug in one ear. There was a chair a few feet from his, but he left her standing.

"Your name, soldier?" He asked it amiably, while aiming a microphone toward her, then watched the monitor on his terminal while she answered. Next he tapped something on his keypad, before looking back at her. "What's your complaint?"

Again she described it. He tapped an instruction, then frowned, listening to something she couldn't hear. Now his fingers tapped a longer instruction. From a box came Esau's voice, then the corporal's who'd sworn them in, and finally her own. The sergeant major cut it off.

"Corporal DeSoto misinformed you," he said. "He told you one thing and did something else. Your husband has been assigned to Company B, 587th Infantry Training Regiment. You have been assigned to Company G, 249th Fighting Vehicle Training Regiment."

Her breath stopped, trapped in her lungs.

"For whatever satisfaction it may provide you, Corporal DeSoto will be reprimanded before the recruiting staff, assigned punishment, and perhaps demoted.

"After you have completed your basic and specialist training, which will require several months, both you and your husband will be assigned to a corps consisting of your own people. Meanwhile you will train in different camps. On the same planet, but he in an infantry center, you in a fighting vehicle center.

Her guts shriveled.

"Or," the sergeant major went on, "you can choose to transfer to the infantry. In that case, considering how you were misled, you and your husband can be in the same platoon and squad. But there are serious disadvantages in that."

Again he paused, observing her relief. "You can also have your enlistments cancelled, on the grounds of Corporal DeSoto's deliberate misrepresentation. In that case you will find yourselves in a civilian labor battalion." He paused. "Perhaps on a colony world, building fortifications. If the invaders arrive there, and the fighting goes badly, an effort will be made to evacuate our fighting units, but it is difficult to imagine a situation in which labor battalions can be salvaged."

He leaned forward, forearms on the table, his tone detached but not unfriendly. "The army is no bed of roses," he went on. "The Commonwealth is in serious danger of being overrun, and the human species eradicated. That includes you and me, small children, old people—everyone. So in the army—or in the labor battalions—the purpose of existence is not pleasure, comfort, or convenience. It is to stop the invader. Defeat him and drive him out. Bloody him so badly he will never return."

She stared round-eyed, understanding enough to get his meaning.

"That is what your training will be about, whether you are an armor jockey, or in your husband's infantry squad. One is about as dangerous as the other. In the infantry, however, the purely muscular exhaustion is much greater. The need for muscular strength results in female recruits being routinely assigned to fighting vehicles, but exceptions can be made." He eyed the wide-bodied, broad-handed young woman before him, clearly from a heavyworld, and wondered how many Terran men were as strong. "You will almost certainly be the only woman in your company," he went on, "and probably in your regiment. And ancient experience has shown that few young women can long stand such isolation from female companionship.

"Meanwhile you would not be sharing your husband's bed. Private moments of any sort would be few.

"As an armor jockey, on the other hand, the exhaustion is more of the nerves, and fighting vehicle regiments have many women."

He leaned back slightly in his chair. "You must decide now: armored vehicle training, your husband's infantry platoon, or a labor battalion."

Her eyes met his, and her voice, though quiet, was firm. "I want to be with my husband."

Sergeant Major Nguva smiled. "Good," he said, and getting to his feet, held out a large black hand with a pink palm. Hesitantly she shook it. "Congratulate your husband for me," he said, "on his good fortune in having so steadfast a wife."

Chapter Sixteen
Puzzles

The two Wyzhñyñy sat in the grand admiral's office, talking. "Our progress?" the chief scholar said. "It is accelerating. We exchange limited sentences now, on a growing number of subjects."

Grand Admiral Quanshûk shu-Gorlak nodded without enthusiasm. "And what of the questions and topics I have listed?"

"I have not broached them yet. They…"

"None of them?!"

The interruption was discourteous and its tone accusatory, but Chief Scholar Qonits zu-Kitku did not lower his eyes. He was the leading scholar in their mutual and extensive tribe, and in this galaxy without a gender peer. But given certain enigmas in the operating situation, he understood the grand admiral's concern. "Your Excellency," he answered, "the subjects I am able to discuss with the aliens deal with everyday experiences, largely physical. I must compile a much broader vocabulary, and refine what I already have, before I can even present the questions you ask. Let alone understand any answers.

"But each day we learn more. As you know, I now spend most of my waking time at the task." He might have added, but didn't, that he'd warned it would take time. Instead he gestured now, palms out and open. "And as I said, progress is accelerating."

Quanshûk nodded. The chief scholar's reply had been as much lecture as answer, but his own impatience had brought it on. Qonits was exalted in more than gender, and due both courtesy and high respect. Pique, impatience, and gender prejudice were inappropriate between them.

"Meanwhile," Qonits was saying, "the ship runs semantic correlations, and presents me with strategical areas to explore." He changed the subject. "It seems that among the aliens there are two parent genders, not one, each gender with fixed sexuality.

You can imagine how such personal—incompleteness—might affect the individual, and that a mated pair might therefore bond very strongly.

"The two larger aliens are a mated pair. The smaller one, who does not speak, seems to be a member of their kin group, and is mentally and physically defective. It was being cared for by a servant—apparently of the nanny gender—when the marines captured it. The bond between servant and child had become profound, and killing the servant traumatized the child severely."

"Ah." This was something Admiral Quanshûk could understand. It was easy to overlook that aliens had lives and feelings of their own. *It would be wise,* he told himself drily, *not to dwell on that.*

<>

Prior to the invasion, Prime Minister Foster Peixoto and President Chang Lung-Chi had routinely met late in the morning, in the president's office. But seldom at lunch, which they'd agreed was a time for relaxation. Government had not been as crisis laden and stressful, nor politics as consuming and ruthless, as they'd been a millennium earlier. Society was less overwrought. Socially and psychologically, the human species had truly evolved and advanced. Stagnated, their remote ancestors would have said. Lost their fire.

But since the invasion, crisis and stress were endemic in government. The prime minister and president had met routinely for lunch and often for supper, specifically to talk business. Time was too precious for relaxed eating. Usually they met in Peixoto's office, and ate at an AG table guided in by an orderly.

Chang Lung-Chi would not have changed jobs with his prime minister for anything. The demands on Peixoto's time and energy were more stringent than Chang liked to think about.

Meanwhile it was Chang who'd come down with the latest new viral pneumonia, quite dangerous, and been confined to the palace infirmary for twelve days. Now Peixoto was updating him on some of the less worrisome matters of interest.

"You may recall my giving Bekr the task of learning

where the 'messages' are coming from," the prime minister was saying. "He has it sorted out now. The Julie mentioned in their conversations can only be a sensitive named Ju-Li Hamilton-Gävle, the wife of a Dennis Bertrand. She is, or was, the attendant of her half-sister, a pre-adolescent female savant named Annika Pedersen." He paused meaningfully, then finished: "Assigned on Maritimus. The people now looking after her—the Yukiko and David on the cube—are a marine biologist and an oceanographer, Yukiko Gavaldon and David MacDonald respectively. MacDonald was also chief of station on Maritimus. Apparently Hamilton-Gävle and Bertrand were killed by the aliens, and Gavaldon and MacDonald, not being trained sensitives, don't know how to control the savant. Bekr is convinced they don't know she's channeling. They think she's simply comatose."

Thoughtfully the president ate a spoonful of cream custard. "How," he wondered aloud, "does Bekr explain a comatose savant who channels automatically? Or could it be on her own volition, at some subconscious level?"

Frowning, the prime minister sipped thick Iranian coffee. "Bekr has said nothing about volition," he answered, "but you raise an interesting question. Each savant communicator is hypno-conditioned to react to a 'psychic touch' by another communicator. *Any* other communicator. Or to make such a touch, directed by the savant's attendant through a hypnotically pre-installed...'switch,' Bekr calls it.

"Judging from the date that Maritimus was captured, Annika did not channel at all for some weeks afterward. Perhaps she was too deeply comatose, and began when her level of consciousness rose to some threshold... Which brings up the possibility that she may stop channeling as her level of consciousness continues to climb. I need to ask Bekr about this."

The president raised another spoonful of custard. "Without an attendant to direct her, how is it her messages get to Ramesh, instead of to someone else?"

"Bekr has an explanation for that. Hamilton-Gävle reported the alien's arrival in the Maritimus System through

Ramesh and Chloë. Via Annika of course. That much we know. Then obviously the aliens caught the mission's base ship before it could escape. Presumably when they stormed it, Annika's attendant made another contact, seemingly cut short either by her death or Annika's injury before our savants here could react. Then, when Annika recovered sufficiently, the latent contact activated. Now, in the absence of an attendant able to direct her, she channels whatever is said in her presence. At least when she is sufficiently receptive; Bekr believes that within her coma she sometimes descends below functionality." Peixoto shrugged. "A sort of sleep within a sleep."

Absently he raised a morsel of preserved pear to his mouth, to be chewed and swallowed. "I have a new savant covering Ramesh's past duties," he went on. "Bekr has set her up in the Lavender Suite. Ramesh is now available only to Annika. As Chloë is at War House."

Chang Lung-Chi nodded. "And what have we learned from this connection, besides a few words in the alien tongue? And their name: the Wyzhñyñy."

"Primarily we are gaining added insights into the aliens— learning what sort of beings they are. While they concentrate on learning our language, which I, at least, find encouraging. War House's AI is working on theirs, but so far lacks a useful key. I'll inform you when we have a significant breakthrough.

"MacDonald and Gavaldon don't discuss their situation. They are undoubtedly monitored and recorded, and careful of what they say to each other. Otherwise when the aliens have an effective translation program..." Peixoto's long expressive hands gestured vague unpleasantness.

"Bekr feels sure the MacDonalds don't realize Annika is channeling. If they suspected, they'd surely have informed us covertly—given us some sort of hint. I've had Burhan undertake to pass an innocuous comment through Annika, to alert the MacDonalds without attracting alien suspicion. It didn't work. Bekr believes Annika is operating as a one-way relay—them to us. Yukiko Gavaldon is clearly not a sensitive, let alone a trained attendant, so that is not really surprising."

He paused. "In fact, as you suggested, we may lose even that one-way contact. Annika no longer has to be helped to use the sanitary facility, and she holds her own drinking cup."

"Without disconnecting?"

"So far."

Hmm. Chang wondered if her present state qualified as coma. He frowned. He definitely did not want that connection lost, but there seemed nothing to be done about it.

He changed the subject. "Has Special Projects had anything to report?"

"No, Mr. President, they have not. Dosado has promised a preliminary report no later than Threeday. The know-how exists; it has for a very long time. The difficulty is, we know nothing about invader physiology. Which does not preclude following through, of course. It simply leaves the result very much in doubt."

Chapter Seventeen
The Home Front

The marchers ranged from elderly to children in arms, and wore no uniforms. They filled the boulevard from curb to curb, and the night with their drums and bagpipes. And Peace Front slogans, chanted in every accent on Terra, some even in the tongues of ethnic forebears. Their weapons were banners, placards, and the Commonwealth flag. And though they threw up no barricades, they paralyzed traffic quite effectively, for they numbered an estimated hundred thousand. The din could be heard for more than a mile.

The demonstration was not remotely spontaneous. It had been carefully planned, and its contingents were rather well coordinated. The great majority who marched believed sincerely that the Commonwealth and its safety lay exclusively in the hands of God. That if the invaders were received by humankind in peace and love, their alien hearts would hear God whispering. And hearing, they'd move on to regions of space unoccupied by humans. So the various peace sects and persuasions had smoked the calumet, the pipe of peace—literally smoked it—agreeing that the important thing was to end Commonwealth defense activities. That only then would God act to save humankind.

Remarkably, the scores of thousands of marchers drew rather few spectators, and these were watched closely from police floaters. The government wanted no incidents that might cause an eruption of violence. Nor did the Peace Front, for the media were there in numbers, along the sidewalks, within the marching ranks, and in floaters keeping the legally required distance, recording with electronic eyes. Any violence would be witnessed worldwide, and video and holo cubes would be podded throughout the Core Worlds. If the marchers became violent, even in self-defense, the Peace Front would be seen as hypocritical, and so large a demonstration would itself be considered provocation.

While if spectators sparked an incident, the government

would be blamed for failure to police the demonstration properly. But if government force was seen as less than highly restrained, the demonstrators next time might be twice as many.

At length the marchers flowed onto the vast pavement of Wellesley Square, which was large enough to hold them all. Flowed onto and across it, their skirling, booming, chanting current carrying them to the force field that, activated for the event, encircled the huge capital complex—a city embedded in a city. There the current stopped, the marchers flooding to both sides to fill the square.

Near one side, this sea of humanity contained an island— "Martyr's Hill"—a large grassy mound with steps, topped by a platform. Which tonight was topped in turn by a microphone connected to Wellesley Square's sound system. Martyr's Hill was 742 years old, an enduring memorial to the demonstrators whose battle and massacre on this very square had led to a military coup, and the overthrow of the old Terran war government. Ending the long "Troubles"—94 years of economic warfare, embargoes, sabotage, terrorism, guerrilla actions, and now and then formal space fights between Terra on the one hand, and her insystem colonies on the other. The mound had held various impassioned speakers over subsequent centuries, but there had not been so many listeners for a very long time.

Paddy Davies was a small man, so with his companion he'd climbed a few steps up on the side of the mound, to see over the crowd. The demonstration monitors allowed it, for the two were the principal members of the coordinating committee. Paddy gestured toward the executive tower, a mile away within the Complex. "What would you bet the beanpole is watching?" He shouted it, to be heard over the din.

"Of course he is," Jaromir Horvath shouted back. "In person, from a balcony. And Chang with him." Even shouted, his words were tinged with scorn. Horvath had founded, and at age sixty-four still led, the quasi-religious Party of the Holy Universe. An organization nominally inclusive, but politically narrow and dogmatic.

So far as anyone knew, joy was foreign to Horvath.

Paddy Davies was an idealist, and a mostly cheerful young man—the executive director of the People of the Glorious Creator. At age thirty-two, he could pass for twenty-five. "The People" was an ecumenical, nontheological religious umbrella beneath which various churches and sects—and any individuals who felt inclined—could merge to pursue common objectives. These days the overwhelming objective was peace. Paddy found joy in political conflict, and had many opponents but not so many enemies.

He didn't trust Jaromir Horvath, nor did Horvath trust him, but they had smoked the calumet, and united two of the more effective activist groups on Terra into a Peace Front. Which they directed, though reckless splinter groups might force their hands.

Together they watched Fritjof Ignatiev climb to the platform atop the mound. Ignatiev was the third leg of the Horvath- Davies-Ignatiev tripod. Horvath was all intellect and bile, a theorist and planner as bitter as Karl Marx, and with far less justification. He might convince, but he seldom inspired. While Paddy was charming and bright, but lacked charisma.

Ignatiev on the other hand—tall, blond, and messianically sure of himself—had a compelling charisma that worked well on crowds. He radiated power, spirituality, and certainty, and his eloquence never ceased to impress. His intelligence, however, was less than ordinary. He listened closely to more powerful minds—notably those of Jaromir Horvath and Paddy Davies—and imprinted their arguments. His grasp of those arguments was often weak, but he delivered them as gospel, and Wellesley Square this night held a sea of true believers, eager to hear.

Simply standing by the microphone and raising his long arms, Ignatiev caused the clamor to fade, the drums to stop. The bagpipes groaned to a halt. He had a magnificent voice. He didn't test the sound system, didn't think about what he was going to say. He simply lowered his arms, opened his mouth, and began.

<>

When he finished, thirty minutes later, the crowd cheered

their heads off. Nothing he'd said had differed in substance from what they'd heard before. Afterward one of the major news anchors termed it "the same tired old bunkum." But Ignatiev had given it a sense of higher truth. And if it did not specify new efforts, it bathed the demonstrators in a lagoon of self-righteousness, strengthened their sense of unity in the cause, and inspired new fervor. While undoubtedly, some among those who watched and listened on television were converted. At least temporarily.

It was, Paddy thought, up to himself and others now to capitalize on it. Create and implement projects that would make a difference. Projects already prepared, that together would change the flow, turn public opinion around, and end this dedication to war. He left uplifted, less by Ignatiev's thirty-minute oration than by its effect on the crowd.

Jaromir Horvath had not been inspired. His cynicism left no room for that. Instead he returned sour-faced to his small grim apartment to plan and write, and channel the movement's efforts. Rarely did he imagine success—the war effort abandoned, the Infinite Soul triumphant, the Wyzhñyñy invasion turned aside. But he would persist. It seemed to him that in another twenty years he'd be dead one way or another. And whether or not the Front prevailed in its struggle with a blind and perverse government, the all-creative, all-seeing Infinite Soul would take him into its loving arms.

Basically, Horvath was really rather orthodox.

<>

Foster Peixoto had watched from his apartment high in the executive tower, as Jaromir Horvath had supposed. But he'd watched alone, and via television, not from his balcony, which was much too far from the scene. When Fritjof Ignatiev had finished, and the cheering had finally faded, only then did the prime minister switch off the set and step onto the balcony. There his tall form was susceptible to a marksman with a long-range weapon, but that was not the sort of thing that worried him. In such matters he was a fatalist.

He considered the Peace Front an annoyance of limited

potential. It could produce mischief, but not revolution. Nothing Ignatiev had said had changed his mind on that. An overwhelming majority of Terrans found the Front's position seriously unconvincing. If history had done nothing else, he told himself, it had demonstrated the creator's disinclination to meddle in human affairs. Humankind would live or die by its own efforts.

Presumably the Front didn't expect to convert the broad public to its point of view. And surely its members were contemplating more than demonstrations. Even now, extremist splinters would be planning serious terrorism and sabotage. Or efforts to lever the political and theological primitivism of refugee labor battalions into strikes and uprisings. That had been his reason for setting up a government cable channel, for and restricted to refugee labor camps. A channel with mostly entertainment, and educational/propaganda programming that would not offend refugee ethno-religious sensitivities.

But a certain risk remained: benign, well-intentioned civic organizations had begun inviting groups of refugee laborers to members' homes on Sevendays. One could cautiously vet such organizations in advance, but they could not be controlled without stirring up civic resentment and uproar. Thus Peace Front agents could infiltrate, as Internal Security agents had. Fortunately the damage the Front might accomplish through such groups seemed limited. His main worry was that the media might fan small flames into something more troublesome.

Foster, he chided, *you have taken steps; let IntSec do the worrying. If they uncover anything, act accordingly. Otherwise do not tire yourself over these matters.*

◇

Chang Lung-Chi had watched the video in his living room, from the comfort of his recliner. When the cheering had died, he switched off the set. *Such delicious self-righteousness,* he thought ironically, then grunted. *In their imaginations, they no doubt say the same of me.* He hoped devoutly they did not create serious problems. Neither he nor Foster believed they would. History showed that *Homo sapiens* had come a long way: it was far less susceptible to having its emotions hijacked by agitators. Though there was still room for worry. So they'd agreed: let the Front march and rant as long as their resistance didn't seriously impair the war effort. Since the Troubles, martial law was anathema. It would do more damage than a hundred Ignatievs. He was willing to tolerate even a certain amount of activist destructiveness, if it came to that.

But if it became serious... The trick would then be to take counter measures that met with broad public acceptance.

Chapter Eighteen
Camp Mudhole

The *Madam Jao*—another converted bulk carrier—emerged from warp space less than two hundred thousand miles off Pastor Lüneburger's World. Brigadier Pyong Pak Singh had been waiting in his cabin to witness the event. Pak, his staff, his regimental commanders and their staffs, and their company commanders had made the trip from Terra "live," sixteen days in hyperspace, then a half dozen hours in equally featureless warpspace. In between there'd been perhaps a minute in familiar F-space, but he'd been sleeping, and missed it.

They'd hardly noticed the lack of scenery. They'd spent six hours a day in class, reviewing the cube of *New Ground Tactics,* produced by War House staff. Each day ended with another six of discussion and simulation exercises.

They needed to know the stuff cold, and see that their troops did. Because if things came together as planned—ship-building, fleet training, weapons delivery, and their own preparation—in nine months they'd take this now utterly green division to its home world, New Jerusalem, to wrest it back from the invaders. Whether or not they succeeded, it would be the Commonwealth's first ground campaign; War House had decided to start ground warfare not defending but attacking. And in the process, for better or worse, they'd learn a lot, both War House and his task force. Though War House wouldn't pay for it the way his people would.

Of course, Pak mused, *that assumes the invaders have gotten that far by then.* Given their progress to date, and the lack of resistance, they should, easily. But who could be sure about the behavior of an unfamiliar alien life form? And how large a battle force they'd leave behind in the New Jerusalem System was anyone's guess. Guesses! He'd take Kulikov's and Sarrufs's guesses over anyone's, but still…

Pastor Lüneburger's World now occupied all but a corner of his screen. Seen from this distance it showed no sign of humanity. It was almost a core world—an inhabited planet within ten parsecs of Terra. Had been Terra's third outsystem colony, and the first and nearest of the first dispersion. But like most worlds of the first dispersion, it had been settled by an agrarian sect, in this case United Mennonites. Even after the century of Troubles had ended, and Terra had finally begun reconnecting with the worlds of the dispersion, acceptance of technology had been slow and selective on Lüneburger's.

Not as slow as some, he reminded himself, thinking specifically of New Jerusalem. Before leaving Terra, he and his entire staff, down to platoon sergeants, had studied a cube on the planet their recruits were from. The ethnologist who'd done the narration had called New Jerusalem an unintentional reconstruction of the United States in the early 1800s.

Pak could feel the ship slowing under grav drive. They must, he decided, be getting close to the F_1 layer. The view before him was probably centered on the gravitic vector they were riding down. Much of the surface was dominated by forest, with the larger rivers visible, and to one side, ocean. He couldn't make out towns yet, but they were there. Pastor Lüneburger's World held some 200 million humans, nearly twenty percent of them townsfolk. Leaving plenty of partially cleared and semi-wild tracts on the fringes of settlement, areas well suited for training.

Somewhere down there was Camp Woldemars Stenders. They'd studied a cube on it, too, showing the Terran 4th Infantry Division in training there. The Terrans had dubbed it "Camp Mudhole." *Within the hour,* the brigadier thought, *I'll see it live.*

In the real world, Pak had never commanded anything larger than a battalion before— no one on Terra had—and under the circumstances it was natural to feel misgivings. But in sim training he'd commanded a corps, so his misgivings were mild.

<><>

The *Madam Jao* sat on an AG cushion five inches above the surface. Herded by officers and sergeants, the disembarking Jerries saw a world looking not greatly unlike New Jerusalem or Terra: the sky was blue, the vegetation green. It had rained not long before, and things even smelled more or less familiar.

Esau was disappointed. It seemed to him a different planet should look, smell, and in general feel more different. He could as well have felt that way when he'd disembarked on Terra, but he'd been too uprooted and anxious then to pay much attention. Now, by contrast, he had a new and major stable element in his life—the army—and some idea of what the future held for him: training. Though what training would be like, he hadn't tried to imagine.

Once on the ground, the recruits formed ranks—they'd learned to do that much on Terra—and were led down a graveled road toward camp, lugging their duffel bags, and sweating.

Camp Stenders was unlike the temporary war-time camps on Terra. Basically it consisted of low-tech huts and sheds—concrete slabs, lumber, and linoleum—though with Plastosil panels from a newly built local factory. War House had earlier provided the camp's administrative staff—the bureaucrats who were an essential if not always appreciated part of the system. They'd kept the place running while the Terran 4th Infantry Division got its basic and advanced training there, then had sent them off to Camp Chu Teh, for unit training exercises with the Terran 3rd Armored.

Most of the key administrative elements were "retreads," retired military personnel from the marines or the small, pre-war, Terran planetary defense force. The company clerks, supply clerks, cooks and flunkies were conscripts not considered suitable for combat. They'd been rushed through three weeks of mini-basic, then enough specialist training to function, and learned the rest of their duties on the job.

The second-tier training cadre were holdovers from the 4th Terran, mature men who'd completed their basic and advanced training right there at Stenders, and earned a stripe or two. They would help the first-tier cadre train the recruits.

<>

Esau and Jael Wesley knew nothing of all that. They did know the name of the world they were on, and the camp; reception center personnel had told them that much before loading them onto a snooze ship. The time of day they could only guess—somewhere in the middle, because the sun was high.

They didn't talk as they hiked—no one had told them they could—but there was lots of observing and more than a little wondering. It seemed to Esau that a pound wouldn't weigh a pound here, either, but closer to it than on Terra; apparently Lüneburger's World had grabbity, too. Meanwhile he was hungry. They'd each been given an energy bar and a carton of apple juice when they'd been wakened, but it hadn't been enough, for him at least. The road brought them to camp, a broad featureless area of featureless shed-like buildings. Companies began to peel off from the column, moving into company hutments. Shortly, B Company 2nd Regiment halted on what they would learn was their company drill field and mustering ground.

The second-tier cadre, who'd marched them in, formed up to one side. All wore at least one chevron on their sleeves. In front of the recruits stood the company's first-tier cadre—commissioned and non-commissioned officers. Like the recruits, they'd just arrived, but been bussed to the company area. A step in front of them stood a large, thick-bellied, fiftyish marine retread, with three stripes and three rockers on his sleeve. "All right, recruits," he bellowed, "listen up. I am Master Sergeant Henkel. To you I am god. You are not part of the 587th Infantry *Training* Regiment, as originally informed. Instead you are Company B, 2nd Infantry Regiment, 1st New Jerusalem Infantry Division. If any of you goddamn sonsabitches can't remember that when asked, you're in deep shit. So I'll repeat it once: this is B Company…2nd Infantry Regiment…1st New Jerusalem Infantry Division."

A voice called from the ranks, loud, clear, and righteous. It was the student speaker of the books, Esau realized, the guy who'd told him about grabbity. "Master Sergeant Henkel, sir," the youth called, "in addressing us, you have twice taken God's name in vain and used several obscenities. Offending everyone, and more serious, offending God. You…"

The sergeant interrupted, his voice soft but easily heard, and dominating. "What's your name, recruit?"

"Isaiah Vernon, sir."

"Come up here, Recruit Vernon."

The young man did so.

"Do you know what pushups are, soldier?"

"Yessir."

"Good. Drop down and give me fifty."

"Fifty sir?" Vernon sounded unbelieving. He'd never been much for sports or exercise.

"Make that a hundred, for backflash."

"For…but… I can't do a hundred!"

The voice almost purred. "Make that a hundred and fifty, and start NOW!"

Suddenly realizing his situation, Vernon dropped to the ground and started. In Lüneburger's relatively modest gravity—1.25 gees compared to New Jerusalem's 1.42—he managed to squeeze out fifteen, then collapsed. To lay there looking up at Henkel. The sergeant's voice became almost kindly.

"Recruit Vernon, you are guilty of backflash, disrespecting a superior, and refusing an order. Considering how green you are, I can overlook your ignorance. But not your stupidity. Common sense should tell you you don't mouth off like that to a superior. And here, anyone with a stripe on his sleeve or an insignia on his collar is your superior. Tonight, report to the orderly room at 2200 hours, to receive company punishment. Now, on your feet."

Vernon struggled pale-faced to his feet while Henkel scanned the recruits. When the sergeant spoke again, his voice was no longer soft. "Look at you!" he bellowed. "You look like some goddamn dog shit you out! STAND STRAIGHT!"

Every recruit straightened. Esau's eyes sized the sergeant up. He could, he told himself, throw down the big tub of lard and sit on him, but he doubted the satisfaction would be worth the punishment.

The sergeant turned sharply to the company commander and saluted. "Sir," he said, "with your permission, I will have the men shown to their quarters."

"Do so," the captain said mildly.

Before getting a break, they were shown to their huts, two squads per hut; assigned cots and open-faced wall lockers; given a guided, familiarization tour of the company area while marching in ranks; then issued bedding, field uniforms, and boots. Finally they were taken to the drill field, where they practiced close order drill for an hour. Esau wondered what possible good close-order drill was.

◇

Finally they were released to use the latrine and wash for supper. The company latrine was a long shed with two long parallel rooms, one with two rows of washbowls and mirrors, the other with a long row of commodes, and long, trough-like urinals. At one end of the building was the shower room, about twenty by thirty feet, with showerheads at thirty-inch intervals all the way around, and wooden duckboards on the floor.

Most of the recruits headed directly for the latrine. Others went first to the huts, to get towels and soap. Jael went to their platoon sergeant, above whose left shirt pocket "SFC Hawkins, A.," was indelibly printed. What SFC meant, she didn't know, but she already knew the three chevrons, and guessed that the two rockers below them stood for increased authority. "Sergeant," she said hesitantly, "where do I go?"

"Go?"

"To—relieve myself."

He regarded her mildly. "There is only the latrine," he answered. "If you are willing, you can use it when the others do. Otherwise you can wait till they're done."

She looked at him with dismay. Dismay and pain, it seemed to him. He made a decision. "Come with me," he said, and turning, led her to the orderly room. There Master Sergeant Henkel ruled. When Sergeant Hawkins stepped to his desk, Henkel looked up at him. "What can I do for you, Sergeant?" he asked.

"Sergeant, I need to speak with the company commander."

"Bypassing your platoon leader?"

Hawkins' voice took an edge. "This is urgent."

Henkel gestured. "Go ahead."

The plaque on the door read C.O. Hawkins went to it and knocked, leaving Jael standing in the middle of the orderly room. Through the door, a voice called "come in." Hawkins went in and closed the door behind him.

"Sir," he said, "something has come up that needs your attention."

"And what is that?"

Hawkins explained.

Captain Martin Mulvaney Singh's red eyebrows rose. "You've already presented her the options, such as they are, but it's not really practical for her to wait. She'll just have to use the latrine when the men do."

"I realize that, sir. But these Jerries are fundamentalist Christians. It may require some setting up. To lessen embarrassment and avoid incidents."

Mulvaney frowned. His briefing on the Jerries hadn't covered situations like this. "Being a Jerrie, she'll find it embarrassing enough anyway," he said, then paused. "Call her in." Hawkins opened the door to the orderly room and ordered her in. She stood before the captain sturdy but forlorn, and with pain that was more than psychological.

I wonder how old she is, Mulvaney thought. *Seventeen? Eighteen?* "Sergeant Hawkins explained your difficulty to me," he said mildly. "He has already told you the alternatives, such as they are. But it will seldom be practical for you to wait, so for the most part you'll have to use it when the men do. However, the company will muster before supper, and I will set certain rules of behavior. Which—" His face turned stern. "Which they will obey, as you will, or receive company punishment."

She nodded. Her answer was little more than a whisper. "Yes sir."

He gestured to a door in the back of the room. "Meanwhile, just this one time, you may use mine if you wish."

"Thank you, sir," she repeated. Her gratitude was too heartfelt to be hidden by her embarrassment.

When she'd entered his little toilet and closed the door

behind her, the captain spoke quietly to Sergeant Hawkins. "What is she doing in this company?"

"Sir, there's another Wesley in the platoon. Recruit Esau Wesley. I believe they're husband and wife."

"Ah. What does he look like?"

"Bigger than most Jerries, sir, and looks—like no one to fool with."

"Um-hmm. Good. And Jerries are supposed to be pretty straitlaced. All right, stay here till she comes out. Then take her outside and dismiss her."

Shortly afterward she emerged, and left with Sergeant Hawkins. Which reminded Captain Mulvaney of something he needed to do. Getting to his feet, he stepped to the orderly room door. "Sergeant Henkel," he said, "come in here please," then returned to his desk and sat down.

Henkel came in and stood at attention. He'd spent thirty years around officers. He could smell when something was wrong. "Yes sir?"

"Sergeant Henkel, the Sikh style of command is different than yours. Therefore I am reassigning your command duties. That will give you more time for your administrative tasks, which in any case have been very much your main duties."

He paused.

"Yessir," Henkel said, but his eyes made it clear that his "yessir" was acknowledgement, not agreement. "You're aware, sir, that my duties are prescribed in our T.O."

Their eyes met, the sergeant's resentful, the captain's mild. But behind that mildness was no give at all. "An old marine gunnery sergeant like yourself," he said, "doesn't need to be reminded of my authority. And the appeal authority is back on Terra. Pod time each way is fourteen days. I have no idea how long the turn-around time is at War House, in times like these, but I'm sure things are prioritized by importance.

"Meanwhile, War House has seen fit to provide field commanders with extraordinary authority. The army, the fleet— even the Corps are recreating themselves, doing things in new ways, to fit the time and resources available. And War House is giving us elbow room to do it."

Henkel's resentment was fading. He'd never had a C.O. like this one before, and there was something about the man he liked.

"Look around," Mulvaney went on. "The two-tier cadre system itself is new, a necessary response to the enormous training load, and the lack of experienced personnel."

Again the captain paused, then spoke with fresh crispness. "Field Sergeant Fossberg will carry out the command duties that you would otherwise carry. Tomorrow, you and he will go over your job description, write up the changes, and give them to me for approval. By 1700 hours."

The old marine saluted sharply. "Yessir, captain," he said. "By 1700 hours tomorrow." He still was less than happy with this surprising development, but it would make life easier, he'd mellowed with age, and the captain held a handful of aces.

◇

The company stood in ranks in the slanting rays of an evening sun, facing the company commander and Field Sergeant Kirpal Fossberg Singh.

"Men," Mulvaney said, "when I call you men, I include the sole woman in the company. It has been brought to my attention that among the people of New Jerusalem, men and women do not bathe together or use a latrine together. However, we do not have separate facilities for the two genders, and during duty hours, the opportunities to relieve yourselves are few and crowded.

"Therefore, it will be necessary that men and women use the latrine together. And the shower." He paused. The company stood at ease, but furtive glances flicked, largely avoiding Jael, who stood fiery faced.

Mulvaney went on. "I have consulted with Recruit Spieler about this. For any who don't know him, Spieler is a speaker of the books. He tells me that your religion forbids people to show themselves naked to others. That means men to men, as well as women to men and vice versa. So using the showers with the other gender should be no worse a religious misdemeanor than using it with others of your own gender.

"Some of you will also be sharing a hut with your female comrade. At appropriate times you'll be changing clothes there. So—" He paused, then raised his voice. "LISTEN UP! When someone of the other gender is naked in your presence, you will not stare, you will not make comments or gestures, you will not touch them, even accidentally! If you do, you will receive company punishment! Which is whatever I say it is, or whatever Sergeant Fossberg says it is, or your platoon leader or platoon sergeant!"

Again the captain paused. "You are in the army now, and you'll find many things different than you're used to. If you have difficulties with this, talk to Recruit Spieler about it. I've appointed him the company's religious advisor.

"Now! Back to business! The mess hall opens for supper at 1730 hours. That's in fifteen minutes. It closes at 1815. At 1900 you will muster here in field uniform for an evening speed march."

He turned to his field sergeant. "Sergeant Fossberg, the company is yours."

Fossberg nodded. "Thank you, sir." He turned back to the recruits. *"Company!"* he bellowed, *"dismissed!"*

<><

That evening the company learned what speed march meant, at least to Sergeant Fossberg, at least on that day. They jogged an easy quarter mile, then walked another, alternating the two for an hour and a half in the warm humid summer evening. And on Pastor Lüneburger's World, the hours, minutes, days, were 1.13 times as long as Terran standard. As they ran, they were joined by the local version of mosquitoes, which came out in force about sundown. And though the recruits had lost essentially zero conditioning during stasis, few had had distance running as an important part of their life style at home. At 2100 hours they were dismissed, slick with sweat. Knowing intuitively that the experience had been just a foretaste of the weeks to come.

Then they headed for the showers. The most difficult thing

Jael Wesley had ever done was go to the shower room with no more than a towel wrapped around her. Wrapped around her chest, it was not adequate to hide her loins, while around her waist it left her breasts exposed. She draped it around her waist, and with a truculent-looking Esau glowering beside her, walked to the shower room. Then of course came the new most difficult: she had to remove the towel to shower. Esau stayed by her, his scowl daring anyone to say or do, or perhaps think anything out of line. If they did, they hid it. Any erections were concealed by turning away.

After a few days, mixed showering would seem routine, though Jael was never totally comfortable with it.

◇

At 2200 hours the CQ threw a switch, and the lights went off throughout the trainees' huts. But the night was clear, and rich in stars, and after a minute, Esau's eyes adjusted. Dimly he could make out the cot next to his, and the shadowed form of his wife. It stimulated him; he wanted her very much. Nonetheless he waited; there were men all around them, not yet asleep.

He lay there for half an hour anticipating, not sleepy at all despite the long day. Then, leaning half out of bed on his left hand, he reached toward her with his right and touched her arm. She flinched out of sleep as if burned, sat half up, then saw her husband's arm, and rested her hand on his. He swung his legs out of bed, and stood. She stood too. For pajamas, the troops wore short, dull-green summer drawers, Jael with a dull-green T-shirt. Esau paused, and from his locker took his poncho. Jael did the same, and they padded very carefully out of the hut. Keeping to the shadows, Esau led her through the night to the latrine building, and around behind it. There was the water heater room, its door without a lock; he'd done some advance scouting. They didn't speak till they were inside with the door closed, and didn't leave for nearly an hour.

Back in bed, Esau thought about how he might get a mattress—something for padding—and stash it behind the large water heater. Jael, for her part, thought about what might happen if she got pregnant. She hadn't in six months of trying back home. What a cruel thing it would be to get pregnant now.

<>

The Wesleys weren't the last recruits to get to sleep that night. Not by a long shot. It was 0255 hours when Isaiah Vernon settled groaning onto his cot. He'd discovered one form that company punishment could take. Under the occasional eye of the charge of quarters, he'd dug a hole some six feet long, six wide, and six deep. In loamy clay, while water seeped in around his feet. Then, when the hole had met with the CQ's approval, he was ordered to climb out, urinate into it, and fill it up again.

He'd been careful not to ask why.

Chapter Nineteen
Another Shortage

In the Office of Military Resource Planning, Captain Bruno Lucas scanned a message on his screen. "It seems we have a shortage, Colonel," he said laconically. "A *critical* shortage."

Colonel Wiktor Kobayashi raised a graying bushy eyebrow and grunted. There were endless shortages, most of them flagged critical. "Is that so? What's this one?"

"Nothing new. An old one getting more urgent." The captain flicked it to the colonel's screen. "With three red flags now," he added.

Kobayashi looked. It was the shortage of qualified warbot volunteers again. Warbots carried the cyborg concept to the ultimate, and lots of them were needed, but qualifying was tough. You needed to have lost at least three limbs, including both arms, or two limbs and your eyes, or be dying from incurable injury or illness, or be serving a life term in prison. The central nervous system had to be functional, intelligence normal or above, and personality profile acceptable. Thus most quadriplegics, amputees and convicts were ineligible, as well as older invalids with significant decline in CNS function.

"Nothing to it," the colonel said wryly. "We'll assign a regiment to meet the evacuation ships with swords, and cut both arms and one leg off everyone on board."

"Sorry, Colonel, but we've got a serious shortage of swords. Would laser saws be all right?"

Kobayashi was rarely sarcastic, and didn't like it when he was. And the shortage of warbots was real and serious; sarcasm wouldn't reduce it. It directly and seriously affected the combat readiness of all infantry divisions, of which 63 were now in training. Some of those divisions had begun or were approaching interactive tactical training -- so-called unit training. Within five months, the plans called for a total of 300 divisions in service or training. And tactics—even strategy—called for each to have a "normal" contingent of warbots.

He was well-informed on the subject, and knew the arithmetic too well. Three hundred divisions, each with eight regiments, each regiment with two platoons of warbots. Forty-eight hundred warbot platoons; some 110,000 bots overall. But the latest figures showed only 4,400 qualified volunteers. If every one of them completed training successfully, that would still mean fewer than two bots, let alone platoons, per regiment. And for most warbot tasks and missions, "organics" -- ordinary infantry -- were not suitable substitutes.

Producing trained warbots took time and care. First the central nervous system had to be extracted from the body. Then came its painstaking neuro-electronic "bottling." Installing the bottled CNS in a battle servo was similarly demanding. And finally a period of neurological, and sometimes psychological detraumatization and "breaking in" was required, before the individual was ready for warbot training.

But the basic problem was the demanding legal qualifications for volunteers.

"Shit," the colonel muttered. The captain was tempted to answer "Yessir. I'll be right back, sir," but he sensed that just now, humor would not be appreciated. Certainly not that kind.

Kobayashi touched a pair of keys and began to dictate.

I see no possibility of providing the necessary warbots without (a) modifying the legal qualifications for volunteers, and (b) promoting intensively. Therefore I STRONGLY RECOMMEND that the army:
(1) Accept candidates with two useable limbs; volunteers with four useable limbs but who are blind; and volunteers with debilitating conditions, even though promising research is underway toward a cure. The latter limitation in particular permits all manner of opinions to block us.

It wasn't the first time Wiktor Kobayashi had proposed that. But previously he'd been rebuffed by government attorneys under political pressures. This time he would add to it. If he became sufficiently extreme—who knew? They might go along with his more moderate suggestions.

(2) Attach recruiters to all hospitals, including emergency rooms, with access to candidates over the objections of hospital personnel.

(3) Accept able-bodied volunteers—if they can pass appropriate mental and psychological tests—and to hell with family approvals.

Number three awed the captain. It seemed to him that reasonable mental and psychological tests would automatically eliminate able-bodied volunteers. And the part about attorneys and family approvals would offend a lot of politicians.

He hoped it wouldn't result in Kobayashi getting transferred. If it did, he'd probably be named to replace him, a dreadful thought.

(4) Before long, we will start shipping divisions to combat sites. There they will suffer casualties, and some will become bot eligible. Therefore I ALSO STRONGLY RECOMMEND that (a) each division carry neuro-electronic conversion teams, and extra BEIUs and servos; (b) *that all organic trainees get effective virtuality training on warbot operations and tactics.* The training they already receive as organics will go a long way toward getting them ready. Let the motto be, 'today's serious casualty, tomorrow's warbot.'

As it now stands, the warbot situation makes a charade of our entire defense program. If prompt and effective measures will not be taken to correct it, I recommend throwing in with the Peace Front and rolling out the red carpet for the invaders. It will save a lot of effort and money, and the result will be the same.

(Signed) Colonel Wiktor Kobayashi, Assistant Director for Human Military Resources.

Captain Lucas stared aghast. Kobayashi scanned his monitor, then pressed *send*. Thereby committing professional suicide.

Lucas blew softly through pursed lips. Maybe a suicide was needed. Maybe somewhere up the line, someone would pay attention. Maybe Lefty Sarruf would lay *his* neck on the block; surely someone would pay attention then. *If it comes down to it,* Lucas decided—*if they can Kobayashi and promote me to the job, I'll send the same goddamn message up lines, verbatim. And fuck the pettifogging, obfuscating, political sons of bitches. It's the survival of the human species they're pissing around with.*

◇

Footnote:

[1] A warbot consists of a mobile, electro-mechanical weapons system termed a "battle servo," or simply "servo," containing and controlled by a human central nervous system sometimes termed the "kiddo" to emphasize its humanness. The kiddo is installed in a life-support system termed a bioelectronic interface unit (BEIU, or "bottle") which is neuro-electronically interfaced with the servo. The composite constitutes the warbot. The individual kiddo is *never* called a warbot.

Chapter Twenty
A Day in the Life

B Company was gasping and staggering when it reached the top of the slope. And sweating profusely, although the sun was still low. This was only their third week, but already their morning run had been extended to thirty long Lüneburger minutes. And this was the first time it had been routed up what the Terrans had dubbed "Drag Ass Hill."

Despite their cadre, who'd snapped relentlessly at their heels, their ranks had strung out pretty badly on the hill. But once at the top, their pace firmed. Through stinging, sweat-blurred eyes they could see the regimental area some five hundred yards ahead, and their company hutment with its orderly rows of small gray buildings.

Almost there, thought Esau Wesley. Grimly. He'd never liked taking orders, even as a boy from his father. And looking back, his father's orders had mostly made sense. But where was the sense of running uphill? Or running at all, if you weren't in a hurry? For toughness, they'd been told. For physical conditioning. He had no doubt he was tougher than anyone in their cadre.

"Hup, hup, hup two three four!" The voice was Sergeant Fossberg's, and seemingly effortless, though he was sweating as much as any. Esau didn't notice. He was too busy being angry. Then, some three hundred yards from the company area, Fossberg shouted. "You're on your own! The last ones to reach the mess hall and slap the wall get punishment!"

Esau snarled his anger—wanted to shout it. Lowering his head, he ran hard. Too hard. With a hundred yards to go, his legs began to fail. He fought it, eyes slitted with effort, his gait increasingly heavy-legged. 2nd Platoon had been second in the column, yet without being aware of it, Esau had fought nearly to the front of the now badly strung-out company. Anyone in his way, he'd elbowed aside. But he staggered the last twenty yards, barely keeping his feet. When he'd slapped the wall, he stumbled aside and fell gasping to the ground.

After eight or ten seconds he looked back. Most of the company was still coming. Some had slowed to a walk, alternating with a staggering trot to avoid being last.

Jael was not one of the very last. Perhaps fifteen or twenty were farther back, most of them from 3rd and 4th Platoons, who'd started out in the rear. Wobbling, she staggered through the fallen and touched the wall.

A few had given up the struggle entirely, and knelt or lay in the dirt along the way. It was their names the cadre spoke into their belt recorders. Esau could hear someone retching— more than one—their heaving dry; the company hadn't eaten breakfast yet.

Although they didn't know it, B Company's trainees had just been through a test. Less of themselves than of the training pace. Was it too hard? How much could they tolerate?

Fossberg didn't let them stay collapsed for long. "Company!" he bellowed. "On your feet! Fall in and stand at attention!"

Their platoon sergeants and ensigns herded them into ranks, where they stood, still breathing hard, facing the company commander and field sergeant. It was Captain Mulvaney who addressed them. "All right, B Company," he said, "stand at ease." As always his voice was effortless but easily heard. "You're making progress. You've got a long way to go, but you've started out nicely. Some not as well as others, but you'll catch up. We'll see to that. It's our job."

He paused, scanning the ranks in front of him. Esau noticed resentfully that the captain wasn't sweating. He hadn't run, just strolled out of his office to watch them arrive.

"Now," Mulvaney continued, "everyone on the ground." To a man, the trainees dropped to their bellies, knowing what followed but not how many. "Give me—twenty-five!" Up from twenty; that was new. The captain began to count, and the ranks of trainees pumped pushups to match. In strict form; they'd already learned the penalties for cheating. Besides, for most, even in Lüneburger's 1.25 gees, twenty-five pushups were readily doable. Farm work or other hard labor in New Jerusalem's gravity had given them abundant strength.

For a few, including Jael, twenty-five were only marginally or not quite doable. But they were young, and with company punishment and New Jerusalem's work ethic, they did their best. And they did at least twenty sets of pushups a day; they were gaining.

"...twenty-four, twenty-five. All right, on your feet!" Mulvaney said, and the trainees stood. "The mess hall opens for breakfast at 0730 hours. You will fall out for muster at 0815 in field uniform. Company dismissed!"

<><

The ranks dispersed, the trainees hurrying to their huts for towels and soap. Captain Martin Mulvaney Singh and Field Sergeant Kirpal Fossberg Singh watched them go. "How is recruit Jael Wesley doing?" Mulvaney asked.

"According to Sergeant Hawkins, sir, she asked if she could go to the dispensary. When he asked her if she was pregnant, she blushed bright red and told him no. And that she didn't intend to be. I'd say she's smart and responsible."

"Or hoping perhaps to be promiscuous?" It occurred to Mulvaney that some of his trainees, removed from their straitlaced culture, might cast off its inhibitions. Though Jael Wesley didn't seem like a rebel.

"Hawkins doesn't think so, sir. He doesn't think she'd find many takers if she was. Her husband is the dominant recruit in their squad. One of the two or three most dominant in their platoon."

"Apparently they've found a way to have intercourse."

"Apparently, sir." Sergeant to sergeant, Hawkins had told Fossberg they snuck off to the water heater room, but Fossberg didn't volunteer the information. Though if Mulvaney had asked, he'd have told him.

"Tell Sergeant Hawkins to be alert for any undesirable effects in their hut. The briefing we received on the Jerries was long on generalities but short on details."

"Yessir, Captain."

Fossberg headed for the noncommissioned cadre's latrine. The captain's questions had inspired one of his own. *How did a young girl like her, from a primitive fundamentalist planet like New Jerusalem, learn about birth control pills?* He decided to ask Recruit Spieler, as circumspectly as he could. These Jerries were turning out to be an interesting experience.

<><

Esau had gotten over having to shepherd his wife to the latrine, though he still hovered watchfully near her in the shower. And as usual, they used adjacent washbowls. This morning while they washed, he murmured to her: "You fell way behind this morning on the run." His tone was accusatory.

"Not till the last," she countered. "When we had to sprint."

"That's what I meant; in the sprint. You embarrassed me."

"I did the best I could." She said it quietly, without apology.

"Your best?" he muttered. "You were way back near the end of 4th Platoon."

She said nothing, and avoided looking at him.

"Let's see if you can do better on the chin-ups this morning."

She didn't answer that, either.

<><

At the head of the mess line were several chinning bars. Before going inside to eat, each trainee was required to do all the chins he could, monitored critically by two or more cadre. This time Esau did thirty-nine, and Jael struggled out eleven, with Corporal Fong watching.

"Good work, Recruit Wesley," the corporal said. "That's up from four the first day." The number identified which Wesley he was talking to.

"Thank you, Corporal," she said.

As the couple entered the mess hall, Esau jostled her. "Don't you have any sense of decency?" he hissed.

"What?"

"You know what I mean," he murmured. "Fong telling you 'good work.' For eleven puny chin-ups! I did thirty-nine, and he didn't say a thing to me. He wants you to commit adultery with him."

He'd turned his face to her when he said it, and without thinking or speaking, she slugged him in the left eye, almost knocking him down. The first cook had been standing with a spatula, serving scrambled eggs, and saw the exchange.

"YOU TWO!" he bellowed, pointing with the spatula. "WHAT'RE YOUR NAMES?"

Esau spoke for them both, glaring at Jael, who stood red-faced but without visible repentance.

"Report to Sergeant Henkel at the orderly room, both of you! Now! And tell him you're not getting back in here till I have his okay. In writing. Now out! OUT!"

They hurried out, aware that everyone in the mess hall had heard and seen their ejection. Esau was about to berate Jael some more, when Lance Corporal Fong called after them.

"Where do you think you're going?"

"The cook just sent us to the orderly room," Esau answered.

Fong pointed at the chinning bars. "You know the orders. Trainees do exit chin-ups when they leave the mess hall."

Esau made no move to comply. "We didn't eat."

Fong's reply was not particularly loud, but it was prompt, and strong with intention. "Recruit, that was backflash. Let's see those chin-ups. *Now!* And they'd better be good." Esau turned to the bars, pivoting violently enough, it seemed to Fong he almost screwed his boot into the ground. The Jerrie homesteader snapped off forty-two chin-ups this time; the corporal was impressed in spite of himself. Fong had trained with the 4th Terran Infantry, and some of these Jerries were already stronger than most of his buddies had been when they finished their training. And *their* cadre had been Masadans!

By the time Esau had finished and was free to leave, his wife was out of sight on her way to the orderly room. Her twelve hadn't taken a third as long as his forty-two, and when Esau had finished his chin-ups, Fong had ordered him to do fifty pushups for the backflash.

At the orderly room, Esau found Jael standing before Master Sergeant Gerritt Henkel, who clearly had been waiting for him. "What kept you, recruit?" Henkel asked.

Asked it like a cat, Esau thought, *waiting for the mouse to move.* He told the master sergeant how many chin-ups he'd done, and about the fifty pushups, not withholding what they'd been for.

The ex-marine looked at the couple appraisingly. "That's quite an eye you've got there, recruit."

Esau said nothing. He looked like he could chew rocks.

"What happened? I'm asking *you,* Recruit Esau Wesley."

"My wife was disrespectful, Sergeant. So I upbraided her, and she struck me."

"Disrespectful? Really! And upbraided! My my!" The mockery was thick. "Tell me what you said, as exactly as you can."

Esau did. The sergeant turned his eyes to Jael. "Is that the way you remember it, Recruit Jael Wesley?"

She nodded. "Yes, Sergeant," she said quietly, and Henkel turned again to Esau.

"Where exactly did this happen?"

"In the mess hall, Sergeant. In line, by the tray stack. Then the cook kicked us out without breakfast."

"Um-hmm. You're in 2nd Platoon, right?"

"Yessir."

"Recruit Esau Wesley, go sit in that chair." He pointed. "Recruit Jael Wesley, you sit in that one." He pointed at the opposite end of the row, then turned to the company clerk who'd been watching with half a grin. "Corporal, go tell Sergeant Hawkins what we've got here. This is his problem. For now, anyway."

The clerk left briskly, and was back in five minutes. Hawkins, on the other hand, didn't hurry. He finished his breakfast first. If Henkel had wanted him right away, he'd have said so.

Meanwhile, for the most part Esau avoided looking at his wife. But he was angry. His left eye was swollen half shut. It would be black, too, and everyone would be talking about it. He shot an occasional, resentful glance at Jael, but she never returned it, simply faced straight ahead, her expression stony. It struck him then how pretty she was in profile. And how strong her character, even if she was in the wrong. His anger softened.

When Hawkins arrived, he took them both outside, without berating them at all. "Esau Wesley," he said, "drop down and give me forty. On my count." As Esau got down, Hawkins continued. "Jael Wesley, drop down and give me twenty-five."

"What!?" Esau demanded, looking up. "Me forty and her twenty-five? That's unfair!"

"And that, Recruit Esau Wesley, is backflash," Hawkins said calmly. "Which will cost you. But not now. Later. And for her, twenty-five is as hard as forty is for you. Harder. Now, on my count…"

When they'd finished and stood before him, Hawkins told them their idiocy had cost them breakfast, because they had less than ten minutes before muster. "Report to me at the orderly room this evening, both of you, at 2030 hours. Among other things, I will tell you then what your punishment is. You, Esau Wesley, for repeated backflash. And you, Jael Wesley, for striking another recruit."

Then Hawkins turned and walked away. They needed more than punishment, he told himself, but he wasn't sure what.

◇

From muster, where the trainees gave their cadre twenty-five more pushups, B Company jogged three-quarters of a mile to a lecture shed, where they dropped down and did another twenty-five before entering. Then they filed inside and took their seats on wooden benches, benches hard enough, the trainees were less likely to fall asleep, despite their heavy exercise regimen.

The presenter was a major from Division, who stood before them in a clean, pressed field uniform. He also wore a crimson turban, instead of the field caps of the company cadre.

"What you're about to watch on the screen," he began, "is a presentation of regimental and small unit tactics. While you watch it, try to spot just what's going on. The better you understand it, the better fighting men you'll be, and the less likely you'll be killed. Afterward we'll go over it again.

"Incidentally, it is *not* a recording of actual fighting. So far as we know, there hasn't *been* any actual fighting with the invaders. They've attacked only undefended colonies. But the animated visuals you'll see" —he gestured at the large wall screen— "are as realistic as they can be made. Realistic enough to be mistaken for real."

The entire company cadre was there, including Captain Mulvaney and Master Sergeant Henkel. The cube was one of a set newly arrived from Terra, via pod, and none of the company staff had seen it before. The major had, the night previous. It had its own audio, but he had a list of questions to expect, and tips on how to deal with them.

The audience watched the whole forty-five-minute first run-through without a pause. Captain Mulvaney would have bet that none of them dozed. Then they got a fifteen-minute break that began and ended with pushups for the trainees, with time to rassle around or use a field latrine in between. Afterward the same cubeage was shown again, but this time with numerous built-in pauses where a voice-over discussed the tactics they were watching. When that run-through was finished, there was another break like the first—pushups, latrine, and more pushups.

Afterward the major took questions, almost all of them from the cadre. That went on till it was time to leave for lunch. Outside, the trainees gave their cadre a quick twenty-five, then double-timed briskly in a column of fours to the company area, where there was just time for another twenty-five and to wash up before their noon meal—broiled ground beef, mashed potatoes and gravy, crisp green beans, bread and butter with apple sauce, rich bread pudding, and coffee.

The first cook didn't say a word to Esau and Jael, and they said nothing to each other. They simply ate as if they'd hadn't eaten for a day. Actually it had been eighteen hours.

◇

After the noon meal and the break that followed, the company mustered, did pushups, then jogged to the regiment's physical training area. 2nd Platoon began its workout on "the log yard." Each five-man fire team had its own log, which massed roughly two hundred and fifty pounds, Terran. Working together, they lifted it to their collective right shoulders, then to arms' length overhead, then down onto their left shoulders, and back onto the ground. From there they repeated the sequence in reverse, and again, and again, until they had to fight it up. Esau was the leader of his five-man fire team, a team that unfortunately included not only Jael, but Isaiah Vernon, two of the three or four weakest in the platoon. Esau had put himself in the middle, between Jael and Isaiah, to make up for their lack of strength. Before they were done, he was gritting his teeth, partly from exhaustion, partly exasperation.

That done, they did twenty-five pushups. Then, driven by barking second-tier cadre, they ran hard to the chin-up bars, a bar per man, where they alternated between sets of ten chin-ups, fifteen pushups, and thirty side-straddle hops, each exercise serving as rest from the one before. After six rounds of those, they jogged to the obstacle course and ran it, climbing walls on knotted ropes, shinnying up rough-textured poles, vaulting or bellying over low fences, crawling through culverts, and ending with a hard, sixty-yard sprint.

They finished on what the Terran trainees had termed "the junkyard." The name had been passed on by the second-tier cadre. It had rows of stout iron pipes, the ends of which had been stuck in tins of concrete before it hardened. Each crude barbell massed roughly seventy pounds Terran, hefting about eighty-eight on Lüneburger's World. The exercises were led by a husky second-tier cadreman, a corporal, who'd finished twenty-six weeks of training only three weeks earlier, and was in superb condition. Mostly they did high repetition cleans and jerks. To rest between sets, they lay on the ground and did leg raises, pushups, and situps.

They'd been on the PT area every day since they'd been at Camp Mudhole (which so far had been more of a dust hole), but never had they been pushed as they were this day. It was on the junkyard that Isaiah Vernon collapsed in the sun. Two cadremen helped him into the shade until an ambulance arrived.

<>

From the PT area, the company ran to "the pond"—a long,

dozed-out depression covered with a foot of sand, then flooded by damming a creek. It was new to them. They ran toward it at a good lope, waiting for their cadre to halt them. No one did, and to their own astonishment, the trainees ran fully clothed into the water. Only when the last of them was in did Fossberg bellow "COMPANY HALT! REST!"

For the next twenty minutes they sported in the water. There was a lot of laughter, splashing, wrestling, some holding under, and a few brief fistfights that were broken up by cadre. When it was over, there were no pushups. Instead they marched back to the company area in their soggy boots and socks, the clothes drying on their bodies. They were even dismissed without further pushups.

◇

They changed clothes before supper, which was preceded and followed by the usual chin-ups. At 1845 hours they mustered again, and marched to a lecture shed where they viewed another cube. This one was an assemblage of pre-invasion scenes from worlds since captured by the invaders. Presumably the people shown, those who'd declined evacuation, were dead now. The trainees left more soberly than usual.

◇

Captain Martin Mulvaney Singh, Ensign Erik Berg Singh, and Sergeant First Class Arjan Hawkins Singh, didn't go with them. They were in Mulvaney's office, discussing the case of Recruit Isaiah Vernon, and whether they'd cranked up the physical demands on the trainees too rapidly. War House wanted them pushed hard, and Division had provided guidelines and schedules, but the company cadre retained considerable latitude. Berg pointed out that most of the trainees were meeting the demands very well. They were not only heavyworlders, and young; they'd worked at farming or other heavy labor. And Hawkins pointed out that the amount of running would soon stabilize. At midweek they'd be issued weapons and pack frames, and march to more distant field locations, carrying sandbags on the march.

They were interrupted by the Charge of Quarters knocking

on the door. "Recruit Isaiah Vernon is here, captain. They just brought him back from the infirmary."

"Good," Mulvaney answered. "Just a minute." He looked at the others. "I'll have him sent in, and question him. It may cast light on the subject." He looked toward the CQ. "Send him in, Corporal."

The CQ ushered a subdued Isaiah Vernon into the room, then closed the door behind him. The commanding officer looked the trainee over. "At ease, Vernon," Mulvaney said. "Let me see your medical release."

Vernon stepped over and handed a sheet of paper to him. Mulvaney scanned it. "Simple exhaustion," he read, and looked up at the young Jerrie. "Not heat exhaustion. Good." He paused, holding the youth with his eyes. "You've been having a harder time of it than the others. Tell me about that."

Vernon didn't hesitate. "The others—lived differently back home than I did," he said. "My father's a speaker of the books, and I was to be one, too. So when other boys were working in the field or the woods with their fathers, or in the tannery or sawmill or whatever, I studied scripture. Instead of lifting and carrying, grubbing stumps and ditching swales, I read and memorized. I did barn chores, and cut and brought in firewood, but that was about it. And I never cared much for games or foot races or wrestling. So I wasn't properly ready for training to be a soldier."

The frown had left Mulvaney's eyes. "I see," he said thoughtfully, then made a decision. The abler trainees shouldn't be held back for the least able. "Recruit Vernon, I'll see about getting you transferred to administrative duties in Regiment or Division. Meanwhile…"

Remarkably the young man interrupted. "Sir?"

Mulvaney frowned. "What is it, recruit?"

"Sir, I can do this training. I can! I quit this afternoon. I just up and quit! I could have kept on. I thought I couldn't, but really I could have. I know that now. I'm learning that when I feel like I haven't got anything left, I've still got a little. And I'm getting tougher and stronger every day."

Mulvaney glanced at Berg and Hawkins, then looked back at the Jerrie. "Very well, Recruit Vernon, I'll leave things as they stand, and give you a chance to show what you can do." He handed the paper back to the young man. "Give this to Corporal Rodin." He paused. "I presume they fed you supper at the infirmary?"

"Yessir."

"Good. The company is at Lecture Shed 4. Do you know where that is?"

"Yessir."

"Go there and report to Sergeant Fossberg. They'll just be starting to show the cube now. You'll see most of it." He clapped his hands. "Now RUN!"

Vernon turned and fled, barely taking time to close the door behind him. Mulvaney grinned at the others. "'Just up and quit!' Hmh! I hope he makes it through. I like his self-honesty. Also he answered my uncertainty about the pace of training. We'll proceed as we have been."

◇

At 2015 hours, B Company was back in the company area, where the trainees showered and lazed around a bit. Some went early to bed.

But not Esau and Jael. Sergeant Hawkins had reminded them before the company was dismissed; they had a date with him at 2030 hours. They walked to the orderly room together, not knowing what to expect. Somehow their mutual hostility had died. They didn't know why, and didn't wonder. It was simply gone.

They arrived several minutes early. The Charge of Quarters told them to sit down and wait, then returned to his novel. Hawkins walked in on the dot. "Recruits," he said, "we need privacy. Captain Mulvaney said to use his office." He opened the door to it, held it while they entered, then closed it behind them.

He pulled two folding chairs side by side, so he could see their occupants at the same time. "Sit," he ordered. They sat. He examined them quietly, ordering his thoughts. "I'm going to call you by your given names," he began, "to save time and confusion. I'll ask questions, and tell you who's to answer." He paused, then spoke more loudly, for emphasis. "The other one will remain silent until called on."

His calm eyes examined Jael. "Jael, why did you punch Esau?"

"Because he said I was playing up to Corporal Fong, and that Corporal Fong had said what he did because he…wanted to commit adultery with me."

Hawkins eyebrows rose, and he turned to Esau. "What did Fong say that made you think that?"

"He congratulated her on her chin-ups. She did eleven. But he didn't say a thing to me, and I did thirty-nine! And I didn't say she played up to him!"

"Hmm. Jael, why do you think Fong congratulated you on your chin-ups?"

"Because when we started doing chin-ups two weeks ago, I could barely do four."

"I see." He turned back to Esau. "None of that sounds very lascivious to me. Has Jael flirted with anyone since you've been here?"

"Not that I've seen."

"Not that you've seen. Do you think she might have when you weren't around?"

Esau didn't meet his eyes. "No sir," he said.

"All right. Jael, you claimed that Esau said you'd played up to Corporal Fong. Esau claims he didn't say that. Which is it?"

"He never said it in so many words, but that's what he meant. Otherwise why would he have said anything at all?"

"Um." The sergeant examined the situation. "What—Jael, I'm asking you this question. What were you and Esau talking about just before that?"

She gestured slightly toward her husband. "He was upbraiding me because I didn't run fast enough this morning."

"Um-hm. Esau, do you think she could have run faster?"

"Most of 3rd Platoon and half of 4th finished ahead of her.

And they started out behind!"

"You avoided the question, Esau. Now answer me. Do you think she could have run faster?"

"She should have."

Hawkins' tone sharpened. "Recruit Esau Wesley, I asked you a question twice, and twice you've avoided answering it. Now…"

Esau interrupted. "But she lied! She said I accused her of playing up to him!"

"That doesn't answer my question. It's flashback, Recruit Esau Wesley, and it's earned you a six-by pit to dig before you go to bed tonight. You've got to break that habit. Another flashback tonight and you'll go without breakfast again in the morning."

Esau seemed to shrink, but his expression was bitter and obstinate.

Hawkins' voice was mild again. "Now, I'll ask you once more. Your last chance. Do you think she could have run faster this morning? Or is it just a matter of she couldn't run as fast as most of the others?" Esau didn't answer at once. "The answer, Esau," Hawkins prompted, his voice soft but ominous. "The answer. Nothing else."

"No sir. It seems to me she ran as fast as she could."

"Thank you, Esau, for your honest answer. So why did you, ah, upbraid her for her late finish?"

Esau looked at his hands, folded on his lap. "I'm the leader of our fire team. I'm responsible for it. And her and Isaiah Vernon are both in it."

"And?"

He looked at Hawkins now, frustrated and upset. "They can't run as fast as the others, and they're weaker!"

"I know that. But do they do as well as they can?"

Esau deflated. "I guess."

"You have some doubts, do you?"

There was a brief lag, then Esau answered. "No. No doubts. She tries all right, hard as she can. And I suspect he does too."

"Are they improving?"

Grudgingly, "Yessir."

"Good. That's what we want them to do. What we want all of you to do. And you Jerries are doing well. You were strong to start with, and you try hard. Your corporals just completed their training here, and they tell us how impressed they are with you all. Jael in particular, because she's a woman. And most young women don't get the kind of physical exercise young men get. Even on New Jerusalem I suspect."

He paused, sizing up Esau, who seemed to be coming out of his black pit. "Tell me, Esau: have you said anything to Isaiah about his running? And his strength?"

"Once or twice."

"Did you ever upbraid him the way you did Jael?"

Esau relapsed a bit. "No sir."

"Why is that?"

"He's not my wife."

"Do you think your wife's running, and her strength, reflect on you personally?"

Esau met Hawkins gaze now, and his voice turned monotone. "It's not that. But I'm our fire-team leader, and because of them, my team is the weakest in the platoon. I'll never make squad leader, or recruit platoon leader."

"Ahh! So you want to be squad leader. At least. Why?"

The question took Esau by surprise. "Why, so things'll be done right, and folks'll give it all they've got. Captain Mulvaney said it himself: we'll have to give it all we've got to win the war."

Hawkins nodded slowly. "Those are good reasons. So let me tell you how that works. You start with the people assigned to you, whoever and whatever they are. Some will be strong, some not so strong, some smart, some not so smart. Some able, some not so able. A leader's job is to work with what he's got, and make them an effective team. To do it with fairness, and a minimum of turmoil and resentment. A fire team and squad live together, work together, defend each other. They're closer and more loyal to each other than brothers.

"We senior cadre will base our final decisions on leadership based on how well you lead. On your ability to handle the personnel you have." He paused meaningfully. "Including your fairness.

"You, Esau, are physically strong. And fast and smart. But those aren't enough by themselves. Just now, Ensign Berg and I have misgivings about your suitability for leadership. You've shown excellent potential, but you have two major weaknesses. One, you are sometimes surly, and take your frustrations out on others. In this case your wife, which is seriously unfair.

"The other is your backflashing. You backflash more than anyone else in the platoon. When given orders, carry them out! Don't answer back, or argue or discuss—except when invited to. You can't be given authority to order others, when you take orders so poorly yourself."

Hawkins got to his feet. "Now. About your punishments— Recruit Jael, for punching Esau in the eye, you will dig a pit tonight, six feet long, six wide and six deep. After lights out. Recruit Esau, you will also dig one, for backflash. The CQ will supervise you. Report to him in the orderly room at 2200 hours.

"You are now dismissed."

◇

Jael and Esau didn't go directly to their hut. Instead they strolled silently along the road that framed the battalion area. Esau's hand found hers, and she accepted it. After a bit he spoke. "At school once, Speaker Farnham chided me for bullying other kids. I denied it, didn't think I did it, till he gave me instances." He stopped, turned her to him, and held her two hands gently. "And this morning I was bullying you. The onliest one here that means much to me. I'm truly sorry, Jael, and I hope you'll forgive me." His voice broke then, taking him by surprise, and he took her in his arms, his tears falling on her hair and upturned face.

"Oh Esau, I do forgive you, I truly do. And I hope you'll forgive me for striking you. That was bullying, too. I'm not sure I'd have done it, if I hadn't known inside that you wouldn't hit me back. So that makes me a bully."

They clung to each other in the unlighted street until Esau

could speak again. "Sweetheart," he husked, "I'm not sure but what I might slip up and talk like that again sometime. I'll surely try not to, but man is a weak vessel, and I might could slip up. So if ever I bully you again, just punch me in the eye. To remind me." His composure slipped again, and again his tears fell on her.

"Honey," she answered without smiling, "I'll pray not to. Because I do love you so."

They embraced again, this time their lips joining.

◇

When the couple had left the orderly room, Sergeant Hawkins went to the hut and told Recruit Isaiah Vernon to come with him, that he had questions he wanted to ask. Then he took him to the dayroom, looking for privacy. At Hawkins' suggestion, they both drew a cup of coffee from the small urn there, before sitting down on opposite sides of a cribbage table. Isaiah had never been in the dayroom before. A sort of recreation room, it was part of a company's normal setup, but the recruits' training schedule left them almost no time to use it. Most had literally forgotten it was there.

"Vernon," Hawkins began, "you said you were being educated as a Speaker of the Books. I suppose by now you realize that we Sikhs don't know much about the Church of the Testaments. As children we're taught the basics of all the major religions, but we don't get down much into the, um, subdivisions. So I may ask you questions from time to time, to give me a better sense of your beliefs." He paused. "Does it bother you that we refer to you as Jerries?"

"No sir, Sergeant. Not me at least, and I've never heard anyone complain of it. It seems like a natural thing to do." He hesitated. "We are not a people greatly given to complaint. And in *The Book of Contemplations,* Elder Hofer taught that we should tolerate and respect…unbelievers."

Hawkins nodded solemnly. Their briefing had mentioned that a North American named Albert Hofer had founded the Jerrie church. "Ah," he said, "we have tolerance in common at least. "Guru Nanak founded the Sikh religion on the philosophy of religious tolerance." He raised an eyebrow. "How do you get along with other religions on New Jerusalem?"

Hawkins knew the answer, but he wanted to learn how frank this youth would be with him. The question didn't faze Isaiah. "Sir, there are no other religions on New Jerusalem. Other religions have their own worlds, or at least a place on Terra, and we respect that. But we keep our planet for ourselves. It's in our charter with the Commonwealth."

He paused. "From *The Book of Origins,* we know that long ago on Terra, different religions fought each other, even massacred each other. Do they still?"

Hawkins smiled. "There's still some intolerance, but Terra got over most of it during the Troubles, eight hundred years ago. There hasn't been any serious violence since then. An occasional fist fight maybe. Intolerance tended to grow out of fear, and when a sect had the freedom to leave Terra and colonize a planet of their own, that fear became less. And the Commonwealth tries hard not to be overbearing toward the colonies."

He sipped the somewhat bitter Lüneburgian "coffee" he'd learned to like. "I want to talk about the platoon now. You grew up differently than the other men. Do they ever give you a bad time about that?"

"Not really, Sergeant. Esau's commented a few times, as the fire team leader, that I need to be stronger and tougher. But he's never been mean about it. When someone's as strong as Esau, and runs as fast, they might not understand why others can't."

"Ah. That brings up another question: How do you feel about Jael Wesley showering with the men?"

Isaiah's face showed no embarrassment. "I've never heard anyone say anything about it. Though they might, a few of them, if it wasn't for Esau. I'm pretty sure they were troubled by it, early on. But what Captain Mulvaney said made sense. As boys we used to sport together in the river, naked as newborns, and hardly anyone fretted about that. We boys didn't." He spoke more slowly now, as if feeling his way into the subject. "But that *is* different from swimming naked with girls or women, because sight of their flesh can make you think about having carnal knowledge of them. Maybe *want* to have carnal knowledge of them. The thing is, here there's no choice. She's a soldier and part of the company, so she should have the same rights. Like I said, I've never heard any of the others talk about it, but I suspect that's pretty much how they look at it."

Hawkins sipped thoughtfully, then nodded. "Thank you, Vernon. You've helped me understand you people better." He got to his feet. "We seem to be done now. You can return to your hut. I may have more questions some other time."

Isaiah got up too. "Yes, Sergeant." He paused. "Sergeant, may I ask you a question?"

"Ask away."

"Do you Sikhs believe in Jesus?"

"Believe in Jesus? Yes we do."

The trainee looked at his sergeant for a long second or two, his eye contact mild. "Thank you, Sergeant," he said, then turned and left.

Hawkins watched the door close, and smiled. *You almost asked me whether we believe he's the Son of God, then thought better of it.* The young Jerrie could have followed his answer—he was abundantly intelligent. But that very question, or rather Gopal Singh's reply to it, had split Sikhism even before the Troubles, the better part of a millennium earlier. Split it into the Orthodox and the Gopal Singh Dispensation. For Gopal Singh's answer had posited something akin to the Hindu *avtarvad,* which Guru Nanak himself had explicitly rejected in the *Mul Mantra.* Gopal Singh had tried to reconcile his belief with Orthodox leaders, but the split remained.

◇

Shortly before lights out, it began to rain. Not a storm rain, but a steady soaker muttering on roof and walls, now and then intensifying briefly. At 2200 hours, Esau and Jael reported to the orderly room, wearing ponchos. The CQ issued each of them a shovel, a short crude ladder, and a six-foot measuring stick. And digging sites some fifteen yards apart. "No talking," he warned. "Just dig. I'll be checking on you out the window." Then he returned to the orderly room.

They dug as rapidly as they could sustain, if only to get more sleep time. Meanwhile the rain continued, and the CQ wasn't eager to come out in it. So when Esau's measuring rod indicated he was done, he tossed out his shovel, climbed wetly from the pit, and went over to Jael's. It wasn't quite as deep yet as she was tall. Without a word he jumped in. As in his, the water was about a foot deep.

"What are you doing?" she asked.

He kissed her. She tasted like rain. "Come to help out," he said.

"The CQ—he'll see. You'll get in trouble."

"To heck with that. We're not only husband and wife, we're comrades in war. Besides, we're eight or ten rods from the orderly room, and it's darker than the inside of a black bull." Then he turned and began to dig. When they'd finished, the CQ still hadn't reappeared, so Esau climbed out and went to the orderly room to get him. The man lay his book aside. "That was quick," he said. "You sure you're done?"

"I'm sure *I* am," Esau answered. "I can't speak for anyone else."

The CQ donned his poncho and they went out to Esau's pit. Nearby, Jael's continued to emit shovelfuls of dirt and slop. Taking Esau's measuring stick, the Terran measured height, width, and depth. "Looks good," he said. "You're done." Then bypassing the ladder, the corporal squatted, reached down a hand, and hauled him out. Esau was impressed. *Stronger than I thought,* he told himself.

They headed for Jael's pit. "Quit throwing a minute," the CQ called. "It may be deep enough." He measured. "Good job both of you. Fill them and tramp them, and you're done. Tramp them every foot or so the whole way. I'll know if you don't, and you don't want to do the whole thing over again tomorrow night."

She came up on her ladder, to see the corporal striding off toward the orderly room. Filling the pits was far easier than digging them had been, and they worked hard and fast. When both were full and well tramped, the rain-sodden couple went to the orderly room together.

"All done," Esau announced.

The corporal donned his poncho again, went out with them to inspect the sites, then dismissed them to their hut.

On their way, Esau spoke. "You know," he said innocently, "we've already lost half our sleep time. We might as well lose another half hour, and go shower off."

She pulled his face down to hers and kissed him thoroughly. "That's a wonderful idea," she said.

In their hut, they hung their wet things on the drying rack— the clothes from the pond were already dry—put their cold wet ponchos on their bare bodies, and ran to the latrine. After a shower, a hot one, they turned the water off and made joyous love on the duck boards before scurrying back to the hut for three hours of sleep.

Chapter Twenty-One
Contract

Dr. Deborah Coonoor arrived at Bangui International Aerospaceport with zero fanfare, her visit and its possible importance publically unknown. Her welcoming committee consisted of one very tall person, Dr. Issa Libengi, who stood in the air-conditioned reception area holding a sign with her name on it. His grin was an expanse of white in a truly black face.

Weaving her way through the crowd, Dr. Coonoor herself was dark enough not to be conspicuous: a glowing mahogany. Her raven-black hair, however, was simply wavy. Her father was from Mysore State, in the south of India; her caramel-colored mother was "black English": Celto-Saxon/Caribbean/Brazilian.

When she reached Dr. Libengi, she extended a slender hand, which he carefully wrapped in his much larger. "Ms. Coonoor I presume," he rumbled. "I hope your flight was agreeable."

She laughed. "It was. Although I confess to being mystified by lunch. I'm unfamiliar with African cuisines."

He took her bag; emergency items in case of delay. She expected to be on her way back to Kunming before evening. Away from the gate area, they followed the flow toward the rotunda. "I was impressed by the flight," she said. "I'd never seen Central Africa before. Even from 5,000 feet, your rainforest looks impressive. I grew up in Brazil you know."

"Seen from within the forest, it is even more remarkable. An invertebrate zoologist like yourself would find your interest quite stimulated. As mine was by your call; more by what you didn't say than by what you did."

Her eyes met his, and she laughed. "Perhaps we can discuss it in your car. Depending on your driver."

"You can trust his prudence absolutely. I drive myself."

Actually she'd assumed that. Universities which originated as agricultural colleges were seldom pretentious, even after centuries of distinction. From the Rotunda, they took a trackway to the four-story parking tower, then a lift tube to the third level, and walked to the coupé floater he'd driven, with the Bangui University logo on its door. Libengi held her door for her, a provincialism she found attractive. Then he stepped around to the other side, got in, and let the cybervalet move them to the floater exit, from which Libengi gently launched the vehicle into the midday air.

"So," he said, "what possible interest can Kunming have in a geneticist specializing in Central African species of Apoidea?"

She detected neither diffidence nor false modesty in the question. He simply wanted to know. "Because that is precisely what we need," she said, "a geneticist specializing in Central African species—a variety, actually—of Apoidea." She laughed without humor. "Particularly one who knows more about the genome of *Apis mellifera scutella* than anyone else. Which narrows it down to you."

<>

Four hours later, Issa Libengi returned his guest to the aerospaceport. By then he knew Kunming's proposal in detail. The confidentiality was not from any fear that the enemy might have spies on Terra. Rather, it was to avoid stirring up the Peace Front, which would be upset by it.

Like a swarm of Apis mellifera_var._scuttella_*stirred with a stick,* Libengi told himself, savoring the metaphor. The project was abundantly challenging, which was why he was so pleased with it. And the potential professional and public recognition were pleasant to contemplate. Even allowing for the multi-project nature of the program, its success could eventually mean prestige, salary increases, grants... And meanwhile, ah the challenges! Dr. Coonoor was well aware of them; her professional bona fides were substantial. "Take it as far as you can," she'd answered. "Interaction among projects should help."

What she hadn't said, and in fact didn't know, was that this was a contingency backup project. The equally vital other half of the program was quite uncertain.

Chapter Twenty-Two
Close Encounter

The debris zone outside Henry Morgan's bolt hole changed from one trip to the next, and the change had become conspicuous. Shoots had sprouted from the base of many broken tree stubs, and were growing vigorously. Some were already more than ten feet tall: the place was beginning to heal. *Wait till the real rains arrive,* Morgan thought. *I'll need a machete.*

Actually he was carrying one on this trip, but not for clearing trail.

He'd been coming topside every week, spending a day hiking out and another back, and from one to three days spying. Among other things, he'd seen and reported several—foals? Cubs? Small playful Wyzhñyñy juveniles, accompanying and occasionally nursing on adults at work in the clearing.

The previous time up, it had occurred to him that the stream flowing through the clearing was much too small to provide water for the invaders on the site. So he'd hiked to the bluff northwest of the clearing, and out onto a point he knew. From there his binoculars verified his suspicion: the invaders had installed what had to be a desalinization plant above the beach. Not large, but presumably adequate, no doubt powered by a geogravitic power converter.

May it be visited by a tsunami, he thought.

But it seemed to him his observations were trivial, except for the hornets. From that had grown two specific hopes: that it would (1) contribute a weapon, and (2) result in rescue. Robert and Connie would surely not be charged with piracy, while he himself... It seemed to him a pardon might be in order.

Terra had been in no hurry to reply to his offer. Then, at his last contact, had come the hoped for word: "Captain Morgan, we agree on the potential of your proposal. Please capture a number of the hornets of which you spoke. Capture some from several separate nests, and if there is more than one species, some of each. Store them alive in stasis, if any of your stasis equipment has survived. Otherwise frozen, or failing that, dried thoroughly at low heat."

Not for breeding then, he thought. With disappointment but also relief. He had no idea how to recognize breeding pairs, if there were such things.

There'd been more to the instructions than that, and questions as well, but the best part they'd saved till last. "Last week we sent a long-range courier to pick you up, along with your brother and his attendant. And of course the hornets. We'll be in touch with the craft from time to time. At some point it will get in touch with you, via your savant, to discuss how and where to meet you. They cannot arrive for forty-nine standard weeks. We wish, perhaps more than you, that it could be sooner."

Morgan seriously doubted the "more than you" part.

That had been three days past. On the first of them he'd returned to the hangar, where various useful material remained, along with tools. Using fiberglass mesh and aluminum, he built a hornet trap he thought would work. The next day he made three of them, modified to serve as cages for transportation, as well.

His limited experience with hornets had been in or near glades -- small forest openings created when a large tree had fallen. A base keeper, Pat Kajimoto, had once said they came out of holes in the ground. With the increased light, the undergrowth thickened, and apparently the hornets preferred to dig their nests in the thickets. In a few months the debris zone might serve, but so far he hadn't seen any hornets there. Probably the shock of heavy blaster pulses had destroyed any pre-existing nests.

So he headed for the clearing. Its south side was near the old resort, and hadn't been extended much. The plateau shelved off there, forming forested slump benches before dropping to sea level. Wisely the invaders hadn't built there. The forest fringe and the slump benches were thick with undergrowth.

Hopefully he wouldn't need to go that far. If he kept his eyes open, it seemed to him he'd encounter hornets along the way, and discover where they emerged from the ground. Then he'd hang around till they holed up for the night, swamp any vegetation out of the way with his machete, set the trap over the entrance/exit, and see how things looked in the morning. And if that strategy failed, there was no hurry. He had most of a year to develop a good capture system.

He hoped, though, that it wouldn't involve getting stung a lot. Tagus hornets packed a wallop.

◇

It was afternoon before he even saw one. Then it was gone, to where, Morgan didn't know. He began to circle, spiraling outward, hoping to find the nest, checking a few thickets as he went. But found no more hornets.

Dusk was just beginning when he arrived at the foot of the knob. After hanging his net hammock between two slender, light-starved trees, he once more took his scope from beneath its log and lugged it up the knob. There was still enough light to scan the clearing by. The invader's crop of whatever it was looked about three-feet high, and was fenced. He recognized the fence generators.

The breeze was pleasant on the knob's exposed top. He took time to sit down and eat his supper—an air-tight container of fruit-sweetened tapioca in rich cream, accompanied by hardtack with peanut butter. Connie had shuddered at the combination, but Morgan liked it, and it was quick, simple, and nourishing.

As he ate, he wondered if panthers had discovered the fence. The "panthers" of Tagus were black, lightly dappled with tan-yellow. They were also smart and wary, and had learned quickly that humans, with their beam guns, should be avoided. It was as if they shared knowledge with one another over a distance. But there was always the risk that some hungry yearling, driven from its mother's range, might make bold. It occurred to Morgan that in none of his spy missions had he heard a panther's moaning, far-carrying cry, and he wondered if the aliens hunted them. There was a lot of jungle. They could easily have hunters out patrolling without his knowing it. He hoped not.

He stayed on the knob till the stars were out, then moved the scope into the open and aimed it at the sky. In its narrow field of view, the stars stared coldly, unseeingly back at him.

Coldly, he thought. *A strange word to apply to stars. Coldly in the sense of no emotions.* He wondered what emotions the invaders felt, looking at the sky, and what star or stars they'd come from. It didn't occur to him they might have come from another galaxy.

He covered the tube of his scope, shouldered it, and picked his way down the knob. Beneath the forest's dense roof, the darkness was utter, impenetrable. Shielded by jungle and the knob, he used his belt torch to find his hammock. Once in it, he activated the repellent on his belt. Its power output was low enough, it seemed highly unlikely to be noticed.

In scant minutes he slept.

◇

He awoke to the dawn chorus of jungle birds and lemur-like "monkeys." Breakfast was like supper, except for an apple preserved "like fresh." After eating, he climbed the knob again for a brief scan of the clearing. With binoculars; they were enough for the purpose. There was little activity; too early, he supposed. Climbing back down, he shouldered his pack frame with its load of collapsible hornet traps, and set off, circling southwestward through the forest to approach the clearing's south edge.

When he was near enough to detect it, he slowed. The south edge had not been cut back at all, and was only about a quarter mile from the invaders' main building. This was by far his nearest approach. Carefully he slipped forward to the thick undergrowth of the fringe, where he lay down and slowly crawled, making no sudden move.

He'd almost reached the edge when he made out movement ahead: two aliens together, less than a hundred yards out in the clearing. Seen through the screening foliage, they seemed almost stationary. Briefly he heard a small tapping sound, then the two moved a short distance. He backed away till he couldn't see them at all, then angled toward a large tree at the very verge. Reaching it, he rose slowly upright, keeping the trunk between himself and the invaders.

Carefully he peered around it till he could see them again.

They had something on a tripod. One of them was peering through it toward the forest—right toward him!—and he realized what they must be doing: laying out some engineering project.

He didn't notice their sidearms till one of the invaders, the one at the instrument, drew his, raising its muzzle toward him. Withdrawing his head, Morgan turned and fled into the jungle. There was no shot. How good a look had they gotten? Hardly enough to know what they'd seen, seventy or eighty yards away.

He slowed to a strong striding walk, not routing himself by the knob, glad his spying trips had gotten him into good physical shape. He'd stay away from the clearing for a while—or for good; find hornets closer to home. It had been foolish to approach so near the clearing. Perhaps he'd stay underground for a while; a few weeks.

◇

It was late afternoon when he reached the debris zone and headed for his bolt hole. When he stepped into its narrow irregular opening, the last thing he did was turn and look back. *To see a floater hovering above the edge of green forest! They'd followed him!* His heart nearly stopped, and slowly he backed into the tunnel, out of the light. There he activated the alarm, then the booby trap, then closed the door and ran down the long tunnel, activating the other booby traps as he came to them. They wouldn't bring the tunnel down, but they'd slow intruders and reduce their numbers.

The survey instrument, he realized now, had been telescopic, and the instrument man had realized what he'd seen. He'd radioed his headquarters, and a scout, no doubt on standby, had been sent up. Knowing his approximate location, it had gotten an infrared fix on him through the forest roof. They could have sent a gunship then, blasted the jungle where he was and almost surely killed him. But they'd wanted to know where he'd go. Now they knew.

Stupid! he thought as he ran. *You stupid, self-destructive sonofabitch!*

In little more than a minute he reached the steel door to the living area, unlocked and spun the wheel, then entered and locked it behind him. For a moment he leaned on it. Connie had heard him, and stepped into the entryway. She started to speak, perhaps to ask him how it had gone, then saw his face and stopped, eyes widening, one hand moving to her mouth.

"What?" she whispered.

He didn't answer at once, just shook his head. Setting his harness and pack aside, he got his pistol from a drawer and put it in his waistband. Connie followed, watching, seeming not to breathe.

"I was seen at the forest edge," he said quietly, "and slipped back into the jungle. I didn't think they knew what they'd seen." He put a hand on her arm. "When I got to the entrance, I turned and looked back. And saw it—a military floater hovering above the jungle's edge. They'd followed me." He stepped past her, speaking more softly now. "They'll have called for a troop carrier."

"What will we do?"

"Let them know on Terra."

She stared up at him; she was barely five feet tall.

"We don't have much time," he said. "Get Robert ready."

She nodded soberly, and followed him into what served now as "the family room." Robert was at the computer, browsing star charts, unaware that anyone had entered. "Robert," she said, "it's time for you to go to work."

Her voice was wooden, but Robert's response was deeply conditioned. Already in trance, he got up, walked to the divan and lay down, folding his hands on his chest while Connie moved a chair beside him and sat. After the connections were made, Morgan began to dictate.

He'd just finished when the alarm buzzed. His final words to Terra were "they're here." Then he stepped to the alarm and turned it off. The first booby trap was small and distant; he neither heard nor felt the explosion. "I'm done now, Connie," he said. "Waken him."

He waited while she and Robert went through the brief withdrawal ritual. Robert sat up, saw his older brother, and grinned. "Hi, Henry," he chirped. "Did you bring me any flowers?"

"No, no I didn't. But I brought you a new story." A scenario was forming in his mind even as he spoke, rooted in an ancient movie, one that had touched him deeply. Initially, in pre-technological times, it had been shot on film, and since then copied and recopied in other media.

"Sit on your computer chair," he said, "and turn off the computer." He watched Robert comply. "Now look at the screen. Keep your eyes on it, and imagine you're seeing what I tell you. Seeing it like a movie."

His order sent his brother into a near-hypnotic reverie. "Do you remember where we lived in Colorado? After father died?"

Robert nodded. "Yes," he said.

"Remember the garden behind the house. With all the flowers, and the lilac bushes. Do you see it?"

He'd made it all up years before, part of an imaginary past to help bury the ugly reality. Robert's head bobbed eagerly. "I see it."

Morgan heard or felt a booby trap explode, a small, dull, distant thump. Whether the second, or the last, or one in between, he wasn't sure.

"All right. Now see mother there. Do you see her?"

"Uh huh."

"Tell me what she's wearing."

The savant didn't hesitate. As Morgan drew his pistol from his belt, Robert answered. "She's wearing her white dress with the blue and yellow flowers." He chuckled. "And she's barefoot. She used to say it let her feet be friends with the grass."

Connie choked back a sob.

Morgan raised the pistol and put the muzzle almost against Robert's head. It wavered, and he gripped it with both hands to steady it. "All right," he continued, "now you and Connie and I are going there to see her. We'll be there in just a second."

He pulled the trigger, the explosion loud in the small room. Connie screamed and lowered her head, covering her eyes as if knowing. He'd saved Robert once before by killing their father. Now he'd saved him again. Small tight sobs, like little chuckles, burned his throat, and his free hand wiped away tears. A much more powerful explosion roared from the other side of the steel door, knocking things from shelves. Morgan held the muzzle close to Connie's head and pulled the trigger again.

Tears blinded him. Then he heard alien voices; the safety door had been dislodged. A blaster pulse struck the family room door, sending a spray of Tuffboard fragments across the room. Morgan put the muzzle in his mouth and pulled the trigger a final time.

Chapter Twenty-Three
Interrogation

Qonits' ranking bodyguard rapped sharply on the door, but not with the butt of his blaster, as he had at first.

Even that had been an improvement. In an early session, a half-hour charade with the chief scholar, David and Yukiko had managed to communicate that they didn't want guards, or even Qonits himself, walking in on them without permission. That it showed lack of respect, and they would not cooperate without respect.

Not that privacy was the point. Video cameras monitored them endlessly. The point they hoped to make was that they had rights. Of course if their captors disagreed, pain was always available to inspire cooperation. Neither David nor Yukiko imagined they could withstand serious torture. But the Wyzhñyñy didn't know that, and might prefer not to risk their deaths, or possibly inspire unbreakable resistance.

When Qonits had left that time, they hadn't known whether he'd understood. But beginning the next day, the guard who'd brought their meals had knocked. And so had Qonits' bodyguard, all without apparent resentment.

"Who is it?" David called.

"It is Qonits."

As far as it went, Qonits' Terran was quite understandable. On the other hand, the Wyzhñyñyç the humans had learned was negligible. For awhile the exchanges had been fairly even, but apparently the Wyzhñyñy had changed their minds and decided not to teach them. At any rate the humans had no artificial intelligence to run endless cross-references, refining and expanding on meanings and nuances.

As shipsmind acquired a working vocabulary, sessions had more and more been built around lists—requests for the meanings of words recorded during earlier interrogations and the prisoners' personal conversations. Words presumably chosen by shipsmind. Qonits' efforts to speak became less halting and uncertain. His main difficulty was understanding what was said to him.

"Come in!" Yukiko called back. She and David made a point of neither being the prime spokesperson. Let the Wyzhñyñy consider them equal to each other in rank.

As always, Qonits' entrance showed what the two Terrans read as dignity without arrogance. They still didn't know whether that dignity and apparent lack of arrogance were idiosyncracies of Qonits, or shared by other ranking Wyzhñyñy. But they'd come to *like* the chief scholar.

"Good morning," Qonits said carefully. "I wish you feel well now."

"We feel very well, thank you," David said, "and we wish the same to you."

The Terrans sat on a couch. Yukiko had sketched one for Qonits, and he'd had it made. His own people had such things, and Qonits could understand that "humans" might have greater need for them. It must, he'd told himself, be tiresome standing on just two legs. He'd wondered at first why they didn't fall over.

"You are welcome," Qonits replied, then paused. "I have—more questions."

David raised an eyebrow at Yukiko; the knowledge master's delivery suggested this might be a different sort of session.

"We are interested," Yukiko answered.

They almost always say that, Qonits thought, *and I never know why. What might they be learning from us?* He wondered how long it would be before he began to actually understand these aliens. Until he did, knowing their words and sentences would be inadequate to understanding their meanings or intentions. What went on in the privacy of those round alien skulls?

"We wonder what is the kind of your empire," he said.

"Ah," said David, and spread his hands. "It is—an empire."

Qonits looked at him warily. "Please tell me more about it."

Yukiko spoke next. "It is many worlds united to permit, and provide for, the separate and mutual satisfaction of each and all worlds."

The focus of Qonits' eyes slanted off into left field, a response the Terrans had learned to recognize: he'd gotten no real notion of what her statement meant. His fingers tapped something into the small keypad hanging from his neck. Presumably he was listening to what shipsmind made of it.

After a few moments, his gaze returned to the two Terrans. "Thank you," he said. *This session,* he told himself, *promises to require much work by shipsmind before I understand their answers. I wish I understood now. My subsequent questions could be more to the point.*

"And what is this empire's government?" he asked.

It was David and Yukiko who felt uncertain now. They suspected the monitoring they were subjected to was more than visual, and they preferred to keep the Wyzhñyñy guessing, uncertain. It was David who answered. "It is a commercial union, to facilitate the members buying from and selling to each other."

As he'd spoken, he began to see where this could take him, and felt a touch of excitement. Meanwhile something was obviously going on with Qonits. Disbelief? Concept overwhelm? David tried another tack. "We call it a commonwealth." He tapped his head as he went on. "Think of it as many self-governing worlds united for their separate individual good. And also for their mutual good—their joint good, their together good."

Qonits' eyes had lost their unfocused look. He was intent now. "Then there will be no effective defense," he said. Even in the Wyzhñyñy's non-human voice, David could hear the mental wheels turning. And sense the distrust.

"That is not correct," David said. "There will be defense." *God there'd better be!* "Defense is one of the primary functions of commonwealth government. Defense, the enforcement of valid contracts, and overall record keeping."

Qonits' nictitating membranes slid over his eyes in a reflex the Terrans had yet to understand. "What is the kind of defense?" the Wyzhñyñy asked. "What kind of things is done by that defense?"

David wasn't thinking his way through the situation now. He was running on creative intuition, winging it. "My wife and I are not informed on defense. We are research scientists. We learn about the seas on new worlds." The nictitating membranes were back again. *This will give his shipsmind something to chew on,* David thought. *He'll be back with a monster word list tomorrow.* "We know the basic principle though," he continued. "Design the defense, or select the defense, which most damages and frustrates the enemy. Keeps them off balance."

Qonits' long tongue licked air. David and Yukiko hadn't figured that one out yet, either. It took a long moment before the chief scholar responded, speaking very slowly, very deliberately. "Then why have we not met such defense? We have now eleven of your planets. Still no defense. Why?"

There was no sense of challenge in the question. *He simply wants to know,* Yukiko thought. "We are a very numerous people," she answered. "In recent centuries—hundreds of years—we have colonized many new worlds. We are a very diverse species, with many different peoples having different wants. They go out beyond the older colonies, find new worlds and colonize them."

The answer stopped Qonits dead in the water. It seemed to her he was about to go catatonic, whether because he couldn't grasp what she'd said, or because he could. She wished she knew what he was hearing on the earphone he wore. "And," she went on, "apparently the newer, farther colonies are being sacrificed." She turned to David. "Wouldn't you say so, dear?"

He nodded. "It seems obvious," he answered.

"Sacrificed," she continued, "while our fleets and armies are being concentrated or distributed, I have no idea which. Preparing to defend our core worlds, with their vast populations."

Qonits mind was signalling overload. He bobbed a nod. "Thank you for valuable information. I now leave you, return at later time." Then he said something to his bodyguards, and they left together.

<>

Quanshûk had witnessed the brief interrogation via monitor, and had understood the key questions; he'd helped define them. What had mystified him were the answers, even though, like Qonits, he was plugged into the ship's growing translation program. Too much of what the prisoners said had made no sense to him, while some had been disturbing. Qonits' physical responses he'd understood well enough.

His own tongue licked air. *We must sort this out,* he told himself. *As quickly as possible.*

◇

Yukiko put her arms around Annika and rocked her, feeling her snuggle in response. *Poor kid,* she thought, then retracted it, as if the savant might read it and be troubled by it. *For you,* she amended, *a stupor is probably best. You don't suffer, you don't worry. It's the next best thing to sleeping through it.*

Then she decided she wasn't sure about that either. Did Annika, in her mind, revisit the events in the *Cousteau?*—the undoubtedly violent deaths of Ju-Li and Dennis? She leaned back to better comprehend the child. *Probably not,* she decided. *When the Wyzhñyñy gave her to us, she was deeply in coma. But since then...* Yukiko shook her head. *Within that stupor, there's something like serenity.* "Annika," she breathed, "I wish you could tell me what goes on with you."

David's eyes had been closed, but he hadn't been sleeping. Now they opened. "What?" he whispered.

She whispered back. "I was talking to Annika. I told her I'd like to know what she thinks about."

"Nothing very exciting I'll bet," he said, and closed his eyes again.

◇

Chang Lung-Chi sat beside the prime minister, watching Ramesh on the wallscreen. Foster Peixoto had viewed either the complete or selected cubeage of almost every language session. This had been more like interrogation. He wasn't surprised at how much communication had taken place. Actually he assumed it had gone better than it had. He didn't realize how much Qonits had understood only vaguely or not at all.

~ 163 ~

After they'd listened to the complete session a second time, Chang frowned thoughtfully. "Remarkable. Those two are playing a game with the aliens. The question is what good it will do."

"I have the same impression. Perhaps they have enough sense of the alien psychology to accomplish something. Hopefully we will get a better sense of it as it continues. Weintraub and Li are studying the sessions carefully. When they have gained some insights, they will share them with us."

Chang was less optimistic. *When? Or if? One can but hope,* he told himself. *At any rate we must monitor this closely.* "And the child," he said, "the savant. Has she shown any sign of shutting down, and depriving us of this remarkable contact?"

"None. And Bekr is optimistic now. Gavaldon has commented to her husband on how much better the child seems. Yet she continues to send. Bekr suspects the condition may be effectively permanent."

"Good! Good! It may be that this will prove truly important." *We were optimistic about Morgan the pirate,* Chang reminded himself, *and now he is lost to us. May he rest in the Tao. He served his species well in his weeks of spying.*

Chapter Twenty-Four
Hard Facts, Hard Decisions

Captain Martin Mulvaney Singh had spent most of the day at Division, being briefed on a duty he hadn't expected. As a training company commander, his main role was executive; to actually train troops was someone else's function. The company's noncommissioned cadre did the hands-on training— notably the platoon sergeants—with the platoon leader a step removed. While lectures, with or without video cubes podded out from Terra, were a function of Division staff. The training schedule came from Division, too, based on a plan from far-off War House. There were open periods in which the company commander could insert whatever he thought best, but his main role was to track the progress of training and the trainees, turning the intensity up or down, and dealing with problems.

A company commander addressed the trainees daily, at morning muster and often at other musters. This kept his presence and authority in their consciousness, and hopefully inspired them from time to time. But lectures? Lectures were delivered by Division staff.

Except for this particular, newly conceived lecture. War House had foreseen possible troublesome effects, and wanted the company commanders to deliver it. If a C.O. was doing his job properly, his trainees knew and trusted him. Division concurred, and Mulvaney didn't doubt they were right. Major General Pak—he'd been promoted from brigadier—took it a step further; he wanted each platoon sergeant to talk it out afterward with his trainees. If the sergeants had been doing their job properly—and Mulvaney was confident his had—they'd have bonded with their Jerrie youths, like experienced and respected older brothers.

Jerries were about as close to homogeneous as a human culture gets, and tended to accept authority. According to the ethnology report, the Jerrie religion was narrow, but persuasive more than restrictive. Its defining book, *Contemplations on the Testaments,* said that wise leaders led by example, gentle teaching, and mild admonition. And like God, exercised "tolerance of the imperfections that are a part of being human."

Gopal Singh would have applauded that, Mulvaney told himself.

He got back to the company area in time for supper; his driver let him off outside the mess hall in a light but steady rain. Sixty feet away, the trainees were doing their pre-supper chin-ups before going in, callused fists gripping wet bars without a sign of slippage. Even with the enforcement of strict form, they were doing so many chins now, he'd tripled the number of bars, to keep the serving line moving.

He watched them for a moment before entering the officers' mess. He'd developed a real fondness and respect for his trainees. This evening he would brief his platoon leaders and platoon sergeants on what tomorrow held. Meanwhile Bremer and Fossberg could take the trainees on a sixty-minute speed march with sandbags, then let them off early.

◇

The next day's training began with the usual run before breakfast. After six weeks they weren't grueling anymore. It was the one part of physical training that wasn't being intensified. Drag Ass Hill seemed neither so steep nor so long as it had. At the end of Week 4 their runs had been lengthened to forty of Lüneburger's long minutes, and would stay at that, neither lengthening nor speeding up. Nor did they end with any more "suicide races."

After breakfast the trainees fell out wearing fighting gear, complete with armored jackets and battle helmets. And of course with the blasters they'd been issued in Week 4. In Week 5 they'd learned to fire them, and had qualified for single-shot firing, set for soft pulses, for safety's sake. But they'd been shown what a hard pulse did to a dummy in a flak jacket. A jacket and helmet might help against shrapnel, or spent or grazing blaster pulses, but that was all.

This morning they marched four miles, burdened not only with their gear, but with forty-pound sandbags to build strength.

Then spent an hour and a half moving carefully through forest, senses alert, firing short bursts at wooden targets that popped up for two seconds from unexpected places. Fired from the hip while walking. Failure to hit your target earned gigs, which, they were told, they'd pay for on their next day off. In Week 5, on slow fire, Jael had scored "excellent." But on quick fire she'd been charged four straight gigs before she'd gotten fast enough, and a couple since when she'd missed in her haste. On this day—Fourday—she got none.

The body armor didn't help, nor did the sandbag. But on the other hand, Esau hadn't missed yet; a number of young frontiersmen hadn't. He'd been hunting with a breech-loading single-shot rifle since boyhood, had learned marksmanship at an age when the reflexes channel readily and deeply. And New Jerusalem's version of squirrels didn't hold still longer than a second. "Shooting blasters in bursts, you can't hardly miss," he'd told Jael, "once you get the hang of it. There's no recoil nor windage, and the trajectory's flat. Durn energy pulse would travel around the world and hit you in the back, if it held together good enough."

It wouldn't, of course, and Esau knew it. It would head into space on a tangent. Lieutenant Bremer, the company XO, had told them that. Nor did the pulses fall to earth. They simply lost integrity after a mile or so, and died—"unraveled" was how he'd put it.

At 1100 hours the company ground out another fifteen pushups—all they were asked for, wearing flak jackets, sandbag and helmet—and headed back to camp. They had no notion of what the afternoon held for them. But there'd be something; there always was.

<>

Pastor Lüneburger's World grew a lot of barley, so the trainees ate a lot of it, as a frequent substitute for potatoes and rice. At the noon meal this day they found roast pork waiting for them, with barley, savory pork gravy, thick slices of hot, buttered whole-grain bread, crisp green beans, and a cobbler of some Lüneburgian fruit. And Lüneburger coffee. All with seconds if wanted.

Afterward they had thirty minutes to recover. Most napped on their cots. Then whistles brought them out in field uniforms for muster, and afterward they had the rare experience of marching to lecture with Captain Mulvaney leading them. Arriving at the lecture shed, they pumped out the now customary thirty pushups, then filed in. Captain Mulvaney was standing in front, at the lectern. When they were seated, his big voice barked "at ease!", and the trainee chatter cut abruptly off.

"Men," he said, "today you're going to see something you've only heard about till now. You'll see cubeage of warbots in realistic simulated combat, coordinating with organic troops like ourselves. You'll find the warbots very interesting. After that you'll see cubeage of how they're constructed, and how they operate. You'll even see one of them interviewed." He paused, turning. "Corporal, begin the program."

The shed lights dimmed and the wall screen lit up. The presentation resembled a full-fledged dramatic production, opening with an interior shot of forest that had not been fought through. Artillery thundered in the distance. Squads of infantry trotted through in fighting gear, blasters in hand. Along with several seven-foot warbots roughly humanoid in form, their movements as smoothly articulated as an athlete's, though a bit different. Their laminated ceramic-steel surfaces were protected by camouflage fields whose color patterns fluctuated as they strode, mimicking the immediate surroundings. It was very effective.

A voice-over narration accompanied the visuals. A few weeks earlier the Jerries would have had serious problems with its language, but they'd been immersed in military life, and had already learned a lot.

Now the point of view followed close behind one of the infantry squads, till the organics reached the forest edge and began digging in. "This organic battalion," said the narrator, "has been bivouacked several miles back in the forest, hidden from aerial detection by a concealment field. Meanwhile, seek and engage actions have seriously reduced the capacity of both sides to launch aerial attacks."

When Mulvaney had first seen the cube, during the briefing the day before, mention of a concealment field had troubled him. The last he'd heard, back on Terra, concealment fields were only theory. But the PR was, science was as fully mobilized as industry, and who knew what might be available by the time they left for New Jerusalem.

As far as that was concerned, who knew what weaponry the Wyzhñyñy had?

The Wyzhñyñy. *How,* he wondered, *had War House learned what they called themselves?*

The camera view cut to panoramic. Ahead of the troops lay farmland, with forest close to a mile away on the other side. A road ran across the middle of the open ground. Now, from the forest on the far side, a wave of armored personnel carriers emerged, supported by armored fighting vehicles. Behind them came another wave, and another—a whole series of them. "The enemy forces are shown in animation," the narrator was saying, "as realistically as technology can portray them."

Mulvaney wondered how close to reality that was. They had to be almost wholly imaginary. But the production was excellent. Neither the animation nor the battle choreography could be faulted. Trashers began to rip the Wyzhñyñy as soon as they appeared, but the infantry held their fire until the Wyzhñyñy had crossed the road, then began to lay intense fire on them with slammers and blasters. Immediately the Wyzhñyñy returned the fire, and the fight became a melee within which Mulvaney's trained eyes could see the basic drilled-in tactics and creative responses of the troops on both sides.

Even the casualties were convincing, though it seemed to him the Wyzhñyñy might be dying in unreasonable numbers. Then Wyzhñyñy APFs—armored personnel flyers—sliced across the field at perhaps two hundred feet. Not a lot of them. The script writers, he recalled, had decimated them during the aerial preliminaries.

The picture cut to an oblique overhead view a few hundred yards back from the forest edge. The Wyzhñyñy APFs hovered close above the trees, lowering troops on individual slings, from doors with short stout drop booms. Then it cut to a view within the forest. As the airborne Wyzhñyñy landed, they triggered their sling releases and began forming up squads.

Suddenly warbots hit them, greatly outnumbered, but fighting with astonishing speed and power. The Wyzhñyñy were slaughtered. The warbots seemed too heavily armored to be harmed by their shoulder-fired blasters. And bots, Mulvaney knew, had a backup "torso" sensorium in case their eyes and ears were knocked out.

Briefly the trainees witnessed special effects sufficient to impress even Terrans. For Jerries who'd never seen dramatic video before—or video at all till they'd come to Camp Stenders—it had to be a truly powerful experience.

The airborne Wyzhñyñy were shown as effectively wiped out, the few survivors dispersed and routed. Only a handful of warbots had gone down. The remaining bots did not linger. As if on command, perhaps received by built-in radio, they turned and loped off among the trees. Mulvaney was skeptical that machines on two legs could move so smoothly.

As the final bots disappeared, the viewpoint changed again, to the close-range fighting in the forest fringe. Wyzhñyñy bodies were abundant, but many humans also lay "dead." *Not as many as you'd expect,* Mulvaney thought. *I suppose War House doesn't want to shock the trainees too badly.* Then the warbots entered the fighting there, too, striking swiftly and powerfully. The Wyzhñyñy gave way, and after a brief desperate moment broke and fled, across a welter of bodies. Three warbots lay disabled, presumably by heavy slammers. The camera watched the surviving Wyzhñyñy gallop all the way across the fields to the forest on the far side, impelled by human fire that added more bodies to those already sprawled.

As the final Wyzhñyñy disappeared into the far woods, the scene froze on the field, and music cut in, restrained but powerful. Mulvaney recognized it as "The Arrival of Alp Arslan," by the Egyptian composer Ibrahim Hakim, in his orchestral suite *Manzikert.* It ended with a dark and powerful closing phrase, as the visual faded and disappeared.

Then the shed's lights came on, and the recorded narration resumed. "This cube was made to show you the basic function—and the great importance!—of warbots in modern warfare. For every regiment, the table of organization calls for two warbot platoons. Without them, no infantry regiment is complete, or fully prepared for combat. You will learn much more about warbots as your training progresses."

The voice stopped. Mulvaney got to his feet and stepped again to the lectern. *Well, Martin,* he thought, scanning his Jerries, *it's time to earn your pay.* "All right men, stand up in place, and stretch. Really stretch, so you feel it."

They did, with a chorus of groans.

Mulvaney grinned. "Now stamp your feet!"

Boots drummed on the plank floor.

"All right, now turn to the men around you; tell them hello, and shake hands with them." After half a minute of confusion and laughter, everyone had been included. "Good. Now tell them you're glad they're here. And mean it." He paused to let the chatter play out. "All right, at ease. Sit down." They stilled and sat. "We have something very important to talk about."

He paused a long moment, letting them wait. "Who of you," he asked, "will tell us why you're here, instead of back home on New Jerusalem?"

A hand shot up. "Recruit Isaiah Vernon," Mulvaney said, "tell us about it."

"Captain, sir, it's because invaders have come, invaders not made in the image of God. They're conquering human worlds, and killing the people on them. If we stayed, we'd be killed, too. Here we're learning to drive them away."

"Right," Mulvaney said. "At last report they'd definitely captured fourteen human worlds, and probably two others. Those we've heard from say the Wyzhñyñy" —he paused, pronouncing the name carefully again— "the Wyzhñyñy were killing everyone they came to, including those who tried to surrender."

Mulvaney scanned his audience again, his eyes stopping

on Esau. "Recruit Esau Wesley, suppose we don't get back to New Jerusalem soon enough, and the Wyzhñyñy take it. What then?"

"Then we'll drive them off, sir."

Mulvaney frowned. "Why not leave in—say a month from now? That should get us there in time."

"Fine, if we're ready. But if we're not, and we go, the Wyzhñyñy will beat us."

"Exactly right. And believe me, you're a long way from ready. You're coming along well, *very* well, but you're far from ready." His gaze found his religious advisor. "Recruit Spieler, you trainees are all from New Jerusalem, so it's obvious why you should return there to defend it. Or regain it. But I'm a Terran. All your cadre are. Why should we go there to fight?"

The somber Spieler got to his feet. As recruits went, he was old, twenty-seven Terran years. "Captain Mulvaney, sir, long ago, God put Adam and Eve on Terra, and they were fruitful, and multiplied. Then, in His own good time for His own good reasons, He shepherded folks out to the stars. But all of Adam's progeny are God's children, created in His own image and saved by the sacrifice of His own son. It is the duty of us all to drive out these" —he paused, struggling with the pronunciation— "these Wiz-nin-ee."

"Well said, Spieler." Once more Mulvaney scanned his audience, making them wait. He was no orator, but he knew how to communicate. "So," he said, changing directions on them, "what did you think of the cube? Anyone?"

"Exciting, sir," someone called. Someone else followed with "We've got some idea now of what fighting will be like."

"Recruit Jael Wesley, what did you think of it?"

"Sir, it made me realize the cost of being in this war. If we lose, we'll all die. But even winning, lots of us will."

"Good observation. Recruit Spieler, what about death?"

"Sir, we'll all die sometime. If not on the battlefield, then maybe in bed. But death isn't the thing to fear. Hell is, and next after Hell, the destruction of the human race." Spieler paused, then went on. "Most of us here—maybe all of us—when we die, we'll go to Heaven and be with the Lord."

"Thank you, Recruit Spieler." Another hand rose as he said it. "Recruit Esau Wesley, what have you got to add?"

"Sir, I was wondering about the warbots. The cube said every regiment was supposed to have them. And those folks it showed would have been in bad trouble if it wasn't for warbots. But I haven't seen or heard of any in our whole division."

Mulvaney stood tall, sure of himself. He made them wait again, tightening their attention. "I was coming to that, Wesley," he said, "but I'm glad you brought it up. What do you suppose a warbot is?"

"Sir, it's a kind of machine."

"Ah. That's right, as far as it goes. But they're more than that." Again he pointed. "Recruit Vernon, do machines have souls?"

"No sir. Only people have souls."

"And brains?"

"I suppose they have artificial brains, sir."

Mulvaney nodded. "You certainly might think that. But actually a bot has both a soul and a human brain."

There wasn't a sound from his audience, but it seemed to Mulvaney he sensed doubt, resistance. "I have a sister who's a bot," he went on. "A different model than shown in the cube. She's a medic bot."

Esau hadn't sat back down yet. "Sir," he said, "your *sister?*"

"My sister. She was a nurse, until she came down with a condition called 'cascade syndrome' —the breakdown of one body part after another. By age thirty she was expected to die at any time. The last time I heard from her was since we arrived here on Lüneburger's World. She'd volunteered to have her central nervous system—that's her brain, her spinal cord and nerve connections—removed from her body and put into what's called a 'bottle.' Then the bottle was put into a machine called a 'servo'—the sort of machine you saw in the cube. Without the human central nervous system, and the soul associated with it, the servo is a useless piece of machinery. It's the combination—

the servo, the central nervous system and the soul—that makes a warbot. Or in Audrey's case a battlefield medic bot.

"And therein lies the reason the 1st New Jerusalem Division has no warbots yet; why no division has anything like as many as it should. People don't get converted into warbots unless they're badly crippled, or they're dying of something.

"Because becoming a bot is final. If someone becomes a bot, and later wishes he hadn't, it can't be undone. So even severely disabled people, who may feel tempted, often can't bring themselves to take that final step. And until the past month, many people who were willing weren't sufficiently disabled to qualify. Now recruitment for what is called 'bottling' has picked up. So the 1st New Jerusalem Division should have at least a partial contingent of warbots when we leave."

There Mulvaney stopped and simply stood, the silence longer than before, as if he were looking for the words to continue. Finally he nodded, as if to himself. "When we get to New Jerusalem, we cannot expect replacements for our casualties. You noticed in the cube that not all the casualties were Wyzhñyñy; not even close. We'll have a medical battalion to treat our wounded; Indis—people from another heavyworld called Epsilon Indi Prime."

Again he paused. "There will also be damaged warbots. We'll have spare servos—warbot bodies—and bottles can be transferred from damaged servos to replacement servos. But in some of the damaged servos, the human inside will have been killed. And we'll need to replace them if we can.

"So—" This was the hard part. His new pause was not for effect; he was groping. "So what we need," he said carefully, "are volunteers. People like you and me, who'll agree in writing that if we're disabled or mortally wounded, our central nervous system—our brain and spinal cord—can be bottled and installed in a warbot. Division will have specialists to do the job."

Once more he paused, sensing his audience was ill at ease with this. "We don't know now which of you will receive such wounds," he went on. "So beginning next week we'll start training all of you in how to operate as a warbot. The training modules are expected to arrive next Twoday. The same ship is also bringing a platoon of real warbots to continue their training here. Later you'll do tactical exercises with them."

A hand shot up. "Yes, Recruit Arvet?"

"Sir, how can we learn to operate as a warbot if we're not—bottled?"

"You'll find out. You'll probably enjoy it." He grinned. "It won't require running up Drag Ass Hill."

He pointed at another hand. "Yes, Recruit Harrison?"

The young man's voice was subdued and tentative. "Where do we, uh, sign the agreement, sir? To get bottled if we're crippled or dying?"

"Right after supper, at the orderly room. Sergeant Henkel or Corporal Tsinijinnie will sign you up." He scanned the room and saw no sign of enthusiasm. "Or at some later time. The sooner we know, the better." Again he looked around. "Any more questions? Cochran?"

"Sir, you said we'd see cubeage of how warbots are made, and watch one of them get interviewed."

"Right. That comes next. Corporal Cavalieri, continue with the cube."

◇

B Company was introverted when it left the lecture shed, but the condition was not allowed to persist. Captain Mulvaney had prearranged for that. Outside, they were ordered to drop down and this time pump out thirty-five. Even Recruit Vernon managed thirty-two. Then Sergeant Fossberg led them on a gallop to the Physical Training Area, where they spent a long Lüneburgian hour and forty minutes deeply in touch with the physical universe—gravity, dirt, fatique and pain. Afterward they trotted back to the company area by a roundabout, nearly hour-long route, chanting from time to time, to disrupt their breathing cadence. They arrived at their hutment sweating profusely, and were dismissed for showers, dry clothes, and a layabout before supper, mostly napping.

After supper but before evening muster, exactly five trainees showed up at the orderly room to sign agreements. If they were severely disabled or mortally injured, and unconscious, the army was authorized to "extract the undersigned's central nervous system, and install it into an interfacing module for installation in a servomechanism, to serve as a cyborg of a model, and in a military unit, deemed appropriate by the army."

◇

B Company's platoon sergeants had been allowed to choose their own site for their evening session. Sergeant 1st Class Arjan Hawkins Singh had chosen a field training site less than a mile from their hutment. There they found a platoon-size bleachers, with trees shading it from the lowering sun. Some second-level cadreman had delivered a folding chair to the site, for Hawkins, to help this seem like a conversation instead of a lecture.

The Jerries had been brought up to disdain war, and according to the briefing handbook on Jerrie ethnology, they put great stock in showing respect to the bodies of the dead, who presumably would be watching. On the other hand, the afternoon's training cube had rubbed their noses in their mortality, and the prospects of being killed or maimed would be more real now. And if five volunteers fell short of a landslide, it seemed to Hawkins that the bonding among the trainees, and their psychological identification with their regiments, would strengthen with time, and make a difference. A shortage of agreements now didn't necessarily mean they'd be lacking when the casualties began on New Jerusalem.

At any rate, Division, Regiment, and Mulvaney himself wanted this to be a relaxed and intimate discussion. The trainees sensed that this would not be another training lecture. For one thing, their sergeant hadn't ordered them to give him thirty or thirty-five pushups before seating them.

Hawkins didn't begin with the usual "at ease" to shut them up. He simply asked, "What did you think of the training cube this afternoon?" When no one volunteered a comment, he pointed. "How about you, Abner?"

It took Abner McReynolds a moment to react. No cadreman had ever addressed him by his given name before. It distracted him enough, he even forgot to address Hawkins as "sergeant."

"Those warbots were something to watch," he said. "I can see why the army wants us to volunteer."

Hawkins nodded. McReynolds didn't sound like someone deeply perturbed by the request. "I'm signing up myself," Hawkins told them. "As soon as we get back in." He looked around, then pointed at Esau Wesley. "Esau, what did you think about the training cube?"

"Sergeant, the thing that struck me most was all the bodies, all the dead and wounded. I knew all along a person could get killed, fighting in a war, but seeing it like that made it a lot more real to me. Those pulses don't pick and choose. If you're in the way, you're a deader. Wounded at least. It doesn't matter if you're the toughest man in the company."

"Good observation. Isaiah, what have you got to say?"

"Sergeant, it's well to be in good standing with the Lord before you go into battle. Of course, it's well to be in good standing with Him anyway, on general principles and for your own soul. As Jesus said in the Book of Mark: we don't know the time when death will come." He shrugged. "Although a battlefield seems a lot more dangerous than being home in bed."

"True. Unless you're home in bed when the Wyzhñyñy arrive." Hawkins paused. "What about death, Isaiah? What can you tell us about that?"

"In *Contemplations on the Testaments,* Elder Hofer wrote that 'death is the door to Heaven and Hell, and each of us chooses in life which one it will be.' So I'm prepared to die defending humankind."

"How about you, Hosea?"

"Well, Sergeant, say you're out deadening timber. And your hound's laid up hurt, so you're out there alone. You hear something and turn, and there's a big old tiger ten foot away, and you'd just set aside your ringing ax. My bet is, you'd be too scared to spit, even if you were spotless as the Lamb of God. The soul might go to Heaven, but the body? It'd stay behind for tiger feed, and don't no way like the prospect."

"Ah! Now there's a good way of putting it. Thank you, Hosea." Hawkins scanned and pointed. "Jael, you look as if you have something to say."

"Yessir, Sergeant. I'm a lot more scared of great pain than of dying. I suspect that lying out there in terrible pain, with maybe my innards ripped open and the flies buzzing, I'd be crying out to God to take me fast as he can."

"Good point," Hawkins said, thinking he'd as soon it hadn't come up. "But if it comes down to it, in combat you'll all have something in your aid kit that will greatly deaden the pain."

Jael continued before Hawkins could call on someone else. "And something else, Sergeant. There are things I want to do before I die. Have children, bring them up, watch them grow. Maybe even be a grandmother."

Hawkins nodded. "A good wish to have; a good ambition. But to enjoy it, it helps to have a safe place to live. There are lots of people who chose to stay on New Jerusalem—many with children—and they're a lot more likely to see their children murdered than grow up. While those who left with children...a labor camp's a hard place to raise a family. But when the war is over, and if we win it, things will work out for them.

"The fact is, the invaders have changed everything for us. I have a wife and two children back in North America. In a city called Madison, by a large beautiful lake. There's a good chance I'll never see them again, but I'll be doing what I can to keep them safe."

"Sergeant Hawkins?" It was Isaiah Vernon again.

"Yes, Isaiah?"

"Where do Sikh's believe they go when they die?"

Don't get into that, Arjan, Hawkins warned himself. *It'll dilute the subject we're here for, and maybe generate contention.* He would, he decided, give them a generality, something uncomplicated but basically valid. "Isaiah," he said, "think of it as returning to the loving arms of God."

◇

When 2nd Platoon got back to the company area, there wasn't any real discussion about their evening. A few comments, but no actual discussion. In fact, the hut was more quiet than usual.

Jael Wesley was the first to take her toiletries bag and head for the latrine to brush her teeth. When she was almost there, she met Isaiah Vernon on his way to the hut. On impulse she stopped him.

"Isaiah," she said, "can we talk? Privately somewhere?"

His eyes widened. "What about?" he asked cautiously.

"I don't want to stand out here and talk about it. Where can we go that's private?"

For a long moment he stood silently. What would Esau think? Jael was so pretty and so nice, more than once he'd caught himself drifting into a fantasy about her. A guilty fantasy. It was well, he'd told himself, that they trained so hard and had so little time to think. "The dayroom," he said at last. "That might be all right."

She knew where it was, though she'd never been inside it. She led off, Isaiah following. No one else was there, and they sat down opposite each other at a reading table.

"It's about agreeing to be turned into a warbot," she said. "If someone's badly wounded and going to die."

He stared at her, then realizing he needed to respond, he nodded.

"I'm thinking about signing," she said.

His mouth opened slightly, but nothing came out for several seconds. "That's something you need to talk to Esau about, not me."

"I will. Before I make any decision anyway. The reason I want to talk to you is, you were studying to be a speaker. So you must have read and reread all the books, and thought about them a lot. And the first thing I need to know is…"

She groped, clarifying her thoughts. "Like I told Sergeant Hawkins, I'm afraid of great pain. And I don't trust myself to be signing for the right reason: to help out in the war. I might just want to be rescued from great pain, or not spend the rest of my life all crippled up. You see. But God might want me to experience those things. To suffer in those ways."

Isaiah's expression changed, showing not worry now, but focus, and his answer, when it came, was expressed as a speaker might have phrased it. "Jael," he answered, "you've read that sometimes God tests people, as in the case of Job, and Abraham. But there's no sign that he'd have punished them if they'd failed."

"But what about suicide?"

"Suicide?"

"If I caused my crippled body to die, on purpose and ahead of its time, would that be suicide? And if my brain got took out and bottled, then when God gathers the blessed to rise, and if I qualified, would I be resurrected as a warbot, or a person?" Isaiah frowned not in disapproval but in thought, then shook his head. "First of all, all I can tell you is how it seems to me. The Testaments don't speak of that, nor does Elder Hofer's Contemplations. But it seems to me a warbot *is* a person. Because it has a soul. And as for resurrection— If a person gets eaten by a tiger, his flesh becomes tiger flesh, but he won't be resurrected as a tiger." Jael shook her head at that, rejecting. Isaiah continued. "And martyrs that were burned at the stake won't be resurrected as smoke and ashes. Nor cripples as cripples. God wouldn't resurrect them all humped over or twisted, or short an arm or leg."

He watched her thoughtful eyes. She was even prettier than he'd allowed himself to notice before. Finally she nodded. "Thank you, Isaiah," she said. "You've been a big help." Then she got up and left, leaving him sitting there.

Feeling guilty, because he hadn't been entirely honest with her. It seemed to him they wouldn't be resurrected in a body at all. He'd thought that when he was a child, and had gradually come to believe that when the time came, folks would have no interest in bodies. They'd just be souls.

Which of course brought up a lot of questions about the Testaments themselves. That was why he seldom let himself think about such things. The thing to do was trust in the Lord, and hope God would forgive his errors. Elder Hofer—and his own father—had always stressed that God was love.

<>

Three more trainees of 2nd Platoon went to the orderly

room that evening and signed warbot agreements. Jael Wesley was not one of them; she wasn't ready yet, if she'd ever be. The company as a whole signed 10 more; given those who'd signed earlier, that made 15. *Now,* Mulvaney thought, *if we can get the other 145 signed up...*

Chapter Twenty-Five
Status Review

The mahogany table and wall panels glowed with golden sunlight, the ten-foot tall window fields adjusting both the intensity and the blend of wavelengths. The entire Commonwealth Cabinet was there, along with several high-ranking officials of War House and the Office of War Mobilization. Elsewhere, selected others watched on live, closed circuit video. Whether in person or electronically, attendance was by invitation only. For some, this cabinet meeting was their first.

Prime Minister Foster Peixoto presided, with Chang Lung-Chi beside him; since the invasion, the president invariably attended.

The Prime Minister began with a brief caveat. "First you must all remember—MUST ALL REMEMBER—that what you hear in this meeting is confidential. Repeating *any* of it without authorization can result in a charge of insubordination or even treason. The Ministry of Information decides what will be released and when, and clears those releases with myself, in consultation with the president."

He looked them over, allowing his injunction to sink in. "Most of you are well informed on one aspect or another of our plans and progress, but not on all of it. What I will do here is summarize major areas. Others may elaborate on them.

"Our central strategy is and must be to stop the alien advance. At some point we must defeat their armada in space, which requires a great fleet well crewed. Which of course we do not have. Meanwhile the aliens are not waiting for us to get ready, and the course of their advance will bring them here to Terra as surely as if they knew where we are."

High on each wall, a screen showed a diagram of the Commonwealth and the alien progress, the captive worlds glowing redly.

"So far we have not challenged them," Peixoto went on. "Until very recently we've had no force that could fight a meaningful action. Even to draw a small demonstration of their armaments, we depended on Morgan's refugee pirate squadron. It was like a mosquito annoying a man, and what we learned from it was very limited. But *very* important."

Amazing, Chang thought, *that he can sound so worried when he and I talk privately, yet so calm and assured when speaking to others. It is a gift from the Tao.*

"Now we do have a significant space force: the 1st Sol Provisional Battle Force, commanded by Admiral Alvaro Soong. It is *far* smaller than the enemy's, but powerful enough to draw a broad display of alien armaments and tactics, and inflict significant damage.

"Soong's ships are ready. What remains is to finish training their crews. The crews of battleships have all handled battleships in test runs. Those on cruisers have flown actual cruisers. Every officer and man has carried out his flight duties and manned his battle stations and damage stations, in a ship of the kind he's assigned to.

"But they have not flown them through battle evolutions; not in reality. What they have done is fight numerous actions in simulation drills—actions in virtual F-space and virtual warpspace. And every officer has manned his station in wargames against every tactic and combination of tactics that generations of officers could think of. Against the weapons we know the enemy has, and others we think he might have, given what is known of physics."

He picked up a glass and sipped, then scanned his audience, the president watching beside him. *Part of the impression he makes,* Chang decided, *is due to his height. And his eyebrows, like crows' wings! But mostly it is his intelligence and honesty. He speaks the truth, so far as he knows it.*

"Within days," Peixoto said, "Soong's force—they call themselves the 'Provos'—will generate warpspace and fly to the outer fringe of the Sol System. There its officers and men will carry out every sort of battle evolution in reality. And when Soong feels they are ready, but no later than four weeks after leaving the vicinity of Terra, they will journey outward to meet the enemy.

"The progress of alien conquests is direct and predictable. The flagship's savant will be in touch with ours, and we will keep the admiral informed of the enemy's progress, world by unfortunate world. At some point, when the alien armada emerges from hyperspace, Soong's force will be waiting for it."

A hand raised.

"Yes Mister Bawadin?"

"Suppose the alien armada breaks up into separate task forces. What then?"

"At present we know little about alien psychology, but the possibility has been considered." He didn't mention the human prisoners on the Wyzhñyñy flagship. It would be a distraction. The few who needed to know already did. And at any rate, though what had been learned was interesting, it was of limited use. "The aliens haven't subdivided so far, except to establish colonies on the captured worlds. And of course, this sector of the galaxy is unknown to them. They don't know what they may encounter. And if they lack instantaneous communication, they'll be very effectively out of touch with each other."

"Suppose they do have instantaneous communication," Bawadin said. "What then?"

"There is every reason to believe they do not. That we have it ourselves grew out of fortuitous observations in unlikely research on unpromising subjects."

Another hand had raised, and Peixoto pointed. "Yes, Ms Syrkin?"

"Why a Sol battle force? Why not a force more broadly integrated?"

"The answer is time and shipyards. Shipyards here in the Sol System were able to begin large-scale production of warships more quickly. Also, the majority of available training cadre were here, thus the Sol System has been able to produce crews earlier than the other core worlds. Construction and training in the Indi and Eridani Systems are well underway now, but their trainees aren't ready yet. In a few weeks that situation will have changed."

"What makes this force 'provisional?' Why not simply call it a fleet?" Syrkin asked. "Do you have misgivings about it?"

"We could call it a fleet. But what we learn from the first action may dictate major changes in force makeup, organization, and tactics. Thus it seemed appropriate to call it a provisional force."

"You said 'action,' not 'battle.' Why?"

"'Battle' suggests sustained fighting. This is expected to be a short series of hit and run actions. Lasting just long enough to record a spectrum of alien responses. You'll have an opportunity to ask Admiral Tischendorf about it later."

Again Peixoto paused to sip. "We are also preparing an action of another sort, to be fought very largely by farworlders: the 1st New Jerusalem Infantry Division, supported by the 3rd Indi Armored Regiment with attached Ground Support Wing, and the 5th Lüneburger Engineers. All heavyworlders; all training on Lüneburger's World. Their commander, a Sikh of the Gopal Singh Dispensation, reports that training is on schedule. And..."

Another hand had risen. "Yes Dr. Corneille?"

"The people of New Jerusalem are pacifist Christians. What makes you think they'll fight?"

"The question has been considered. The *founders* of New Jerusalem were firm pacifists, and their descendants have been inculcated with the beliefs of the founders, as filtered and adulterated by time and frontier living. But until the alien invasion, war was only a concept on New Jerusalem. And their most holy book, the Christian Bible, is replete with descriptions of patriotic wars and warrior folk heroes of the remote past. Intrinsic cracks in their pacifism.

"True, many on New Jerusalem stayed behind. Some refused to believe that aliens were coming. Others believe that God will protect them. But 77,000 adults, with their children, left farms and often family behind, and fled here. Those who volunteered for military service were well aware that it meant fighting a war.

"There is no indication that their cultural pacifism will prevent them from fighting. Certainly it has not interfered with their training. General Pak is confident of their willingness and toughness."

He didn't stop with that. "The Sikhs themselves, under their founder, Guru Nanak, began as fervent pacifists, but in time became notorious warriors as a matter of survival. While in his time, Gopal Singh was a peacemaker, if not quite a pacifist." Peixoto grimaced. "During the Troubles, many of Gopal Singh's followers resigned their positions in the military, on the basis that it was an unethical war. And spent years in prison for that dedication to what they regarded as right. But there have been no—*no* Sikh resignations in this war. Not one."

It occurred to Chang that his friend had never mentioned his own spiritual persuasion. Probably deist, he thought. Flavored by other doctrines, deism predominated on Terra.

"In about fifteen weeks," Peixoto went on, "when the troops are ready, the New Jerusalem Liberation Force will begin a five-month voyage to New Jerusalem. By the time they arrive, it will have been in alien hands for some time. And besides the ground and air units, there will be a space force, under Admiral Apraxin-DaCosta, to deal with whatever space force the alien armada left in the system."

He then described the Apraxin's Task Force. When he'd finished, a hand thrust up, and Peixoto pointed. "Yes, Doctor?"

"Mr. Prime Minister, that is a rather modest force. What makes you think it can do the job?"

"Most of the conquered planets informed us of the number of alien emergence loci, so we know how many fewer they have been from world to world. Some of the ships left behind with the conquering colonists are undoubtedly transports, and supply vessels left to support the conquerors until they can support themselves. But others are warships; Morgan's squadron provided information on how many to expect."

Peixoto's gaze had been on the people in the room. Now he scanned the faces on the monitors. He had their attention.

"Also, judging from the elapsed time between worlds, the

armada remains in the system's fringe for about a standard week.

"We also assume that they expect us to make a stand farther within the Commonwealth. If so, they probably leave behind no more fighting ships than they consider necessary."

He scanned the people in the chamber. "We've had to make numerous assumptions, and add modest safety margins. While keeping in mind that the ships of the Liberation Task Force will not be available to Admiral Soong's Provos."

He pointed at an upthrust hand. "Yes, Senator Bomboulis?"

"Why send a liberation force to New Jerusalem? At this time, I mean. Why not send Apraxin's force with Soong's? And hold the New Jerusalem division to help defend some other world?"

"We have two reasons. One, we lack knowledge of how the enemy fights. The ground units we land on New Jerusalem will be accompanied by several savants, as will Apraxin's and Soong's space forces. They should give us very important information on how the alien fights. And two, if we undertake to defend a world on the ground, the alien can send in more and more forces to overwhelm our own. While if we land a liberation force well after he's left, the alien defense is unlikely to receive reinforcements. As I pointed out earlier, we have compelling reason to believe that they do not have instantaneous communication."

More hands had popped up; the prime minister waved them off. "Now we will hear from our director of industrial mobilization, and our minister of war. Please jot down any further questions; I will invite them afterward. Our time is limited, and Mr. Shin and Mr. Stavrianos will no doubt anticipate many of them in their presentations."

◇

The director of industrial mobilization spoke first, followed by the minister of war. When the meeting was again opened to questions, the first hand raised belonged to the Chief of Senate Liaison. The prime minister pointed. "Senator Bomboulis," he said.

"Wouldn't it be simpler and less expensive to make warbots

in the form of floaters? Because human soldiers walk upright on their hind limbs doesn't make it the optimum design strategy."

"A perceptive question, Senator," Peixoto said, "but I believe you'll find it *is* the best design strategy. General Kulikov, why don't you explain."

The general rose; he preferred to speak on his feet. "The human nervous system," he answered, "evolved to operate an erect, bipedal body with upper appendages which manipulate objects. And beginning in infancy, each of us spends years mastering their function. The warbot servo is designed to operate using those same neural circuits in the manner for which they evolved, and in which the person learned to use them.

"In the late 28th century, when warbots became feasible, alternative design strategies were tested. All but the bipeds presented serious training problems, while biped servo design proved less difficult than expected.

"So when the present emergency struck, we went with a biped design. Plans already existed for large-scale production. Have I answered your question?" Kulikov finished.

Senator Bomboulis nodded. "You have, General. Before my election, I was a professor of history at the University of Kaunas. So I am well aware how little appreciation and support your peacetime defense efforts received—both your predecessors' efforts and your own. You have my sincere admiration and gratitude for your dedication, foresight and ingenuity." He paused, then chuckled wryly. "Not to mention your thick skin."

◇

When the meeting was over, the president walked to his office, briskly as always. He was thinking about something Kulikov had failed to mention. A bot design, loosely speaking, only recently in production, and not bipedal at all. Not a fighting bot in the conventional sense, though in its way, military. But it wasn't time yet to make it known, even to the cabinet. A leak would result in problems he would gladly do without.

Chapter Twenty-Six
Warbots

On their way to various training areas, B Company's trainees had seen the new building grow from bare, bulldozed earth to a completed structure in under four weeks. The largest in the regimental area, it even had two stories. They'd wondered what it was for. Now, obviously, they were about to find out.

Entering it, they filed into a small lecture hall and sat down on its benches. It smelled like newly-sawn lumber and fresh paint. Then someone, *something* entered and stepped to the lectern. "I am Lieutenant Mei-Li den Uyl-Gurejian," she said, "from New Netherlands, in Spain. That's on Terra. I have two children, and for four years I was a lecturer in history, a teacher, at the University of Barcelona. Until I was afflicted—and I do mean afflicted—by cascade syndrome, the major killer of young adults on Terra." She spread her arms. "So when I had a chance to contribute to the defense of my species and my children, I took it. Without hesitation."

A mother! thought Jael Wesley. *More than seven feet tall, and steel! Here to protect her babies.* A thrill ran through her. Glancing sideways at Esau, she laid her hand on his.

Gurejian continued. "Two years ago I was five feet four and weighed 125 pounds. In secondary school I was a competitive gymnast. It developed excellent balance and coordination, very useful for warbots. Now I'm seven feet three, and weigh 447 pounds; perhaps less than you thought. In the core worlds, materials engineering is quite advanced.

Jael didn't understand everything the warbot said, but she got a sense of it. And she was impressed by the bot's clear female voice. She'd expected a baritone, a voice like the bot's on the cube they'd watched.

"I see one of you is female," Gurejian added, and Jael felt herself blushing. "As I still am in all but body. My viewpoint remains essentially female—a female soldier's—and my feelings are still female, though in some respects different than before."

Her fingertips passed down her body almost to the knees; her arms were long. "Obviously I'll have no more children, but I've had my quota, and with cascade syndrome I couldn't have had more anyway. Nor could I have mothered the two I had, much longer; I was expected to die within weeks at most. But now, if I survive this war, I can be with them. I may very well not survive, but if we lose the war, my children would die."

She paused, then laughed. "They've seen me like this, incidentally. I had five days leave before I shipped here. They're eight and five years old, a girl and a boy, and at first they were very shy with me. But within a couple of hours, the shyness was gone, replaced by curiosity. Argop loved using my arm for a chinning bar. We did some hugging and kissing, too," she added chuckling. Jael found herself loving this seven-foot metal woman. "Kissing went better for me than for them. My sensorial package—the senses built into this servo—includes a good sense of touch and being touched. And my brain translates it into familiar feelings. But touching *me?* I'm afraid I'm not the best for snuggling with." Her audience laughed nervously. "Krikor, my husband, says he'll be glad to get used to it, but I told him he should find a female companion anyway. One who'll be a good surrogate mother for our kids, and that I can get along with when the war is over."

She sounded almost serene as she said it. It struck Jael that this woman had needed to examine her feelings and make adjustments fast. But then, having a deadly disease, she must have gotten used to doing that. And now she had a life again, and a purpose.

It also occurred to Jael that she herself might never have known such thoughts, if she hadn't left New Jerusalem, and the life and farm they'd had there. The realization took her by surprise.

Mei-Li den Uyl-Gurejian hadn't been killing time, talking about herself. Part of her job was to make herself human for her listeners. That accomplished, she went on to prepare them briefly for the training they'd begin when she'd finished.

They could not, she told them, learn to operate a servo—a

bot body—while still organics. What they could do though, was learn and get used to what warbots did in combat, especially individual and small-unit tactics.

"Some of it," she said, "is much like the things you already do. Every day, while training as organics, you learn things that warbots need to know. And most of the time, in combat, warbots work with organics, and need to know what you know and do. So those of you who make yourselves available for warbot service—in case you're ever maimed or fatally injured—will already know much of what you need to know. You'll have it stored in your brains. And what you learn in the training you begin tonight will teach you the rest.

"The main thing you'll need to do, after being bottled and installed, is learn to operate your new body, the servo. And that's not so much learning as it is simply practice. You'll find that your arms and legs will work very much like they always have. Intend them to do something and they'll do it. But your center of gravity will be higher, so your sense of balance will feel a little off at first. Also your arms will be considerably longer, and you'll have to get used to that. You'll weigh a lot more, so it will be harder to dodge. And you'll be a lot faster, a *lot* stronger, and a lot more durable. Meanwhile, some things you'll have to be more careful about, till you get used to doing them in your new body. And some things you can be less careful about."

A teacher, Jael thought. *No wonder she's good at explaining.* She wished she could get to really know this woman, this giantess.

"What you'll begin here this evening," Gurejian went on, "is called 'virtuality training.' You'll wear a special helmet, and sit in a little room, seeing and hearing a realistic video scene all around you. Seeing it as if through bot eyes, hearing it as if through bot ears. The sounds that go with the scenes will be partly the sounds of battle, including orders from officers. And partly it will be the voices of your trainer and your coach, telling you what's going on and what to do. As an imaginary warbot, you'll seem to move around and fight within that scene, but without ever leaving your module. Your coach will be seeing the same things you see, and talk to you through your earphones. It'll be awkward at first, but that will soon pass."

Abruptly she went from being a professor to being a sergeant or whatever. "And that," she said, "is it. End of lecture. On your feet! Sergeant Burlingham will take you to the training section."

Burlingham was another bot. As the company followed him down a corridor, Jael had a nervous stomach.

Chapter Twenty-Seven
Messages

Encrypted pulse OSPCO
2912.07.13/14:16G
Bloemfontein to all AMS program labs
Subject(s): venom studies
We have what appears to be the appropriate insertion loci to work from, to increase broad-spectrum venom virulence in AMS. Exploratory work is underway. Suggestions?
— Marijka V
(Issa, can you send me 12 of your best clone for some exploratory work? MV)

Encrypted pulse OSPCO
2912.07.13/14:46G
<u>*Lusaka*</u> to Bloemfontein AMS; copy all AMS program labs
Subject(s): venom studies
Suggest *Selenarctos thibetanus* as a test species. They are reportedly less venom-sensitive than any other Ursidae, even the honey bear. Availability of test material may be a problem. Check with Institute of Biosystem Research @ Dehra Dun. If they can't advise you, no one can.
— Jabari H

Encrypted pulse OSPCO
2912.07.13/16:03G
Bangui to all AMS program labs
Subject(s): 1. reproductive enhancement (fecundity of queens); 2. security break.

1. We have an enhanced clone whose queens, under Hesselink B conditions, averaged 3,873 viable inseminated eggs per day over 14 days. A busy lady! See attachment.
2. Minutes ago, university received E threats from "Peace Front"

re program, so the cat is out of the bag. You will be hearing from the Bureau soonest, if you haven't already.

— Issa L

(Marijka, 12 princesses are on their way to you. IL)

Encrypted pulse OSPCO
2912.07.13/16:27G
OSP to AMS Nairobi; copy all AMS program labs
Subject(s): Foulbrood project
Kanika, given the update by Marijka on the venom project (shudder), and by Issa on the fecundity project (shiver), I certainly hope you folks are making good progress.

— Benny

Encrypted pulse OSPCO
2912.07.14/03:23G
OSP to all AMS program labs
Subject(s): NSS 12
At 03:05G this date, NSS 12 reported passing the halfway point (eccentricity 1.06) to Tagus. Looks good so far, but don't depend on it.

— Debbie C

◇

"Excuse me," said Major General Pyong Pak Singh, and took the call on his privacy receiver. "Pak," he said.

"Sir, this is WO-3 Kiefer." Yolanda Kiefer sounded very young, something he hadn't gotten used to. She was older than he was. "Dierdre just brought a message from War House," she went on. "About two minutes worth. I can read it to you if you'd like."

A savanted message. "Just a moment, Kiefer," he said, and turned to his visitor, Mayor Ritala of nearby North Fork. "This will take perhaps two minutes."

The Lüneburgian nodded.

"Read it to me," Pak said. "I'm ready."

"From Lieutenant General Titu Cioculescu, deputy chief

of staff, Commonwealth Army." *Cioculescu,* Pak thought, impressed. *Lefty Sarruf's right hand.* "To Major General Pyong Pak Singh, commander, New Jerusalem Liberation Corps. Greeting. When you have reached New Jerusalem, you will provide War House with three Wyzhñyñy prisoners alive and unwounded. Do not rely on serendipity. Develop a plan, and train teams accordingly. You will be informed later on how the prisoners are to be processed. Personnel will be provided to handle and transport them. You will be further informed as appropriate.

"(signed) Cioculescu"

◇

Frowning, Pak pursed thin lips. "Thank you, Kiefer. Is that it?"

"Yes, General."

"I'll answer him when I've seen it in writing."

Reaching, the general disconnected, wondering what War House wanted with prisoners. It seemed highly improbable they had a translation program for whatever language the Wyzhñyñy spoke, or whistled, or gestured, or however they did it. It didn't occur to him that the questions might have originated from an agency he'd never heard of: the Office of Special Projects. And that the answers would come not from questioning, but from chromatographs and other tests.

He turned to his visitor. "Mayor Ritala, I appreciate that your merchants would like my troops to come into town more often, and I'm glad their behavior meets with your approval. But we are on Pastor Lüneburger's World to train, preparing to fight a very dangerous foe. The present schedule of passes on alternate Sevendays will have to suffice, and at any rate it's about as often as their very modest pay permits." He paused. "Is there anything else?"

The general's voice held a tone of dismissal; his closing question was clearly rhetorical, a courtesy. A thought passed through the mayor's mind: to invite the general to his home for Sevenday dinner. But somehow he didn't. This soldier was too single-minded for that.

It also occurred to him that single-mindedness was desirable in generals, given the circumstances the human species found itself in.

Chapter Twenty-Eight
Qonits Answers Questions

Instead of answering, Yukiko Gavaldon got calmly to her feet and faced him. "Qonits," she said, "it is not appropriate that you ask all the questions. Now it is time for us to ask questions, and for you to answer."

David had learned to conceal his surprise at his wife's sometimes off-the-wall responses. "Yes," he said, backing her. "It is disrespectful that we are not given a reasonable chance to question you. It becomes increasingly so as the imbalance grows."

Qonits stood for several long seconds without responding. This was something new from the captives. When at last he replied, it was slowly. "But we are the victors. You are our captives. You are obliged to do as we order."

Yukiko shook her head firmly. "That is incorrect. There are two categories of victors. One is barbarians. The other consists of civilized beings. Barbarians are inferior sophonts who do not care whether they behave properly or not. Civilized beings do care. And you have shown yourself to be civilized."

She stood with arms folded, her features firm.

The two Terrans had learned to read Qonits somewhat. It seemed to David that the chief scholar was unsure of himself now. "There should be balance in all things," he added. His voice was mild, even kind. "Not absolute balance; that is hardly possible. But sufficient to show respect."

Qonits looked at him warily. "What questions would you ask?"

It was Yukiko who began. "Where in the galaxy are you from?"

Qonits' head jerked three times, as if with Tourette Syndrome—a reaction that seemed too extreme for the question. But he answered it. "Shipsmind says this not our galaxy. We jumped here in—no elapsed time."

David frowned; this had to be a language problem. "Not

from this galaxy? How can that be?"

"We do not know. We crossed from our old spiral arm to another—very far voyage, eleven years—then emerged from hyperspace. At that time, shipsmind knew exactly what place we were, and where our home sector was. Then we entered a star system to explore…and suddenly…"

He stopped, his hide twitching weirdly, alarmingly. Yukiko got quickly to her feet and placed a hand on Qonits' arm. "It's all right," she said softly. "It's all right. You are with friends."

Qonits didn't answer for a full minute while his twitching subsided, but he remained agitated. "Suddenly," he went on, "the view, the stars, all things was different. And the ship's…" He gestured frantically, as if digging for the word with his hands. "Numbers that appear."

"Readouts," David suggested.

Qonits seemed not to hear. "Ship said we were in different galaxy—*and no time had passed!*" He paused. The twitching had begun again, and he breathed heavily, seeming to hyperventilate. More than his nictitating membranes had closed. His eyelids had clenched shut, and he stood without saying anything more until he'd calmed somewhat. Finally, eyes open again, he continued. "Ship was searching for known objects in space, as fastly it could. And was recognizing nothing.

"Some of our people lost…" Again his hands pawed as if digging. "Some even died."

The chief scholar's reaction stunned David. Granted the experience must have been a shock, it seemed to him that humans—certainly spacers—wouldn't have reacted so strongly.

"I'm sorry my question led to painful memories," Yukiko said. "I had no wish to distress you. I was simply interested in the world on which your people originated. Is that where you're from?"

The question seemed to calm Qonits somewhat. He stood as if digesting it. "Wyzhñyñy began on a world whose name would have not meaning to you, and hard for you to speak. We say Kryzhgon. My tribe would start long later, on different world. Kryzhgon had hard history to live with. Much danger.

Much fighting."

"Fighting?" said David.

"Kryzhgon had three sapient life forms, each on different part, with ocean between. One already had water ships. Came to our land on them. Two-leggers like you; we do not say their name. Had better weapons than Wyzhñyñy, but Wyzhñyñy more numbers." Qonits had begun to shiver again. "They tried to kill us, have all land for themselves. War was a very long time. Gradually, enemy grew more. But as they grew more, we made weapons like theirs. Better weapons. Our...old fathers?"

"We say 'forefathers,'" Yukiko told him, guessing.

Qonits picked it up without comment, as if deeply into the story he'd begun. "Our beforefathers fought hard, tried to kill them all, be safe from them."

Yukiko thought of pointing out the parallel between that ancient invasion and what the Wyzhñyñy were doing in the Commonwealth, but decided not to.

"For long time," he went on, "more enemy came across ocean, but beforefathers grew stronger. Finally no more enemy came, and Wyzhñyñy killed all that were there. Hunted them down till all were dead. Then beforefathers built water ships— explored, learned where enemy came from. Built fleet and went there. After many generations, and many many Wyzhñyñy killed, Wyzhñyñy killed last one of enemy. That enemy.

"But Wyzhñyñy still not safe. On another land was third sapient life form. Small." He gestured, indicating a height of perhaps twenty inches. "Six limbs, like us, and very quick, very fierce. Very clever." Qonits tapped his cranium. "Our long-time enemy had gone also to small one's land. Then small ones came to ours."

"At first they fought old enemy, and us only when we met. After old enemy all dead, we fought small ones a long time; many generations. Both sides learned explosives. Wyzhñyñy became much more numerous than them, but it took very long time before killed the last one." Qonits paused, gestured a sigh. "Over many lifetimes, the small ones ate Wyzhñyñy. But not since a very long time now."

With that, Qonits stopped talking. He looked emotionally drained. Yukiko patted his arm. "The Wyzhñyñy had a very difficult history," she said. "I am glad our life form is not so savage as the enemies of your past. We will not try to destroy you, but I don't expect you to believe that. Not after the long suffering of your people."

David nodded emphatically. "Now you have balanced your relationship with us," he said. "It is time for you to ask us questions again, before we must exercise Annika."

Qonits bobbed his upper body. After consulting with shipsmind through the speaker in his ear, he began.

◇

Nine hyperspace months away, Chang Lung-Chi and Foster Peixoto sat awed by what they'd heard. "Amazing!" said the president. "Two oceanographers, prisoners of the enemy, yet they are providing us with information beyond anything we could have hoped for. Seemingly without realizing it."

The prime minister's nod was subdued. "Two oceanographers and a traumatized idiot savant." He paused. "What do you make of the alien's statement that their ship inadvertently jumped between galaxies?"

Normally Chang Lung-Chi answered questions quickly and with certainty. This time he lagged. "It seems to me…" he began, "it seems to me the creature told what he thought was the truth, I have never sensed subterfuge in anything he's said. And his grammar and pronunciations became poorer. As if he were strongly agitated."

Either that or the knowledge master is a good actor, Foster Peixoto thought. But that made no sense; the alien had no apparent reason to mislead his two captives in that. "I wish I could have seen him as he spoke," he said.

Chang nodded agreement, and for a moment the two men sat silent. Finally Peixoto spoke. "Wyzhñyñy history makes it psychologically more difficult to exterminate them. What we plan for them is much like what they did to their enemies, long ago."

Chang grunted. Humanity was the likelier candidate for

extermination. "But if they had not attacked us," he said, "we would have accepted them peacefully. And even after they'd attacked us, if they hadn't been so focused on extermination, we could have negotiated."

Peixoto examined that. They'd become so deeply involved in the war effort, they'd never followed through on the question of negotiations. "Negotiations?" he said.

"It was you who first suggested them."

"What terms would you offer, now they've done so much harm?"

"They must remove their colonies from the worlds they've captured, and leave this sector."

Peixoto nodded thoughtfully. "That willingness, that preference, is what makes us civilized. But given the experience of their forefathers, what would it take to get their agreement?"

"We will need to dominate their fleet first, and route them from enough of their colonies that they know they cannot hold the rest. Then perhaps they'll agree to leave."

Peixoto sighed. Victory felt unreal to him, and so did Wyzhñyñy agreement. "Let us hope we can do it," he said quietly.

"We will," said Chang Lung-Chi. "We will." But saying it produced second thoughts. Could they trust such a life form anywhere in this part of the galaxy? Even with a peace treaty? And they "knew" only one Wyzhñyñy. How representative was he?

◇

Quanshûk watched the monitor screen as Qonits left the captives' room. The prisoners had been a major disappointment to the grand admiral, or their information had been. Even now, with shipsmind's knowledge of the human language growing rapidly, and Qonits' expanding proficiency in its use.

It would mean a lot simply to learn how large their empire was. A hyperspace year in diameter, one of the humans had said, but the body-field monitor insisted he'd lied. Obviously they wanted their empire to seem larger and more formidable than it really was.

In a way, the lie had been reassuring. It established that the monitor worked. And why make small lies? To that question anyway. So say they'd doubled the actual size, and the true diameter was half a hyperspace year. Considering how far his armada had already penetrated, that was conceivable, though barely.

It never occurred to Quanshûk, nor to Qonits, that the human, to make himself more believable, might have deliberately described the commonwealth as *half* its actual diameter, not twice. And that the volume of human space was roughly sixty-four times what he himself was assuming.

The watch officer's voice broke Quanshûk's preoccupation. "Lord Admiral, the F-space potentiality indicates another stellar gravity field coming into range."

Quanshûk's gaze moved to the red view screen. Perhaps two hours ahead and to starboard, a white gravitic isoline formed hesitantly, a segment at a time. So many stars, and so few suitable planets; detouring and emerging to examine them slowed his armada greatly. Fortunately, some could be dismissed without doing either. Like this one, which promised to be a white dwarf.

What he really wanted was to reach a system with a human defensive fleet, something he could deal with. Not an empire too vast for his capacity to subdue and occupy.

Quanshûk, he chided himself, *you worry needlessly. No empire can be that large.*

<><

Annika now had easily recognized cycles of sleep and waking. But her waking state was definitely not normal; mostly she lay on one side or the other in a fetal curl, her eyes open. From time to time she'd get up on her own to use the latrine, though it was Yukiko, or occasionally David, who cleaned her up. Or she'd sit up and repeat the single word "eat," until she was fed. Fortunately for her health, she'd stand up when Yukiko asked, and allow herself to be walked around their fifteen by twenty-foot chamber. Recently she'd even done simple exercises when led. But she was nothing like the happy child she'd been aboard the *Cousteau.*

Yukiko had been tempted to impose herself on Annika's odd state, and see if she could break her free of it, but the temptation was easily resisted. As David had said: what good would it do? The girl seemed content as she was.

He broke his wife's thought now with a whisper, breathy and without sibilance. They weren't sure whether the monitor picked up such whispers or not, but they needed *some* means of confidentiality. "What did you say?" she whispered back.

He repeated even more softly than before. "It was spooky, the way Qonits acted when he talked about the ship being jumped between galaxies. Do you think it actually happened?"

"I have no doubt at all." Yukiko barely breathed it.

Snuggled beside her, Annika neither doubted nor believed. She simply, unknowingly, passed it on to Kunming.

Chapter Twenty-Nine
Night Surprise

The night was moonless, the galaxy a banner of frost half seen through bare branches and twigs. Boots crunched recently-fallen leaves, loudly enough, it seemed to Esau, to be heard a hundred feet away. Until it rained again, there was no chance at all of slipping quietly through the woods.

His helmet gave him a choice of two night-vision enhancements. One provided positive night vision, which worked even in heavy forest and under thick clouds, but might be detected by an enemy. The other amplified natural starlight, moonlight if any, and whatever other light there might be. The army preferred the latter, when there was moonlight or enough starlight.

Isaiah Vernon had wondered aloud whether the Wyzhñyñy might have a way of detecting starlight vision, too. And of course no one knew, or would know till they fought.

At any rate Esau could see in the dark. See Jonas Timmins ahead of him, it being Jonas's time to lead the squad. Off to the left, twenty yards or so, was a meadow, with thin wispy fog on it. *Odds are,* Esau thought, *it'll thicken through the night.*

Ahead of Timmins was the rest of the platoon, and ahead of it, Ensign Berg, Sergeant Hawkins, and the point man.

Esau was a little irked that Timmins was leading 4th Squad tonight. He considered himself the rightful squad leader. But the ensign was giving others the experience, which Esau realized made sense. And Timmins was probably the next best leader after himself. Timmins and Jael. His wife had surprised him with her willingness and ability to make decisions and give orders. And to his further surprise, he liked her even better that way.

Somewhere up ahead, the ensign or Sergeant Hawkins raised an arm, and the file of trainees stopped silently. This was a simplified problem, Esau realized, one suited to their training level. Somewhere on the other side of the meadow, the platoon's scouts had spotted the enemy outpost. The platoon was to capture it. The problem had no broader context, strategic or tactical.

An order spoke in their ears, and the file became a rank, slinking toward the meadow's edge. Halfway there they dropped to their bellies and stopped. To lie waiting, while Timmins and the other squad leaders moved forward in a low crawl, to examine the ground with Hawkins and the ensign.

After a couple of minutes, Timmins spoke to his squad on their own frequency, ordering them to the forest edge. When they'd reached it, he spoke again. "4th Squad, we'll start out crawling; the vegetation'll cover us. And don't bunch up. See that pointy-topped fir sticking up above the hardwoods?" On Lüneburger's, the Jerries called any evergreen a "fir." "I'll guide on that. If anything happens to me" —they were being as realistic as they knew how— "Esau takes command. When we come under fire, proceed by teams. The teams that are covering, really pour it on."

They'll have starlight vision, too, Esau thought. *They'll spot us by the way the weeds move when we crawl through them.*

Timmins continued. "That worm fence down the middle is the sticky part. If anyone's over there, that's where they'll spot us. If we haven't come under fire before we cross it, climb over. Anyone not over before they start shooting at us, pull the fence apart and advance by crawling. Everyone that's across, lay down covering fire."

It was, Esau judged, about a hundred yards to the fence. Where he saw a complication: pulling the fence down would be easier said than done. The meadow hadn't been grazed that spring and summer; that was obvious. The livestock had been removed when the area was made a military reservation; that's why the vegetation was so tall. Along the fence, he could make out a row of naked saplings—probably a row along each side. Unbrowsed they'd flourished. Many were six feet tall or more, he judged. They'd tend to hold the rails in place.

He wondered if Sergeant Hawkins had spotted that. It would be like him to see if they came up with it themselves. If they didn't, he'd point it out later. Or maybe not. From things he'd said, Hawkins had grown up a town boy. He might miss something like that.

"2nd Platoon, listen up." This voice was Ensign Berg's, activating the platoon command frequency. "When you reach the fence, stop. Squad leaders tell me when your squad is there. Now move out."

Timmins moved out at once, on elbows and knees, his blaster cradled in his arms. The rest of the squad followed, almost even with him, losing themselves at once in the thick, falling-down meadow growth. From time to time Esau raised himself high enough to see the fir tree. *Either they're blind over there,* he told himself, *or they're waiting for us to reach the fence. We'll be better targets then, for sure.*

They were all good crawlers. They'd practiced a lot, and it didn't take long to cover a hundred yards. After a bit, 3rd Squad's leader announced his arrival at the fence. Almost at once, Timmins reported his. Esau and the rest of 4th Squad reached it at almost the same time. Then 1st and 2nd Squads reported.

"All right," the ensign said, "squad leaders send your squads."

"4th Squad," Timmins said, "1st Team over."

Esau got quickly to his feet, blaster in one hand, and bellied over the chest-high fence. He hadn't hit the ground before firing came from the woods ahead, the staccato popping and thumping of blasters and slammers, loud in the aggregate, each kicking out soft pulses at several per second. None had hit him; even soft pulses had an impact, and except for their helmets, they weren't wearing armor on this patrol. He took up a squat-firing position—the vegetation was too tall for firing prone—and began to shoot back. Near him on his right, Jael, the squad's grenadier, was launching a series of dummy phosphorous grenades, the butt of her launcher on the ground, braced against a foot. Behind him he could hear obscenities as 2nd Team struggled to pull the fence apart.

Ensign Berg ordered the platoon to move forward by

squads. Adding "keep low!" Crouching, Esau sprang forward, ran six strides, then dove for the ground, taking the impact on the butt of his blaster. Rolled sideways, then returned to the squat position to lay fire on the defenders. To his right, Timmins yelped—hit, Esau supposed. The red warning light on his HUD, his heads-up display, told him he needed to change his blaster's power slug. He did. Then Timmins shouted "1st Team go!", and Esau was on his feet again, ran another six strides and hit the ground. This time he remembered to squeeze off a burst while running.

Their cycle of rush, give covering fire, and rush again was repeated several times, and still he hadn't felt the impact of a blaster pulse. He wondered how many had. Surely if this was hard fire, some of them would be lying bloody behind him.

They were almost to the forest when warbots attacked, the weapons attached to their forearms pumping bursts of energy pulses. From their seven-foot height, they could easily target the trainees in the vegetation. Esau felt soft pulses slap him in chest and thigh. Without thinking, he fired a burst at the nearest bot, at the primary sensorium on the head, then dove, wrapping thick-muscled arms around its ankles. The bot crashed down, and he scrambled over it, grabbing at the head, going for the sensors. But stronger arms than his wrapped around him. "Gotcha," said a voice. Instead of giving up, Esau struggled.

Then cadre whistles shrilled; the exercise was over. The arms that pinioned him relaxed, and the warbot got up, rolling Esau off. For a moment he lay stunned, not from any blow, but by what he considered an unfair trick. Warbots! No one had said anything to them about the Wyzhñyñy having warbots!

◇

The platoon leaders were taken back to the regimental area by floater, to evaluate the exercise. The trainees marched back, led by their platoon sergeants. They marched "at ease" (no talking), left to their own thoughts, double-timing once they reached the road.

It was a lecture shed they went to, and did fifty pushups before going inside. 1st Platoon was also there; it had been their adversary in the game. The two platoons sat on opposite sides of the center aisle. Four bots were also there, sitting farther to the rear. It was Captain Mulvaney who reviewed the exercise with them.

"All right men," he said, "at ease." He looked them over. "Who here got hit, by any kind of weapon? I'm talking about before the warbots attacked."

Esau looked around. On 2nd Platoon's side of the aisle, nine hands raised. Considering all the shooting, he was surprised there weren't more. 1st Platoon had only four, but it had been dug in.

Mulvaney questioned everyone who'd raised their hand. Of the thirteen organics who'd raised theirs, eight would very probably have died.

"And who was hit during the warbot charge? Keep them up so I can count you."

Esau didn't try to count them. All four bots had been hit. They'd charged into the middle of it, been big targets and drawn lots of fire. "Seventeen," the CO said, "plus the bots. Okay, take them down. Your ensigns and Division's umpires all agree: 2nd Platoon, you carried out your approach and attack very professionally. 1st Platoon, you dug in effectively in the limited time you had, and fought a good defense."

He looked toward the bots. "Corporal Sciacca, where were you hit?"

"In the head, sir, by a blaster. A hard pulse would have ruined one of my ocular sensors. I also took hits on my chest and left leg, but even if they'd been hard pulses, neither one would have done damage."

"Thank you." Mulvaney paused, turning his gaze entirely on 2nd Platoon. "What did you think of the warbots?"

Esau's hand shot up. "Esau," the captain said.

"Sir, it wasn't fair to use warbots against us like that. No one told us the enemy had any. We didn't have a chance."

"War is seldom fair," Mulvaney answered, "and surprises are part of it. So far as we know, the Wyzhñyñy don't have warbots, but they'll have something dangerous we don't expect.

When fighting an enemy we know so little about, we can expect more surprises than usual, mostly unpleasant. This evening you got some notion of what it can be like.

"Some of you responded very well, incidentally."

Mulvaney turned his attention to 1st Platoon. "1st Platoon, Division's umpires estimate you took twenty casualties from phosphorous burns. You've seen demonstrations of what that can mean, so you can be grateful this was an exercise, with dummy grenades."

He paused, scanning both platoons. "The reason we didn't have you feign death when hit was, we didn't want you to forego the complete action. In combat, of course, when you're hit, you're hit. When you're burned, you're burned." Another pause. "History tells us that many soldiers go through numerous actions without being wounded, but there are also actions where casualties are very heavy. The best chance you have of coming through, of winning and surviving, is by working as a team." Again he paused. "Let's hear you say it: 'We work as a team!'"

"We work as a team!" they answered.

"Say it like you mean it!"

This time they shouted: "WE WORK AS A TEAM!"

Mulvaney grinned. "Good. I got that. And there are other things: we keep the enemy under heavy fire. Say it!"

"WE KEEP THE ENEMY UNDER HEAVY FIRE!"

"We maintain contact with the enemy."

"WE MAINTAIN CONTACT WITH THE ENEMY!"

"We are aggressive."

"WE ARE AGGRESSIVE!"

"All right! You will learn more about all these things over the weeks to come, including when and where they *don't* apply. You will practice till doing the right thing is as natural as breathing. And when you first go into battle, you'll be as good as you can get, short of actual combat experience." He paused, raised his voice. "You want to know what surprise really is? Surprise…" He slowed, his voice softening, becoming confidential. "Surprised is what the Wyzhñyñy will be the first time they tangle with you. They're going to wish they'd stayed wherever they came from."

He hadn't anticipated the cheers he got. Inwardly it shook him. He'd have given his life to cancel this war and send his trainees home, but it wasn't an option. For anyone. The Wyzhñyñy had come, and there was nothing that would cause them to leave, short of defeat. And there was no reason to expect even defeat to drive them away. If they had to be hunted down and wiped out on each world they'd occupied, this would be a truly hellish war.

Chapter Thirty
"And God Created Humankind in Her Own Image"

Over the past century, summers had shortened and cooled substantially as far south as the Dakota Prefecture. And the Keewatin Ice Sheet—actually the fifth-year firn line, deep in metamorphosed snow—had reached the north end of Canada's Reindeer Lake. The previous winter's snow had survived the summer southward almost to Lac La Ronge. Four hundred and fifty miles north of Reindeer Lake, near the heart of the ice sheet, soundings reported an average of more than eighty feet of ice, with plastic flow on slopes.

Not surprisingly, Saskatoon's population was less than a third that of 250 years earlier. Over the past two decades, a congregation of the Reformed Church of the Holy Mother (Gaean), had formed there, centering on the campus of a defunct Church of the Divine Liturgy. The long decline of real estate values had attracted members of the sect from all over Terra, making Saskatoon the RCHM capital of the world. One of its activities was the production of "The Daily Worldwide News Roundup," broadcast from warm and pleasant Oaxaca, Mexico, by Gaea Worldwide, an ecumenical network of Gaean sects. It claimed a listener base of 80 million—roughly point-zero-seven percent of the planetary population.

Worldwide was part of the Peace Front, but Jaromir Horvath and Paddy Davies seldom listened to their program. The Gaean sects had not been major players. But the two leaders had been notified that the Gaea Worldwide would release a shocker on the Roundup, at noon Greenwich and at intervals afterward. So both men were tuned in, Horvath in Kunming, and Davies in Sydney. They'd discuss afterward whether to follow through on it.

The roundup began with a summary of refugee labor battalions: their locations, projects, home worlds, and the number of refugees "enslaved." Old stuff, thought Horvath. Obviously not the promised bombshell.

Next was a report from "an anonymous source high within the government." Horvath's ears perked up; Gaea was trying to add authority to what came next.

A different voice read it, the accent British. "Kunming," it said, "has inaugurated a new and unspeakable outrage against humanity and the Holy Mother. This station has previously uncovered Kunming's unconscionable use of mentally handicapped persons as slaves for War House. Now the government has taken those vile, soul-corrupting acts a long and evil step further. They have conscripted a large number of severely handicapped children and have…" The voice stumbled, paused. "Have *murdered* them!—butchered them like animals, then ripped out their brains and spinal cords and transplanted them into what are termed…'bottles!'" He almost choked on the word. "Bottled innocence! Human beings designed by Gaea's holy evolution as the ultimate life form for Planet Terra. In bottling the pitiful shards of these sad creatures, Kunming, under the leadership of Chang Lung-Chi and Foster Peixoto, has not only enslaved the souls of these children. Their very humanity has been stolen. They are being installed in guided missiles, and assigned to Kunming's war fleet for use in the brutal war against our visitors from deep space.

"This incredible atrocity proves the utter depravity of our elected government. I urge everyone listening to waste no time in spreading the word, personally and electronically, to everyone you know."

Horvath's first reaction was how incredibly cliché-ridden the script was. It discredited the story, and would deflect uncommitted listeners. But he believed the underlying claim, and muting the audio, called Paddy Davies in Sydney.

<>

Foster Peixoto's phone trilled. "Yes, Ilse?"

"You have a call from Director Al-Kathad, sir."

"I'll take it." It seemed to him that an unexpected call from the Director of Internal Security would not bring good news. "Peixoto," he said.

"Mr. Prime Minister, this is Nabil Al-Kathad. I have a recorded radio broadcast you should hear, broadcast ten hours ago. It was just now brought to my attention. I recommend you record it."

Peixoto touched a switch. "Very well, the recorder is on. Let's hear it."

The director began with a brief rundown on Gaea Worldwide, and the Reformed Church of the Holy Mother (Gaean). Then he played the cube, his eyes on the prime minister's long thin face, reading annoyance in it.

When it was over, Peixoto thought for a moment. "I want you here in my office in thirty minutes," he said. "You and Chief Kumoyama."

In his office, thought Al-Kathad. *Unusual.* "Certainly, Your Excellency."

The prime minister disconnected at once, and his fingers rapped out another number, this one at Special Projects. "Dr. Franck," he said, "I need you here in thirty minutes, to meet with the president, myself, Director Al-Kathad, and his Chief of Investigations." He paused. "Meanwhile I want you to hear a radio address, broadcast by a station in Oaxaca, Mexico. Please record it."

He gave her a moment to activate record mode, then turned on the cube with the director's comments and the Gaean broadcast. He listened again himself, while watching Dr. Franck's slender brown face. When it was over, she switched off record mode and was about to speak. The prime minister cut her off. "Be in my office in twenty-five minutes," he said, and disconnected.

He could deal with this without the president, he told himself, but Chang would want to be involved. A long finger tapped a dedicated switch. They'd eaten lunch together half an hour earlier; the president would be at his desk now.

"President Chang's office."

"Good afternoon, Setsuko. This is the prime minister. I would like to speak with the president please."

"I believe the president is indisposed for the moment.

Shall I interrupt him?"

Chang, like himself, had a phone in the private bathroom off his office. But no. "I'll wait," Peixoto said.

"Thank you, sir. It shouldn't be long."

An anonymous source, Peixoto thought. *If we have a traitor, we need to know who.* From the comments it wasn't a highly placed source. Someone overheard something in the office, or at lunch, and made up the rest. *Installed in missiles for godsake!*

He became aware he was grinding his teeth, a habit he'd defeated years before. Stopping, he took three long breaths: in, one two three; hold, one two; out, one two three four... *Our first concern is to counter this attack,* he told himself. *It is not one we can ignore. Detecting the source comes second.* He fidgeted impatiently, his mind moving back to the leak. *The most direct approach would be to interrogate the Gaeans who obtained the story, but they are unlikely to inform.* An investigation of staff would distract from the many jobs at hand, but it would also tend to increase their awareness of the risks. On the other hand, if actual treason was uncovered...

His phone warbled again, and he reached for the switch, wondering what the president would say.

<>

When their meeting was over, Peixoto was glad the president had attended, for the strategy they'd agreed on was Chang's. They would not attack the Gaeans. They would take the issue away from them. Broadcast a prime-time special, publicizing the project as giving dying children a chance at extended life in a—call it a "life module," or something like that. *Not* a "bottle." While at the same time filling a vital, non-violent defense need. The truth would outweigh Peace Front ranting.

There was no need to feel apologetic about defense; the polls confirmed that regularly. A promotional video would be made, beginning with crippled, mentally retarded children declining toward death. Afterward they'd show newly "converted" savants functioning as communicators. And painting, doing mental computing, listening to music…whatever their personal play might be. Franck, at Special Projects, would assign and oversee production responsibility, and run quality control.

Chang was confident it would work with the public. Peixoto, on the other hand, could visualize it backfiring if it wasn't done well. Franck assured them it would work beautifully, and that she knew just the producer for the job. Al-Kathad and Kumoyama hadn't volunteered their opinions; they'd been there to discuss the security problem, and how the source might be found. But Al-Kathad's face suggested skepticism. He was skeptical by nature, of course; it went with his profession.

With some misgivings, the prime minister had given the go-ahead on the project. They'd know soon enough how successful it was.

Chapter Thirty-One
Airborne!

The sweat shed had had only the body heat of the trainees, initially twelve platoons, to warm it above the frosty morning. Twelve platoons, one selected from each company in the regiment. Captain Mulvaney had chosen 2nd Platoon.

The shed was large and strange, as well as cold, with no lecture platform and no "pulpit"—the Jerrie term for lectern. But Esau had gotten used to strangeness. By now he felt at home in the army, though it was a lot different from his favorite army in Scripture: Gideon's, whose warriors had lapped water like a dog.

He smiled inwardly, imagining Gideon's Hebrew warriors sitting crowded on benches, with parachutes strapped on their backs. A strange thought, even though Sergeant Hawkins had said their airborne trainers were themselves Hebrews, from a world called Masada. A world whose people still spoke the Hebrew tongue; now *that* was strange.

It was also strange to have their Sikh cadre—even Captain Mulvaney!—training with them, with Masadans as instructors. The division's Sikhs had all been airborne trained, Hawkins had told them, but War House had decided they'd retake the training.

Esau's eyes focused on Hawkins a couple of benches ahead, and he wondered what his sergeant was thinking about.

◇

Hawkins wasn't thinking; that is, he wasn't processing data. He was meditating. He'd begun by focusing on his breathing cadence, which from long experience produced a deepening calm. And a viewpoint exterior not only to events, but largely to his own personality. Nonetheless, he was aware of his surroundings. He saw a door open—the benches faced it—and a Masadan sergeant stepped in. Heard the man call for C and D Companies' platoons, and watched some eighty men get to their feet. Burdened with chute packs and hampered by harness, they sidled to the aisle and filed out. Most of the benches had already been empty; the Masadans had begun with K and L Companies' contingents, and were working their way toward A and B.

Despite that calm exterior viewpoint, Hawkins could flip out of trance and into action instantly. In more profound trances, a meditator might be oblivious to physical events, but Sikhs didn't court oblivion or bliss. Gopal Singh had advocated meditation to enhance living, not avoid it.

◇

Isaiah Vernon often sought to enhance his life by silent prayer. For the most part he'd lived life cautiously, and stepping out of floaters far above the ground was seriously out of character for him. But dedication and duty were very much in character, and he was determined to be a strong and effective soldier for God and humankind. To calm his fear of jumping into what he thought of as nothingness, he sat praying and reciting Scripture in the privacy of his mind. At the moment he was repeating: "The Lord is my shepherd, I shall not want. He makes me lie down in green pastures; he leads me beside still waters; he restores my soul...."

◇

Jael Wesley dealt quite differently with her nerves. In her mind's eye, she'd been jumping from a floater—without a chute—and watching the ground rush up at her. At the last moment she snatched herself away, back inside the floater, then jumped again, and again, until she was bored with it. The technique was nothing she'd been taught; it had simply occurred to her.

◇

Beside her, Esau sat calmly unconcerned. He thought about the briefing Captain Mulvaney had given them, on why they were being trained as paragliders. Paragliding was an ancient technique, something the Wyzhñyñy were unlikely to expect. So on New Jerusalem, paraglider platoons would come silently down into Wyzhñyñy positions at night, and with luck, wouldn't be detected till they were on the ground raising Cain.

He was glad that 2nd Platoon had been chosen. In his mind, paragliders were special.

Paraglider raids would be particularly dangerous of course, but Division didn't intend they do a lot of it. The main reason for doing it at all was that War House wanted Wyzhñyñy prisoners. The Wyzhñyñy had rejected human surrenders, so they probably wouldn't surrender themselves. Getting prisoners would take special measures, and paragliders seemed the best bet.

The danger was something Esau knew mentally, but not yet viscerally. He couldn't recall ever being afraid for more than a moment; not in his entire life. His most intense emotion in life had been anger, and for whatever reason, during the course of military training his temper had grown more moderate and less frequent. Which pleased him. He'd wondered if daily contact with Sikhs had anything to do with it.

The shed door opened again, and a burly Masadan called in. "A and B Companies on your feet and file out!"

2nd Platoon, along with Captain Mulvaney and Lieutenant Bremer, shuffled to the nearest aisle and out into the autumn sunlight. There'd been a shower the day before, and this morning the ground was frozen. *Only thinly though,* Esau thought as they walked to the floater. No more than a crust. It hadn't been cold enough to freeze solid.

The transport floater was ten feet wide but low, a semi-cylinder flattened on the bottom, with a wide entry/exit at the rear, where a ramp had extruded for boarding. The troop compartment was a more solid version of the roughly-made stationary mockups they'd practiced in. There were two long benches, one down each side. When all the trainees were seated, the Masadan jump master murmured to the pilot via the microphone strapped to his wrist. A moment later, the seventy-foot armored floater lifted on its silent AG drive and they were on their way. Esau wished there were windows to look out of.

He ran through the jump drill in his mind. It was simple enough; no one was likely to screw up. Refuse to jump maybe, but not screw up. Captain Mulvaney had said that anyone who couldn't do it should stay in their seat and not interfere with the flow to the doors. Esau glanced at Jael beside him. It occurred to him that being a woman, this might be too much for her, and that if she couldn't jump, she might be transferred to a different platoon. But he reminded himself that when she decided to do something, she wasn't one to back down.

It was a ten-minute flight to the drop area. The word was, it had been plowed, then harrowed, to provide softer landings. Also, for safety, the trainees wore no equipment except their chutes. They'd been told that with the parachutes they wore today, they'd fall faster than with parasails—about twenty feet per second in Lüneburger's gravity. That seemed awfully fast, but they'd been assured that on mass jumps, these chutes were safer than parasails. There was less risk of tangling in each other's lines.

A buzzer sounded. "Stand up!" called the jump master. On both sides of Esau and across the aisle, trainees got to their feet—*but to his dismay, his own legs failed to obey the order!* For a horrified second, Esau couldn't move. Then Jael's hand was on his sleeve, pulling, and somehow he managed to stand, his mind a fog of utter shock and confusion. Upright, his knees felt watery, as if he might sink to the floor.

"Hook up."

It was all well-drilled. On its own, his hand unhooked the static-line snap from its D-ring, hooked it onto the jump cable overhead, and tugged sharply. His mind, however, was frozen. "Sound off for equipment check." Each jumper, including Esau, checked the chute pack of the man ahead of him, and reported. "Twelve okay!" he called hoarsely.

"Stand to the door!" The two files shuffled toward the ten-foot wide exit, each jumper sliding his static line along his file's jump cable. Esau felt paralyzed; Jael's hand on his back helped him move. Now the first man in each file stood in the exit looking out, a jump master beside him, eddies of cold wind snapping at his trousers. The others crowded behind. Esau's guts churned, and it seemed to him he was suffocating. Actually he'd stopped breathing.

He didn't see the light flash above the exit, didn't even hear the buzzer. He knew only that Masadan voices were shouting "Go! Go! Go!" The men in the doors had stepped out, the trainees behind them following quickly. Jael's helping hand was pushing, and somehow Esau kept pace. Then 3rd Squad was out, and the exit's lip was at his feet—the exit and empty air. For just an instant he hesitated. His jumpmaster's meaty hand slapped his shoulder, and his feet obeyed, his traitorous mouth wailing feebly. He felt the jolt as his chute opened...and suddenly he was floating beneath its mottled green canopy—with a sense not of fear but exultation! Beneath him—2,300 feet beneath him—was the ground. He laughed aloud. His mental paralysis of a moment before was gone as if it had never been.

He gave it no attention, simply looked around. Parachutes formed irregular twin lines in the chill air. Invigorating! *Pay attention,* he reminded himself. *You're supposed to be learning.* As if paragliding, he examined the field for non-existent obstacles. As he approached the ground, it seemed to accelerate toward him, a false apparency they'd been warned about. *Don't reach for it,* he reminded himself. Landing straight-legged destroyed knees. At almost the last moment he looked ahead, then felt the impact, and reflexively did a proper landing roll. Coming to his feet, he pulled in his risers and suspension lines, collapsing his chute. It was over.

He'd have happily gone back up at once, and jumped again.

◇

"At once" was not an option. The rest of the day they went back to the physical regimen of infantry training, harder than ever, as if to make up for an easy morning. After supper, they did a ninety-minute speed march with sixty-pound sandbags and flak jackets. But at 2130 that evening, the platoon and its company CO and XO, were back in the sweat shed, waiting for the platoon's first night jump. No one had failed to jump that morning. Esau wondered if any of the others had felt as he had. It seemed to him he wouldn't have made it without Jael.

I sure as heck won't let that happen again, he thought, and behind the thought was total warrior intention.

This time the selected platoons from A and B Companies were tabbed to go first. As 2nd Platoon shuffled to its carrier, Esau noticed the brisk breeze. When they'd arrived twenty minutes earlier, it hadn't been half as strong, he was sure. They'd been told in their first lecture that for safety reasons, War House had decreed that no training jumps be made in wind stronger than 18 knots. On New Jerusalem there were no anemometers, and he had no real sense of what an 18-knot wind felt like, but it seemed to him this might be stronger.

Still, he told himself, the Masadans knew what they were doing. Aboard the floater, he felt as calm as he had that morning when he'd boarded. But this time, he knew, there would be no water-kneed paralysis. Reaching, he squeezed Jael's hand in reassurance. Eight minutes later, the jump master ordered them to stand, and they went through the drill again, Esau grinning widely. He literally dove from the exit, and with his head-down attitude, the opening shock jerked him viciously.

He hardly noticed. The night was clear, quiet, dark— *peaceful!*—and seemed more beautiful than any he'd ever seen before. The sky glittered with stars. The wind began oscillating him like a pendulum, and he reached the ground on the upswing, softening the landing. Then the wind in his chute was dragging him briskly on his side, and he half-twisted onto his belly, powerful arms pulling in his front risers and suspension lines, spilling the air from his canopy.

He stopped. Jerking the safety clip on his harness, he hit the release sharply, gathered chute and harness into a great wad of fabric and cords, then strode toward the headlights of the bus coming to pick them up. He felt big enough, powerful enough, to eat the world.

◇

The next day was Sevenday; for B Company, a pass Sevenday. They slept in till 0730 and there was no morning run. After breakfast, Speaker Spieler held a religious service for the trainees. An early lunch followed, then those who wanted to, rode trucks in to North Fork. Esau and Jael among them. Since week seven, when they'd become eligible for passes, they'd spent their free afternoons in a by-the-hour room at a small hotel. With so much night training, they hadn't been visiting the water heater room much.

When they'd spent themselves, they dressed again and went outside to walk, holding hands. Old wives' summer lay on the land. The air was still, the sun soft with autumn haze, and Riverfront Park was carpeted with fallen leaves.

"What was it like for you yesterday morning?" he asked. "Jumping and all."

"Not too bad," she said, "until I started toward the door. Then I felt really scared."

"Really?"

"Really."

"Not as scared as me, I'll bet. If you hadn't helped me, I couldn't have done it. My brain was froze, and my knees were like water. I wouldn't have been any scareder with a tiger chasing me." He paused. "But as soon as I was out the door—bang! No way can I tell you how great it felt! When I got down, I wanted to go up and do it again. Right away. And last night was just as good. Maybe better, because the sky was so beautiful."

"It was, wasn't it." Jael paused. "About being scared that first time, scared of going out the door— Remember what Hosea Innis said that night, when we talked about warbots with Sergeant Hawkins?"

"Remind me."

"He said if he'd ever come across a tiger and didn't have so much as his ax, why even innocent as the Lamb of God, he'd be scared to death. Because while the soul goes to heaven, the body knows it's going to get killed and eaten." She looked up at her husband. "It was our bodies were scared. They did *not* want to jump out that door! And when they found out it was all right, the relief was so big, we felt really really good." Esau nodded thoughtfully, then stopped and kissed her. "You know what?" he said. "I'm married to the wisest woman in the world."

She chuckled. "How about the prettiest?"

"That too," he answered, and kissed her again. "You know something else I really really like?" he murmured. "Better than jumping out of a floater?"

This time she laughed out loud. "Let's go back to the hotel," she said.

◇

Over the next two weeks, each of the paraglider platoons made three free-fall jumps with parasail chutes. The first was by daylight from 4,000 feet, wearing high-altitude jump suits. The trainees needed to get used to them, and even at only 4,000 feet, these autumn days were freezing, or close to it.

Combat jumps would be at night, but the Masadans, demanding though they were, knew the value of training gradients. The trainees had been given a target to hit, a hundred-yard circle a mile from the flight path. Every jumper in 2nd Platoon came down inside the circle. And they all liked the parasails, which set them down less hard than the mass-jump chutes they'd used before. The second parasail jump was at night from 12,000 feet, their target a ring of unlit cloth panels eight miles away, invisible till they were near it. Until close in, they'd been guided by passive gravitic matrix detectors, read as a heads-up display on the face plate of their jump helmet. They'd done it in virtual training, but needed to experience it for real.

Two missed the target, and were taken back up immediately, to try again.

Meanwhile of course, they continued their infantry training, which was extended two weeks to accommodate the addition of paraglide and warbot training.

◇

On the following Oneday, 2nd Platoon made its graduation jump. By then, Camp Voldemars Stenders was no longer Camp Mud Hole. Or Dust Hole. Deep-freeze temperatures had arrived, hardening the ground like stone.

It had already been decided to run this exercise in the subtropics. Their target would be an abandoned paddock, on an artillery range five hours by floater from Stenders. The operation was to be as realistic as feasible. There were even unwilling prisoners to be captured. Meanwhile an enemy might very well have detected the floater, perhaps even recognized it as hostile, but they'd hardly connect it to the intended capture site. The floater would pass it twenty miles to the west.

◇

Forty miles short of the jump point, the carrier had slowed to 200 mph, hopefully still fast enough not to draw suspicion. The jump would be made at the same speed. And until they were on the ground, the only electronic gear the jumpers would activate was their heads-up displays.

They had run and rerun this mission on sand tables, complete with imaginary enemy responses. But this was no sand table. Now they sat on bench seats 30,000 feet above the ground, in a nearly silent floater. Some stared at nothing, their attention inward. Some slumped, dozing. A buzzer sounded, loud and coarse, jerking them alert.

"One minute to amber!" The voice was the pilot's.

This time they had no Masadan jumpmaster. Ensign Berg stood at one side of the exit, Sergeant Hawkins at the other. The floater arrived at the ready location. Above the door, the amber waiting light flashed on. The trainees got to their feet and did an equipment check. Static lines weren't used.

The amber light flicked off, and the green ready light came on. The double doors spread, and the two files of trainees shuffled toward them.

Exhilaration flowed through Esau Wesley; this was the life! Again the buzzer sounded, the red light flashed and the files moved, jumpers disappearing out the exit at a measured pace, one of Ensign Berg's, followed by one of Sergeant Hawkins'. Then Esau was at the lip, felt the ensign's hand slap his shoulder, and stepped out. The slipstream snatched him, then released him, and for a moment he seemed to hang suspended in the starry night. They'd been warned of the illusion. He maneuvered his arms and legs for a good opening position, then pulled his ripcord and felt the fabric feed out. There was no shock; he simply swung forward. Even the oscillation quickly damped and disappeared.

He spoke the words "activate hud" to his helmet, and his heads-up display turned on, hair-thin lines lit against the backdrop of night. A red X showed near the top; the target. Near the bottom was a green arrow point, himself. The arrow pointed to the right, so he pulled lightly and evenly on his left control line until the arrow aimed at the X. Small numerals at bottom-left read 29,612—his altitude, referenced to the landing site. Next to it was the wind vector, an unobtrusive arrow with a shaft, the windspeed indicated by the shaft length and small numerals. At his altitude, there wasn't much wind at the moment. Then he jettisoned his reserve chute and its weight.

They'd been forbidden to activate their comm headsets till they were on the ground, in case the electronic signature was too strong. Again two keywords activated his night vision. Peering around, he could see other parasails, higher, lower, ahead, behind... Deactivating it, he settled down for the long, slow glide to the target. He could already sense the cold around him.

◇

Isaiah Vernon felt his usual pre-jump tension and post-jump exhilaration. Glancing up, he saw his black canopy against the stars, then unclipped his reserve chute and let it fall, just as he would on a combat jump. But did it out of sequence; he hadn't checked his HUD. When he did check it, the position arrow was rotating, not pointing somewhere.

Pulling on a control line—either control line—made no difference. Something was seriously wrong! His first impulse was to radio his predicament, but this exercise was to simulate reality. Besides, there was nothing anyone could do for him, and once he was down, he could call for help.

Again he checked his canopy, this time with night vision. His problem was a lineover, presumably due to faulty packing. Two suspension lines had gotten across the canopy, and instead of one large airfoil, he had what amounted to three small airfoils. One was ejecting air sideways, producing the rotation. His HUD showed him falling much faster than he should.

He responded quickly, climbing a riser hand over hand. When the connector link was in his reach, he pulled on its suspension lines. His thickly gloved hands were clumsy and the lines thin, but he was strong, and under the circumstances, driven. He continued climbing, partly collapsing his parasail, his rate of fall increasing markedly. Reaching the skirt of the parasail, he struggled to dislodge what seemed to him the lineover most susceptible to dislodging. What he succeeded in doing was collapsing the canopy entirely.

He let go. A moment later the sail caught air and reopened, but still with the lineovers.

I am going to die, he told himself, then shook the thought off and looked again at his HUD. His rate of descent was sixty-seven feet per second. At that rate, he thought, he'd end up mush when he hit. They'd bring him in in his helmet. Then he remembered a Masadan officer telling them the nearer they got to the ground, the thicker the air would be. That should slow him, but would it be enough? It seemed highly unlikely.

His rate of fall slowed to 64 fps. Possibly, just possibly… On the elevation readout, the tens column was a blur. The hundreds were peeling off rapidly, and the thousands inexorably. He jettisoned his blaster, his rucksack, and everything else removable, slowing to 47 fps.

Speaking to his helmet, he switched off all displays and deactivated his night vision. "Father in heaven," he said quietly, "into your hands I commend my spirit." Briefly he looked downward. A few miles to the north was a town, electric lights in its windows. There were people there—families, children—living their lives and worshiping the same God he worshiped. For a moment he felt love swell in him for those unknown Lüneburgians. It seemed the most natural thing in the universe to do.

Then he turned his attention to David's most beloved psalm. "…Even though I walk through the valley of the shadow of death," he recited, "I fear no evil; for you are with me; your rod and your staff—they comfort me. You prepare a table before me…."

<>

Jael Wesley was intent on her HUD. She'd timed her forward speed well; she'd make the paddock nicely before she hit. Hopefully without having to spiral in.

Briefly she activated her night vision. Too far to see yet; she switched it off. The HUD gave horizontal distance to center target as 2.07 miles, and altitude 915 feet. At this level there was an eight-knot breeze, not enough to worry about, as long as she didn't have to buck it. The paddock was said to be about one acre. At one mile she slowed her forward speed, and at half a mile tried her night vision again. Now she could see the intended prisoners clearly, scattered but mostly near the fence. She'd hoped they'd be bunched up.

Deactivating her HUD to avoid distraction, she adjusted her speed and direction by night vision. Her job was to land at the far side of the paddock and suppress fire from outlying "enemy guard positions." She swung wide, sizing up the guard positions while button-hooking to use up altitude and avoid the fence. Somewhere out there, A Company should already have arrived, and be lying in support, ready to attack the guards.

But A Company made too much noise, and from the enemy outposts came blaster fire, directed not toward the paddock, but outward. In response, A Company's grenade launchers flashed, followed quickly by the pops of training grenades around the guard positions. No sooner had the grenades landed than with blood-curdling shrieks, A Company's raiders rushed the enemy positions with fixed bayonets, blasters spewing soft pulses. Jael freed her rucksack and felt it jerk the dangle strap.

She was almost down, and braked. Her feet touched lightly, three running steps using up her momentum. She hit her harness release, released her blaster tie-down, and crouched by the fence, ready to provide supporting fire as needed.

The capture teams were already in action. The intended prisoners consisted of twenty calves, each weighing about 250 pounds Terran. Unarmed though they were, the calves resisted, running madly to avoid would-be captors, and struggling when caught. One nearly trampled Jael. She fired a burst of soft pulses as it careened toward her, so that it fell skidding in its effort to turn. Someone grabbed it, threw it back down, and struggled to tie its hooves. After several minutes of running, rassling, and whooping with laughter, the capture action ended with the landing of two floaters inside the paddock. Jerries dragged the tied "prisoners" to the ramps, then cut the ties and let them go. All that was left to do was muster, board the floaters and leave.

The mission was over.

◇

It was at muster they learned that Isaiah Vernon was not with them, and no one had seen him since they'd jumped. Nor could anyone there pick up his transponder. Using one of the floaters' high-powered radios, Captain Mulvaney called Division.

Yes, he was told, Isaiah Vernon's transponder had activated, giving his geogravitic coordinate. An ambulance floater from the artillery range had already picked him up, and he was being rushed to the division hospital.

Why Division? Jael wondered. *Didn't the artillery training camp have a hospital? Or perhaps his injuries weren't so bad.* Somehow though, it seemed to her they were.

◇

They learned the next day how severe they were, when Captain Mulvaney reviewed their graduation exercise with the entire company. Division's umpires had given B Company's paragliders a grade of "very good." Then he told them about Isaiah. "Apparently trainee Vernon's parasail malfunctioned," he said gravely, "after he'd jettisoned his reserve chute. He hit the ground very hard; his knees and leg bones were shattered. He also had broken lumbar vertebrae and critical internal injuries. The medics kept him alive with life support equipment and an injection of Stasis 1. They assured me there was no chance at all that he'd have lived long in that devastated body."

Mulvaney paused, and when he continued, used the trainee's given name. "Isaiah signed a warbot agreement last SixMonth, so he's been bottled. When the sedative has worn off, he'll undergo therapy for neural trauma and be tested for neural functionality. But the conversion team doubts that he can function as a warbot."

After the CO had finished, Speaker Spieler led the company in a prayer for Isaiah—not simply for his survival, but beseeching God that their brother could fight as a warbot.

Afterward, more than thirty new agreements were signed by B Company trainees.

◇

Esau considered signing, and talked to Jael about it. "That's fine, if you want to," she answered. "But I've decided not to. I want to have babies if I possibly can, whether I'm crippled or not."

Esau nodded. "Well then," he said firmly, "I won't either." And chuckled. "Because if you have babies, I want to be the father."

Chapter Thirty-Two
The War at Home

"Mr. Garmisch, Supervisor Reinholdt will see you now."

Paul Garmisch got uneasily to his feet. He didn't know what this was about, but a guilty conscience had made him wary. The production supervisor's receptionist was indicating a door. It had opened, and a neatly-dressed, athletic-looking man waited by it. He was not Supervisor Reinholdt, but neither was he an office assistant. He looked too hard, too sure.

"Come in Mr. Garmisch," the man said.

The words, the tone, were mild, but to Paul Garmisch they sounded sinister. Garmisch was addicted to adventure cubes, and now he realized what this man reminded him of. He looked like the CIS men on shows about crime detection.

Garmisch entered the office. It was not Production Supervisor Reinholdt who sat behind the desk. It was a woman, someone Garmisch had never seen before. Reinholdt stood to her left, somewhat removed. "Please sit down, Mr. Garmisch," the woman said, and beckoned toward a chair. To her right, also not close, was another man, seated in a chair with a monitor arm and keypad. A small, brown, wiry man with probing, deep-seeing eyes; inwardly Garmisch squirmed, trying to escape them. A foreign immigrant, he thought. Perhaps a Malay. He'd known a Malay family once. The parents had looked somewhat like this man.

The woman repeated herself. "Please be seated, Mr. Garmisch. I am Ms Sriharan."

She did not identify her function. The omission troubled Garmisch, and so did the chair she'd indicated. He'd never seen one like it before. It stood apart, on a low, apparently portable platform. He stayed where he was. "What is this about?" he asked. His tone was neither challenging nor indignant. It was wary. Frightened.

"I am about to tell you. But first, please sit down." She still sounded affable, looked affable. Her name was foreign, perhaps Asian he thought, but from her blond hair and blue eyes, she could be pure German. Garmisch did not consider himself hostile to non-Germans. "Let them live here, work here, vote here." He'd said it more than once. But he regretted genetic mixing, certainly with non-Nordics.

It was, he knew, much too late to be prevented. Non-Nordics had been trickling in for centuries. Perhaps as far back as the Troubles. (In school, history hadn't taken with him.) After a few generations, little remained of their origins except foreign surnames, sometimes dark skin. African hair. He himself was of mixed origin; it was hardly avoidable. But in his case, so far as he knew, his non-German ancestors were Aryan: Moldavian, Polish, and Croat. In school he had even taken German as one of his electives, learning it well enough to carry on limited conversations.

"Mr. Garmisch," she said. Her voice was still mild. "If you do not sit down, I must arrest you."

Garmisch looked at her, then at "the CIS man," then the Malay. *What is a Malay doing here?* he wondered. *And what is he thinking?* Hesitantly he stepped to the chair and sat. Perhaps, he told himself, the questions would not be about what he feared. Perhaps he had no reason to worry.

"Thank you, Mr. Garmisch. Let me complete the introductions." She gestured toward the supposed Malay. "This is Forensic Technologist Balaug, and the gentleman who admitted you is Senior Investigator VerDoorn. Both are of the Commonwealth Internal Security Directorate. You already know Supervisor Reinholdt, of course. He was kind enough to let us use his office."

The security directorate! The confirmation added weight to the stone in Garmisch's belly. He looked from one to the other. Ms Sriharan leaned back in her chair like someone who'd just eaten a very fine meal. "It has been brought to our attention," she said, "that military blasters assembled on your line have been found defective. The assembler program had been altered, and a small but essential component was omitted, converting each blaster to a small but quite deadly bomb. A man died testing one; it blew his head quite off, and his arms to the elbows. We trust you can enlighten us on how this came to be."

Garmisch looked at Production Supervisor Reinholdt, who looked back at him grimly. Garmisch's gaze turned to his knees, and stayed there. It seemed to him that at the very least he would be discharged from his position. It was a good position. In these days, of course, there were many good jobs, but if they decided that what he had done was deliberate…

"First though," she continued, "let me advise you that you are not required to answer our questions. What you tell us may be used against you in a court of justice. Or to exonerate you, as the case may be."

They know. They surely know. I prepared the assembler program. I am in charge of it. Perhaps if I help them… Otherwise, it seemed certain he would be put in prison, where there were dangerous people who might harm him, beat him up for pleasure, or stab him to death so he could never tell what he knew. Inwardly he shivered.

Ms Sriharan was looking steadily at him, as was Supervisor Reinholdt. And the Malay, and the senior investigator, whose names had not registered with him. They were all looking at him, waiting for him to speak.

"I have a neighbor," he said softly, as if not wanting to be overheard. "Sometimes he asked me into his apartment, where we would drink beer together, and talk. It is very nice to drink beer with someone and talk. One time he asked me if I would like to go to a football game with him. He had tickets. 'There is always a party afterward,' he said. 'There will be women, some of them looking for a good man….'"

<>

The prime minister's office, 5,000 miles from Leipzig, was considerably larger than Supervisor Reinholdt's. And the people gathered there were interested in the broad issue of sabotage, of which defective blasters were only a part.

It may be time," the prime minister said, "to take the issue to the public. Saboteurs have presented us with several cases having the potential of great harm, including defective equipment in warships and armored floaters. Even defective stasis lockers on troopships. All potentially serious, and a drag on the defense effort.

"Now, from Lüneburger's World, we have a case in which several parachutes arrived from the Indonesian Autonomous Republic improperly packed. One of them was used in a training exercise, and a soldier nearly lost his life—a nineteen-year-old from New Jerusalem. His body was effectively destroyed; he would not have survived the day, had he not signed a warbot agreement."

Foster looks worn out, the president thought, *and the day has little more than begun; he needs more sleep.* He would not, however, urge it on him. Defense of the human species took priority. Perhaps if his ability to function seemed threatened... But his friend would never agree to ease off. He'd argue that in Terran gravity, Lunies habitually looked tired.

"I have heretofore been reluctant to bring the sabotage problem to the public attention," Peixoto went on. "Publicizing crimes sometimes does more harm than good, by stimulating others to commit similar acts. Especially political crimes by extremists. But numerous inflammatory Peace Front harangues on the ether and the broadcast media make this consideration less compelling than it might be. And now we are able to give the issue a suitable human face, an earnest, 19-year-old face. While at the same time promoting the warbot program."

He scanned the faces around the table. "Any questions or comments at this point? Nabil?"

The director of internal security had thrust his hand up, like Thor raising his hammer. He stood to speak, his words emphatic. "Declare martial law," he said. "Outlaw the Peace Front, and imprison its leaders for sedition or treason. Hold them incommunicado in special prison camps. Charges such as leading or organizing a demonstration, or burning the flag, deserve imprisonment at hard labor for the duration of the war. The most severe crimes—sabotage, mutiny, or inciting to mutiny—should bring sentences of hanging."

He remained on his feet for two or three more seconds, all

eyes on him. But the prime minister showed no sign of replying while Al-Kathad still stood, so the director sat down.

"Thank you, Nabil. Martial law is an option, one I hope will not become necessary." He gazed mildly but unblinkingly at the director. "Imprisonment is appropriate, but not the death sentence. Historically, many fanatics have embraced execution to promote their cause. Often effectively."

Peixoto's gaze moved to the minister of justice—a one-time senior jurist, and Al-Kathad's boss. "Bikel, how would you implement martial law from the viewpoint of justice?"

Bikel Wong remained seated while he spoke. "Let me begin by agreeing with Nabil that martial law is advisable," he said. "Peace Front activities are building momentum. Its leaders are determined; they will not give in short of success—or their removal from the social/political environment. By which I mean imprisonment. Incommunicado.

"Membership in Peace Front organizations, including subscribers to Peace Front talk groups and newsfaxes, is less than two percent of the Terran population, and even lower on the other core worlds. However, polls indicate that as many as fifteen percent have reservations about defending the Commonwealth. Mostly on the grounds that we cannot succeed, and might do better leaving it in the hands of the All-Soul. On Terra, fifteen percent means some 1.2 billion who are more or less susceptible to Peace Front propaganda.

"At the same time, however, punishments for obstructing defense activities must be moderate and judicious. I recommend the use of civil tribunals, each consisting of three prominent and respected judges, sitting in closed sessions to evaluate the charges and evidence. And to pass sentence where appropriate." He paused, seeming unhappy at the prospect. "Nabil agrees, we do not want imprisonment based on rumors, nor an open season on dissenters. Or witch hunts. And people must not be arrested, then simply disappear. As for being held incommunicado— approved representatives of humanitarian organizations should visit the camps regularly, and question whomever they please. But complaints must be taken only to Justice, not to the public.

"And finally," said the justice minister, "all sentences should be reevaluated at the end of the war, when the pressure is less and our perspective greater."

Chang Lung-Chi grunted to himself. *Justice delayed,* he thought wryly, *is better than no justice at all.* He got to his feet without asking to be recognized; he was, after all, the president. "I recommend against martial law," he said. "Though I may change my mind later, the lessons learned from the Troubles advise against it. It is enough that our prime minister has extraordinary war-time powers.

"Today's activists are not the seasoned, well-schooled insurgents of eight or ten centuries ago, and I do not believe they pose so serious a threat. Certainly not yet.

"And let me say this about martyrdom. Peace activists are innately self-righteous. True believers. They will condemn any sentence, whether passed in closed or open courts, and deny all evidence, however compelling. They will declare—they will trumpet!—that everyone sentenced is a martyr. They are already our dedicated enemies, regardless of what we do. So in dealing with saboteurs, we must have two goals: first the suppression of sabotage, and second, the winning of at least acquiescence by those who have misgivings about defense."

He paused long enough that Nabil took the opportunity to speak. "If we imprison their spokesmen…" he began.

"If we imprison their spokesmen simply for speaking, we create additional martyrs and new spokesmen," the president said, "which we cannot afford to do. Certainly not yet. Arrests and punishment should be limited to those who commit crimes widely recognized as such. Meanwhile we must strengthen public recognition that sabotage, terrorism, and the destruction of property are felonies. And that it is destructive to pass them off as simply differences of opinion."

Again he paused. "This means a bluntly honest exposure of Peace Front fallacies and lies. It means promoting the validity of our defense activities, and establishing that they are necessary and efficacious. And these efforts need to be headed by someone whom the population as a whole trusts and respects."

With that the president sat down. From beneath arched brows, Foster Peixoto's eyes rested on him quizzically. "Indeed. And are you willing to *take* the job? While seeing to your already existing responsibilities?"

"I am. Though you may very well come up with a better candidate. Meanwhile I am the head of state, not the head of government. If I have difficulties handling it all, I will delegate my ceremonial and other less essential duties, and give priority to this more critical work. But we should not create a special office. It should be done within the existing structure of government."

Nabil Al-Kathad listened glumly. He recognized the factors the others had pointed out, but saw himself as ultimately responsible for enforcing the law and suppressing crime. *I'm damned if I do, and damned if I don't,* he thought. Meanwhile there remained the matter of appropriate and effective punishment.

This time he raised his hand, and the prime minister recognized him. "Yes, Nabil?"

"I still believe it is appropriate to execute criminals for high war crimes. It establishes their gravity in the public mind.

"Mr. Prime Minister," said Chang Lung-Chi, "if I may?"

"Go ahead, Mr. President."

"Nabil, my good friend, in cases sufficiently extreme, I would be willing to consider loading the guilty into a hyperspace courier and shipping them, without stasis, to a system in the path of the Wyzhñyñy. There they would be shuttled to the surface of an enemy-occupied planet to negotiate peace. The minimum terms being Wyzhñyñy withdrawal from the world they have taken, and from the general bounds of the Commonwealth sector."

With that the prime minister asked for further comments. As these were people with strong demands on their time, within five minutes the meeting was adjourned.

Chapter Thirty-Three
Camp Bosler Nafziger

The third oldest deep-space colony, Pastor Lüneburger's world began as an agrarian religious settlement. Over the centuries, its original Mennonite doctrines had blurred and weakened, but low-tech agrarianism persisted. About fifty percent of its people still lived on farms, about thirty percent in rural hamlets, and twenty percent in market and industrial towns. The only colleges were seminaries. Trades and professions were learned by apprenticeship, with professional and trade associations providing optional certification.

Technological introductions were further hampered by disinterest in products. Nonetheless, over recent centuries, technology on Lüneburger's had gradually, and more or less unintentionally been upgraded. The slowness was largely a matter of cultural inertia, rather than Luddism. "Burgers" tended to like things as they were, and new things, to be successful, had to fit into the system. This was something the benign elected government considered very important in granting import licenses, especially the importation of technology.

On Lüneburger's World, railroads were thought of as "new." Actually they'd been used there for centuries, but only during the past eighty years had they spread beyond the mining regions. While "trucks"—steam-driven rigs that burned coal or wood—were a phenomenon of recent decades, filling the newly felt need for hauling heavy freight to the expanding railroads.

Most Burgers with serious interest in technology migrated to the Sol, or Epsilon Indi, or Epsilon Eridani systems. The Lüneburgian government had established a small trust to help finance their off-world education. (A trust quietly supplemented by the Commonwealth.) On Lüneburger's, this was considered Christian Kindness, not a means of developing a cadre of technicians and scientists. In fact, the expatriates were not encouraged to return.

Some did of course. Lüneburger's had a number of

engineers who'd trained offworld, or apprenticed under someone who had.

Given the circumstances, Lüneburgian farmers and craftsmen, especially in frontier areas, tended to be innovatively practical with the materials at hand. They could drain a swamp, or build a house from scratch. A small crew of farm boys, using hand tools and a work horse, could bridge a deeply-cut creek in an hour, and drive a loaded wagon over it. While those exposed to machinery quickly became decent jackleg mechanics. Thus given a handful of trained officers of whatever origin, Burgers were proving to make excellent engineering troops.

The threat of alien conquest had already brought changes. Most new military training camps, Camp Stenders for example, consisted of buildings whose prefabricated sections and modules were assembled on site by local entrepreneurs. Such practices would not have been accepted earlier. But in warmer climates, military camps were primarily tent camps. Administrative buildings and lecture sheds were prefab, but living accommodations consisted of acres of squad tents on raised wooden floors.

Camp Bosler Nafziger was sited in a region where winters were mild enough to live year-round in tents. The Lüneburgian government had condemned nearly 40 square miles of rural land there for military use, including a village which was left intact. The Commonwealth had compensated the landowners liberally, and leased an additional 440 square miles of adjacent forest.

When the Jerries finished their advanced training, they were sent to Camp Nafziger for twelve weeks of unit training: combat exercises on battalion, regimental—even divisional scale. These were to be carried out in conjunction with the Indi 3rd Armored Regiment, camped six miles down the Bachelor River. The Lüneburgian 4th Infantry Division, camped ten miles upstream, would provide opposition forces in conjunction with its own unit training.

<><>

Major General Pyong Pak Singh had arrived by floater several days ahead of his division. He'd spent four days inspecting the camp and its facilities, getting acquainted with the Lüneburgian staff in charge of maintenance and other services, being briefed on the military reservation itself, and finally reviewing the training plan with his general staff, and the Masadan commander and staff of the Indi 3rd Armored Regiment.

They were four gray, chilly days, with sporadic, wind-driven showers. His division arrived on the third, fourth, and fifth days, mostly by rail. On the fifth afternoon and evening, Pak inspected each regiment separately in a cold drenching rain.

The Indi 3rd Armored, with its Masadan cadre, had also traveled mostly by rail. He'd inspected them, too, at their own encampment.

<>

The sixth morning had dawned gratefully clear, with a Fahrenheit temperature of 45°, and a predicted high of 63°—much warmer than the Jerries had been having at Stenders. At 0815, he started off in an open command car, gloved, jacketed, and capped, with a map book on his lap, and a driver behind the wheel beside him. Pak had developed his trip itinerary in consultation with a Captain Hippe, a Lüneburgian engineering officer. Hippe had assigned the driver, and Pak had given the man his itinerary.

As they drove through the encampment, Pak gave his attention to the infantry companies standing in ranks on their mustering grounds. Shortly they'd march to lecture sheds for a two-hour orientation on the Camp Nafziger military reservation—a video lecture with large-scale topographic/vegetation maps and aerial photos. That would be followed by a two-hour talk on unit training, with an upfront caveat that the specifics might be changed.

Just now Nafziger's roads were puddled and muddy, but the car rode an AG cushion at the default height of four inches—enough to buffer it against irregularities in the surface. There was no splashing, and of course no rutting. And at the camp speed limit of 25 mph, even the puddles were little disturbed by the vehicle's air wake. Another main road crossed the one they'd been on, and the driver turned south, passing a cluster of prefab buildings—a regimental headquarters.

Ahead, the Bachelor River flowed through a stepped, steep-sided channel, its terrace forest jutting winter-bare treetops above the terrain break. Moments later the car crossed the break and skimmed down the forested-bordered road to the terrace, and thence to the wooded flood-plain.

The river itself was about two hundred feet wide, crossed by a timbered bridge whose stone piers jutted from murky swirling water. On the other side, the car crossed the same levels in reverse order, until both road and forest spilled over the rim onto the plain above. Pak examined the open map book, checking road designations, and watched to be sure his driver turned west at the first crossroads. Corporal Müller was unfamiliar to him—a Burger assigned from the camp's driver pool, and supposedly familiar with the reservation's roads.

The river was like a boundary. The south side was mostly forest, the farms in small clusters, their buildings abandoned intact. A mile or so farther south, high hills rose, with forest shown as unbroken, except by occasional wet meadows. The car took them past several junctions, with rutted spur roads leading southward at half-mile intervals. According to the map, the spurs didn't reach the hills. Then they came to another road, this one graded. Müller turned onto it. When they reached the first ridge, the road angled up its long slope.

Stumps, most of them large and old, were scattered throughout the thick forest. Many of the remaining trees were quite large. Obviously the people here logged lightly, entering the forest now and then to harvest trees that met certain criteria, probably of species, size and condition. Here and there along the road were small openings, some overgrown by saplings, others with little more than coarse weeds matted down by winter's rains.

"What are the openings?" he asked the driver.

"Landings, sir."

"Landings?"

"Places were logs were decked, sir. Dragged out of the

woods and piled. They load the logs on trucks there, and haul them to the railroad."

That, Pak thought, *helps explain the railroad coming here.* "Couldn't they float them down the river?" he asked.

"Most logs are sinkers; too heavy to float."

The forest changed little for several miles, then the road doubled back eastward. The driver surprised him by turning onto another spur road that went south, and the general unfolded another map.

"Where are we going now?" he asked.

"To the edge of the virgin reserves," said the corporal. "Captain Hippe said you'd ought to see it."

Hippe, Pak recalled, would be briefing officers today.

Half a mile later, the spur ended in a loop, a turn-around. The driver stopped, and they got out. "Everything south from here," Müller said, "is the reserve. That there," he added pointing, "is the boundary."

"That there" was an east-west line of blazes hacked on trees, apparently with an ax. South of it the forest had many large old trees. Slowly the two men strolled into it a short distance, their eyes exploring. It would, Pak thought, be beautiful in summer: green with foliage, and no doubt bright with birdsong.

"The number of people keeps growing," the corporal told him, "and the need for wood along with them." He gestured at the surrounding forest. "When it's needed, the government'll open it up for cutting, but for now it's wild; no farms, no roads, nothing but woods from here on. Folks hunt in here, of course, as much to keep down the wolves and lions and bears as for wild meat. And sport. Otherwise there's too many would spill out across the river and play hob with the livestock." His right hand slapped his sidearm. "And boars; they're worser'n mean if you come across one. They can gut a man in a minute."

He pointed to a tree whose otherwise smooth bark was vertically scarred to about seven feet above the ground, as if by large claws. "That there is bear sign; made about two years back, judging by the callus. Some he-bear marked it to warn off others. Lions mark by spraying piss on things. Hasn't been a lion reported north of the river for ten, fifteen years; they don't much tolerate people. But they're in here. Folks hear one screech from time to time."

Wolves. Bears. Lions. Boar. Pak wondered what manner of beasts the Burgers applied those labels to. Nothing trivial, he supposed. He was surprised he hadn't been shown pictures of them. He'd have to correct that when they got back to camp.

"Hunting helps keep predators leery of folks," the young man went on, "and out of the livestock. It's rare that one of them jumps a person, but now and then they do raise Cain in a pasture or sheep pen, or paddock."

He grinned at the general. "Your Jerries need to be ready to switch their blasters to hard fire."

It occurred to Pak to wonder if Müller would dare pull a general's leg. It seemed unlikely. "Are you from around here?" he asked.

"Yessir, General. My family's steading was just about where division headquarters stands now."

"Ah. It must have hurt to have your land condemned for a military reservation."

The corporal shrugged big shoulders. "There's some folks sour over it. But if the Wyzhñyñy get this far, we'll lose it anyway, and worse. As it is, Terra paid us good money for it, more'n anyone else would've. And when the war is won, if it gets won, we get it back for free."

The young man had seemed to turn inward as he talked. Now his eyes met the general's again. "Pastor Lüneburger told us to care for the land, the planet, and treat it with respect. Not abuse it like our long-ago forefathers did on Terra." He shook his head. "But he never foretold any alien invasion."

Pak nodded. "Few did," he said. "Few did."

They walked back to the car in silence and continued the tour, getting back to camp for lunch. Pak realized more fully now how suitable a range of conditions Camp Bosler Nafziger provided: forest, open farmland, rugged hills, small and large streams, even swamps and marshes in the north. And a sizeable section that was essentially virgin. All in all, it resembled conditions described for New Jerusalem.

Chapter Thirty-Four
Reunion

Esau Wesley lay still on sodden leaves, peering across a forested draw. *With the sun up,* he told himself, *they're not hard to see. Not this time of year, with the leaves down.*

Not all the leaves were down, of course. There were patches of evergreen shrubs whose stiff leathery leaves looked nearly black at a hundred yards. And some trees had kept their leaves, mostly dead and brown. He could hear them rustling dryly in the breeze overhead, a breeze that scarcely touched the ground.

Much of the hundred-yard separation between ridgetops was unobstructed, for the two ridges were steep, and looking across the draw was mostly looking through empty air. His narrowed eyes could make out folks dug in over there, obscured by undergrowth and not moving around. *If those are enemy,* he thought, *we could open fire and really play Tophet with them. Blasters, slammers... Heck, our grenade launchers would reach that far. The umpires would charge them heavy casualties.*

Friend or foe, that was the nub of it. *If this was for real, it'd be easy to tell. Something that walks on four legs with the top half of something like a man stuck on the front—that'd be easy to recognize.* But playing war against other humans would have to do.

Just think of them as the enemy, he told himself. Whoever, whatever they were, they were dug in. Esau wondered if the real Wyzhñyñy dug foxholes. It would, he thought, be awkward for folks like them. And how would they climb in and out?

◇

"Can he get close enough without being noticed?" Ensign Berg murmured it from a corner of his mouth, as if for secrecy.

Hawkins too only murmured; a nod involved movement. "He scored higher than anyone on the stealth tests."

That didn't really answer the question, Berg thought, but visor magnification didn't fill the bill. Two much obscuring undergrowth. "All right," he said, and triggered his helmet mike with a syllable. "Esau," he murmured, "cross the draw farther up, and get close enough to see whether those are our people or enemy. Then back away and let me know. If they are enemy, and see you, cover yourself with a smoke grenade. Then we'll give them something else to worry about."

The Jerrie's voice answered in his ear. "Yessir."

Not yessir, Ensign, just yessir, Berg observed. *Terse. Good stealth discipline.* Even so tiny and short range a source of electronic activity as an ultra-short-range helmet transmission on low might be picked up at 200 yards. He'd risked their security himself, with so long an order, but delivering it in person was a greater risk.

Carefully he turned his head in the young man's direction, but couldn't see him. Some evergreen brush was in the way. He'd already learned, though, that to give Lance Corporal Esau Wesley an order was to start a prompt response chain. He decided to talk to the CO about promoting Esau to full corporal. And to buck sergeant when they left Lüneburger's, unless he went sour along the way. And he wouldn't, not Wesley. Not seriously.

◇

The first thing Esau did was crawl backward over the crest of the ridge. Slowly, with short pauses. Any movement might catch the eye. Protracted movement held the attention, with greater risk of recognition. Once behind the crest he arose, ran off to his left 200 yards, then crossed it again on his belly. When well below the skyline, he moved in a low crouch. Here the ridges were somewhat less steep, and the draw between them considerably less deep. Thus the forest provided a thicker screen than at the point from which he'd left.

He understood without being told why the ensign wanted him to identify the people on the other ridge. The draw opened into a grassy glen, a sort of natural travelway. Both 2nd Platoon and the force across the draw could lay down fire on armor or anything else using it.

He didn't think the fact. It was simply there, an operating datum. Once atop the other ridge, he'd need to get close; see whether those others wore gray-blue Burger armbands on their left sleeves, or yellow-brown Jerrie armbands like his own. He didn't intend to get close enough to hear their accents. Even though they'd shown no sign of having seen 2nd Platoon, any talking they did would likely be quiet.

His advances continued smooth and intermittent, even as far up the draw as he was. He moved from cover to cover, down the slope and up the other, taking advantage of evergreen shrubs. At every pause, his eyes scanned. The "enemy" would have sentries out. Human sentries; electronic sentries were "noisier."

At one pause he peered long and carefully across the draw, toward where he'd come from. Spotted the outline of a helmet against an outcrop. Some folks had trouble getting it through their heads that the camouflage pattern on your uniform wasn't enough. A little brush, strategically attached, made a lot of difference. He'd mention it when this was over.

He still couldn't see the folks on this side. Some forty yards ahead, a rocky prominence hid them from view. It was a good place for a lookout, too, lying low beside a tree, watching for someone like himself. Esau didn't move again till he was satisfied with his surveillance. He couldn't afford carelessness. With back-country like this, there'd be skilled hunters among the Burgers.

After long seconds he moved on. The wet leaves on the ground made effectively no noise, and the dry leaves rustling in the treetops helped cover the occasional wet twig breaking. When he reached the outcrop he paused again, then slipped past it on his belly. He spotted his first "enemy" thirty yards away, and stopped. He couldn't see an armband, but if he…

What caused him to look aside just then, he would never know. What he saw was something he'd only heard about, but he knew what it was, and it was looking right at him. It gathered itself, and for just a moment Esau froze mentally.

Then the lion rushed him, and Esau's paralysis transformed into action. Not to turn his blaster and fire. That would have taken too long, for he was prone, and the lion was to his right. Instead he twisted onto his back, coiling, interposing the weapon between himself and the predator, while loosing a shout at the top of his lungs. Then the 300-pound feloid was on him, and Esau had jammed his blaster sideways into its mouth. He felt the front claws not as pain but as deadly threat. For a moment it tried to reach him with its jaws, but the blaster was in the way, and the young man's powerful arms held them off. Then it tried to move around him, flank him, and he pivoted on his back in desperation.

He didn't hear the popping of blasters across the ravine, firing soft pulses at the "enemy"; 2nd Platoon had misconstrued his shouts. He could only fight. Salvation came as unexpectedly as the lion. Steel fingers, numbingly powerful, penetrated the ruff, gripped the hide beneath, hauled the predator back, then swung it, slamming it hard against a tree, so quickly and overwhelmingly, the lion didn't have time to twist and fight back. Swung it again, and again, till it lay broken on the ground, hissing coarse bloody hisses at its metal assailant. The warbot set its right-arm blaster on full, and fired a single pulse, putting the lion out of its pain.

Esau stared up at the cyborg. It looked back down at him. "Hello, Esau," it said quietly. "You took us by surprise."

◇

The "enemy" turned out to be 1st Platoon, E Company. Its ensign radioed 2nd Platoon B, and the firing stopped. Meanwhile 1st Platoon E's medic cut off Esau's torn camos, poured antibiotic on his lacerations, bandaged him, gave him an injection, and wrapped him in a casualty blanket. Then Isaiah Vernon picked up his ex-squad leader and carried him down the slope to the meadowed glen as if Esau were a child. Within ten minutes an evac floater was there, and carried the injured man to the division hospital.

2nd Platoon was told that Esau's wounds weren't serious. Jael asked Sergeant Hawkins if she could go with her husband. He'd told her no, that she was a soldier, and this was part of war.

That evening Hawkins came to her while the platoon ate. The ensign had just gotten a message from Esau: he was fine, and expected to be back in two or three days.

◇

The estimate was Esau's, not the doctor's. He rejoined the platoon and his wife five days later, when the regiment returned to camp. That was also the day Isaiah Vernon went to 2nd Battalion headquarters and asked to see the CO. He had the permission of Sergeant Henry Okinwobu, his squad leader, an ex-marine medically discharged for cascade syndrome.

The battalion sergeant major looked up at the towering metal-and-composites human standing in front of his desk. "What's this about, Vernon?"

"Sergeant Major, it's about my old platoon. I'd like a transfer to 1st Battalion, so I can work with it. I trained with it. I even jumped with it. My best friends…"

The sergeant major cut him off with a gesture. "Just a minute, Vernon," he said, and touched a key on his desk comm. "Major, a personnel matter has just come up, something not covered by policy. You might want to consider it." He listened to something Isaiah couldn't hear. "It's Corporal Vernon of the bot squad." Again he listened. "Yessir, that's him. He went through basic and part of advanced training with 2nd Platoon, B Company, before his 'chute malfunctioned. The guy he rescued from the lion is one of his old buds. Vernon would like to be swapped for one of 1st Battalion's bot squad… Yes major, that's the key to it. We're not likely to get a replacement with his level of infantry training, but… Yessir. Thank you, sir."

He jabbed the switch and looked back up at Isaiah. "Sit down, Corporal. I have another call to make."

Isaiah sat. In five minutes he had an answer. It wasn't all he'd hoped for, but it might work out. Technically, a warbot platoon was assigned to a regiment as a tactical reserve, which meant the regimental CO could use it any way he wanted. But Division had ordered them divvied out to the battalions. "So if you can find someone in 1st Battalion's bot squad willing to switch," the sergeant major said, "the major will take it up with the colonel." He paused. "But if you're going to do it, do it no later than tomorrow."

Isaiah got to his feet. "Yes, Sergeant," he said. "I'll get

right on it."

Sergeant Major Pieter Fuentes Singh watched him leave. According to the grapevine, Captain Chatterjee, Division's technical specialist, had said that even bots weren't strong enough to swing 400-pound lions by the scruff, and beat them to death against trees. But this one had.

Fuentes shook his head. Apparently the adrenalin analog system built into them was more effective than the specialists had realized.

Meanwhile, Private Isaiah Vernon had laid to rest any reservations Fuentes might have harbored about the basic humanity of warbots. They felt the human bond. Certainly this one had.

Chapter Thirty-Five
Hanging Around Sagenwerk

This was the third Sevenday in a row that Joseph Switzer had hung around the depot to watch soldiers on pass pile out of coach cars. If he'd gotten to Lüneburger's World a few weeks earlier, he wouldn't be in this miserable village. He could have gotten his business done in North Fork.

On Terra, even a backwater like Sagenwerk would have a square with trees, planters, maybe a brass sundial on a granite pedestal. A good bookstore and a nice cafe with outdoor tables, bright awnings, a friendly waitress. And there wouldn't be a railroad reeking with soft-coal smoke, and gritty soot.

The depot here had no amenities except a weedy path leading to an outdoor privy with back-to-back rooms, one for men, one for women. Until the soldiers had come to Camp Nafziger, passengers were few, and most trains had only a single coach, inserted at the head of a string of log cars, lumber cars, or box cars.

Switzer dug his watch from a pocket and snapped the lid open. It was twelve minutes past time, but the train wasn't in sight or hearing. On Lüneburger's World, schedules were casual.

Grunting, he rotated his shoulders. He'd gotten a job at the sawmill, stacking lumber, and was still a bit sore. In North Fork he'd found work as a freelance engineer, but with eleven thousand inhabitants, North Fork was an important regional center. Sagenwerk's only excuse for existing was the sawmill that provided its name. Its population was said to be five hundred. Here a freelance engineer would draw too much attention, and he'd make too little money to pay for the one-room shack he rented. The war had caused prices to rise.

When he'd left Lüneburger's, twenty years earlier at age sixteen, he'd intended never to come back. On Terra he would get an education and interesting work, and live in the 30th century instead of the 19th. And he had. Then this corrupt war had come along, an affront to the All Soul, fouling the mother world with chauvinism and godless self-justification.

Actually, North Fork hadn't been so bad. It was civilized, with electricity, plumbing, green lawns, shrubs and flowerbeds. The streets were shaded by overhanging trees. Its main lack was people who could carry on a modern conversation; even the All-Soul congregation there was provincial. But the only language you heard was Terran, unless you hung around one of the dwindling old-order congregations.

Here in Sagenwerk, on the other hand, you were more likely to hear the old *Bauerndeutsch* than Terran, and got scowls if you didn't understand. *Bauerndeutsch!* A blend of 18th and 19th-century peasant *Plattdeutsch, Switzerditsch, Volgadeutsch*...and old church German. Along with a sprinkling of recent Terran, and a mixture of archaic, germanized Anglic—words necessary to function in 19th and 20th century North America. Gawd! Even then, a millennium ago, *Bauerndeutsch* had been dying out. The early colonists had revived it as part of their blockheaded ethno-religious chauvinism, as if Jesus had spoken a broken-down peasant German! But gradually it had receded again.

And worse, Sagenwerk was a stagnant pool of bigots! Mention the Church of the All Soul and you risked a black eye. Say that being "born again" referred to reincarnation, and you'd lose your job before you could pick up your lunch pail. Refer to Jesus as an avatar of the All Soul, and some ignorant fool on the green chain, who didn't know the meaning of "avatar," was likely to break your face in the name of God.

The town was changing—a result of the war—but even the changes weren't good. Greed was flourishing. The railway had brought in twenty coaches to shuttle soldiers on their days off, though the village was less a magnet than its people had hoped. The rundown old tavern faced competition from a new beer garden. There was a theater still smelling of fresh lumber and paint, and two large houses, refurbished, had been supplied with women and girls from Landfall and other "cities."

Joseph Switzer shook his head. It was his own fault he was here. The project had been his idea in the first place, and no one else in the organization was suited for the assignment. He knew Lüneburger's World, and he knew its people. With a little care he still passed for one of them.

The wail of a train whistle jerked him from his revery, and he looked down the tracks. It was in sight half a mile west, its locomotive spewing thick black smoke. Unconsciously he curled his nostrils. Instead of stepping out on the platform, he remained beside the depot door, well apart from the collection of young women who also waited. From there he'd be able to see if any of the Jerries he'd met at North Fork got off. Hopefully Wheeler, who'd been responsive and very promising.

Slowing, hissing, sighing, the train drew alongside the platform. Brakes squealed, couplings clashed, cylinders released steam. A conductor swung down from the first car, followed by a stream of uniformed soldiers. And there, the very first of them, was Wheeler, conspicuous by his height.

Instead of going out to him, Switzer waited. Wheeler was walking and talking with another soldier whom Switzer recalled. Elijah somebody. As they passed him, he spoke. "Good morning, Moses," he said. "Good morning, Elijah. Good to see you again."

Today he would get down to business.

Chapter Thirty-Six
Charley Gordon

Admiral Alvaro "Spanish" Soong pressed the button beside the door and waited. *An admiral waiting to be let in!* he thought. *On business, on his own flagship! Ah the universe we live in.*

There was no real irony in the thought. Courtesy was almost always appropriate, within the bounds of circumstance, and rare resources could require special treatment.

The door opened, and Ophelia Kennah looked out at him. As a savant's attendant, she was old style: her personnel file said she was psychic. The briefing he'd been given on savants stated that many of the new savant attendants were simply empaths trained to act as nurse, hypno-technician and companion. Also, Kennah was fifty-one years old, though slender and still graceful, with calm observant eyes.

She stepped back, and he entered. "Good morning, Ms Kennah," he said.

"Good morning, Admiral."

The room was large for a ship's quarters, and impressed him as the most aesthetic on the flagship. Though if asked, he couldn't have said why it seemed that way. Near one side stood a sort of wheeled stand, with a 30-inch-long module mounted on it. The module contained cube ports, and on its top a multi-sensor set. Just now only one of its sensory status lights was on.

"What's he listening to?" Soong asked.

"'Concierto de Aranjuez,'" she answered. "By Joaquin Rodrigo. It's quite old; 20th century."

Spanish, Soong thought. He didn't speak the language, beyond a few courtesies—family heirlooms. His mother's clan had long since abandoned both Spanish and Catalan.

He wondered if he'd ever heard the concerto. He enjoyed music when he had time, but seldom paid attention to who'd composed what. Probably Ophelia Kennah could set the player so she heard it too. She'd probably been listening when he'd rung, and switched off the room speaker before opening the door.

"I need his services," he told her.

"Of course." She stepped to the stand and touched switches. Two additional status lights flashed on. "Charley," she said quietly, "the admiral needs you."

Charley Gordon, that's the name. Presumably he'd been given it at the Institute. Soong wondered how that had happened. The savant's one-page personnel brief listed him as Male Infant Doe, followed by a registration number. A designation dating to when he was processed into the Institute.

"Ah! The admiral!" said Charley Gordon. "Good day, sir. I'm happy to be of service. Do we have a moment?"

The response astonished Soong. His impression had been that idiot savants were invariably retarded, by definition. And till now, Charley had never spoken in his presence except in trance, channeling messages from War House. Now this request for 'a moment.'

Soong answered solemnly: "A moment, yes. Then I must have your help."

"It is my privilege to serve." The statement sounded, and might well have been sincere. Certainly Soong discerned no irony in it. "Meanwhile," the voice went on, "I shall take advantage of my moment." It paused. "You never visit me except for my services. Perhaps if I invite you, you will. Therefore, will you visit me? For friendly conversation, man to man?"

This question too took Soong off guard. "Why… If you'd like, yes. We'll soon enter hyperspace again, this time for an extended period. I'll visit you then."

"Thank you, Admiral. I will hold you to that." Again Charley Gordon paused. It seemed to Soong the savant had turned his gaze to his attendant, though the ocular sensors were immobile. There had to be a means of directing visual attention. "Ophelia," Charley Gordon said, "I am ready."

"Good," she replied, and paused. "We will now start. Begin the session." She looked expectantly at the admiral.

"Begin the session" was the standard formula that triggered Charley Gordon's trance. Soong began his message.

It had an unspoken context, one familiar to both himself,

the prime minister, and War House. Soong had been given a four-week limit to finish training his battle force, then reluctantly granted a four-week extension. He was still not fully satisfied with its exercises in cross-dimensional combat. And it was entirely possible, if unlikely, for a battle to involve rapid transitions between warpspace and F-space. But his people had become basically competent, and three days earlier Admiral Tischendorf had told him there could be no further extension. The Commonwealth and the human species couldn't afford it.

Thus, Soong's message to War House and the prime minister was expected and succinct: "At 1100 hours Greenwich, this date, the Sol 1st Provisional Battle Force will generate hyperspace and proceed to the vicinity of the Nei Frieslân System. There we will determine what further jump seems appropriate for the effective interception and engagement of the enemy armada. Meanwhile I will contact you at appropriate intervals, and of course remain receptive of your orders and advices. Admiral Alvaro Soong, Commander."

A minute later, his message acknowledged, Soong left the savant's quarters. Thinking not of his responsibility, nor of his force's battle readiness, but of Charley Gordon, his strange power, and his seeming intelligence.

Soong often learned a great deal about people from their faces—their expressions and their eyes. But Charley Gordon? At least until very recently, savants had faces too. The only savant he'd seen before, he'd observed at War House before getting his present assignment. Chloë was tiny, deformed, and severely retarded, but her face, unexpressive though it had been, had permitted him to watch her consciousness shut down when her attendant spoke the brief hypnotic formula. Her features had fallen slack, and he'd known she was in trance.

Charley Gordon's apparent intelligence was far more interesting. *I'm glad he invited me to visit him,* Soong realized. I would never have thought to invite myself.

◇

He decided to make his visit that evening, and calling Ophelia Kennah, arranged for a specific time. Then asked a question: "Is Charley as intelligent as he seemed to be this morning?"

"Just a moment," she replied. He imagined her looking toward her charge, to see if he could overhear. Apparently he had his external sound sensor turned off, perhaps listening to music. "Charley's intelligence is an enigma," she answered. "He does—indifferently on intelligence tests which measure reasoning ability, though better than any other savant I'm aware of. But he does exceedingly well on rote memory tests, as do many other savants."

"Interesting. He memorizes things then."

"If by 'memorize' you mean an effort to imprint a visual or auditory experience, or to create a mnemonic to assist recall—no. He simply experiences things, then recalls them exactly. He can recite extensively and verbatim from biographies of great composers."

"So he reads."

"He does, but prefers audiobooks. He plays them at a rate incomprehensible to me—a high-pitched twittering. Faster than I can read them silently."

The admiral stared. She paused. "I haven't finished answering your first question. A test of intuitive intelligence was being circulated before we left Terra, a preliminary version for testing and professional critiques. I tried it on Charley. His score was nearly the highest possible. I sent a report on it to War House, but when we left, I hadn't had an answer. It seemed to me he might be of greater value there than here.

"Formal tests, of course, do not correlate perfectly with life performance. Charley sometimes produces marvelously logical replies to questions; produces them intuitively. If he is allowed a hand in directing your conversation with him, I do not doubt you'll be pleased and impressed. On the other hand, if you arrive with a list of questions, you may be disappointed. I recommend you simply open the conversation and let things develop as they may."

Soong wondered what Ophelia Kennah's intelligence score was.

She paused, then added: "Charley tires rather easily. The central nervous system tires; that's one reason students need rest and recreation. Channeling and other psychic activities tire it more than most. Typically, psychics hold up reasonably well during the activity, but if it's protracted, they may collapse afterward.

"Excitement may also tire Charley. He's not used to it, and having an actual visitor will be exciting for him."

Alvaro Soong's attention had been hooked by the mention of psychic activities. Like many people, he tended to respond skeptically to the word "psychic." The field of psychodynamics had risen above alchemy and Freudian psychology, to about the level of the phlogiston theory, but had yet to bring forth its Newton or Lavoisier. A few psychic applications had become routine in the world, but these were no longer thought of as "psychic." The term tended to be reserved for fringe activities and fakery.

But what the communication savants did was genuine enough. And the instructions on the management of savant communicators had warned against overworking them.

"Are there subjects I shouldn't bring up?" Soong asked.

"Charley is emotionally quite stable," Kennah answered. "I know of no subjects you should avoid. He is perfectly willing to discuss his condition and history. And yours, if it comes up."

◇

The admiral's appointment was for 2000 hours, and he was there on time. To find Charley not listening to a cube; he was waiting, ready. "Hello, Admiral," he said. Pleasure and anticipation were apparent in his voice.

Remarkable, Soong thought, *that his equipment reflects emotion so well.* "Hello, Charley," he answered. "Or would you prefer I call you Charles?"

"Charley, please. I have never been Charles, though it is a nice name. Please have a chair, Admiral, and be comfortable."

Soong pulled one to face Charley's sensorium.

"I've been studying your open file, sir," Charley said. Brightly. Eagerly. The announcement took Soong by surprise.

Kennah must have gotten it for him, he decided. Meanwhile Charley continued. "It says almost nothing of your life before you attended the space academy. Born near Terrassa, in the Catalunya Prefecture, and attended the space academy in the Colorado Prefecture—twenty years in just a few lines!" He added the last almost merrily. "Then graduated with high honors; one more line! After that it summarizes your service record. Surely there is more to be told than that."

"Not really," Soong replied. Untruthfully of course, but it wouldn't be very interesting. Except possibly to a student of social and professional acculturation and family iconography. "I'll tell you what," he added. He was surprised at what he found himself saying. "I'll have some spare time for a while. Enough to sit down some day soon and record a few items of my childhood and youth for you. Things that may provide amusement, or insights."

He took a different tack then, to get his own questions answered. "You know more about me than I do of you. I read a bit on savants years ago. My impression was that most of them were children."

"*Idiot* savants you mean," Charley answered. "The adjective is apt, and typically accurate. Many of us are severely defective physically as well as mentally, and die as infants or children. Typically with our potentials undiscovered. Historically, especially before the Enlightenment, others were killed—sometimes burned—as being possessed by the devil. And later, many were put away, out of sight in institutions."

Charley sounded quite serene as he recited, as if he'd long since come to terms with the facts.

"As for me— I am thirty-three years old, and spent my life in an institution from perhaps two days of age until the War Mobilization Directorate learned of me."

"Was that when you were installed in a bioelectronic interface unit?"

"To understand that, you need to know my origins. As far as they *are* known. I was found abandoned in a trash bin, in Rio de Janeiro, in the Brazilian Autonomy. Seemingly in my first day of life. The police delivered me to a hospital, which passed me on to another, which forwarded me to the Sacred Heart Research Institute. Where I remained for more than thirty years."

Sent to a research institute at what? Five days of age? *There has to be an interesting story behind that,* Soong thought.

Charley paused. "As for being bottled… My early years involved a continuous struggle on the part of the Institute's personnel, to keep me alive. Because of the physiological imbalances that continually afflicted me. Finally they arranged with another research organization to extract my central nervous system and bottle it. An operation quite illegal then, even for research, and carrying severe penalties. But I was beginning to show signs of the hormonally driven syndrome referred to as adolescence, a period of powerful physiological changes. My staff guardians doubted I could survive it."

"They didn't call my bottle a bottle, of course, or even a bio-electronic interface unit. They called it a modularized life-support unit. It was hoped that that and being a monastic order would protect them, if the act came to the attention of the secular authorities. But it required extraction of a living central nervous system, which legally made it bottling.

Again he laughed. "And now, all these years later, here I am in my technological glory, and some would say middle-aged. Incidentally, what you see before you is my third module. The technology does progress, you know, albeit covertly."

The admiral sat without speaking. *I'll have to digest all this,* he thought. *Sleep on it, see how it looks in the morning.* Meanwhile Charley seemed to be waiting. "How did you go from being 'Male Infant Doe' to 'Charley Gordon?'" Soong found himself asking.

"Ho ho! You have opened a new area there! In the beginning it wasn't known that I was a savant. I was simply a medical challenge, not in the Savant Division at all. What set me apart from most critically defective infants was surviving my first day. Despite having been discarded. The neighborhood I was found in was quite degraded. I could easily have been eaten by rats.

"My savant status was first suspected before my third birthday, when I showed a love of good music, and recognized and asked for certain numbers. It was also determined that I could be educated to a higher level than supposed. The highest of any wards of the Institute, actually.

"Finally, at age twelve, my physical condition became quite precarious, and I was bottled."

Charley paused long enough that it seemed he'd finished. "You were about to tell the admiral how you came to be called Charley Gordon," Kennah said.

"Oh yes. Excuse me, Admiral. One of my mental weaknesses is a tendency to lose track of the subject. I have noticed that normal people sometimes do the same thing, but I excel in it. If I may use the word 'excel' in this sense.

"Now, where—oh yes. I was named Charley Gordon after a person in a story: a retarded man who became a genius."

He paused, then spoke again. "I really should tell you the rest. Otherwise it's not very meaningful.

"The study that discovered my ability to learn, was a by-product of research on a theory of psionics. You might even say that savants are to psionics what fruit flies were to genetics—the key to a breakthrough. And as one of the study subjects, it was determined that I had 'the talent,' as it is called. I might then have been assigned to the Commonwealth Ministry, and sent to an embassy on some colony world. But because bottling was still a felony—even my existence was illegal—I remained at the Institute, occasionally taking part in research projects as a subject or advisor. Until the invasion surfaced, and the Office of Technical Recruitment learned of me."

Again he paused. "Admiral, I'm afraid I'm a poor host. I have not offered you food or drink. Ophelia, would you please?"

"Of course, Charley. Admiral, I do not have an alcoholic beverage to offer you, but I do have a mixed fruit drink, and some hors d'oeuvres."

"Thank you, Ms Kennah," the admiral said gravely. "The fruit drink will be fine, and I'm sure I'll like the hors d'oeuvres as well. But I shouldn't stay long. I didn't tell the bridge where

I'd be."

She saw the statement as an excuse. He could easily call the bridge and tell the officer of the watch where to reach him. "Of course," she replied. "Perhaps you could select your own hors d'oeurves in the kitchenette."

The suggestion sparked his curiosity; it seemed lame. He wondered if Charley saw through it. Or didn't it matter to him? *Either way,* he thought. If she wanted privacy...

The kitchenette was small but not tiny. The door closed itself behind them. The hors d'oeurves were on a tray. "Ms. Kennah..." he began quietly.

"Call me Ophelia if you'd like," she prompted. "Or Kennah without the miz. Or Ken; that's what they called me at the Institute. Actually I prefer Kennah."

"Well then, Kennah it will be. How long have you known Charley?"

"Since he was only days old; as soon as he came out of intensive care. I was a seventeen-year-old apprentice nurse, assigned to watch him eight hours at a time, with a half-hour lunch break. It was then I learned to love him, when he was still a tiny baby. Before it was recognized how truly special he was. He *is* special, you know. The whole staff came to feel it. All the children are special, and loved, but Charley more than any. His fight to live was so brave. As if he knew he had a special gift to share." Again she shrugged. "And he was so cheerful! Did you know a sick infant can be cheerful? You can hardly imagine what he went through. For years! And his growth as a person and a personality have been equally outstanding."

Perhaps I can imagine, Soong thought. *Surely to some degree.* He took a tiny three-cornered sandwich and tasted it. Goose liver paste, he decided, its seasonings close to perfect. No doubt the makings came from the command officers' mess. "Was that why you wanted me to come into the kitchen?" he asked. "To give me that insight into Charley?"

She shook her head. "No," she said. "You need to know something he has done. He mentioned it just yesterday. You may not approve."

He frowned. "Yes?"

"He hasn't been listening to music as much as I'd thought. Playing it, yes, but quietly, as background. He'd…broken into shipsmind, into the battlecomp system; he said it wasn't difficult. For weeks he's listened to your battle exercises. He told me it was the most interesting thing he'd ever done; much more interesting than battle dramas." She shrugged. "He's always liked battle dramas and histories, and war games when I smuggled them to him at the Institute. Patients were not supposed to have them, nor staff as far as that's concerned."

She paused, calmly accepting the admiral's eye contact.

Soong nodded slowly. "I see. Thank you for being forthright."

They returned to the living room, Charley's room, Soong carrying another sandwich and a glass of fruit punch. "Ophelia is quite skilled in the kitchen," he said, using the name Charley used for her.

"I'm sure she is," Charley answered. "Before you leave, I'd like you to have a cube. Of the early, magazine version of 'Flowers for Algernon,' translated from the original Anglic. It is the story of the original, fictional Charley Gordon. My dear Ophelia read it onto the cube for me. It is sad, but it is also beautiful. It is rich in love."

<>

When Soong left the small apartment, it was soberly. It was not surprising that in Charley Gordon's mind, love was associated with sadness. Meanwhile he needed to have the battlecomp checked for anything Charley might have done to it.

<>

That evening, a careful rundown by Lieutenant Commander Bedi Chen, the flagship's senior computer specialist, found nothing out of order in the battlecomp. Chen was curious as to why the admiral had asked for the check; the system monitored itself constantly, and at frequent, random intervals ran all-inclusive scans. But he didn't ask, and Soong volunteered nothing.

The admiral was glad, in fact, that Charley had done what

he'd done. What *he* needed to do now, he told himself, was find ways to (1) check his operating assumption, and (2) find a way to make use of it. While not allowing himself expectations. Hopes, yes, but not expectations.

Before he went to bed that night, Soong read "Flowers for Algernon." It *was* sad, and it *was* beautiful. Normally the admiral was not fond of sad, but in this case he made an exception. Perhaps because it seemed to him that Male Infant Doe, aka Charley Gordon, himself showed considerable love. And in the physical universe—the world Alvaro Soong knew— there was generally too little love.

Chapter Thirty-Seven
On a Different Flagship

Tension had worn on Grand Admiral Quanshûk, tension born of incongruities and enigmas—of a situation and life form beyond comprehension.

Only a very potent life form, powerful, vigorous, and technologically advanced, could have spawned so many colonies so far. A life form strong enough, confident enough, smart and ruthless enough to have overcome and destroyed its sapient rivals on its world of origin. And on any other attractive world it found.

He didn't actually think the concept of ruthlessness. In the Wyzhñyñy worldview, ruthlessness toward rival life forms required no conceptualization. It was an underlying truth.

So far his armada had penetrated only the outer zone of the human empire. That was obvious, despite the distance of that penetration. Somewhere ahead he would encounter the old, long-settled body of the Commonwealth, and there, if not sooner, meet resistance. The prisoners had admitted it.

He'd considered coercing more information from them, but Qonits had recommended against it, reminding his admiral that the two humans were simply marine scientists. Obviously most humans were not fighters. Their warrior gender, called "soldiers," seemed missing from their colonies. And clearly their other genders were untrained—probably unsuited—for war.

Quanshûk and Qonits had reviewed the situation repeatedly, particularly since the passage of time made it both clearer and more enigmatic. The landing forces had met essentially no resistance, and had already captured twenty-one planets. The human empire was truly vast. Humans must be bound together by unbreakable loyalty for such an empire to exist, a loyalty deep within the genes. The enormous volume of space involved, the time requirements even for hyperspace pod communication, the impracticality of effective policing—all made space empires impractical without such inborn loyalty.

But loyalty extended in both directions, from the ruled upward to the rulers, and from the rulers downward to the ruled. Quanshûk believed that implicitly. It was logical, and it was true to the experience of his species.

Over their long history, the Wyzhñyñy had known and destroyed a half-dozen space-faring species. Two of which had created large empires, though neither with a radius that approached the distance he'd already traveled in this one. And both had responded to invasion with a united ferocity that could only grow out of such loyalty.

Yet the humans had not. Why had that loyalty not manifested? Or perhaps manifested so strangely?

From the very first human world his armada had reached— clearly a picket world—three, perhaps four craft had escaped. And beyond doubt had homed inward to warn their empire. They would have come out of hyperspace a day or so inbound, and launched message pods to the nearer inhabited worlds. Which in turn would have spread the message: invasion!

Pods were intrinsically faster, because they carried no life forms. Nor did they need to detour and emerge, to examine systems for habitable planets. Nor cover an invasion flotilla when such a planet was found. So surely the human core worlds knew by now. Should have known months ago.

Unless their empire was vast beyond imagination! The possibility gnawed on Quanshûk. What sort of empire had he invaded? With how many core worlds? How many fleets?

Yet he'd encountered no enemy force at all. None! And clearly the humans had hyperdrive. Without it they could not have begun to colonize so far.

This lack of resistance had to be a strategy. But what strategy? Was a vast human warfleet being gathered, while his armada was being sucked in as if by some enormous singularity? The thought squeezed his heart like a giant fist.

And on the other warships, his officers had surely hatched and brooded those same fears.

The responsibility was his though, and it was taking its

toll. He was on medication now for arthritic hips and tarsal joints. The ship's chief physician had advised him to stay off his feet as much as possible, so he'd reduced his time on the bridge, and worked more from his stateroom. Which, after all, had full access to shipsmind, which meant to everything on board.

A time or two he'd wondered if his anxiety was worsened by the presence of humans on board. He'd even thought of jettisoning them from an airlock, but his troubles and fears would not die with them. And as Qonits had pointed out, "We have learned much from the prisoners; to kill them would be to throw away a resource. Soon we will meet the humans in battle. It is unavoidable. Then further questions will occur to us, and without our captives, we would have no one to ask. They can make the difference between success and failure."

And to that, Quanshûk reminded himself, *I had no conclusive reply. Not then, not now. Shipsmind has found no substantial inconsistencies in what they have told us. I can only await what happens, and when the time comes, fight skillfully and very hard.*

◇

Fortunately the admiral's mood was not always so dark. But never was it bright. It hadn't been since they'd somehow been cast across intergalactic space, into this galaxy so impossibly far from home. That such a thing could happen… His view of the universe, and his confidence in himself, his fleet, his science—his reality!—could never be the same.

◇

Qonits quickstepped down the corridor, his bodyguards close behind. The chief scholar shared Quanshûk's concerns, but not his responsibilities. And in temperament he was a scholar, not a master, driven by an urge to know, not to rule.

Arriving at the prisoners' door, his senior guard knocked, and Qonits identified himself.

"Come in," David answered. Qonits opened the door and entered, his guards stopping just inside.

"My friends," said Qonits in Terran, "we will do something different today."

David's eyebrows rose. "Different? In what way?" Both he and Yukiko had adjusted to the monotony, but Qonits' visibly good spirits suggested that the change would be pleasant. Or at least well intended.

"I shall take you to see more of the flagship. You shall see the place of command and control, and the place where the, um, the ship's workings are accomplished."

"Ah! The bridge and the engine room."

Qonits peered carefully at the human male. "Perhaps. Where we go, I will show you things, and you will tell me their names."

Yukiko spoke next. "Qonits, we would like very much to do those things, but we cannot leave Annika alone. You have seen how much better she is now than when we first arrived. If we leave her, I'm afraid she will relapse—get worse again. She might even die."

Qonits' expression changed into one they had not seen before. A Wyzhñyñy grin? "I have," he told them, "foreseen the problem." Turning, he spoke in Wyzhñyñy toward the open door, and in from the corridor came another guard, pushing an AG seat large enough to accommodate Annika. "You will bring her with us," he said. "On this."

Yukiko examined it, testing its stability, poking and pushing on the cushions, inspecting the seat belt, its adjustments, and the simple fastener. "Oh Qonits!" she said, "a stroller! It's lovely! It should do beautifully!"

It wasn't "lovely," of course. It was strictly utilitarian. But her appreciation was genuine, and Qonits felt it. He and David waited while Yukiko took Annika to the potty stool they'd had made for her, and waited while the girl relieved her bladder. Then David buckled the savant into the stroller, and the humans left with the chief scholar.

They hadn't been outside the cell since they'd been put in it, nearly ten Terran months earlier. They'd eaten in it, slept in it, exercised and bathed—even on occasion made love in it. Told stories to each other and to Annika, to fill the time and amuse each other. By now they felt no discomfort at being nude among these people, these aliens who themselves wore no clothing.

First they visited the bridge, and for the first time saw a Wyzhñyñy master. Three of them, in fact—the grand admiral, the ship's master, and the watch officer, though the humans didn't know those identities. Like Qonits, all three were blue and red, but their crests were considerably larger and showier than any scholar's. They guessed Quanshûk's identity from his ornate harness. The bridge watch, to the best of their ability, pretended to ignore the visitation, but all managed a look. Almost none had seen the prisoners before, even on a monitor. Only Qonits and the prisoners spoke, and only to establish the Terran terms for the bridge's equipment and furnishings.

Next the Terrans were shown the engine department. Both thought they recognized some of what they saw, and by asking questions, were able to provide names, probably correct. Shipsmind, meanwhile, heard and saw everything, including the uncertainties. It stored, dissected, parsed, assigned tentative evaluations based on known roots and contexts, and ran correlations. Iteration was a major tool.

Next they visited a beam gun battery, then a torpedo battery, and finally the shield generator. Little guessing was needed.

The last technical visit was brief—the stasis section, where the equipment was even more unmistakable. Their final stop was the officers' galley, where a grinning (surely that was a Wyzhñyñy grin!) chief baker gave each of the visitors what the baker regarded as a treat. It was crunchy and rather dense— rather like something they often received at meals. But this was also sweet, its flavor reminding them of maple sugar. His eyes watched intently, expectantly, and he spoke to them in Wyzhñyñyç.

"He asks if you like it," Qonits interpreted.

"Oh yes," Yukiko said. "Delicious," David added. Annika gnawed silently, without cerebral response. The baker spoke again, Qonits interpreting. "He says he will send some special food to you each day."

Then they left the galley, and the chief scholar led them back to their cell.

◇

Afterward Qonits went to his own quarters. Shipsmind would already have analyzed, organized, and formatted the additions, but he was in no hurry to examine them. After mid-meal would be soon enough. Meanwhile he would close his eyes and nap briefly.

He felt good about the tour. The prisoners had benefited from the change, and the ship's human vocabulary had expanded in an important area, filling a hole. It seemed to him there couldn't be many holes left. More and more they'd worked on the nuances that separated synonyms. Important work but less vital, for now at least.

The human language seemed more complex than Wyzhñyñyç, but less so than either of the two exotic languages previously deciphered. It was basically oral, and many of the nuances were verbal, as in Wyzhñyñyç. But even more than Wyzhñyñyç, it seemed to him, it had many visual nuances, including postures, arm and hand movements, head movements, facial expressions, eye movements... Qonits wasn't sure how many of those signals were deliberate and how many subliminal.

If the time comes when we must negotiate with their rulers, he thought, *then the nuances will be critical.*

He hadn't voiced the thought of negotiation to Quanshûk. It would be dreadfully inappropriate; circumstances would have to do it. But with the translation program developing so nicely— surely the possibility had occurred to the admiral. *We negotiate among ourselves,* Qonits thought. *Surely we can negotiate with others. Even if we never have before.*

◇

On his closed command monitor, Quanshûk had watched the tour after it left the bridge. Had seen Qonits say goodbye to the humans, and leave them in their prison. *Shipsmind will have analyzed the whole thing by now,* Quanshûk thought as he entered his quarters. As for the prisoners... None of it had surprised them—the bridge stations and their screens, the strange-space generator, the beam guns... Which strongly suggested that human science and technology were much like his own. They'd hit the wall in much the same places.

He didn't know whether to feel relieved or disappointed.

<>

The cube showed only the savant, Ramesh, lying in trance on his couch, with Burhan sitting attentively beside him, while words issued from the savant's lips in a variety of voices. As usual, the president and the prime minister viewed it in Peixoto's office, unedited except that the brief silences had been compressed. Now they viewed it again.

When the cube had played out, the two men looked long at one another. It was the president who broke the silence. "The Tao has been good to us, allowing us to hear that. And today I learned more than Wyzhñyñy technology. Those are people we must war against."

Peixoto pursed his lips. "But it does not change the situation. Alive or dead, they must leave the Commonwealth. And even if they were Eve's children, they would hardly leave unforced. They have too much invested, too much at stake."

"It seems so," Chang said. "But we agreed that if we could, we would negotiate. It was you who said it first. And the Tao is full of surprises."

Peixoto's inner reaction was bleak. *Full of surprises, yes,* he told himself, *but surprises fitting probability equations and natural laws. Some things simply do not happen.*

He kept the thought to himself though. There was no point in throwing negativity in anyone's face; certainly not his best friend's. And if an opportunity arose—if the Wyzhñyñy were willing to negotiate—he would approach the task honestly.

Chapter Thirty-Eight
Ruckus in the Morgue

Esau slogged forward, blaster in his hands and grenade bag over a shoulder. He hadn't slept for thirty hours—hadn't eaten for nearly twenty, except for an energy bar. His belly, he told himself, must think his throat had been cut. But his red-rimmed eyes moved constantly, from the forest half a mile ahead, to the farm woodlots that broke the croplands and pastures, to the Indi tanks moving ahead on their AG cushions. To both left and right stretched other 2nd Regiment companies.

Not all of 2nd Regiment was in his line. The lead rank was 1st Battalion; 2nd and 3rd Battalions followed at thirty-yard intervals, while 4th Battalion sat in APCs as a tactical reserve. Esau was glad he wasn't in an APC. They tended to draw heavy fire when they showed up. They weren't supposed to be committed before the tanks and "legs" had the enemy fully engaged, and even then, the enemy would give them serious attention.

As a rule, Esau could immerse himself in these training maneuvers as if they were the real thing. As he was supposed to. He never glanced back at the umpires on their grav scooters, following the action. The sight of them, even the thought of them, weakened the illusion.

No shots had been fired yet from the distant forest, nor from the building and woodlots nearer at hand. Which might mean no one was there, but that seemed unlikely. Surveillance buoys showed things like that. And if no one was there, 2nd Regiment would have crossed in APCs. Only if serious enemy fire was expected would they cross on foot like this.

At that moment, firing broke out from forest, woodlots and steadings—crackling, hissing, thumping—and a voice spoke sharply in his right ear: "Bogies from the rear! Bogies from the rear!" Esau flattened himself as low as he could, then hazarded a glance back past his shoulder. A rank of killer craft swept across the field, slammers flickering. Esau felt a soft pulse strike about at his tailbone, and obediently rolled over, playing casualty. The umpires' instruments recorded all hits, along with the victims' identities, the virtual force, and points of impact.

The assault craft swished by overhead, most of them. A few must have taken "crippling hits" themselves; they landed obediently as casualties. If they hadn't, and promptly, the "enemy" would have been penalized, and the pilots put on report. The ground was cold but the sun bright, and Esau put a forearm over his eyes. He wondered if Jael had been hit, and if perhaps they should have signed up for bottling. If this had been a real fight, he told himself, and the hit he'd taken had been a hard pulse, signing wouldn't have made any difference. Because surely that had been a slammer. It would have blown his guts, lungs, heart and spine, all to Tophet.

He was aware of 2nd and 3rd Battalions passing him, trotting now. The sound of firing remained intense. It seemed odd to be lying there out of it. He was going to miss some of the action. It occurred to him to sit up and look around, see what was going on. Their own floaters should be up again, suppressing enemy fire.

But it was easier to just lie there with his eyes closed, feeling himself drift into sleep. Then a medic gripped his arm, and he wakened.

"Where are you hit?"

"Tailbone, from behind. It would have been one of the killer craft. If it was real, I'd be deader'n Tophet."

"Okay. I'm going to give you a shot for the pain, just in case."

The man pretended to inject Esau in the side of the neck, then taped a fake syringe to his patient's field jacket and hurried on. Esau let his eyes close again. Who knew, he thought, what would happen when they got into real combat, back home on New Jerusalem. Wyzhñyñy weapons were thought to be pretty much the same as human weapons. "Physics is the same everywhere," Sergeant Hawkins had said. Jerries weren't taught physics, but Esau had gotten the basic idea; only certain things were possible. But the Wyzhñyñy had four legs under them, and might be stronger than him. Might all of them carry slammers.

"Esau," said Brother Crosby, "they are way to heck stronger than you are." He patted his horse on the shoulder. "They're near as big as this fella, with arms in proportion."

Esau decided to keep Clancy with him for protection, and looked around for the big hound, but couldn't see him anywhere. Then realized he'd begun to dream. Clancy was a long long ways off, and so was Brother Crosby. *It don't matter,* he told himself. *You're already dead anyway.*

Shortly afterward an armored ambulance landed a few yards away. Without speaking, two medics lay him carefully on an AG stretcher, then took him to the ambulance, where another medic secured the stretcher on brackets and turned on the "warm field."

◇

Soon afterward they arrived at a field "hospital" in the forest, a complex of tents beneath the trees. It was supposed to be protected by a concealment screen so the enemy couldn't find it from the air. The tents were like shallow, upside-down bowls, protected by colors generated by their camouflage fields. The medics moved quickly and smoothly, transferring the casualties to a receiving tent. Calling him dead on arrival, they put Esau in a body bag, and moved him to a morgue tent.

The activity had wakened him again, and because he actually was alive, the bag had been pressed shut only to his waist. He sat up and looked around. There were no attendants in this tent, but the trainee on the floor beside him was also looking around. "Well," the man said. His voice was quiet. "So this is what it's like to be dead."

"Not hardly," Esau answered.

"What's your company?"

"B, 2nd Platoon. Name is Esau Wesley. Yours?"

The other didn't answer at once, as if thinking about it. "Simon Justice," he said at last. "E Company, 3rd Platoon. Can you say bunch of foolishness?"

"What do you mean?"

The man's gesture took in the tent, perhaps the whole

hospital, or planet. "All of this. Pretending to fight, pretending to get shot, pretending to be dead. All of it."

Esau decided he didn't like Simon Justice. Didn't like his tone of voice, didn't like his pretense of superiority. "It's not foolishness," Esau replied. He didn't expect to change the man's mind, but the statement required an answer. "We'll be glad we've gone through it when we get back to New Jerusalem."

"Huh! We'll never get to New Jerusalem. The government's going to send us somewhere else, to put down an uprising." His tone suggested scorn for anyone who didn't realize that.

"Where'd you get that notion?" Esau asked.

"Why, it's plain to see. A four-legged critter with a man stuck on the front?" He snorted his scorn.

"That's no more unlikely than what you said." Esau paused. "Are you calling Captain Mulvaney a liar? Or General Pak?"

"That's about right. Yeah."

Esau moved his hands to the open edge of his body bag, separating the closure all the way to his knees. And got up. "Get out of that bag and we'll talk about this," he said.

By that time others in the tent were watching, their eyes on Esau now. The man who called himself Simon Justice, on the other hand, had decided to lay back down again.

"What's the matter?" Esau demanded. "You were big on talk, with all that bullshit."

"It's against regulations to fight," the man answered. "Otherwise I'd get out of this bag and teach you a lesson."

With a single step, Esau was leaning over him, gripped him, pulled him to his feet and jerked him close, bag and all. "Simon Justice," he said, "you're a liar and a coward. And unless you take all that back…"

Another soldier was on his feet now. "A bigger liar'n you know," he said. "He's not Simon Justice. *I'm* Simon Justice. He's not even in 3rd Platoon. E Company, yes—I've seen him around—but not in 3rd Platoon. So if anybody beats him up, I'm the one ought to do it."

Esau's eyes widened, then he barked a laugh, and grinned

at the real Simon Justice. "Well well! He's all yours. Have at it!" He let go the counterfeit, who dropped to the floor in self protection, gripping his body bag closed and yelling at the top of his lungs. "HELP! HELP! MURDER!" waking whatever corpses weren't already awake.

Before either Esau or the real Simon Justice could decide what to do, a Terran medic stepped inside. His sleeves had sergeant's stripes, and above his jacket pocket the name Sinisalo, Urho E. "What the hell's going on in here?" he barked. "You! And you! Get back in those body bags."

While they did, he murmured softly, as if to someone invisible beside him. Then he looked down at the false Simon Justice. "Are you the one who yelled?"

"Yes sir," the liar answered softly. "They said they were going to beat me up." His voice was almost too faint to hear. He realized his situation. There were maybe a dozen—at least several others in the tent who'd heard the exchange. He'd never in the world lie his way out of this situation.

Sinisalo frowned, then looked around and pointed to a watching, listening corpse. "You," said the medic. "What happened in here?"

The man told him, closely enough.

Sinisalo looked down at the liar. "Give me your dog tags."

Only the liar's eyes moved.

"That's an order, soldier!"

The liar shook his head, encouraged by the apparency that he wouldn't be beaten up.

A lieutenant hurried in, a Sikh wearing a white turban and Medical Service insignia. "I'm the provost marshal," he said to Sinisalo. "What's going on here?" The provost marshal's post was only one of several he covered, the one he'd least expected to require his attention. His military police unit consisted of one man—himself. When he'd gotten the call, he'd grabbed a stunner, a belt recorder, and a set of handcuffs, and hurried to the morgue. But he was a Sikh, with five years military experience, and a cram course in the basics of the provost marshal's job. He'd make it go right.

When Sinisalo had described what he'd found and heard, the provost marshal stood over the liar and reached down. "Your dog tags," he said.

Again the liar refused, clasping himself with his arms. The provost knew Jerrie strength, so he turned to Esau. "Sergeant, take his dog tags."

Esau crouched beside the liar, pulled open the body bag, grabbed the man's field jacket and hoisted him to his feet. Hurriedly the liar gave up his dog tags. Esau handed them to the provost marshal, who read them and scowled. "Private Thomas Crisp," he said.

He manacled the now compliant Crisp, then went around the morgue with his belt recorder and got the name, serial number, and unit of each "corpse" there.

"All right," he said, "Wesley, Justice, Crisp, come with me. You other casualties, continue in your roles." He turned to Sinisalo. "Sergeant, you come too." As he herded his three corpses toward the hospital admin tent, the provost marshal drew his belt comm and called for an MP floater from Division. The hospital had no place to incarcerate anyone.

<>

Before the lieutenant had finished questioning his three Jerries, two other things happened. The MP floater arrived, with six MPs led by a sergeant. And an orderly arrived to report a genuine casualty. A trainee in the maneuvers had been shot in the back with a hard pulse, a slammer pulse. It had scrambled his innards—bones and organs. And all the power slugs used in the maneuvers, including those in the aircraft, had supposedly been for soft pulses.

Saboteurs again! the lieutenant thought, thinking of the parachute incident, the major ordnance and equipment-checking project that had grown out of it, and what was found. When the floater had taken off with the prisoner and the principal witnesses, the lieutenant returned to the morgue to get statements from the other corpses.

<>

Esau fell asleep again even before the MP floater took

off; almost as he buckled himself in. *Take advantage of your opportunities,* he'd thought as they'd walked out to it. He'd heard how it worked for "casualties," from guys who'd gone through it the past couple of days. In an hour or two he'd be reclassified from corpse to combat replacement, and flown to some company other than his own, to fit in as best he could till the exercise was finished. On New Jerusalem, of course, there'd be no replacements, but the general didn't want his casualties to miss out on the training.

Actually it was a dozen hours before he was reassigned. Division's provost marshal let him sleep for eight hours before questioning him. And learned nothing he didn't already have on cube.

Chapter Thirty-Nine
Digging for Roots

The weather had been pleasant for the Mühlbach maneuvers, with mostly sunny days, and temperatures reaching into the 60s. The nights had been near 40, with brilliant starscapes. The trainees might have enjoyed their Fiveday test, if they'd had enough to eat and at least a few hours a day of sleep. But the maneuvers were more than a test of tactics, leadership, and readiness. Their commanding general wanted them to discover their tenacity, and endurance of privation, so he'd cranked up the hardship factor.

They'd handled it well.

Maneuvers were the heart of unit training, and at least as vital for General Pyong Pak Singh as for his troops. Pak had never experienced actual combat; never directed a battle except in electronic games. So he lived maneuvers as realistically as he could. He directed his division from a floater; camped in the field, was often on the move, ate field rations, and caught catnaps when the situation allowed. Though he slept more than his men. His alertness, or lack thereof, was important to every man in his "corps," his expanded division—Jerries, Indi Armored, killer wing, and Lüneburger Engineers.

He'd delighted in the competition with his opposing counterpart, Major General Pauli Nachtigal of the Lüneburger 4th Infantry Division. And found strong satisfaction in his troops, who'd performed well. Even E Company, 2nd Regiment, which with fifteen men in the stockade was shorthanded, and perhaps a bit demoralized by the defections. While the opposing Burger infantry division was really good; Masadan trained.

Now that the Mühlbach maneuvers were over, and everyone had had a long night's sleep, the troops were enjoying a day off. In camp, for there'd be no passes till the matter of defections was sorted out. A day off with naps and base food: all the roast pork, the barley with pork gravy, freshly baked still-warm bread with butter and jam, pie with good cheese from Lüneburger's

Mennonite dairies…and all the ice cream they could eat! Few if any of his Jerries had seen ice cream before they'd joined the army. Few had even heard of it. It had become their favorite, if infrequent dessert.

If the troops had the day off, their general didn't. He was at his desk at 0730, working his way through his *In* basket. At 0930 he met with his division provost marshal, Captain Raymond Coyote Singh; and the CO of 2nd Regiment's 2nd Battalion, Major Amar Kalnins Singh. Of urgent necessity, the subject was the defections—the refusal by fifteen members of E Company to serve. Briefly the three officers reviewed the basic known facts, without speculating on the roots. Then Major Coyote reported on E Company's Private Thomas Crisp, and his clumsy attempt to spread disaffection in the field hospital's morgue. He had his own cubes and those recorded by the hospital's provost marshal, with accounts provided by Sergeant Sinisalo, and by Wesley, Justice, and the bystanders. And by Crisp.

The meeting was interrupted by chirping from Pak's intercom. His monitor told him it was Administrative Sergeant Major Watanabe. Frowning, Pak spoke to his pickup. "What is it?" he asked.

The answer came via the pickup in his right ear. "General, Corporal Isaiah Vernon is here, with information that may be important to the defections matter. Vernon's a bot attached to 2nd Regiment, 1st Battalion. Would you like to see him now?"

Pak knew the name. "Bring him in, Sergeant," Pak said, then broke the connection and looked at Coyote. "Captain, record this. Apparently it's information on our problem."

The sergeant major opened the door. A seven-foot warbot stood behind him. "General," said Watanabe, "this is Corporal Vernon."

Vernon stepped inside and stopped. "Thank you, Sergeant Major," Pak said in dismissal, and the door closed. "What do you have for us, Corporal?"

"General, the night before we went on maneuvers, Private Jeremiah Spieler, *Speaker* Spieler, came to my hut and told me a story. He and I were friends. We'd been in B Company together, and back home I was a student speaker. He told me that the evening before, after lights out, some men came to his tent and woke him up. They told him they needed his advice. So he went outside with them. It turned out they didn't want advice. They wanted him to help them spread a message in B Company. Quietly, to men he trusted.

"The one that did the talking said the Wyzhñyñy were sent by God," Vernon went on, "to overthrow a corrupt and Godless Commonwealth government. And that God wants his people—all colonists and Terrans who follow his commandments and the leadership of Christ—to turn against the government. Refuse orders and stand against evil, even at the risk of their lives."

The Peace Front line all the way, Pak thought. "Why isn't Spieler telling me this himself?" he asked.

If there was a way of reading a warbot's reactions, comparable to reading an organic's face, Pak didn't know it. But the two or three-second lag suggested surprise. "Why General, sir, Speaker Spieler was killed in the maneuvers. Someone shot him in the back with a hard pulse. From a slammer, I'm told."

The statement stunned Pak. He'd heard there'd been an accidental death, a shooting. This story made it seem deliberate. "Did they—the men who talked with Spieler—did they say who told them all that?"

"Jeremiah didn't say. They did tell him they were part of a group headed by speakers, but he was sure the man who did the talking wasn't one. Because when he tried to quote scripture, he got it all wrong."

"Hmm. This was—what then? A week ago?"

"Six nights ago he told me about it, sir."

"Why didn't Spieler, or you, inform your sergeants?"

"The speaker said he was afraid of them, sir. And he didn't know who they were. I asked. He couldn't see their names in the dark, nor their faces well enough. All he could say was, the one who did the talking sounded like us—like someone from New Jerusalem—but taller than just about any of us gets. As tall as Captain Mulvaney, he said."

Hmm. That would be more than six feet, Pak thought.

"Afraid. Did they threaten him?"

"Not exactly. They told him to be careful not to say anything about it to anyone he didn't trust. They'd tell him when it was time. But Jeremy said it sounded like a warning."

"But Spieler told you."

"Yessir. I guess he needed to tell someone, and knew he could trust me."

"Why didn't you tell someone? Your sergeant."

"I should have. But we had breakfast at 0630 the next morning and left on maneuvers. And it seemed like just talk; I didn't suppose anything would come of it. Surely nothing like someone shooting Jeremiah. Or that anyone would quit the army. And we'll be leaving for home in another month; I told myself that when we got there, the facts would speak for themselves."

Pak nodded thoughtfully. "Thank you, Corporal. You've been very helpful. Say nothing to anyone about talking to us. And if you see anything, or remember anything that may help us identify the traitors, report it to your battalion commander promptly.

"You may go now."

A gentle giant, Pak thought as he watched the warbot leave. *I wonder how he'll do in combat.*

Well enough, he decided. Major Somphavanh Ruiz Singh, CO of the division's bot contingent, was an excellent officer who'd given special attention to selecting his noncoms. But he'd ask him about Vernon and see what he said.

◇

After Pak closed the meeting, Captain Coyote went to his computer and checked on several things. Near the end of advanced training, the various company commanders, in conference with their platoon leaders and platoon sergeants, had evaluated their troops for promotion. And Spieler had not made lance corporal. His platoon sergeant had characterized him as very conscientious, and hard-working, but passive. He'd probably make lance corporal at the end of unit training, and go no further.

He already knew that all fifteen men who'd "resigned" were in E Company, as Private Crisp was. The tallest man in E Company was a Private Moses Wheeler, who at five-feet eleven was one of the tallest Jerries in the division. He was one of only four in his squad who hadn't defected. He was also 4th Squad's slammer man, and a troublemaker from the start. He'd done nothing extreme, at least not till now, but he led 2nd Battalion in the number of times on company punishment.

Coyote then called up the information on Spieler's death. The pulse had struck him in the left side of the left buttock, below the flak jacket, destroying the left pelvis. Overall the damage indicated an impact vector diagonally upward, out through the ribs on the right side, shattering the right humerus. The overall damage could only have been done by a slammer. It must have been after the troops had hit the dirt in response to the air attack, but the angle practically guaranteed it had not been fired by a killer craft. So. Something else then.

Coyote asked his computer for the regimental formation during the advance across the fields of Müller's Settlement. Spieler had been in B Company, 1st Platoon, 4th Squad. E Company had been about 30 yards behind B Company, and one position to its left. Wheeler had been in 4th Squad, 4th Platoon, but with almost all his squad locked in the stockade, he'd probably... Yes. He'd been attached as an augmentation to—2nd Squad, and from his position there, could easily have fired the pulse that killed Spieler. Judging by the angle, the only one else who could have, given the high-powered weapon used, was 2nd Squad's slammer man. The provost marshal saw no clear way, yet, to prove that Wheeler was the murderer, but this established opportunity, and greatly reduced the apparent alternatives.

His next step, Coyote decided, would be to have Wheeler brought to him for questioning, and meanwhile have his belongings searched. If they were lucky enough to find an M-6 power slug... Then talk with E Company's 4th Platoon sergeant, and learn who were Wheeler's close associates. They were probably in the stockade, he thought. *I'll have them wired before I question them. See how they read. Maybe that'll lead somewhere.*

He was reaching for his comm switch when it occurred to him: *What was the* source *of this Peace Front line? Could some Jerrie have come up with it independently?* It seemed doubtful.

◇

The good weather had broken near midday. Then Joseph Switzer had worked in the rain, piling slabs. The rain had turned to thick wet snow—a rarity at Sagenwerk—as wet as the rain but colder. Switzer's blanket-lined jacket had soaked up about five pounds of ice water, or so it seemed. At the end of the shift he headed home without stopping at the tavern. His nose had begun to run. His heavy work shoes were saturated. He'd have to dry them by the stove, and grease them in the morning. He'd stay home tomorrow, sleep, and nurse whatever he was coming down with.

He looked around him and grimaced. He had never, he'd decided, hated any place as much. Sagenwerk was a backwater without any backwater charms. In general, Mennonites liked flowers, liked to grow things, kept their buildings and yard fences painted. But Sagenwerk—ugly, weedy, and filled with truculent, narrow-minded people—Sagenwerk, he told himself, was where the mean and spiteful were reincarnated as punishment. Even sunny and warm he didn't like it. And in weather like this…

He shut out the surroundings he slopped through—rain, slush, weed-edged streets, slab fences… A chill shook him, and he wiped his runny nose on a sleeve. But as much as he'd like to, he didn't feel free to leave. Not yet. Private Moses Wheeler had arrived at their third meeting not only with his mind made up. He'd arrived with a plan! His own plan, and therefore the only plan he'd consider: work through the speakers. They had influence, and authority in religious matters.

Actually it made sense—except that Wheeler had telescoped it. He wanted to build Rome in a day.

Maybe he could. Joseph Switzer hoped devoutly that he could. If confidence—positive thinking—meant much, he might. For Moses Wheeler was a maverick, and a bomb waiting to go off. The problem was his fuse. Once lit, there was no way that he, Switzer, could do anything about it—control, guide, or even advise. If he'd realized, when they'd first met, what an arrogant asshole Wheeler was, he'd have made his pitch to someone else. But Wheeler made a good first impression. He was big, fearless, and had an aura of power. And he'd seen what Switzer was leading up to while Switzer was still feeling him out. Had taken over and made the mission his own.

In a way, Switzer told himself, he'd suffered from Wheeler's problem—one of Wheeler's problems—over-confidence. Now, though, he wasn't confident at all. Wheeler, on the other hand—he couldn't imagine Wheeler losing confidence. And if Wheeler showed more patience than seemed probable—if he let the speakers do their thing in their own time—the Jerrie army might be compromised enough that War House would be unwilling to send it to New Jerusalem. That was the theory. It was what he'd intended, and what the Front had financed him to do.

The only reason he was hanging around was to learn the results. The Front would expect him to. Word might well never get to North Fork, and almost certainly wouldn't surface on Terra except through him. And quite a few civilian workers at Camp Nafziger came into Sagenwerk on their days off, full of gossip.

Through gray rain and gray introspection, Switzer reached his shack near the tracks at the east edge of town. Stepping onto the rough stoop, he dug his house key from a pocket. With red trembling hands got it into the keyhole and turned it. Pushed the door open, then closed and locked it behind him. That was another thing about Sagenwerk: there were thefts.

Inside it was half warm. The single room was small enough to heat with the cookstove, which he'd banked with coal before work, then closed both damper and draft to hold fire. After stripping off his sodden jacket, he dug coal from a sack and put it on the embers.

Someone knocked on the door. Switzer's guts knotted; he had no friends here. "Who is it?" he asked.

"Nockey Brant."

Brant? The constable? "What do you want?"

"You. You going to let me in, or do I kick the door down?"

Switzer thought of the pistol in his bag. But if he shot Brant, and they caught him... Maybe it was about that tool theft at the sawmill. He was an outsider; maybe they thought he'd done it. Brant would search the place, and when he didn't find the tools, that would be the end of it. Then he could fix his supper; eat and go to bed.

"Just a minute."

He stepped to the door, turned the key, then the knob, and pushed. As it opened, Nockey Brant grabbed and held it. He was broad and extremely strong, a veteran of the green chain. Behind him were two MPs from Camp Nafziger. Brant grinned a stained, spade-toothed grin. "Couple of soldiers want to talk to you," he said. "About conspiracy, and being an accomplice before the fact of murder."

With his other hand, the constable gripped Joseph Switzer by his wet shirt and pulled him out onto the stoop. One of the MPs brought forth a pair of handcuffs and secured Switzer's wrists behind his back. Then they pushed him ahead of them in the direction of the depot. No one locked his door. He supposed his stuff would be stolen before the night was over.

Not, he realized, that it would make any difference.

Chapter Forty
A Change of Plans

General Pyong Pak Singh finished reading the summary of evidence, then cleared it from the screen. The case was cut and dried, he told himself: simple, nicely tied together, and unbeatable. He'd send Switzer back to Terra tomorrow, via an embassy courier craft, for a civil trial in Kunming.

Ignorant, well-intentioned Switzer. In the "theology" of the Gopal Singh Dispensation, the evolution—genetic, social, and spiritual—of the human species grew from the interplay of individuals of every type. Remote interplay, and direct, immediate interplay. Joseph Switzer was part of it, and was not—was *not* faulted for that by THE ONE. Persons like Switzer were not only inevitable, but necessary to that evolution. But it was entirely valid for him to be tried and punished by social authority, also as part of that interplay.

Intellectually, Pyong Pak Singh knew and accepted all that. Emotionally, however, he felt offended by what he considered gratuitous troublemaking like Switzer's. He always had, he thought ruefully, and probably would throughout this lifetime.

The nature of the charges made Switzer subject to the court system on Terra. And when informed, the Lüneburgian chief magistrate had declined to claim him. Though born on Lüneburger's, Switzer held resident rights on Terra, and had come to his birth-world on a visitor's visa. He hadn't applied for more. On a world as loosely administered as Lüneburger's, a visitor's visa might be overstayed forever.

On Terra, according to Coyote, Switzer would almost surely be imprisoned but not executed.

Here on Lüneburger's, the courts martial of the division's fifteen defectors would begin, and no doubt end, next Threeday, the day after the officers of the court returned from the Maple Mountain Maneuvers. The trial of the five conspirators would have to wait till the day after, as three of them were among the defectors. That trial might require two, or possibly three days of argument and deliberation.

The murder trial would start the day after the conspirators' trial ended, because Wheeler was a defendant in both. Considered with other evidence, the used M-6 power slug found folded in a towel in Wheeler's foot locker would probably clinch a murder conviction, even if none of his co-conspirators testified against him. Actually his mouth had killed any chance he had.

After the murder trial, Pak would ship the conspirators to Terra, because sentencing would have to consider the death penalty. And because Lüneburger's World was (1) not a war zone; and (2) had no military appeals authority. And where capital punishment was an option, a prompt, automatic appellate review was required before sentencing, except in a war zone.

The whole mess has been a distraction, Pak told himself. *I should be at Maple Mountain right now. Though Frosty's undoubtedly enjoying running the show. And it's good experience for him, so it's probably for the...*

His intercomm chirped. "Pak here," he answered.

"Sir, the ambassador wants to speak with you. He's got a message from War House, via savant."

Pak frowned. "Switch him through."

The ambassador himself required only a minute. Then they both listened live to the embassy's savant, channeling Lefty Sarruf—Sarruf's words in a remarkable mimicry of Sarruf's voice. All together, the exchange took nearly thirty minutes, followed by another twenty or so with Admiral Apraxin-DaCosta of the admiralty's Liberation Task Force.

There had been a change in the training schedule of the New Jerusalem Liberation Corps. Apraxin's space force had been engaged in battle exercises in the neighborhood of Lüneburger's System for more than a week. Now War House had decided they'd all trained enough—both the admiral's force and Pak's soldiers. The invasion of New Jerusalem had been moved up two weeks. After Pak's Corps had established itself on New Jerusalem, the task force was to leave, to rendezvous with Soong's provos as soon as possible after Soong's attack on the Wyzhñyñy armada. Apraxin-DaCosta would leave an "adequate" force to back up the troops on the surface.

The corps' transports would land on the Sixday following the Maple Mountain Maneuvers, bringing several savants. His troops would begin loading out at once.

When the conference was over, Pak half whistled a gusty sigh. He'd still send Switzer to Terra the next day, but the courts martial would have to wait till his corps was outbound. The trial and sentencing would be held aboard his flagship, in hyperspace, then the prisoners would be stored in stasis as long as necessary.

He'd rather sentence them to service in a punishment unit, assigned to high hazard duty. Let them experience the Wyzhñyñy first hand. It didn't seem right for them to sleep in stasis while the men they'd betrayed put their lives on the line. He decided to ask Captain Coyote about the possibility. If the provost marshal sounded encouraging, he'd run it past Lefty Sarruf, by savant. But he wasn't optimistic.

Continued in SOLDIERS! Part Two

THE END

Books Published by Sky Warrior Books

Purchase them through online resellers and better independent bookstores everywhere. Visit us at www.skywarriorbooks.com **for news and upcoming books and promotions.**

Alma Alexander

2012: Midnight at Spanish Gardens (E-book, Trade Paperback)

Embers of Heaven (E-book, Trade Paperback)

S. A. Bolich

Firedancer (E-book, Trade Paperback)

Seaborn (E-book)

Windrider (E-book, Trade Paperback)

M. H. Bonham

Daemons and Shadows (E-book)

Prophecy of Swords (E-book)

Runestone of Teiwas (E-book)

Samurai Son (E-book)

Serpent Singer and Other Stories (E-book)

John Dalmas

The Signature of God Part 1 (E-book)

The Signature of God Part 2(E-book)

Soldiers! Part 1(E-book, Trade Paperback)

Soldiers! Part 2 (E-book, Trade Paperback)

The Second Coming (E-book, Trade Paperback)

Deby Fredericks

Seven Exalted Orders (E-book)

Carol Hightshoe (Editor)

Zombiefied: An Anthology of All Things Zombie (E-book)

Gary Jonas

Acheron Highway (E-book)

Modern Sorcery (E-book, Trade Paperback)

One-Way Ticket to Midnight (E-book)

Quick Shots (E-book, Trade Paperback)

Frog and Esther Jones

Grace Under Fire (E-book)

Michael J. Parry

The Oaks Grove (E-book)

The Spiral Tattoo (E-book)

Phyllis Irene Radford

Healing Waves: A Charity Anthology for Japan (Editor) (E-book)

Gears and Levers 1: A Steampunk Anthology (Editor) (E-book, Trade Paperback)

Gears and Levers 2: A Steampunk Anthology (Editor) (E-book, Trade Paperback)

Lacing Up Murder, A Whistling River Mystery (E-book)

So You Want to Commit Novel (E-book, Trade Paperback)

Dusty Rainbolt (Editor)

The Mystical Cat (E-book)

Deborah J. Ross (Editor)

The Feathered Edge (E-book, Trade Paperback)

Laura J. Underwood

Ard Magister (Book One of Ard Magister) (E-book)

Dragon's Tongue (Book One of the Demon-Bound) (E-book)

The Hounds of Ardagh (E-book)